Young Digby Swank

Growing up Gay and Catholic Sure is Hell!

Owen Keehnen

Praise for
Young Digby Swank

" *Young Digby Swank* is a story about real life, a story of a Gay Catholic boy coming of age and trying to find himself while living in a messed up, crazy world, one where God was always watching… Think of The Catcher in the Rye but with a gay Holden Caufield."
The Gayly Post

" Owen Keehnen gives us a wonderful character in Digby… I found myself identifying with Digby through most of the story and not only laughing at and with him, but laughing at and with myself."
Amos Lassen

Young Digby Swank

Growing up Gay and Catholic sure is Hell!

Owen Keehnen

WILDE
CITY
PRESS

WILDE CITY PRESS

www.wildecity.com

Young Digby Swank © 2013 Owen Keehnen
Published in the US and Australia by Wilde City Press 2013

Published by Wilde City Press

ISBN: 978-1-925031-00-0

Cover Art © 2013 Wilde City Press

For my Father who gave me a deep appreciation for humor. I'm still in awe of his amazing ability to capture any character through a gesture or expression. It was truly genius.
I miss you Dad.

1 - Birth

Digby's parents were typical Catholics with typical Catholic shortcomings. They were indecisive and guilt ridden, but more to the point, they had an unshakable faith in the rhythm method.

Pregnancy past forty seemed, at best, an inappropriate gift. His mother and father were resentful and shocked in equal measure. The timing was all wrong. Their other children were finally using the toilet, dressing themselves, and blessedly toddling off to school. Shackle by shackle, those initial burdens of parenthood were falling away. Freedom had seemed almost tangible. And now, this. Diapers and feedings and feedings and diapers were all that either one of them could really think.

At the precise moment of Digby's conception, his mother, Lila, recalled opening her eyes, which was indeed memorable since she always kept them closed during the sex act. She looked at the ceiling and gasped, not due to any great pleasure or feeling of sparked life in her womb, but because there was a patch of paint starting to peel near the light fixture. "That will never do," she said. Usually the Swanks had sex with the lights off, and having the bedroom ceiling in such a state was one more reason to do so. She put it somewhere on a lengthy mental to-do list, and closed her eyes once again.

"When I first became pregnant, I thought I was going through the change," confided Lila. "Not that I was any stranger to pregnancy, mind you. But this one didn't feel the same. Something just wasn't sitting right. Looking back, it made perfect sense. Digby always was a loner. Being pregnant with him was more formal, like I was subletting a furnished room. There wasn't the maternal bond I'd had with the other kids. Or maybe I just wasn't feeling too maternal at the time."

Lila discovered her pregnancy about six weeks into term. Her obstetrician, Dr. Darren Dix, told her the news with a big smile on his face. Lila smiled back, then the nurse came in smiling and gushing congratulations. Lila gripped the bottom of the examination table, and maintained the same frozen smile. It was all just such a surprise. Her eyes were tearing up, and those tears weren't from joy. The truth was, she felt like screaming.

"Oh, you're going to have a little one!" squealed Nurse Susie.

"Yes, I am, and I'm so thrilled," said Lila, who tried to equal Susie's tone, but sounded mocking and sarcastic instead.

Nurse Susie was a sensitive girl due to her club foot, and took Lila's tone as a personal affront. She was always a little cold to her after that. Whenever Lila called for an appointment, Susie made a habit of putting her on hold while she straightened the magazines in the office.

The day she got the news about her pregnancy, Lila decided against breast feeding. No more milky bras for her. She never felt comfortable with the whole nursing part of motherhood. That latching on and suckling was just too primal for her tastes. She'd tell folks her milk was bad. She hoped saying so wouldn't make folks think any less of her. She wondered, in retrospect, if Digby had sensed her decision to bottle feed, and that was what caused him to be so aloof.

Though she hadn't said a word about how she was feeling, everyone kept saying her attitude would change. That upset Lila all the more. Was her lack of enthusiasm that apparent? Folks said a baby would be the best thing for her. They told her time and again that it would take ten years and twenty pounds off of her. Proving them wrong on both counts gave Lila a smug satisfaction.

She'd never experienced pregnancy depression the way she did with Digby. The fact that she was glowering instead of glowing only made her feel more guilty. She knew what she was feeling was wrong. There were no two ways about it. Catholics should be joyfully pregnant every chance they got, and smile right up to and through the birthing. "The Lord loves a brooder" was meant in regards to fertility, not attitude. If He felt differently, He wouldn't be against birth control. Lila knew she should've been grateful, but she just didn't want that miracle happening inside her. Not now. Not again. Wasn't having her womb as the vessel of three blessed miracles enough? She hoped the fetus knew it was nothing personal. That this was about being pregnant, not about being pregnant with him or her per se.

Rog, her husband, was no help. He acted as though her getting pregnant was something she'd gone and done behind his back, which certainly would have been a unique way of doing things. Around that time, Rog was just plain miserable and stuck smack dab in the middle of a midlife crisis. His career was leading nowhere, and every day was the same as the day before. Lila knew that Rog wasn't himself.

Rog used to say monotony was the spice of life. He started drinking more than he should have around that time. Drinking was the only routine in his life that he didn't seem to resent. He worried about money around the clock, and found himself covered in sweat despite the fact that it was the dead of winter. He was in and out of the hospital with nervous stomach problems throughout half of Lila's pregnancy. Thank heavens for the company's insurance coverage.

Lila was amazed at how some folks slept nights without insurance. Luck was something you only thought you had until events took a turn for the worse. Health was the same thing. Living without insurance all but ruined the Treacles down the block. Last year when Sandy Treacle fell carrying that half-lame dog of theirs up the front steps during an ice storm, she broke three ribs and suffered a nasty bite on the nose. That mishap gobbled up ninety percent of their savings, and the Treacles knew how to stretch a nickel. Rumor was that when it came to keeping up with the savings plan or paying the insurance, Arthur let the policy lapse, and instead lit extra votive candles. Fat lot of good that did them!

When the medical bills started coming due, Arthur Treacle caused a scene. Not one minute after old Mr. Berman, the mailman, slipped the Saturday delivery through the Treacle letter slot, Arthur flung open the door, chased the old man down the sidewalk, and threw the mail right in his face. People were sympathetic, but they couldn't have things like that going on.

After all, Mr. Berman was a decorated war veteran who sold the most affordable live bait in town. Dolly Steiner saw the whole incident from her front window, and whipped up such a stink about it that eventually the Treacles had to get themselves a post office box.

Lila shook her head, recalling the incident. It all just showed that insurance was nothing to take lightly. It could bleed a bank account, and ruin a reputation. "A body is tempting fate to do something like that," she thought. That was one of the reasons she married Rog. He never tempted fate. Rog always expected the worst, and did what he could to prepare for it.

Though she was hardly one to ask for an objective opinion on the subject, Lila thought her labor lasted a lifetime, or at least much longer than she would have liked. Even with the newfangled drugs and whatnot, it bordered on the ridiculous. The infant didn't seem at all anxious to come into the world. Finally, Dr. Dix, a man not known for his patience, grew red-faced and exasperated. He'd had just about enough. Swearing beneath his breath, he finally got hold of Digby's head with a pair of forceps, braced a foot against the table, and with a grunt, yanked that baby out of the womb like a cork from a jug.

"Shit," he said, wiping his brow and slowly putting his foot back on the floor.

Dr. Dix already had one arm out of his surgical gown when he slapped Digby's rear end with the other. He never bothered to press the boy's head into an acceptable shape, leaving the child with a skull the approximate shape of a lemon drop. He didn't have the time. Dr. Darren Dix had a fishing buddy honking in the parking lot with baited rods all ready to go. He wanted another prize catch to mount alongside the walleye in his waiting room. He was fond of pointing to the fish and saying to his expectant mothers, "You've got it easy. Imagine giving birth to something like that!"

Bathed in sweat, Lila laid back on the pillow. Digby was howling. He obviously didn't appreciate being yanked out that way. She supposed it wasn't the warmest way to welcome a newborn into the world. She knew just how he felt. The drugs they gave her might have worked to numb her lady parts, but they couldn't numb her to all her other worries. She was too upset to even pray. Rog came in and bent to kiss her. He rubbed the knobby crown of the infant's head. Lila could smell the whiskey on his breath.

"Hello...sport," said Rog. "What's his name?"

Lila eyed him blankly.

With everything going on, they hadn't even bothered to think about baby names. After less than two minutes of deliberation, they decided to call him Digby. Neither one especially loved or even liked the name, but more importantly, neither one disliked it to the point of protest. That was more than could be said of Ned or Todd or Delbert or Vincent. Choosing the right name for the child was less important than filling out the paperwork as promptly and completely as possible. Lila was getting an awful headache with the drugs wearing off.

Digby would do, but then the infant's middle name would have to be that of a saint if he was going to be properly baptized. The Church was unyielding about that. For his middle name they chose Timothy. Given Rog's recent ailment, Timothy seemed a wise choice. He was the patron saint of gastrointestinal and stomach disorders. Thank goodness that God, in his infinite wisdom, had created a patron saint for most everything.

After Rog left, the baby moved and almost at once commenced to clawing himself. Despite the aftermath of the drugs, Lila remembered yelling for Dr. Dix's assistant, Susie, for a full ten minutes before she finally came sauntering in the hospital room on her club foot. The nurse pursed her lips in a slight sneer, and put the infant mitts on him. Susie held a grudge, all right. She had a memory like an elephant, and at least one ankle to match.

2 – Afterbirth

According to family lore, Digby rarely moved as an infant. He smelled fungal. His sister, Katie, claimed he always looked startled, as if he couldn't quite believe the things that were happening around him even as a baby.

At a time when most babies smile, giggle, and coo "goo goo," Digby did something very different. He smirked. The smirk was cute at first. Look at what the baby can do! However, the charm proved short-lived. Most adults were intimidated when confronted by a baby wearing a knowing look that sometimes even included a cocked brow. It was unsettling. Some felt their secrets were being exposed, and that the oval-headed infant was peering into their very soul. It seemed indecent, especially to those who had indecent things to hide. Even his own parents felt sinful and exposed by his smirk.

Lila Swank followed through on her modern woman decision to bottle feed. "This store is closed," she thought with a decisive folding of her arms across her chest. There were repercussions. Smirking as he suckled the plastic nipple, Digby drove her to guilty tears on a rather regular basis. A friend said her response could be hormonal, but that was no consolation. The Church really didn't believe in hormones, especially the female ones. Eventually Lila found his bottle feeding impossible to watch. Instead, she positioned her chair alongside the canopied hood of the bassinet, and blindly reached over, poking about with the bottle until she found the infant's mouth. This method brought only a slight reprieve. Even his post-feeding burp seemed accusatory. On one particularly trying day, Lila was rumored to have said, "I may as well have tossed him to a dog with a spare teat."

Digby spoke early. His first utterance was not "mama" or "dada," "doggie," or even "hi." The first word he spoke was "me." The infant seemed to never tire of saying it, and would repeat it incessantly amidst claps and giggles. Squealing "me" brought a great joy that was only eclipsed when he learned the word "I" the following week. He mastered "want" and "no" in the days soon after, and that was where his patter paused. Digby seemed quite content with his limited vocabulary. It was weeks before he used any new words. When he did, the next one was "hurt."

By the time the boy was two years old, the financial pinch of being a single income household had become a rather nasty bruise. At this rate, the Swank family dream of converting the basement into a rec room would never be realized. So with minimal hesitation and a not-so-secret sigh of relief, Lila got out her heels, did up her hair, clasped on her "genuine pearls" and dove back into the secretarial pool with steno pad in hand. Given her skilled use of Pittman shorthand and an impressive words per minute typing average, Lila promptly found a position with a reputable Running Falls insurance firm.

There was only one bump in this smooth transition into a two income household, and that was finding someone to care for Digby. After some low-voiced deliberations, a perusal of the sparse Swank savings (not counting the rec room fund) and a few phone calls, his parents arrived at a solution. Grandma Swank would move in and care for the boy.

To say that Grandma Swank came with issues was a gross understatement. Her baggage could have easily classified as freight. Lizabeth Swank was a severe woman. Her husband had drowned after falling through the ice on the Fulton River years ago, leaving her with four small children and a mortgage. Overnight, her world became a dismal country song and remained so for years.

Rather than buckle to hardship, Lizabeth Swank accepted her misfortune with ample resentment. She then took that resentment, divvied it into four parts and passed it on to her offspring, along with a tendency for thinning hair and creaky knees. Luckily, none of the offspring inherited her lazy hands. Her mitts often fell asleep to such a degree that with a banshee's scream, she'd go running to the nearest sink and flop-turn the faucet to run hot water over them in order to get the circulation going. One of Digby's earliest nightmares was of someone madly running after him, wielding two dead fish.

Circumstances molded, or perhaps revealed, Lizabeth Swank

as acrimonious and uncompromising. She was a cold woman who seemed to warm only in anger. Naturally, she was religious, but in the sort of way that conveniently suits the embittered. Righteous was a better word. Love thy neighbor translated into love thy neighbor unless…or love thy neighbor only if… Everyone and everything seemed under her scrutiny and judgement.

Her severity was understandable given her circumstances, but Lizabeth Swank assumed her particular brand of harshness with an undeniable zeal, taking to it like a house on fire. Loss ripened rather than changed her. Stringency fit her like a very tight glove. She was so downright stern and unpleasant that most folks figured it couldn't have been solely the result of what had happened to her. Some even speculated that her husband got a taste of what lay in store at the cold hands of such a woman, gave a shiver and a shrug, and jumped through that patch of ice of his own accord.

"You didn't hear it from me, but circumstances being what they were, I can see how death by drowning might hold some appeal. Lizabeth Swank was mean as a three-legged barn cat," whispered a former neighbor, nodding towards the old Swank farmhouse as she pulled her shawl closer about her shoulders. "Mind you, that's only my opinion, but people seek my counsel on matters for two counties over, so my way of seeing things is nothing to sneeze at."

People like Lizabeth Swank do not soften over time, they harden like bread heels and cow pies. In the forty years since her husband's demise, Lizabeth's child rearing tactics grew even more rigid. She suffered no fools, tolerated no nonsense, and granted no indulgences. She frowned upon all toys with bells, whistles, or horns, and forbade excessive frolic unless it was done on tip-toe with a closed mouth, which was not the nature of frolic at all. Play was permitted in young children provided it was done quietly and out of her way. Being seen or heard was considered intrusive and disrespectful. Imagination was also frowned upon.

"The sooner a child learns its place in God's world, the better," she reasoned. Lizabeth Swank felt that good children should have the sense to age silently and quickly.

Duty dictated that Digby love Grandma Swank. He was told time and again that she was his flesh and blood, and yet he couldn't help but think that he wasn't the one his parents should be talking to. She was the adult. Every day in her presence made the task of loving her all the more difficult. Saying "I love you, Grandma Swank" was the first consistent lie Digby recalled telling. They both knew better. When his parents prompted him to say the dreaded words, Grandma Swank might roll her eyes or touch him with an icy hand. If there was an audience she might scowl and say, "Not as much as I love you." The curl of her lips and the way she said it gave him nightmares.

Grandma Swank was partial to wearing a black housedress with a frayed white collar. She moved about the Swank home like a domestic in the house of the dead. She took the lows of wallowing to new highs, and many about her were swept up in the grim apron of her misery. Her aggressive melancholia filled the air like a bitter perfume that smelled mostly like mothballs soaked in stale beer. She drank, but that was something that was never discussed or acknowledged. Beer was never actually added to the grocery list, but was always a part of buying groceries. Usually six or ten longnecks were chilling in the fridge at any given time. Two cases were always stacked in the corner of the kitchen. They were kept beneath a tablecloth and a spray of plastic Bird-of-Paradise flowers. Grandma Swank drank throughout the day, and typically went through a case from morning until night. Often times, by the next morning the tablecloth was crookedly rearranged, and the artificial flowers were scattered on the kitchen floor.

Most people loosen up, become garrulous, or soften into a sort of despair when they drink, but not Grandma Swank. For her, getting tight was literal in many ways. Her mouth got smaller, her eyes narrowed, and her hands balled into fists. Sometimes the drinking would also bring on her "dead hand" spells, which made her crazed drunken runs to the nearest faucet especially menacing. Digby was knocked to the floor more than once by her massive form, and the heavy arms flopping at her side.

One of the few bright spots in Lizabeth Swank's dismal world was Digby's brother, Tom. He reminded her of her dead husband. The resemblance increased with her consumption of beer. Whenever she went grocery shopping, she bought Tom treats but never bothered to do so with the other Swank children. She patched Tom's pants, consulted him about dinner, and rarely raised her voice to him. "He's a Swank," she'd say to Rog with a wink.

Once she actually knitted Tom a scarf, which she worked on in the evenings. He unwrapped it for his birthday, and lifted and lifted and lifted the dour brown garment from the gift box. It looked like the sort of scarf that a drunken near-sighted woman with peripheral neuropathy might knit. It measured four feet long and not quite four inches wide. It was perfect for playing tug of war with the dog, or served as a treehouse ladder or a makeshift finish line for foot and bike races.

If Tom was the light of Grandma Swank's life, then Digby was her darkness. He was the latest of her many lifetime hardships. He was a thorn in her side, and a flabby cross for her to bear. She considered him a spoiled baby and frivolous toddler. He cried too often, ate too slowly, fussed for attention, and soiled his diapers at purposefully inconvenient times. She considered him "soft," which in her mind, was the lowest of the low. Soft meant weak. Soft meant vulnerable. Soft meant wearing your insides on the outside, and under different circumstances, it meant he might not have survived.

When Digby's left-handedness revealed itself, Grandma Swank was in the midst of one of her selective religious binges. Those phases came around at regular intervals like the warp in a phonograph record. Jesus was her on-again, off-again savior. She loved and worshipped him, but felt he had abandoned her. He seemed like a lot of men in her life.

Digby's left-handedness only confirmed his link to Satan. It justified what Grandma Swank had been feeling all along. "I knew it," she nodded, narrowing her eyes and giving her rosary a squeeze. At the times of her periodic salvation, the rosary was her weapon of choice. She swung it about as a blessed switch, as the nunchucks of the Lord. Whenever Digby reached with his left hand for a toy or, God forbid, a doll, Jesus on the cross would whoosh through the air and hit his hands. As far as he could recall, this only happened during the day when they were alone. It wasn't until later that he discovered the holy beads were on a rosary for more than just ballast. The crucifix at the end was the most painful; it smacked bare legs and naked arms. Jesus hit whatever was in reach, and when Grandma Swank's rosaries broke and the beads scattered, Digby was blamed. "Look what you have done to our Savior," she'd screech. "Each of these beads will be another ten years in Purgatory for you."

He sat terrified every Sunday when the Swanks went to Mass. He thought everyone held rosaries in church just in case some sinner or child got out of line and needed a good whipping. Given what was happening at home, he always assumed that he was that sinner. He knew the feel of one rosary. He cringed to consider the pain of dozens of rosaries. It would be like a stoning-on-a-string.

3 - Grandma Swank

As the weeks fell into months and accumulated into years, Digby maintained the belief that Grandma Swank's disdain for him could be changed. Codependent before there was a word for it, Digby vowed to win over the crotchety old woman. Elevating her opinion of him became his new goal, along with learning to whistle, and sticking his entire fist in his mouth. He would eventually fail at all three.

Things between them improved when he learned to use his right hand, though he only did so when performing tasks in front of her. She now saw him as merely inept instead of demonic. Recognizing a slight change in her customary scowl, Digby reasoned that there must be even more he could do. However, doing more did not guarantee results.

For Lizabeth Swank, it was a matter of pride, as well. She swore that what she thought of her grandson was more than just an opinion. She claimed to have visions and manifestations regarding such things, though oftentimes her visions came after a few beers. Tolerating Digby's behavior and shameful ways was ignoring her obligation as a good Christian woman. Convincing Lizabeth Swank of something she didn't already believe was considered foolhardy by most that knew her. "You can lead Lizabeth to water, but you'll never convince her that it's wet," was a joke that several folks from her hometown whispered about her. A change of heart required an openness to change, as well as a functioning heart.

Digby was young, and oblivious to such things. He wasn't aware he was asking for a borderline miracle. All he wanted was to be a distant second to Tom as Grandma Swank's favorite. Any rise in the ranks would've been a vast improvement. Even being the third favorite of four, behind Tom and Maynard, the gravelly-voiced eldest, would be fine. The only possible contender for the title of "Least Favorite" was Katie, whose lack of focus aggravated Grandma Swank. Lizbeth considered her dawdling frivolous and sinful. "That girl certainly likes to linger over her ham and eggs," she might say with a scowl in Katie's direction. Such moments filled Digby with hope.

Despite his good intentions, Digby's efforts were systematically met with disaster, resounding failure, or utter indifference. When Grandma Swank's allergies flared, Digby brought her wildflowers. When she was napping, he tried to tiptoe, which made him clumsier and louder. He tried to shower her with compliments: he told her the mole near her mouth looked "just like a chocolate chip," and that he liked the way her chin and upper arms hung and wiggled. When her hands went limp, he rushed to throw hot water on her. When she was sick, he told her not to worry. He'd sit by the phone and call the morgue as soon as she died. None of this pleased Grandma Swank, and most of it angered her even more.

She wanted him simply to ignore her, but she was too indignant to say that. Digby was simply expected to know. The Swanks were that way about things. If someone didn't understand what someone else was feeling, it was just another sign of inconsideration, and all the more reason to be resentful. Unfamiliar as yet to the particulars of this unspoken code, Digby persevered. He wrote her a poem, which was especially outrageous since poetry was something boys simply did not do. His precocious ode went something like this:

You are old but I don't care
If you wear a wig and I have hair.
It always seems that you are near
to slap me right or grab a beer.
So what more is there to say
but Grandma Swank is set to stay.

The poem made her smile, though the truth was that Grandma Swank was illiterate and smiled mostly because she was embarrassed about her inability to read. She wondered if Digby was mocking her by giving her the paper with the "chicken scratch" across it. He was not. No one knew her secret, though her inability to read explained why she never followed the grocery list, ignored the notes by the phone, and never took messages.

Her habit of sitting with the Bible cracked open on her lap was a clever ruse. Perhaps the heft of it brought more comfort than reading the words inside. God was the genie held between its covers. She quoted it frequently, though for Lizabeth Swank, quoting the Bible meant assuming a certain tone and language before lifting her chin in a precise manner. Scripture was part attitude, and part intonation.

She assumed she didn't need to know what was inside to make a righteous point. Instead of a tool for guidance, she used it to suit her purposes. She quoted verses when it came to chores, eating before dinner, and watching too much TV, especially when there was something she wanted to watch on another channel. The Bible according to Grandma Swank was much more improv than actual text.

Misunderstanding her small smile at receiving the poem, Digby eagerly tried to build on his supposed success. He decided to buy her something nice from Woolworths for her birthday. That would require money. In need of funds, he set up a makeshift refreshment stand. Since this was Running Falls with its smoke stacks, sooty brick, and heavy haze, a lemonade stand would've been a complete waste of time. In Running Falls, the saying went, "If life gives you lemons, have a beer." Thusly inspired, Digby dragged a case of Pabst to the corner, and sold longnecks for ten cents apiece. He'd already made seventy cents from the on-the-way-to-work crowd, when Grandma Swank came outside and chased him from the curb with a fly swatter in one hand, and a rosary in the other. Her curses sounded like the gobbles of an excited she-turkey, an apt comparison, given the hang and sway of her chin pouches. Once inside the back screen door, Grandma Swank turned her rheumy eyes heavenward, and asked why before swatting and rosary-slapping Digby a final time.

Shamed by her display and stinging from his punishment, Digby nonetheless persevered in his mission to buy her a birthday gift. The next afternoon he tiptoed into the kitchen, and gingerly opened the drawer that held the precious Swank cache of S&H Green Stamps. These promotional stamps were given when purchases were made from participating vendors, and then pasted into booklets. Those booklets could then be redeemed for various household items. It was a perfect plan for a financially strapped seven-year-old. The booklets had been in that drawer for ages. Digby put them in a grocery bag, and snuck out the back door. Surely the suitably named Redemption Center two blocks away would have something to win Grandma Swank's favor.

Bells rang as he opened the door. It was hot inside, and smelled stale and flowery, like a rotten handkerchief. Enid Snares sat reading a romance novel at the counter. Folks said she was a spinster on account of her one droopy eyelid. All Enid wanted out of life was to pay off her double wide trailer, and die in a dry climate. Most folks saw her as a dreamer.

Digby approached Enid, and dumped the contents of the bag on the counter. Enid retrieved her glasses from the end of the chain about her neck, peered over the top of them, and with the pointing of a bony finger, said he could choose from any of the items on the third shelf of the opposite wall. He was disappointed when Enid told him they most certainly did not sell liquor. With a slightly peeved jab of her finger, she once again pointed to the third shelf.

The merchandise looked as though it was arranged by a small child playing store. The shelf held, among other things: a cane fishing pole; a small suitcase with a variety of curlers; a pendulum on a black wooden frame; a plastic flower arrangement stuck in a plastic Grecian pedestal planter; a rotating holiday color wheel; and a sunburst wall clock.

Digby paced from one end of the shelf to the other for almost a half hour. Twice he chose items, and turned to approach the counter before turning back around to place them back on the shelf. Enid let out a whistle of frustration, and her eyelid drooped all the more before she turned back to her romance. Finally, Digby chose the jewelry box on the very end. When the lid was opened, a ballerina sprang to attention off the red felt and danced at a less than perpendicular angle to a tinny rendition of Mozart's

Piano Sonata in A Major.

Digby gave the gift to Grandma Swank the moment he got home. She looked at him suspiciously, and finally thanked him. He thought for a moment he saw the trace of a smile, which may or may not have been Grandma Swank's own version of a smirk. He told her he wanted to give her something special for her birthday. He never saw the jewelry box again.

No one ever questioned the missing stamps. Lila assumed it was part of a Mother's Day gift, and Rog assumed it went toward a new fishing rod for Father's Day. As more stamps continued to accumulate, the missing books and the supposed surprises were eventually forgotten. It was only mentioned years later when the booklets were redeemed for the sunburst wall clock that adorned the Swank rec room. "I could have sworn we had more of these," was all that Lila had said.

Though only the left-handedness has been mentioned, Grandma Swank had other reasons for her disdain of Digby. He was odd and nervous and manic and silent. Had he been born a few decades later, he would have been one of those children medicated into an acceptable middle ground. As it was, he was a queer duck, and always off by himself. His head was never where his body seemed to be. He was either lost in a fantasy, or on to the next thing, or hopelessly stuck on something from hours or days or weeks ago. The boy was branded a dreamer, which was not very practical.

As a result of his malady, he rarely lifted the toilet seat to pee, and liked to stick his fingers in cakes and pies. He walked into doors, sat in the middle of the floor, and never hooked the gate when he went out the back. He was the absentminded sort—leaving toys on the stairs, tripping over the garden hose, and forgetting to hang up the telephone.

Sometimes his absentmindedness was preferable to his flights of fancy. He liked to lie behind the couch and surprise people a moment before they sat down, or hide behind things and play spy, absorbing forbidden bits of information. He made messes relentlessly. He fashioned a wig made of mud for the family dog, and tore all the newspapers in the basement into long strips for his own New Year's Eve party in July. Grandma Swank found it all quite intolerable. Even when she could stand no more of his unacceptable behavior, more was yet to come.

No one would forget the evening Aunt Lucy and Uncle Willard came for dinner. By family standards, they were well travelled and cultured. They'd just returned from a vacation to Las Vegas. Standing behind the long curtains in the living room, as he sometimes liked to do, Digby overheard his mother say something along the lines of, "I hope we're not too boring, after the casinos and shows. Lucy and Willard saw stars like Marty Allen and Mitzi Gaynor there."

Lila was always competitive with Lucy. Lila married into a life she knew, but Lucy married into a life she wanted, or at least one a step farther in that general direction. Lila felt Lucy lived beyond her means, and Lucy knew Lila was envious. Their bond as sisters had a hook on either end.

Even as a child, or perhaps because he was a child, Digby sensed this. He knew his aunt and uncle were coming over to brag about their vacation. Four postcards from Lucy and Willard's trip were already spread out across the face of the refrigerator, and they'd only been in Las Vegas for three days. The evening would be nothing but talk about the Four Queens, and the Stardust, and the Flamingo, and the Dunes, and all the glitzy Mitzi and Marty times they'd had in the lush carpeted wonderland of Vegas. Digby had overheard his parents say as much. "They're coming to rub our faces in it because they know I can't afford Vegas. Thank goodness our slide projector is broken," said Rog.

Lila shuddered. Rog only saw things that way because she'd explained it to him like that during a weak moment after Lucy and Willard's trip to Niagara Falls two years before. She shouldn't have said anything. Rog was always easier to keep in check when he was in the dark. "Don't say anything and please don't mention our projector. If it comes up, don't let Lucy know that anything we have is broken."

"My lips are sealed."

Unfortunately, Rog's promise did not fill her with confidence. Lila knew that Rog's sealed lips could be easily lubricated with a cocktail or two.

Digby loved his parents and, wrapped in the folds of the living room curtains, he decided to help. He'd make sure the dinner was a memorable night for everyone. Come Friday night, he'd put on an extravaganza of his own, one his aunt and uncle wouldn't be seeing anytime soon, even in Vegas.

Digby slinked from behind the curtains to his favorite thinking and napping spot, crouched in the corner nook behind his father's easy chair. All he needed to succeed was a sensational act, and all that really required was a gimmick. He must've fallen asleep, because the next thing he recalled was his brother Tom saying, "Now that's entertaining!" By the music, Digby knew that Tom was watching Hawaii Five-O. Digby peered over the back of the chair at the new Zenith Living Color TV. His eyes widened. It was a sign, perhaps even divine intervention. He had heard of such things described as "lamp posts that light the Lord's path." Ignoring them was a sin.

For his scheme to succeed, he'd need a costume. He started by taping two-ply toilet paper strips to his belt in layers, even using some of the "special" pink tissue to make the skirt two-toned. The pink toilet paper was for "the ladies" and used primarily for Lila's bridge club. The sheer draping of the skirt allowed for plenty of movement. It flowed. Once his skirt was completed, Digby used one of his mother's sequined scarves as a bandana. Lila would go through periods in which she'd purchase flashy items of clothing, and then promptly consider them too Bohemian to wear or even return. The sequined bandana was one of those items.

To enhance the costume, Digby added a couple of his mother's beaded necklaces, and toyed with the idea of heels before opting for a more authentic look by remaining barefoot. He still felt something was missing. Seeking inspiration, Digby lifted the embroidered lid of Grandma Swank's sewing box. On top was a sheath of gingham, dull by even Amish standards. Beneath the gingham, he discovered a woven sleeve containing a small framed picture of a handsome, somber-faced man in some sort of naval attire. Beneath this were a couple balls of yarn, knitting needles, a pincushion, and assorted fabric scraps. There were also two doilies of festive yellow felt with a white, lacy back border. The circles were bright, and reminded Digby of the sun. They'd be perfect for a top.

Digby eyed himself from the left and from the right before the full length mirror, and smiled. He was the absolute embodiment of pizzazz. Aunt Lucy and Uncle Willard could brag of Las Vegas until they were blue in the face. He was about to show them that the Swanks had a flashy star-spangled revue under their very own roof. Since he assumed this was God's idea, Digby was certain of success. There was no reason to think otherwise.

On the night of the dinner, Digby waited until all the adults had downed a few cocktails and retired to the living room. Positioning his bright red Close N' Play Phonograph just outside the arch of the dining room, he put the Hawaii Five-O single on the turntable. His brother Tom had bought The Ventures' 45. Digby turned the volume a bit beyond High. Promising endless future favors, he convinced Katie to flip the overhead light on and off. Lowering the lid of his sound system, he shook the tension from his fingertips, and breathed deeply. He could hear the soft scratch at the record's start. He took a couple of deep breaths through his mouth. No need to worry. He was doing the Lord's work. He was filled with the Holy Spirit.

Digby nodded to Katie. With the flip of the lights off, the living room grew silent. Before anyone could utter a word, Digby leapt into the center of the room and the lights turned on, the accompanying gasp in sync with the opening drum roll. Digby began his wild hip gyrations to the flip of lights. The sequins caught the flashing light. His toilet paper skirt fluttered in a blur of pink and white, parting just enough for quick flashes of flesh and underpants. The yellow doilies covered his chubby boy-breasts.

Digby smiled. He was sure Mitzi Gaynor never wowed an

audience in quite this way, and indeed he was right. Just when it seemed he had them in the palm of his hand, Grandma Swank leapt from her chair. Screaming that those were her doilies, she ripped them from his chest, and accused him of going through her things. In the midst of her tirade, Rog went to shut off "that damn music." As he rounded the corner, Katie stopped laughing and flipping the light switch. Seeing his anger, she burst into tears. "Oh Papa, I didn't know. I thought it was okay." Katie was daddy's little girl. Crying could get her out of anything.

Aunt Lucy and Uncle Willard shared a look. Lila saw it, and knew just what it meant. A moment later, she grabbed Digby by the arm and dragged him into the kitchen. His little toilet paper skirt came undone, leaving a trail of pink and white across the carpet. Already teary and in serious nipple pain, he began crying. He told his mother he was trying to entertain Aunt Lucy and Uncle Willard. He said he was just trying to make her proud by being a show-stopper and showing that the Swanks weren't second best. The frankness of his comment caused Lila to stiffen and reach for a cigarette. Digby explained that he'd overheard her saying she hoped they wouldn't be bored.

"Oh, I am sure they weren't bored," replied Lila with an uncharacteristic display of irony. She exhaled a column of smoke and picked a bit of tobacco from her tongue.

"I was only doing God's work," he added.

Lila looked at him, and smiled. Rather than find out just how God was involved in all this, explain why his dance was inappropriate, or address the issues in any way that might be comprehensible to a seven-year-old, his mother handed Digby a stack of cookies, and sent him off to bed. That was just how the Swanks dealt with things.

When Lila returned to the living room, everyone was talking about how dry the summer had been, except for Grandma Swank, who sat scowling beside the liquor cart. The silences between comments stretched. Aunt Lucy and Uncle Willard finished their drinks in gulps. Lila could only imagine how they rehashed the evening on their drive home.

Grandma Swank was livid about Digby's behavior. She claimed to have been enraged by the display, when in fact she was much angrier over his "rampaging" through her things. She quoted scripture that was not scripture, and muttered about the incident for weeks, under her breath and over the vacuum cleaner. Soon, every relative on her side knew all about his lewd native dance. She spared no details in her recounting, and even added a few of her own. In her version, Digby was nude and wearing make-up. "And that boy wasn't even punished! He was rewarded with food. As though that one needs another ounce of feed. Can you imagine? Why, if he was my boy, I'd have him shipped off to military school tomorrow."

Though everyone knew how she could be, when Grandma Swank fumed and seethed, people listened. It was always easiest to agree with her, and sharing her outrage was really the only way folks knew to bond with her. Most felt closest to her when third parties were being maligned.

Grandma Swank made a grand show of throwing her doily pattern into the trash. Actually, she threw it into the garbage and promptly fished it out when nobody noticed. When she threw her doily pattern away the second time, it was accompanied by a sigh so huge that it bordered on a breathy scream. She claimed she could never make another doily without recalling that evening, and that heathen child's nakedness.

"Then I guess we'll just have to rely on coasters," shrugged Lila, who'd had quite enough of her mother-in-law's theatrics. Doilies were so old-fashioned anyway.

When Digby braved a peek inside Grandma Swank's sewing box a few days later, the picture of the handsome man in naval attire was nowhere to be found. Years later, Digby learned that Grandpa Swank had never been in the armed forces.

After months and years of this sort of conflict, an unspoken compromise developed between Grandma Swank and the boy. In general, they steered clear of one another as much as was humanly possible in the modest Swank family home. Digby stopped trying to please her and, for the most part, she ignored him. The latter had grown easier with the onset of her macular degeneration, which Digby intermittently heard as spectacular and immaculate degeneration. He frequently hid and watched, waiting for her degeneration. Would she melt or rot? Would she break apart and slowly ascend? Maybe she'd just disintegrate without making a mess. He had no idea what to expect, or even if the result would be gruesome or divine.

Avoidance became an unspoken rule between Digby and Grandma Swank, but like all rules—spoken, written, or implied—there was an exception. For Grandma and Digby, that exception was Dark Shadows. For one half hour every weekday, a truce was called on the foggy grounds of gothic romanticism. The eerie lull of the opening melody drew them to the television, and they were both in place daily for the opening line, "My name is Victoria Winters..."

Dark Shadows nourished each of their ample dark sides. Though no Collins blood flowed in her icy veins, Lizabeth Swank imagined herself as Elizabeth Collins Stoddard. She would oftentimes smile in a superior manner after viewing an episode. Her aspiration of being a powerful matriarch with her hair piled high was transparent. If the phone rang after an episode, since no one who knew her would dare to call during, Grandma Swank would "ahnswer" in Stoddard's grandiose tone. She paused at windows during thunderstorms, and cocked her head when the wind howled. She all but climbed and descended the stairs with a candelabra. At her advanced age and in the midst of her supposed degeneration, Grandma Swank had finally found a role model.

Digby was enchanted by the gloomy atmosphere of Collinwood, as well as "the old house." It was a magical land of graveyards and baying hounds, the tumultuous sea and omnipresent thunderstorms. There were crypts and curses, seances and shadowy facades shrouded in cobwebs. In Collinwood, any sort of creature might be encountered, and most were simply part of the social fabric. Even left-handedness was acceptable. Digby longed for a real life that was as otherworldly as the daily soap. He knew it would suit him. Grandma Swank felt the same way.

Digby could sense a commonality between them, and perhaps for the first time, he somewhat understood her. They both shared a desire for a more dismal reality, or perhaps a world that more accurately reflected the darkness each harbored inside. Both wanted vampires, ghosts, werewolves, runes, time travel, the undead, and the mysterious I Ching. When the creepy theme returned and the credits rolled at the end of each episode, the two inched back to opposite ends of the couch, and everything returned to its usual state in the Swank house.

Then without warning, this routine weekday scenario changed. As soon as Digby had awakened one day in early June, he heard the words everywhere: ROBERT KENNEDY SHOT! The Democratic hopeful for the 1968 presidential nomination had been shot three times in the kitchen of the Ambassador Hotel in Los Angeles. His life hung in the balance at Good Samaritan Hospital.

Things looked grim, but Grandma Swank looked even grimmer. Teary-eyed, she watched the ongoing television coverage. Robert Kennedy reminded her of her dead husband, though not as much as JFK had. Digby stared at her on the couch. He was in unspeakable awe, shocked that any event or circumstance could make Grandma Swank cry.

Digby's gut reaction was to cry as well. Instead, he tried to make his grandmother feel better by smiling. He should have known she'd be immune to his charms. Instead of a smile, Digby's fateful smirk appeared. Grandma Swank took it as mockery. She stopped her sobbing long enough to reach from her end of the couch and slap him across the face, and then slap him again on the return. Digby touched his cheek in shock, and then his other cheek in double shock, before running upstairs. He wasn't used to this sort of abuse. Usually, he saw it coming or heard the jingle of the rosary beads. Grandma's sobbing turned to sniffles. Moments later, he heard the squeak of her sensible heels as she moved towards the telephone. He heard the sound of the rotary dial. He crouched at the top of the stairs and listened, hidden in the shallows of his own breath.

She made several calls. In every quivery recreation of the

Kennedy tragedy, Grandma Swank included the episode with Digby. She spread word among the Swanks that he was a spoiled child with no respect for his elders, his peers, other people's privacy, or even for life itself. She said he'd laughed when he heard that Kennedy was shot. "Now to me, that's downright unholy."

She pulled one and all into her foxhole of hate. Digby wanted to yell from the top of the stairs that it wasn't true, that she was just some salty old fossil who loathed him no matter what he did or said or felt. He wanted to yell that all this was evidence of her factual degeneration, but it was too late. He sat helplessly in the wake of her curse. The witch had used words instead of magic. He'd already been bad-mouthed and labeled several times, but this label was even more severe—unholy. This was even worse than being left-handed. Her accusation caused him to question just who he was, and how he felt. Maybe she was right. Maybe instead of being maligned, he'd simply been revealed.

Feeling completely misunderstood, he ran outside to his fort. In the clatter of the back door's slam, his tears fell. His fort was more a refuge than an actual fort since it was discovered rather than built, but Digby went there when he felt the world, or at least the superpowers in his world, were against him. Given his circumstances, he went there a lot.

His fort was beneath the heavy shroud of a large weeping willow in the backyard, along the alley. He loved to sit sheltered on the dirt where the sun didn't shine, and look out upon the world through the canopied greenery. He felt invisible there rather than merely overlooked. Invisible meant safe.

That afternoon, he parted the hang of branches as he'd done countless times before, and plopped onto the worn ground. He hunched into himself as his tears fell upon the dirt. He jabbed at the ground with a stick. The hostile world was out there, spinning in its wretched orbit and full of terrible things that he didn't understand. In here nothing could harm him, or so it seemed. He saw the smattering of teardrops, and then felt something. A prick. At first he thought he'd sat on a stick. Then came another prick, sharper this time. Something was very wrong. His safe haven had been compromised. Bees! Unknowingly, the boy had sat directly on the hive. His fleshy buttocks were all but smothering the nest. The hive was having none of it. The queen ordered her minions to retaliate, or at least that's what he imagined. Perhaps they did not need a queen's okay when it came to pressing issues like having a big ass squishing you. Perhaps some things even workers and drones could decide for themselves.

At once, dozens of bees were upon him. Digby leapt from his cross-legged pose, and ran in a loop about the backyard before charging through the battered back screen door, screaming and sobbing. He tripped over a loose edge of the yellowed linoleum, and sprawled across the floor.

Grandma Swank put down the phone, and came to see what all the noise was about. He blubbered about the bees and his red swollen hind end. She eyed him coldly. Now it was her turn to smirk, and her turn to sting. "Ho, ho, look who's crying now! Those bees were there for good reason. God's messengers is what they were, the honey of the rock, a swarm of retribution." She quoted a Bible verse that was not really a Bible verse, and said she considered it his just desserts. She even said as much to the party on the other end of the phone line when she walked back to continue her call.

"Then God's messengers are jerks," Digby shouted after her.

She scoffed, and asked the listener if they'd heard. She covered the receiver with her hand. "Sometimes the sword is swift, boy. Sometimes Christ himself leads the cavalry." Turning her back, she finished the call, and walked into the kitchen to make a pickle sandwich for herself. She refused to care for him in any way, and was clearly thrilled to be indifferent. It was a small moment of pleasure for her amidst that period of national shock and sadness.

Digby got up from the floor, ran to his room, and flopped onto the bed. He hurt so much and in so many ways. It seemed he'd done nothing to deserve any of it. He was still there crying when Lila got home. Her office had closed early on account of the Kennedy shooting. The Kennedys were the closest thing the Irish Catholics had to royalty.

Lila knocked lightly on Digby's door, so lightly he hardly

heard her. Lila was subdued. The Kennedy thing had made most folks much quieter. She brought ointment for his stings, and a plate of windmill cookies as well. She eventually fed most of his pain away. He didn't say a word about Grandma Swank. If his parents didn't know by now, they didn't want to know, and if they didn't want to know, they must not care. It only confirmed what he already suspected.

In addition to thinking him a Godless menace and a snoop, Grandma Swank considered Digby a borderline idiot. "Not the sharpest tool in the shed, is he?" she'd sometimes say with a wink at Tom. Some folks agreed with her, but some folks agree on a lot of things that aren't necessarily true, sometimes because they're stupid, and sometimes because they just want to be agreeable. Digby was sensitive and creative, and may have even seemed a bit off, but he wasn't stupid. More accurately, he was misunderstood. Sometimes, he thought too much or got distracted, or was two steps ahead or three steps to the side, or had a tendency to mix up what was true and what was make-believe. As a result of any number of factors, he sometimes did stupid things.

Robert Kennedy remained in extremely critical condition for twenty-six hours, before his death was announced. In the week that followed, everyone was in a state of glum despair, even though it was widely suspected that Robert Kennedy had easily bypassed Purgatory with so many prayers and masses being offered in his name. In that time of national bereavement, Digby did a lot of thinking, but little of it concerned Robert or Ethel or "those poor children." He wasn't even concerned with the length of the mourning dresses worn by the Kennedy women, an issue of great concern among many parishioners at Holy Martyrs.

In the midst of this dolorous maelstrom of black tulle and tears, Digby had been thinking mostly about himself. He knew he'd never find acceptance where he was—not in his house or on his block or in his parish. The people of Running Falls didn't understand him, and for the most part, he didn't understand them, either. After stewing on the subject, he decided that he needed to find a place where there were people like him, people who were misunderstood or outsiders or perhaps even stranger than he was. He needed to find a place where even the freaks belonged. He'd leave Running Falls, and run away to the only place he knew of where he thought he would find acceptance. He'd flee to Collinsport, Maine—to the land of Dark Shadows.

His dream was to reside at Collinwood Manor amidst the haughty likes of Elizabeth Stoddard Collins, Roger Collins, and the rest of that brooding, shadowy bunch. But sometimes dreams need to be compromised. He couldn't just waltz into the grand foyer and plead for adoption, or ask to have the west wing opened. He had to be realistic, if he was to survive in a world that he'd been repeatedly told was a cruel and difficult place.

He decided that he would live in Collinsport proper, and survive there by whatever means necessary. He could get a job washing mugs at the Blue Whale, help Maggie out at the coffee shop, master the art of inserting ships into bottles, become a lighthouse keeper, or maybe just become someone's child. Maybe he could be David Collins' or even the ghostly Sarah's friend. He'd sort out the particulars once he arrived. Getting to that coastal fishing village was his big chance for happiness, or at least acceptance. If people didn't understand him there, he didn't know what he would do. Perhaps he'd have no recourse but to throw himself from the cliffs at Widow's Hill, just as Josette had done when the townsfolk didn't accept her.

In order to reach that austere seaside paradise, all Digby knew was that he needed to head northeast. He'd been given a compass the previous Christmas. Unfortunately, his portly neighbor, Bob Van Camp, had sat on it a couple of weeks before, and shattered the face. Mr. Van Camp didn't even apologize. His wife, Ginny shook her pin-curled head and said, "Oh Bob!" The Van Camps were his parent's best friends, so they did all sorts of things without apologizing. Bob and Ginny Van Camp laughed when they listened, laughed when they spoke, and still managed to be assholes.

Digby reasoned that a broken compass was better than no compass at all. At least a broken compass gave him the illusion of direction, and that can be important at the start of any journey.

Besides, he had a good idea of which direction was northeast. That was in the general way of his father's office.

With the words "My name is Victoria Winters" resounding in his head, Digby left for Collinsport the next day after school. That would give him plenty of time for a good start before nightfall. If he set his course and kept walking northeast, he'd eventually arrive in Collinsport. After two hours of winding his way through the red brick byways and back ways, he reached the outskirts of Running Falls, ambling along the stretch between Loaf and Flounder Lakes, which bordered town.

Here the land opened up to a marshy stretch of low trees and lake brush on either side. This area stunk like the Band-Aid factory that sat upwind across the lake. Situated along this sparse road was Doebbler House, the closest thing Running Falls had to a genuine haunted mansion. As with most Running Falls reputations, this one was based solely on appearances, confirmed by hearsay, and soon accepted as fact. Truth be told, it did look as though it could house spirits. Digby had gone by the derelict residence plenty of times. Oftentimes, one of his brothers would grab him as they passed to try to make him jump. Most times they succeeded.

Doebbler House was quite different from the usual Running Falls residence, which was either boring, trashy, or had an attached carport. The horror of most Running Falls homes was nothing mysterious or otherworldly, but the simple reality of having to live there. Doebbler House, on the other hand, sparked the imagination. It was a gabled and dilapidated wooden monstrosity of dark brown, dominated by a sagging wraparound porch. The shutters were typically drawn, except for one in an attic window that hung menacingly by its hinges, creaking in the wind. Doebbler House was perched squarely on a hill leading down to the larger Flounder Lake. It was no Collinwood, but it would have to do for now.

Digby approached the house, and noticed the placard with the creepy white hand against a black background in the window. That was the Helping Hand, a sign he recognized from his first grade class. If he or any of his classmates were ever lost or in trouble, they were instructed to go to a house bearing the Helping Hand in the front window. They were told to say that they were Roman Catholic, and mention Holy Martyrs, the name of their parish. Sister assured them that by doing so, they would find assistance. Knowing the name of his parish was such an important part of his upbringing, that for years Digby thought Holy Martyrs was part of his formal address.

Sister Anthony had let out a slight hiss and shushed him when Digby asked why people who wanted to harm kids didn't just put a Helping Hand in the window to lure them. "It could be a trap," he said, turning to his classmates for support but finding none. Even as a first grader, Digby was accused of "complicating the issue." He suspected they would understand such things in Collinsport, where complicating issues was a daily affair. However, he doubted the steely, severe seaport had Helping Hand signs. In Collinsport, he'd probably see a talisman suspended on a string over a threshold, perhaps cloves of garlic or a crucifix carved from whalebone.

The steps of Doebbler House creaked as he climbed nearer the front door. The shutter banged overhead. A crow cawed from a bent, rusted laundry tree, cutting through the hum and chorus of croaking frogs. Digby was unsettled by it all and still suspicious of the Helping Hand, but trap or no trap, he was tired and a bit cold. Chips of curling paint fell at his feet when he knocked on the door, lightly at first and then with a bit more force. The crow took flight with the parting of a yellowed curtain to the side of the door. The frogs grew silent. Digby heard the creak of floorboards inside.

An elderly man in shabby gray clothes and saggy gray skin opened the door. With a thoughtful scratch of his head, he introduced himself as Harry Doebbler and asked the boy's name. Digby considered using an alias as a way of covering his tracks, but he only thought of doing so after he'd already given his real name. With a small nod, the elderly gent ushered him inside. The house smelled like old man. Digby pondered the exact components of the odor—something like mildew and powdery sweat, or death and Old Spice, or mothballs and mashed bananas.

Harry offered the boy iced tea, and shuffled out of the room in slippered feet. He returned in a few moments with the tea on a little metal tray. It tasted awful, but Digby drank it anyway. Harry wasn't much of a talker, so they sat mostly in silence in the front parlor. The clock on the mantle ticked and chimed. The wind howled outside, and the shutter banged erratically. His rocking chair squeaked. It was a very long twenty minutes.

When the clock chimed six, Digby heard honking outside. It was his father's car. Rog and Grandma Swank were inside. Digby gave Harry a look. The old man's gaze drifted over Digby's head and out the window. Digby got up and thanked him for the tea. The old man may have ratted on him, but he did serve refreshments—though the tea tasted like crap. Digby dragged his feet down the front steps of Doebbler House, and reluctantly got in the backseat of the car.

He was humiliated. There was no need to lecture or cuss him out. Instead, his father pulled out of the drive, and asked him where the hell he thought he was going. When Digby said, "Collinsport," Rog said he'd never heard of it, and he knew all the towns in and around these parts. Hearing the name, Grandma Swank turned in her seat and stared at the boy for a long time. "Idiot," she finally muttered.

Digby gave her a cold stare before looking out the window. She might not be willing to make an effort to find a place where she belonged, but that wasn't going to stop him. Maybe her immaculate degeneration had drained her of the will to try for anything better. It didn't matter. One day he'd make a pilgrimage to his promised land, his Elysian Fields. One day, he'd find a place where he was happy and accepted.

Realizing that Grandma Swank saw even the attempt foolhardy, caused a shift in Digby's perception of her. He saw how terrible life must have been for her. Seeing the world as such a hopeless place had made her bitter. The thought of becoming like her, with her dead hands and hopeless life and spectacular degeneration, suddenly seemed terrifying. The only thing worse than being unhappy, was being unhappy and unwilling to do anything about it. Sitting in the backseat, Digby shook his head.

Idiot yourself, he thought before adding That will never be me.

Perhaps it was an obsession with miracles, or his interest in the supernatural, or the folly of youth, but Digby refused to let even the laws of nature determine his behavior. That was when he started having the flying dreams, or rather, when he started acting upon them. Actually, they were more floating than flying dreams, since he glided more than soared. These recurrent nighttime visions were surely a sign. Maybe they meant he was an angel.

In dream lore, flying supposedly symbolizes that things are about to "take off." Given his grim support system and limited life prospects, Digby doubted that was the case. He interpreted the dreams in a flat, literal fashion. He prayed that it was real and true, and that the key to human flight had simply yet to be discovered.

Digby loved the feeling of those flying dreams, of being unattainable and free and able to shit down upon it all. There was power there. Maybe Collinsport wasn't the answer. Perhaps above was where he was meant to be. Maybe all it took was the gumption to try.

Eager to find a home in the sky, he climbed atop the garage one especially windy Saturday afternoon. About to bridge the species of man and bird and make his dreams come true, he took care to wear loose fitting clothing so as not to constrict his limbs. That wouldn't do. In his flying dream, the wind caressed him beneath his arms. As it gently lifted him, he'd rise on tiptoe, then a bit higher, balanced and equipoised. Finally, he'd be aloft, soaring over the trees, trailers, houses, the Band-Aid factory, the tannery, and all the dismal lives in the small-minded backwater of Running Falls.

He moved to the very edge of the garage roof, his sneakers at the gutter, then on the very lip of it. He waited perhaps a minute or so for a good sustained gust, and he rose on his toes. His shirt expanded just a bit more in the wind. He'd almost found that point of letting go. He heard a creaking. Almost there. He looked to the sky and wished with all his might, just as the crumbling gutter gave way. Screaming, he threw up his arms, and in less than a second, fell into the line of metal trash cans below like a big, fat, wingless stone.

Hearing the racket, his parents ran outside. "Digby Timothy Swank," screamed Lila, looking at Digby lying amidst the garbage before taking a quick look around for any prying eyes. Though they were their best friends, the Van Camps liked to push their boy, Johnny, forward as a normal youngster. "Our Johnny is all boy," they'd say, shaking their heads and smiling at Johnny's latest boyish doing. Johnny was the same age as Digby, but he seemed almost a different species. The Van Camps already thought Digby queer. Something like this would surely be fodder for haughty sympathy or outright laughter.

Rog followed quickly behind Lila. He had a rake in his hands. He scratched his head to see Digby atop the garbage. He thought the raccoons were back.

Lila looked upon the sprawl of trash cans, thankful that her son seemed unhurt, and equally thankful that no one else was about. "What the blazes were you up to?"

"I thought I might fly."

"You thought you could fly?" asked Rog incredulously.

"Well, I thought I might at least float or something," Digby managed weakly, looking down to brush off his trousers. Suddenly it all sounded so foolish.

Grandma Swank was just approaching when she heard his words. She promptly caught Rog's eye as if to say. "See, I told you that boy was at least a little retarded."

Understanding Digby's desperation to leave Running Falls requires a deeper understanding of the place itself. The town stunk. The smell came partly from the adhesives used at the Band-Aid factory across Loaf Lake, and partly from the tannery that lay on the outskirts of town. But Running Falls was more than just an offensive odor. It assaulted any number of the senses. Perhaps the statistics spoke most eloquently. Running Falls had the highest teen pregnancy rate, and greatest average number of offspring per parent in the state. Even more telling, the residents were proud of those statistics, so more accurately, Running Falls boasted the highest teenage pregnancy rate and greatest number of offspring per parent in the state. Needless to say, it was very Catholic. Every other house had a rusted car on cement blocks in its front yard. It was a town of kitchen haircuts, double-negatives, and bloody hoop earrings found on the sidewalk. It was the perfect place to grow up, only if you liked living in your imagination.

Longtime Running Falls resident and Chamber of Commerce chairperson Donna May Greenshaw shared a different opinion of her hometown. "Running Falls is a nice place to raise your young. There are parks. There is a school system, and the largest automobile junkyard in the state. It is neighborly. There is every food cuisine imaginable, at least every one within reason. There is a roller rink, and the statewide snowmobile races. There is even the World's Largest Hairball, and a stuffed wildlife diorama at some museum downtown. There are also over a dozen rifle ranges. There are things for folks of all sorts and inclinations to do."

Being smallish and insular, Running Falls was also a natural hotbed of gossip, much of it true. It was a "calling across the front yard with a baby on one hip" sort of town. There were domestic disputes on front lawns, business transactions evolving into brawls, family feuds, girl gangs, and babies born in the toilet on prom night. There were breakups in bowling alleys, and lap dances at the high school. There was every ingredient in the hearty stew of hillbilly love and hate. Running Falls had lots of relationships with hyphens and dashes. It was not unheard of for students to have brothers for fathers, uncles for cousins, and teachers as girlfriends, and that was the Catholic school.

Running Falls had everything that comprised the rich tapestry of modern society, but given the town itself, it was less a tapestry and more like the tarp over a big top. Running Falls had a one-legged go-go dancer, a court stenographer with Tourette's, the fattest triplets in the state and, appropriately enough, a clown guild. Mayor Wilson of Running Falls mostly legislated from a bar stool, and was photographed vomiting out his car window on more than one occasion, once even on Election Day. His winning campaign slogan for upwards of twenty years was Vote for Wilson: He Hasn't Burned The Town Down Yet.

In Running Falls, the school system standards were more a formality than any real kind of expectation. The smart ones tended to leave town anyway, so the Board of Education figured it was in the town's best interests not to let the students learn too much. "No good will come from having a bunch of children being too smart for their own good," former school board president Vern Johnson was recorded as saying in the minutes from one board meeting. Though many would call it unethical, Mr. Johnson was only being realistic. Smarter people were more likely to get dissatisfied. Besides, it didn't take a college or a high school degree to work at a convenience store or a gas station or at the Band-Aid factory. The jobs in Running Falls were mostly factory work, or providing services to other service providers. The only folks outside of those interlocking loops were there by family, or connections, or due to a religious calling. No one really worked their way up in Running Falls, they worked their way out.

4 - The Real Thing

Digby's other grandma and grandpa lived across town. They rented. Grandpa Vint was a former saxophonist, with none of the glamorous decadence typically associated with big band musicians. He wasn't a name dropper, or a boozer, or a skirt chaser. Grandpa Vint became a novelty on the touring circuit after losing an arm in the Great War. A saxophonist who gave an arm for his country deserved a hand. He was a true patriot, and a symbol of the great bravery and sacrifices of millions of "our boys." As a result, he became a very bankable act in the postwar era. "Booking gold," was what they called him. Fans adored him, and his frequent mistakes in playing only made him seem all the more courageous. Women often wept right in the middle of the dance floor. Men clapped him on the shoulder, and offered cigars. The novelty tapered off after a few years, and he gave up touring after Aunt Lucy was born. Then he became a one-armed accountant.

When Digby was young, his grandfather's lack of an arm frightened him. The boy never grew accustomed to its absence. It was strange to consider that a man's most distinguishing characteristic was something that he lacked. Usually it—or the lack of it—was covered, but once, Digby saw his grandfather shirtless when he was changing before a family function. The flap of flesh at his shoulder horrified him. Digby expected it to be a dollish form of amputation, a simple tab where an arm could be popped back into place. Digby didn't expect a sort of boneless flipper. When he caught sight of it, the normally pallid boy paled all the more, the room whirled, and all sound seemed to round and echo as though he was listening to the world through a paper towel tube. The spell promptly passed, but in the aftermath, Digby worried that this startling "lack" would somehow befall him. One day he might hop out of bed to began his day, and turn to find his arm still beneath the blankets. Sometimes his arm even felt gone when it went to sleep.

His brother laughed, and told Digby his grandfather's arm

had been blown to bits by a bomb. "Grandpa said there was a flash and then a pop, and then he felt the blood trickling, and then it went numb. Grandpa said his arm was full of metal chunks and springs and parts of clay pots, so they had him drink a bottle of brandy and then they sawed it off while he bit on a muddy boot." Though unbearably gruesome, the story reassured Digby. Tom loved stories like this. Tom read comic books about war, and his favorite TV show was Combat! Sensing that Digby was not of the same mind, since his favorite television show at the time was That Girl, Grandpa Vint never told him the story.

In addition to having one arm, Grandpa Vint was also obsessed with condensing and breaking down garbage. "Now, who put this cereal box in here?" he'd ask accusingly. With a small smile, he would fold the box flat before taking pains to fold it again several times lengthwise. The task was especially challenging for a one armed man, but perhaps that was part of the gratification he found in doing it.

Though he certainly knew how to pack a trash bag, Digby felt that Grandpa Vint's best quality was that he was married to Grandma Rose. Digby loved Grandma Rose. Saying so was not an obligation, as it had been with Grandma Swank. In fact, telling Grandma Rose he loved her was the truest thing he recalled saying. It didn't come from his brain. It came without thinking.

Grandma Rose put his crayon drawings on the refrigerator, and never made a fuss that he went outside the lines. "It's perfect just the way it is," she would always say. She didn't scoff when he wanted to play tea party, and even suggested that they wear hats. She showed Digby how to extend his pinkie when lifting the cup, and said that was how the society ladies did it. Sometimes Grandma Rose shared stories of her girlhood and growing up in Ithaca. "In autumn, it was the most beautiful place in the world, with the maple and the walnut and the oak trees. Those fields I used to play in seemed so endless." When she spoke of her life, she usually mentioned how it all went by so quickly. "In the blink of an eye, nothing more than that. And here I am, a grandmother."

Grandma Rose smelled of talc and lilac. Those scents sometimes still brought her face and the feel of her to mind, as did fresh baked oatmeal cookies. He often saw her in his mind's eye wearing a burgundy sweater, and seated in a darkened parlor. He remembered her large, moist eyes and gloved hugs, and the gentleness of her voice. She was warmth. She was softness. She was security. Being with her was the perfect place to be. To Grandma Rose, his left-handedness was just that and nothing more. She wasn't frightened by his smirk. Grandma Rose had nothing to hide. She knew he smiled differently and thought differently and behaved differently, and she loved that difference. She actually seemed to love him for all the things that made him unique. She said that made him her own.

Grandma Rose died violently. Digby was playing on the patio when the county sheriff's deputy car pulled into the driveway. He hid behind the hedge, and watched a uniformed man knock on the door. The busted screen door creaked as Rog ushered the officer inside. Digby watched through the screen as the patrolman told Lila the news. She moaned and crossed herself before her legs promptly buckled, and she collapsed upon the new Maytag. The metal gave a great hollow boom, and Digby backed away from it all with a primal unease. Something was terribly wrong. His mother was not the sort to collapse for no good reason, much less upon a major appliance. Fear churned in Digby's gut, snagging his breath and making his heart thump. Sound became only the pumping of blood in his ears. He had to flee. He had to stop thinking. Whatever this was, he didn't want to know.

He ran into the woods out back, leaping over the underbrush and ducking beneath branches. Being relatively uncoordinated, he stumbled over a termite mound. He skidded on his chest. The fall knocked the wind out of him, like a slap or a punch or being thrown from flight. Wiping the dirt from his face, he sat up. Nothing was quite real. Sound had returned, accompanied by a numbness. He scooted closer to the termite mound, and watched those black bodies scramble over the sandy cone. If he blurred his eyes, the mound seemed alive, consumed with darkness. Maybe if he blurred his eyes, everything would be alive. Maybe nothing would die if his sight was bad enough. He remembered thinking it then, even though he still didn't know. There's no way of telling just what he had heard, and what he'd blocked. Instinct and intuition can turn the truth into whatever is necessary.

Tom finally found him. "He was out back in the woods, about half a mile away. I tracked him, but it wasn't too hard. He broke branches and left prints as deep as a cow in heels. When I found him, his hand was stuck down a termite mound, like he was reaching deep for something. He was covered with the damn things. I wiped them off the best I could, but they'd bitten him up pretty good, and his hand had swelled to twice its size. Mom and Dad wanted us kids to stay home while they made the arrangements and all. That night, we all went fishing at the Loaf Lake landing. Even with his swollen hand, Digby managed to land a whopper catfish. It was nearly half his size, and he was a chubby kid. Seems almost tragic that we never got that fish to a taxidermist, but with Grandma dying and the funeral and all, it was a pretty hectic time."

A good-sized catfish was no fair swap for Grandma Rose. She was suddenly and mysteriously gone. Digby knew something horrible had happened, but nothing was explained. Everyone became very sad and abruptly muted whenever her name was spoken. During all of this, his mother changed as well. Lila moved like a heavy fog about the house, silent and without genuine substance. She would pause on stairs for no reason, and sometimes sit in the kitchen by herself. She found it hard to be both a mother and a grieving child.

Lila sighed to recall that time. "My mother's death was such a shock, and just so sudden. It's mostly a blur. I didn't know beans from bananas for about a year. My mother was a kind and wonderful woman, but Digby saw her as something more. He thought she hung the moon and stars. I knew what her death would mean to him, and I knew he needed to know what had happened. I wanted to tell him so many times, but the words weren't there. There weren't words for much of anything I was feeling at that time."

Grandma Rose was gone, and all Digby knew was that he shouldn't ask about it. Questions could bring answers, and he was afraid that the answers would make it worse. Had Grandma Rose done something awful or shameful or unspeakable? Did she just leave? Digby wondered if it was because she loved him, or because he loved her. He wondered if the love of a left-handed child who lived too much in his head and was born in a state of sin was reason enough for her to suddenly disappear.

Grandma Rose was gone, but in a way more present than ever. Framed photos of her appeared all about the Swank home—on the mostly knickknack laden bookshelves, on a wall in the hall, and behind the bar cart. She was suddenly everywhere, and nowhere. Grandma Rose smiled at Digby from all of the photos. He stared at the pinpoints of light deep in her dark eyes, but pictures couldn't capture what she was to him. Having her under glass wasn't the same. Things under glass can't touch or be felt. They have no smell. Things under glass are hard and preserved and removed by a cold, solid layer. Being under glass made Grandma Rose into all the things that she wasn't, and removed her in a way that seemed even more complete than merely having her gone.

Weeks later, when he was in the midst of playing dress up, Digby found a Virgin Mary at Lourdes prayer card with Grandma Rose's birth and death dates above The Prayer of St. Francis of Assisi tucked in his mother's jewelry drawer. It took a moment for him to realize just what he'd found, and another moment to take off the clip-on earrings and absorb what that discovery meant. Once the repercussions took hold, he slumped to the bed and stared at the card for what seemed an entire afternoon. Now everything was clear to him. She hadn't abandoned him because he loved her, she'd been taken from him because he loved her. Digby was sure it was all about him. His sinfulness had finally come home to rest. He put the card back where he'd found it. Mother didn't like him playing with her jewelry, even though it was okay for Katie to do.

Digby found Grandma Rose's brush farther back in Lila's jewelry drawer. He took several hairs snared in the bristles, sure the silver strands were Grandma Rose's. He held them to the light. They seemed to glisten and cast a light all their own. Like the tinsel on a Christmas tree. Like the hair of an angel. He smelled them and pulled those thin pieces of her through his fingers.

"I finally realized he knew about the accident when I found a shoebox beneath Digby's bed," explained Katie. "I wasn't snooping. I was looking for my saddle shoes, and whenever I was missing a piece of clothing or jewelry, chances were awfully good that was where it would be. Well, instead of my shoes I found some sort of charm box for Grandma Rose. On a bed of dead flowers were some bobby pins, some gray hairs and a photo of grandma. There were also two small teacups and a medicine bottle of dead termites."

A few days later, Digby tore a sheet of paper from his Big Chief tablet and wrote a note to Grandma Rose. He said he missed and loved her, and that he was sure she bypassed Purgatory. He said he hoped God was treating her okay, and that paradise sounded great with the clouds and the harps and the ice cream in assorted flavors. He wrote that he bet it was even better with her there. He ended by saying he was sorry if she'd loved him too much. He decorated the letter with colored circles and a crayon portrait, and taped some hairs from the brush to the bottom of the page.

That evening, while everyone was engrossed in The Ed Sullivan Show, he snuck onto the patio. Dousing the letter in lighter fluid, he burned it in the backyard grill. He felt a flash of heat on his face. The blaze died quickly. Digby looked at the curling ash and rising cinders, and recalled the huge catfish. So many questions were still unanswered, and they all curled and coiled about one another like a bag of sticky ribbon candy, or his Barrel of Monkeys game. His eyes followed the last bit of blackened smoke as it rose heavenward. Even the sky looked dark and troubled. He wanted to cry, but didn't see the point. Crying only felt good when he knew there was an end to his tears. Death was such an awful sort of gone.

After the death of Grandma Rose, his parents were convinced that the entire family would die in a car accident. Rather than take this as sound reason to drive less, the Swank reasoning was instead to prepare for the worst. Though never formally stated, the Swank family motto was some dire version of You can't stop horrible things from happening, but you can at least prepare for the horribly inevitable.

Overnight, a beige Jesus appeared on the Swank dashboard. The Savior stood on a metal disc with a sticky no-slip bottom. Dashboard Jesus (DJ) was a sort of sacred liability insurance to oversee the lives and souls of all those who rode in the Buick. Whenever Digby was left alone in the car, Dashboard Jesus would have endless adventures that often included a bat-like scaling of the metal under dash, and a fight with the bobble-head dog in the back window. Go Bulldogs! Less than a fortnight after his appearance and even before finding Grandma Rose's prayer card, Digby innocently decided to give DJ a makeover.

He thought he was serving God by dolling up His Only Begotten Son. Using the paints from one of Tom's model kits, Digby went to work. By the time he snapped shut the plastic lid on the palette tray, he'd transformed the Savior into a ruby-lipped, azure-eyed brunette in a flowing green and yellow robe, with red shoes. Digby had been meticulous with the detailing. With his makeover, Jesus really came into his own. He was nobody's Son anymore. The next morning when Digby got into the car with his parents, he wore a sly smile. He'd hoped to be praised for his handiwork. That did not happen. Instead, Digby was chastised and given a stern lecture on the respect due to the magnetic Christ. "That is an icon, not a knickknack, young man," Rog had said. Lila told Digby that cosmetic enhancement was a bad thing. "But you wear make-up," he had countered to Lila. He was told that was different, she was a secretary. Digby was told Jesus was a boy, and boys don't wear make-up or dress flashy and wear red shoes, especially when that boy is the Son of God. "In pictures, you never even see Him wearing prints," Lila explained.

The next day when Digby got in the car for the weekly family outing to K-Mart, the flashy yet fashionable Savior had been replaced by another bland beige Dashboard Jesus replica. He might be able to perform miracles, but it seemed that even the Son of God had to obey the boy rules, sighed Digby. That thought made him sad. They had a whole bin of DJs at the hardware store for $2.99—two for $5.00. A piece of cardboard on the bin said, For the Home or for the Automobile. The Perfect Gift for Christians on a Budget! The icons without the magnetic base were one bin over. Those were less than half the price.

Dashboard Jesus was not the only change when it came to Swank auto travel. In the wake of Grandma Rose's death, the family now also said the rosary every time they entered the car, or at least every time the car was shifted into drive. This proved to be extremely time consuming. Oftentimes, the destination was reached well before the prayer ended. When this happened, all family members were instructed to remain in the car until the final Amen.

Hail Mary, full of grace, the Lord is with thee; blessed art thou among women, and blessed is the fruit of thy womb, Jesus.

Holy Mary, Mother of God, pray for us sinners, now and at the hour of our death. Amen.

Saying the rosary was a complicated process. Ten of the above added up to a mystery, and there were five each of the Glorious, Sorrowful, and Joyful Mysteries. In other words, either The Joyful Mysteries (The Annunciation, The Visitation, The Nativity, The Presentation, and The Finding of Jesus in the Temple); The Glorious Mysteries (The Resurrection, The Ascension, The Descent of the Holy Spirit, The Assumption, and The Coronation); or Digby's favorite, The Sorrowful Mysteries (The Agony in the Garden, The Scourging, The Crowning With Thorns, The Carrying of the Cross, and The Crucifixion) were recited every time the family climbed aboard that coffin/chapel on wheels. The sort of mystery incanted depended on the day of the week. The Swank obsession with saying the rosary occurred years before Pope John Paul II added The Luminous Mysteries to the roster, which even the most liturgically conservative Swanks felt sounded like a line of Revlon beauty products, which was apparently something the Son of God would definitely not wear.

As rosary leader, Lila would begin, "Hail Mary, full of grace, the Lord is with thee; blessed art thou among women and blessed is the fruit of thy womb, Jesus." Rog would chime in a second before Lila finished, at about the first syllable of Jesus. "Holy Mary Mother of God, pray for us sinners, now and at the hour of our death, Amen."

The first time Digby saw this prayer in print, he was surprised to see that those sentences were actually punctuated. In the Swank get-it-done, check-it-off, and let's-get-out-of-the-damn-car version of the prayer, it was all a single mumbled, and often indecipherable, run-on. For instance, Digby always thought Lamb of God in this prayer was Lamaga which he assumed was some hitherto unknown deity who was going to take away the sins of the world.

In addition, The Swank's supposedly pious practice was often punctuated with audacious outbursts of secularism. "Hail Mary, full of grace...would you roll up that damn window!" Lila might shout, turning in the seat while attempting to cover her hair with her hands. "I just got it set on Tuesday, and I don't want the lake gnats getting stuck in it."

"Holy Mary, Mother of God pray for us sinners...Christ on The Cross, that son of a bitch cut me off without even looking! Go to hell buddy! Yeah you! Now where was I..? Oh, now and at the hour..."

Saying the rosary seemed interminable. No one enjoyed reciting it or hearing it, but it was common knowledge that a good Catholic became a better Catholic by not enjoying things. The burden was the joy. Digby would often make himself carsick simply to break the monotony. The only supposed benefit of reciting the rosary in the car was that doing so might save their souls in the event of a fiery crash. Digby wondered why they needed Dashboard Jesus. "So what exactly does he do?" he finally asked. Digby was promptly shushed by Lila who whispered, "Never you mind" as though the plastic icon might overhear and take offense. The purpose of DJ was a minor quibble for the boy. Digby had greater concerns. The thought of a broken and bloody body housing a saved soul was not a great comfort. Saying the rosary in the car terrified him for what it implied.

During his father's cryptic portion of the prayer, Digby would often peer fearfully out the windows, scanning for a bleary-eyed drunk driver or a runaway semi careening their way, terrified that the very words at the hour of our death could bring about the sounding of the grim reaper's alarm clock.

Even among Catholics, the Swank children were well aware that this practice of "saying the beads" was freakish, medieval, and morbid. Other families listened to the radio. Some even had conversations. Once the practice of reciting the rosary began, the Swank children never asked their parents for rides to school or to the movies. Friends were certainly never chauffeured about. The thought was too shameful to even imagine. To the children, Rog and Lila may as well have begun each car ride by handling serpents while speaking in tongues, and flailing about the interior of the Buick. At least that would have been less monotonous.

Rog and Lila Swank took pride in saying the rosary despite the fact that it deviated from the norm. It broke their sacred "act like everyone else, and no one will be the wiser" behavioral guideline. This deviation alone qualified the rosary as somewhat of a glorious mystery. However, the fact that it was used as leverage made it much less mysterious.

The Swanks would often casually mention having just said the rosary. Doing so might have seemed more boastful, if it wasn't typically used as a damage control tactic. If Rog got tight at a social gathering, Lila might say, "Rog is overly tired. He wanted to nap in the car on the way here, but we were saying the rosary." Or Lila might ignore the situation but still stress the religious aspect; "We were just saying the rosary on the way over and I thought, thank goodness for friends like Dick and Arlene... Let's offer up a Station of the Cross for them." Though Digby was still in short pants and lacking a full set of adult teeth, the obviousness of it all made him blush.

5 - Death Is So Cool

The year following Grandma Rose's death, Grandma Swank got sick, disappeared, and was dead within a week. By the time they knew what was wrong, the shadows inside her had spread. She'd probably been dying the entire time she lived with them. Her death was not kept from Digby. "She's safe in her Savior's arms," was the phrase they used to break the news to Digby. It was pancreatic cancer, just like the family dog the year before. When he asked, Digby was told the two were not related. He was also told that the cancer had nothing to do with her degeneration, immaculate or otherwise.

The night before the funeral, Digby's brother, Tom, told him that they sew dead people's mouths closed. He said that was why ghosts always moaned instead of spoke. "It's the stitches that cause it." He also said sewing them up was done to help curb the zombie population, since the dead couldn't consume the living with a sewn mouth. That thought gave Digby little comfort, only nightmares. That was, of course, Tom's intention.

Digby didn't know what to expect at his first visitation, but it wasn't what he thought. Visitation sounded more social than it was. Wake made even less sense. If death was eternal rest, wasn't a wake the opposite of that? They entered from the back, stuck their fingers in the red sponge of the holy water font, and crossed themselves before entering the room single file. Digby didn't expect all the chairs to be facing one direction. The casket was at the front of the room on a pedestal. That was her? Digby was confused. The waxy woman in the padded box sure didn't look like Grandma Swank. She wasn't wearing her glasses or her black housedress, and she was smiling.

Digby jumped when he saw her close up. He was surprised her famously grouchy facial muscles could even be manipulated into that position. He wondered if the tight smile was on account of the undertaker being short of thread. To a stranger, Grandma Swank may have appeared sweet or even nice, but to those who knew her, that smile had a sinister bend, as though she were privy to some pending calamity from beyond. I know when and how each of you will die! Hehehe. Somewhat unnerved, Digby looked from her stitched mouth to the caked powder of her cheeks, and down to the tight grip of her fingers on the rosary. He'd never been whacked by that rosary before.

He knelt at the casket a bit longer than customary. Seeing her this way was creepy, but once he got beyond that weird smile and the way her chin tilted into her neck on the satiny pillow, it was really cool. He imagined Grandma Swank stalking graveyards with the undead, living a Dark Shadows life, and making John F. Kennedy (and maybe even Robert) her lovers of the night. He saw Grandma Swank rising from her grave during thunderstorms, shedding her housedress for a sheer nightgown and bounding in voluptuous slow motion across the grounds of Collinwood beneath a shroud of fog, as wild dogs howled in the distance. She was no longer frightening. Death had made her glamorous.

Lizabeth Swank's niece, Cora Lynn, who married fairly well despite having the tiny, haphazard teeth of a fruit bat, sat a bit straighter in her chair as she recalled the visitation. "Digby sauntered right up to the coffin. Well, child or no child, you can be sure there were some gasps since near-about everyone had heard the stories of what he'd done to Lizabeth with his spying and nakedness and all. As if that weren't enough, the dim-witted boy had the nerve to hold up the entire respects line by kneeling two full minutes at the coffin! And how he knelt—just plopped his big hind-end back on his heels. Lila and Rog didn't say a word. Not one word! Well, I was brought up different. I was taught that sloth was a deadly sin! In our parish, that butt-cushion way of kneeling was a sure way to become a pariah, but it seems anything goes at Holy Martyrs. Personally, I wouldn't be caught dead having my funeral there."

With at least two vehicles in the cortege needing extensive muffler and exhaust work, the rather loud and smoky procession wound its way out of town and to the Eternal Salvation Cemetery. The graveyard stood on a hill, with nothing but sloping farmland stretching out in every direction.

Standing graveside as Grandma Swank's coffin was lowered into the ground, Digby looked around the cemetery. He saw tombstones, and barren trees, and a wrought iron fence with spade posts, and a rusted decorative gate with an interlocking E and S. The wind cut through the grass, howling as a cloud passed before the sun. Digby felt a thrill down to his toes. This world of death was even better than Dark Shadows! The mystery of it all became a whispered secret that Digby was eager to hear.

The next month, one of the kids in Katie's freshman class died suddenly. Shawn Schlummer was an awkward boy who mixed his plaids and lived in the neighborhood with his parents and his sisters, Ginger and Candi. Shawn grew nearly a foot in the last year of his life, and the strain on his knees required him to move about with the aid of a single crutch covered with duct tape. He was resoundingly teased with taunts of "Stretch" and "Tiny."

At the time, there was a rumor in the high school that putting peanuts in a cola drink caused a chemical reaction that resulted in drunkenness. Naturally, all the kids furtively slipped peanuts in their colas during lunch period, and would subsequently act tipsy. Insecure about his giantism and eager to belong, Shawn attempted a cola buzz one Friday evening at home. Unfortunately, he neglected to shell the peanuts first, so when he took a big drink from his glass, several of the nuts got wedged in his normal-sized throat. He choked to death right there in his kitchen. His parents never understood why three unshelled peanuts were wedged in his windpipe. Digby wondered if the undertaker had just figured "the heck with it" and left the peanuts in place when he sewed Shawn's mouth shut. Digby wasn't invited to that visitation. It was a "family only" affair, which put off some folks in the neighborhood.

Thereafter, Mrs. Schlummer broke down every year she saw the dancing Mr. Peanut in the Running Falls Thanksgiving Day Parade. "It was a sad display," was all anyone would say regarding her annual hysterics, though no one ever tried to talk her out of going. In fact, many situated themselves along the parade route just so they'd have a good view of Harriet Schlummer. Seeing her kicking and screaming and being held back from attack soon became a highlight of the day's festivities.

Lots of folks saw death as tragic. Digby did not. Cemeteries had became his new obsession and, to Digby's delight, there was a graveyard right at the end of the block.

Calvary Cemetery crowned the rounded end of Aldo Boulevard. One hundred and twenty years ago, Calvary Cemetery had been on the outskirts of town. Now it was situated between a nameless strip mall and the Martinique Exotic Show Lounge, which was actually part of a second strip mall called Canfield Corners. Despite its location, Calvary Cemetery was still exceptional, with dozens of upright stones, obelisks, monuments, and crypts. A few mausoleums stood like little homes with tiny porches and pillars and windows. Digby loved to peek inside those houses of death, and see a vase of dried flowers amidst the cobwebs and shadows. He would stick his nose through the grates that covered the broken stained glass windows. They all smelled stale and damp and cool. They smelled like elsewhere because that's where they led. He'd heard that when the dead passed from this world to the next, they left the door to the other world slightly ajar.

Calvary Cemetery was a far cry from the flat, treeless burial plazas now in fashion. The folks buried at Calvary knew that your life and legacy were only as big as your headstone. Many of the tombstones were Irish, and very old. A few were weathered so smooth, that who or what lay below was a mystery. Most of the graves were sorely neglected. Those folks had been dead too long to have mourners among the living. No flowers were ever brought there. Calvary Cemetery was no longer a reminder of individual lives, but a collective reminder of the inevitable.

Digby's time at Calvary transformed him. Magic was within those wrought iron borders. He could feel it in the wind and the trees, and the ground itself. Digby gathered leaves and stones and bits of glass from the grave plots. He built crude altars, sure that the collected debris would help amass the power of the dead. Catholicism had taught him the importance of ritual.

On the corner of the lot, there was a gothic shack for the groundskeeper, but Digby never saw anyone about. Someone made a customary pass with the mower, but clippers were never used. There had also been some gathering of larger branches and limbs, as evidenced by the pile of brush on the southwest corner of the back wall.

Digby did what he could to maintain the graves. He picked up paper, and collected the rubbish in stray plastic bags. He hoped to win over the dead by caring for their grounds. He thought maybe if he worked and prayed and built enough altars, the dead would share their secrets with him. Maybe then they would tell him how to see Grandma Rose. Even seeing her in his dreams would be wonderful. Digby had been praying for it to happen for weeks. Grandma Rose had told him that every dream was a message from God, but in this matter, God had been no help. Maybe the dead had less on their plate. Grandma Rose had become little more than a concept and that frightened Digby. He didn't want to forget or lose what little he had.

The dead proved to be as uncooperative as God. Digby soon found that even his wholehearted commitment was not enough. More garbage was always blowing over the wall from The Martinique Exotic Show Lounge dumpsters, and at night, bands of Running Falls teenagers frequented Calvary Cemetery as a make-out and partying spot. Digby retrieved beers cans and condoms and cigarette butts, but despite his efforts, the dead maintained their silence. He went there almost every day, sometimes all day on Saturdays. Time was never an accurate measure of his visits. Once he got inside those gates, the world fell away, and he was elsewhere. As a result, he felt ghostly and invisible, but unfortunately, the latter was not the case. The neighbors began to talk.

Dolly Sterner liked to keep her formal, full-length curtains tied at either side to keep an eye on things. She didn't like the thought of anything going on in the neighborhood without her knowing about it. When she witnessed Digby's graveyard visits, she was scandalized. "Well, it was none of my business, but he was going there all the time. I could see him right out my dining room window wandering around between the graves, and sitting here and there, and even lying right on top of the dead, sometimes. It was downright indecent. I'm not one to gossip, but it seemed to me he was talking to himself. It just wasn't normal, and I knew queer behavior like that was nothing Rog or Lila would approve of. It was my Christian duty to say something."

The next day, Rog and Lila appeared in the doorway to Digby's room. They said they wanted to talk to him. Since they were both there, and his parents rarely wanted to talk to him, he was fairly certain it must be something important. Wearing stern expressions, they exhaled in unison, and with a series of pointing gestures they looked slightly over his head, and then slightly to the right and left of him while proceeding to make the graveyard off limits.

"But why?"

Since his father was loose but not drunk, he didn't avoid the issue. Fortified with two healthy doses of sixty proof courage, Rog told Digby exactly why. "It's a fact of life. People won't like you if you're not like them, and people just don't spend their days in graveyards. They go there and then they get out. It's no place to linger. It's best to just go about your business, and ignore death. That's what sane people do."

Things of this nature confused Digby. Doing what sane people supposedly did wasn't natural for him. The fact that his behavior strayed from the norm was certainly nothing unusual, but the entire episode caused a good amount of confusion. Did that mean he wasn't sane? He couldn't recall ever asking himself that question before, but he'd find himself asking it many times in the future. Differentness and insanity had never been linked in his mind before. He'd always been evil or a freak, and somehow those two things didn't seem half as bad.

His mother added, "That place is off limits, young man. Dolly and Lucas are going to call if they see you again."

Digby's ears perked. Dolly and Lucas Sterner lived on the lot to the side of the Swanks. Digby should have known this was their doing. The Sterners were so unhappy with their own wretched lives that making others miserable seemed their only solace.

There was very little about the Sterners to like. Dolly radiated sneakiness. Her small, unblinking eyes were set so wide that they appeared wedged on either side of her head. When she moved, her bony form seemed to scuttle sideways like a crab. Digby suspected chronic gum disease had made her bitter, or perhaps the bitterness had caused her teeth to rot. Lucas Sterner's halitosis was even worse, but unlike his wife, Lucas's eyes converged in the center of his face like two chocolate chips melting into one. He moved in a way that was both careful and vacant, as though thinking and walking were never to be done simultaneously. Walking behind them when leaving church was to be avoided at all costs. Their mincing, diagonal gates prompted low curses from even the most devout of Holy Martyrs' parishioners.

Digby would not forget this graveyard betrayal. Because of the Sterners, the portal to the beyond was being closed. Because of them, he might not be able to communicate with Grandma Rose. Why did it matter to them anyway? He swore that someday they would have their comeuppance, if he had anything to say about it.

Rog sat swaying at the foot of Digby's bed, and explained that it was best to be aware of what other people did, and then just sort of play along by doing the same thing. "That's how you get through life."

Digby knew what his parents were saying. That message of "be like us by trying to be like them" came through loud and clear. Rog and Lila lived their life inside a mirror, and seemed only concerned with what was reflected. It was nothing new. Assimilation was their life's work, and all things to the contrary were best kept under wraps. Life was just easier that way. They didn't realize that acting like everyone else and blending in with the crowd was impossible for Digby. It always had been. He was incapable of being a mirror. He warped all reflection. He was always softer, always stranger, and always something quite apart from the norm in his behavior, his interests, and in his very being.

6 - Christian Charity

Though they claimed to ignore death, Digby's parents were certainly interested in one's place in the afterlife. Eternal damnation and/or salvation was apt cause for concern, and the signs of that importance were abundant. As Catholics, every Swank child had received the sacrament of Baptism before they could sit up or even roll over unassisted, so Limbo was not an option.

Thank goodness for that, since The Vatican would "officially abolish" the eight hundred-year-old concept of Limbo in 2007. This begs the question, So then what happened to all those non-Christian and unbaptized baby souls?...

The family periodically tried to be proactive regarding the eternal state of their souls. Besides saying the rosary, fish on Fridays, observing Lent, bimonthly trips to the confessional, and keeping sacred the Sabbath as well as other holy days of obligation, a good Catholic could do other things.

Decor was one option. An abundance of sacred art and bric-a-brac never hurt. In addition to Dashboard Jesus in the car, the Swank home hosted an array of blessed knickknacks. Two wall crucifixes mounted atop palms from Sundays past were on either side of the dining room. Both crosses had secret sliding compartments that housed a vial of supposed Holy Water.

Maynard had actually used one of the vials to see what would happen when he poured Holy Water on a frog. Expecting the amphibian to burst into flames or vanish or glow or at least die, he was disappointed when the frog merely blinked and hopped away. Maynard promptly filled the vial with water from the garden hose and returned it to the niche behind the sliding panel. Both Tom and Digby had been sworn to secrecy over the incident.

On the other walls in the Swank dining room were two paintings: an elegantly framed Jesus in the Garden rendering, opposite a Sacred Heart of Jesus print. In the latter, Christ pointed to his exposed heart with a sort of "Check this out" cock of his brow. That painting always bothered Maynard. He said in real life there would be blood, lots of blood, and that "there was no way that Jesus would just be standing there."

Though the dining room was sort of ground zero for hallowed tchotchkes, divine doodads were everywhere. Besides having a crucifix in every bedroom, there were a pair of praying hand salt-and-pepper shakers in a kitchen cabinet, a painting of angels carrying dead people into the clouds over the clothes hamper, and an unused set of pink and purple Advent Candles shoved in the tablecloth drawer. There were also two worse-for-wear Virgin Mary statues; on one, her blessed hands had been broken off at the wrists, and on the second, a thin seam lined the Virgin's neck. She'd been decapitated one rainy day when Tom and Maynard were playing catch indoors.

Despite Grandma Swank's destruction of several rosaries in her disciplining of Digby, at least five or six more sets of beads were lying about. Katie always seemed to be winning a rosary in school for one accomplishment or another. She was also rewarded with holy card bookmarks, and a Holy Family book cover. At least a dozen scapulars hung on her bulletin board. Maynard and Tom loved to torture her by hiding them. "Why don't you pray for me to give them back to you," one or the other would tease.

Lila also kept several veils in the top drawer of her bureau, beside her jewelry. Though touted as a symbol of humility, Digby heard Lila speak a bit more frankly about her use of veils to a friend. "I have a few, but I've never found one that did a thing for me. Besides, they always stick to my hairspray, and they're so flimsy you can never just toss them in the wash." As a result, Lila wore veils mostly as a sign of her vanity rather than her lack of it. Though she would never admit to such a thing, she would only bobby-pin a veil to her head when her hair didn't turn out quite right. "Oh this is hopeless," she'd say, tossing her brush aside with a grunt and grabbing one of her veils with a defeated sigh.

Though the evidence of a Catholic life and a Catholic home were displayed all about, even this was sometimes not quite enough. Rog and Lila's fleeting fears of actual or probable lapses and subsequent damnation could be rather intense. The worry and free-floating Catholic guilt would accumulate. Once or twice a year, they would sit at the kitchen table and whip one another into a frenzy regarding the spiritual life of the family. These evenings tended to prompt immediate action to avoid the eternal damnation that seemed to be forever nipping at their heels. Sometimes the solution was as simple as a generous financial donation to the Church. When this was done, Rog always dropped the check on the top of the pile in the offertory basket without the discretion of an envelope. What was the use in giving if it was going to be kept a secret? Sometimes when financial generosity was not an option, Lila would offer to help clean the altar and Pledge the pews. One Saturday, they even offered to have Maynard and Tom come by the church and rake leaves. Unfortunately that good deed was undermined when the boys, along with two cronies, were caught smoking cigarettes from a pack they had found tucked behind a statue of St. Ignatius in the convent courtyard.

At other times, the repercussions of these reactionary episodes of Christian charity were far more drastic. In an exceptionally weak moment, Rog and Lila once signed some special Catholic housing literature, and before you could say God Help Us, a fetid stream of socially peripheral folk began residing in the Swank home for indefinite periods. No one in the family found any joy or humanitarian satisfaction in doing this, but once the flourish of signing the volunteer form had passed, Rog and Lila could not stop the unyielding wheels of Catholic charity. Their commitment was all but etched in stone.

Saying they'd changed their minds or had a weak moment or had misunderstood was not an option, especially after receiving a special mention of thanks for their Christian kindness in the diocese newsletter. Failure in the eyes of God was one thing; failure in the eyes of the parish was another thing entirely. To backtrack on their decision would mean social and spiritual disaster. Instead of reneging on the agreement, Rog and Lila simply did what all good Catholics do in such situations; they persevered with quiet resentment, mumbled curses, and more guilt. For one terribly long year, their home became a flophouse for the Lord.

During this time, Digby noticed that when his mother couldn't express her annoyance outright, as was often the case given the circumstances, she slowly and very consciously blinked her eyes, as if briefly obliterating whatever lunacy was happening before her. The act seemed to indicate an unrealistic but faint hope that when she "raised the shades," the disagreeable bit of business would be gone. Lila blinked slowly a lot during that year.

The poor souls came and went with great frequency throughout that period. No sooner were the linens in the sunroom changed, than some new unfortunate was shuttled over from the Catholic shelter. Few were with the family for more than a couple weeks. Many were only put up while in preparation for long-term housing elsewhere. The family never knew quite what to expect, and even if they did, they were always surprised. Most of these transient souls made a lasting impression.

Few Swanks would soon forget Miss Doreen, the bug-eyed toll taker who was on disability due to bad knees and a thyroid condition. She was constantly drenched in sweat, and spent most of her time sighing in front of an open window even though it was February. Rog tried to be a Christian about it, but all he could see was his hard-earned money going right out the window every time the furnace kicked on. Miss Doreen always wore a pair of either green or yellow stretch polyester shorts. One pair of her gigantic stretchy pants was always in the wash. Digby and his brothers often danced about in her shorts with sofa cushions wedged in the front and back. One time, all three of them climbed inside her giant green pants and started fighting. The outcome was no surprise. Lila was horrified when she saw the torn shorts. She told Miss Doreen they must have gotten hooked on a nail. Miss Doreen put a tiny hand under one of her many chins. "Well, I have to have another pair. I can't just walk around in my underpants." With a slight shiver, Lila agreed that she most certainly could not, and promptly drove seventy-five miles to find another pair that size. Slightly resentful of the task as well as having to pay the $3.98 for the shorts, Lila did not say the rosary on the drive. "This act is penance enough," she fumed. Miss Doreen only stayed with the family for ten days.

The unfortunates came and went as the weeks and months crept by. There was Red, the knuckle cracker who could get motion sickness from walking too fast, or even by seeing someone else walk at a brisk pace. The shades were drawn in the sun room during his stay. If Red even heard the squeal of a car on the street or on TV, he'd become ill. Eventually Rog said, "No offense" and put a bucket of sand beside his chair. Red was followed by carbuncle Barb who, despite her mammoth neck boil, sat on the window sill in their sunroom and smiled at passersby. She tried to cover her grotesque abscess with a flowery scarf. Even more than usual, the Swanks dreaded to consider what the neighbors might think. Seeing her seated there, Lila seethed "Perched in the front window just like a Dutch prostitute." Barb broke through the screen one night and ran away. Rog called the parish office, and they called the police. Barb was discovered crouched in a neighbor's bushes wearing only her floral scarf and a dirty bra. She never returned to the Swank sunroom. "Amen," thought Lila when she was told Barb wouldn't be coming back.

The next tenant was Doomsday Dietrich, who wore rosaries like necklaces and whose conversational skills were limited to an ongoing monologue of grim pronouncements. Trapping one of the family members in a corner, one or the other of his lazy eyes would circle randomly as he pointed a bony finger and said things like, "This is what not reading The Bible brings to the world— death." "This is what vanity brings to the world—death." "This is what being homosexual brings to the world—death." "This is what smoking marijuana brings to the world—death." Meat on Fridays, eggs on a Tuesday, heels, cologne, bellbottoms, and even pantyhose were all avenues of death and subsequent damnation, according to Dietrich. He made Digby cry more than once. Dietrich never seemed to sleep, so during his stay, the family retired for the night behind doors with a chair wedged securely beneath each knob. The entire family breathed a collective sigh of relief when Catholic Charities reclaimed him in less than a week.

The guest who stayed the longest and also made the greatest impression was a man known as Grandpa Clifford. He was not their grandfather, nor any Swank relation, and his name was Bill, so the family had no idea why he requested to be called Grandpa Clifford. Nonetheless, the Swanks complied. Grandpa Clifford was a man devoid of all charm. His cheekbones looked ready to poke through the waxy skin of his face, especially when he pursed his lips in disagreement, which he did with great frequency. His disagreeable nature soured all the more with the onset of the holiday season. His yuletide reign of terror began with a criticism of the festive decor. He complained of allergies, even though the tree and the assorted evergreenery was fake. He scoffed at the energy expense of holiday lights, as though he contributed one penny to the household budget. He mocked the sentiments scrawled on the holiday cards: "Have a Joyous Holiday Season—my ass!" "Blessings at this Joyful Time—bless this, you idiots!" He even took great pleasure in poking the presents beneath the tree with his cane. "We never had that many toys when I was a kid... Oh, I think I just broke that one."

Katie tried to help him by turning on a TV showing of A Christmas Carol in the faint hope that some ghost of Christmas something or other would scare some sense into him. The story was lost on Clifford, who only enjoyed Scrooge prior to his "going soft." He snickered throughout Scrooge's angry refusals to let Bob Cratchit leave work early on Christmas Eve, and snarled at his clerk's invitation to spend the holidays with his family. After Scrooge visited his grave and emerged from the cemetery a changed man, Clifford actually uttered "Bah!" before launching into yet another litany of complaints.

All this seemed little more than a disagreeable prelude to his atrocious Christmas Eve behavior. On that day, the Swanks embraced the typical "food equals love" tradition, and put cookies and milk on the kitchen table for Santa. We love you Santa...so eat! Seeing the glazed and sprinkled cookies, Clifford's eyes narrowed. Scowling, he hobbled to his room. He returned a moment later with a rifle he laid across his lap. He narrowed his eyes and stroked the barrel with his hand. "I'm going to sit right here, and if anyone comes down that chimney, I'm going to shoot the son-of-a-bitch."

Being older and wiser, Digby's siblings rolled their eyes.

They knew the gun was a fake. They also knew the mystery and identity of Santa. Digby did not. That precious illusion of jolly benevolence had yet to be crushed. Digby turned to Grandpa Clifford with his mouth wide, and his eyes silvered by tears. Clifford's comment hadn't registered right away. When it did, Digby's first thought was, "No presents!" Then came thoughts of St. Nick splattered across the shag carpet on Christmas morning. "We'll be blue-balled!" he screamed, meaning blackballed, of course. How could his parents, of all people, permit such a thing? The stigma would haunt them. That's them, there's the family responsible for Santa's massacre! Digby held his breath and stomped his foot and threw a shoe, and displayed several other forms of misbehavior. His parents assured him that Grandpa Clifford was only "joking."

Digby wanted to believe them, but how could he be sure? How could they be sure? Until a month before, they'd never met this man. He was obviously psychotic. He relied on the good will of Catholic strangers like the Swanks for good reason. Rocking in his chair, wearing a wicked grin, Grandpa Clifford continued to mutter, "We'll see how much of a joke it is when I bury a round between them bushy brows of his. He's breaking and entering, plain and simple. In my day, we shot trespassers. This gun has brought down a grizzly and more than one buck, so this Santa character should be no problem."

Seeing only one solution, Lila gave Digby some peanut brittle and a dozen frosted gingerbread cookies. Such measures had a success rate of over ninety percent. The child's nerves weren't calmed, but the sugar coating certainly took the edge off. In moments, he was riding a glucose wave into a manic, magic land. His tears dried as he laughed wildly, and ran in circles around the dining room table waving his hands about his head, shouting, "Woo hoo, Woo hoo."

Though buzzed, Digby still hadn't forgotten about Grandpa Clifford. He'd wait up as well, with a plan of his own. When he heard the clatter of hooves on the roof and that hearty "Ho, Ho, Ho," Digby planned to run from his hiding place behind his father's chair and stab Grandpa Clifford with a butcher knife before the old geezer could fill Santa full of lead. "This one's for St. Nick," he would say, sinking the blade to the handle. As a result, Digby imagined that he would be proclaimed a hero by children everywhere, and score extra toys for saving Santa's life.

He awoke the next morning in a panic. He'd fallen asleep. Damn that processed sugar crash!

Did he?

Had he?

Was Santa?

Digby peeked over the top of Rog's easy chair, sighing when he saw a surplus of presents beneath the tree, and a lack of blood and bone bits littering the carpet. Blessed be, it was a carnage-free Christmas morn. Santa had managed to skirt the crosshairs of Grandpa Clifford's hunting rifle. When he saw Grandpa Clifford a couple hours later, the old man winked and offered the hint of a smile. "That damn weasel slithered by me last night, but there's always next year."

Though a somewhat reliable cliche, in this case "there's always next year" wasn't true. Grandpa Clifford died mid-January. Tom was home from school that week with the mumps, and Lila had stayed home to take care of him. When Digby got home from school, Tom pulled him aside and whispered that at about noon, two guys had come in an ambulance, ripped off Grandpa Clifford's shirt, and then pounded the crap out of him. Tom said Grandpa Clifford turned blue, then gray, then those guys finally zipped him up in a garment bag. Tom said it was really cool. Digby listened wide-eyed. Tom could tell he was jealous. In a show of brotherly love, Tom offered to spit on Digby so he'd get the mumps too, and get out of some school. But before Digby could answer, Lila came in and hustled him out of the room. "I don't want you getting sick as well. I've missed enough work down at the office as it is."

Once they were in the hallway, Lila explained that Grandpa Clifford was in a better place. Digby was doubtful. If Grandpa Clifford had made it to Heaven, all bets were off.

Grandpa Clifford's cane stood in the Swank umbrella rack for years. To most, it was invisible and forgotten; for Digby, it was a grim reminder of mortality.

Christmas was always confusing for Digby. Every year he made his wish list along with a duplicate, and sent both in separate envelopes to Mr. Santa Claus c/o The North Pole. He wasn't sure if his letters had been lost, or if there had been a processing mix-up at Santa's Toy Shop. He only knew that something was amiss. He never received any of the things on his toy list. Instead of his requested Chatty Cathy or a giant troll doll, Zig Zag Sewing Kit or Happy Family Dollhouse, he always got more boy toys. Digby recalled opening the Little Handyman Tool Kit and thinking, "Did Santa get the wrong list again?" The man may have been jolly and that was great, but he also seemed fairly incompetent. Digby could understand mistakes given the work load, but this was ridiculous.

He wondered if the unrequested toys were part of the "naughty or nice" argument, but that didn't hold water. As far as he knew, Original Sin didn't count. Besides, children far worse than Digby still received the gifts they wanted. His brother Tom was misbehaving all the time, but most of his gifts seemed to arrive. Maynard had thrown a snowball at a nun and took a crap in the neighbor's garage, but he still got his BB gun and Combat! gear. It wasn't fair. Something was wrong somewhere. The entire fiasco made Digby wonder if maybe he was being naughty in a different sort of way.

Despite his frustration with St. Nick, discovering the truth about Santa was a horrible shock when it happened the following Christmas season. Prior to this, he'd had suspicions that generated countless questions. The simple logistics of that one night sleigh ride baffled him. Santa left the North Pole with all this stuff in a sleigh pulled by nine flying reindeer who cruised over Canada to the USA, obviously his first stop, before heading east to Europe and hitting the rest of the Northern Hemisphere, then venturing south of the equator. Santa hit every house, even those without chimneys, and was back at home before dawn.

That was the story anyway, but Digby had questions: What about the people without homes? What about kids who get things bigger than a chimney chute? How big could Santa's sack possibly be? Did he stash things at different warehouses around the globe? Digby was also baffled by the fact that some of Santa's presents appeared under the tree early wrapped in the same paper his folks used in their gifts to one another and to the neighbors. Certainly that was an odd coincidence, or maybe it was just another unspoken Christmas miracle. He found it odd that no one seemed to give all this much thought. Digby would often cross-examine whomever happened to be in the room whenever any of his many Santa questions occurred to him. There was an unspoken Swank rule not to tell the boy, but someone had to crack.

Then one Saturday when playing spy, which he did by standing motionless behind the "romantic length" curtains in the living room, Digby overheard Maynard tell Katie that he knew where their parents were hiding the presents.

Digby scrunched his forehead, and tripped into visibility over the folds of heavy green drapery puddled upon the carpet. "What do you mean?"

Katie and Maynard eyed each other. Weary at the mere prospect of what was inevitably to come, Maynard decided that enough was enough. "What do you think I mean, dork? The other presents, the ones that come on Christmas Eve."

"Those presents aren't hidden. Santa brings those presents."

"My ass he does, you little butt face."

Digby drew his mouth into a tight button. "He does so."

"He does not, twerp."

"Does so! Does so! Does so!" Digby screamed with his fingers wedged in his ears. Many arguments in Running Falls were often won in just such a manner. When Digby asked Katie to back him up, a panicked look filled her eyes. She said she had to make a phone call.

Digby had heard quite enough of Maynard's nonsense.

Marching promptly into the kitchen, Digby asked his mother to tell Maynard he was wrong. Lila was busy trying to fix dinner while talking on the phone to Sears about a recent bill. "Mom, is there a Santa?"

"What?"

"Maynard said you were Santa."

"Grow up, loser. Move on," Maynard yelled from the other room.

"Stop it, both of you!"

"He started it," Digby whined. "So tell him there is too a Santa Claus!"

"What?" Digby couldn't tell if she was talking to him, or the apparently not-so-helpful Sears phone representative.

Digby was stomping his feet and shouting by this point. "Santa! Isn't he real? Isn't it all real but still magical and a miracle? Isn't Santa Claus real and like a funner version of Jesus?"

Finally, his mother brushed a forearm across her forehead and covered the phone receiver. She'd had enough. "That's it, okay! There is no Santa. He doesn't exist, alright? Now go play!"

This couldn't be happening. Digby's stomping feet slowed, and stilled like a wind-up toy running down. He stood frozen for a moment before his bottom lip trembled, and he started to cry. To avoid Maynard's teasing, he ran back behind the curtains. Another of life's illusions had been shattered in an instant. It would not be the last.

Weeks later, Digby was bored and rummaging through a chest of drawers in his parents' room. He stood on a chair, and opened a tiny top drawer. He felt something, and heard a slight jingle. He lifted a plastic bag. It was filled with teeth. There must've been two dozen inside, some still speckled with dried blood. What was going on?

Terrified by his find, Digby once again ran to Lila, who attempted to calm his hysterics by telling him the truth about the Tooth Fairy. Another shoe had dropped. Another series of lies

- 64 -

had been revealed. In and of itself, this Tooth Fairy bulletin wasn't all that devastating. In fact, Digby always found it unsettling to consider that fairy scavenging beneath his pillow as he slept, especially since he usually only got a quarter out of it.

Looking back, the perpetuation of the Tooth Fairy myth seemed perfectly understandable. It was simply part of being a parent. It did, however, seem very odd to save all the teeth. Of what use could they be? Was his mother hoping to craft a charm bracelet someday? "These are all from my children's skulls," she'd say with a jingling shake of her wrist. Digby shuddered at the thought.

The cumulative effect that the Santa and Tooth Fairy disclosures had upon Digby's young psyche was significant. It made him suspicious. Digby didn't know what to believe. Was his entire perception of the world built upon sand? What other icons were nothing but charades? What other things in the world were simply myths conceived to make life more palatable? Was Bob Hope a hot air balloon and Lucy nothing more than a colorful bundle of rags? Was Nixon a mere hand puppet? Maybe his parents were masquerading as them all. Were Jesus and God just two more fairy tales concocted to make sure he was nice and not naughty? Maybe on Judgement Day, the archangel Gabriel will blow his horn, disappear in a puff of magician's smoke, and all will go black. Skeptics aren't born; they are hatched from experience. Digby couldn't understand why he was coaxed to put faith in all these deceptions, only to have them ultimately torn away. These grand, orchestrated schemes were cruel and humiliating.

"That's just the way children are taught," his mother said by way of an explanation.

Digby nodded, though he had no idea exactly what lesson he was supposed to have learned. All he knew was that the teaching was more than a bit sadistic.

7 - Digby Is A Lying Fembot

Digby had always been different. As an infant, he was fussy unless dressed in frills, picky about the flavor of his baby food, and favored flamboyant, glittery toys. He used extravagant gestures almost as soon as he started to speak. Though everyone was aware that something was amiss, no one had said a word. That wasn't the Swank way, and in this case, words were unnecessary.

Children are perceptive creatures. They sense all shades and variations of love, anger, and shame with great acuity. Once Digby became aware that what came naturally to him was wrong, he muted and amended his behavior. The world became a stage where he underplayed or attempted a different role altogether. He quickly learned through observation that pleasing his audience was more important than being himself.

As a result, Digby did what any normal Catholic sissy boy might do. He spent massive amounts of time and energy loathing himself, feeling guilty, and trying not to be everything that he so obviously was. Often, he was simply too impulsive for such thoughtfulness. He was more likely to examine, dissect, and scrutinize his behavior after the fact. Though determined to ignore his instincts and be like everyone else, it was no use. Who he was betrayed him with an alarming regularity.

When he was asked in kindergarten what he wanted to be when he grew up, instead of the typical fireman or astronaut or Band-Aid factory foreman, Digby said he wanted to be a beautician or run a cash register at the Safeway. He could tell he'd said the wrong thing by the look on Sister Clementia's face. Trying to make up for his error, he said that actually he wanted to own the first beauty parlor in space. His amended comment was met with nothing more than the brusque click of Sister's tongue upon her hard palate.

Try as he might, his queerness could not be stifled. It was a big juicy fart on a Naugahyde chair. It erupted and reverberated, and was beyond disguise. He was a nancy boy, a girl, and a femme. The "otherness" circled him like a hoop skirt, apparent in how he thought and created and spoke. It was in the way he arranged his crayons by hue, the jaunty way he wore his scarf and cap in wintertime, and how he rode the carousel horse sidesaddle. If all that went unnoticed, no one could mistake the fey way he ran or ignore his high-pitched squeals whenever he was chased. He could scream much louder than any of the girls on the playground.

Sister Clementia even made regular comments on Digby's apparent over-pronunciation of the "ess" sound in his s's and soft c's. "Ssss. Ssss. Ssss. Did a serpent sneak into my classroom, Digby Timothy Swank?" she often said with an arched brow in his direction. "Perhaps we should all offer a prayer to St. Patrick to gather his s-s-s-staff and drive the s-s-s-snakes from S-S-S-Sister's class-ss-ss-ssroom." T's and the "th" sound were cause for ridicule by Sister as well. Mockery changed nothing about the way he spoke. It only made him self-conscious and frequently silent.

Regarding the sometimes questionable teaching methods at Holy Martyrs School, Teresa Corbell, the former Sister Vivienne (who has since dedicated her life to yarn and crochet craft) explained, "In all fairness, not all Catholic schools are alike. Some Catholic schools are chock full of compassionate and supportive instructors who foster spiritual inquisitiveness. But none of those teachers were at Holy Martyrs. In fact, when I was there, a body would be hard pressed to find a more sadistic and intolerant institution of learning. Any nice or even mildly pleasant nun promptly sought transfer. As a result, the convent became a sort of bitchy old 'virgin' sorority house. The priests who taught there typically had something to hide. And most of the lay teachers lacked options and/or credentials."

Digby's gayness was deeper than words and their pronunciation. It seemed to emanate from him. He even had a tendency to turn his toys gay or transgender. After GI Joe's initial stripping, which came quicker than you could say "boot camp cavity search," Digby got out the model paint kit and added some color to Joe's lids and lips. He added an Egyptian contour around

Joe's eyes, and a green dot on each earlobe for earrings. Digby fashioned a wig out of discarded yellow yarn, and kept it in place with a band-aid that he hand-painted to look like a turban. The overall effect was very Casbah and cosmopolitan. All Joe lacked was a cigarette holder and martini glass. Digby was pleased to discover that with minimal effort, Joe was able to slip into several of Barbie's capes and looser gowns. Skipper was a size too small. In Joe and Barbie's world, genitalia was a non-issue. The same raw materials were used for both sexes. Gender was only a matter of which plastic mold was used. The rest was marketing.

In the real world, gender was apparently a much bigger issue. Ignoring his gut, Digby experimented a bit with cross-dressing. "Look Mommy, see how pretty I am in your heels and beads," he said, turning from the mirror with a lipsticked smile. He'd also added painted strips of Scotch tape to his fingernails. Lila had come into the bedroom to get some money from her purse to pay the paperboy. Lila's initial gasp was followed by dead silence and not one, not two, but three slow blinks. She said, "Wait here."

When she returned, she was a bit more composed, but still not pleased. She was upset by Digby's behavior and for graver reasons than his overuse of jewelry. Lila slumped on the foot of the bed. This was an instance where something needed to be said, no matter how unpleasant. With a determined sigh she helped him undress, and as she did so, said, "Boys don't do that."

"But why?" In so many of his childhood memories, Digby recalled earnestly asking those two simple words. Often, he found no reason why. So much didn't make sense.

"They just don't."

But he did. He was only trying to make what he felt on the inside the same as what he saw on the outside.

"Boys don't pretend in that way."

Digby nodded like he understood, but pretending was an odd word to use for something that was really truer. The idea that it was wrong and not done led him to the simple conclusion that the "wrongness" was more than his actions. It wasn't what he did, it was who he was that was inherently wrong. This went beyond misbehaving. It was mis-being. Boys did not do the things he did just because they didn't. The tangle of logic baffled him. He was a boy. He had a thing! For something so small, the simple existence of "it" seemed to dictate so many things about his life— his clothes, his hobbies, his friends, what he was allowed to enjoy. It didn't seem fair. "Just because," seemed no real reason at all. Katie had played dress up all the time when she was younger. She hadn't been forbidden to do so.

In a similar vein, Digby was never directly forbidden but was strongly discouraged from doing double-dutch or playing jacks or turning the manger scene on the mantle into a seasonal dollhouse. Dolls were taboo as was an Easy-Bake Oven. The ignoring of his Christmas lists made a lot more sense with this new understanding of things. Santa, or his parents as Santa, refused to be accomplices in allowing him to be who he was. Lila and Rog felt it was for his own good. As a result, Digby was given more boy toys and things he couldn't make queer quite so easily, like toy dump trucks and slingshots and tool sets. His parents hoped a bombardment of male identified toys would activate his dormant maleness, and butch him up a bit.

What boy doesn't enjoy a Cowboys and Indians set?

Digby was even an exception to the Cowboys and Indians rule. When he was cajoled and eventually forced to play "frontier games" with Tom and Maynard, he broke tradition by always wanting to be a Native American. Indians loved the environment and cried at pollution. They wore fringe and beads and headbands with feathers. Cher was an Indian. Digby always played a peaceful squaw who wore robes as (s)he scouted the land, guarded the hearth, and did things like summon the winds. At the lifting of a pistol from either of his brothers, (s)he would lay down his/her bow in peace. This was not the sort of thing Tom and Maynard had in mind. Since Digby wasn't much fun at the game, they rarely asked him to play.

His Rock'Em Sock 'Em Robots were fun, but Digby made playing with the action game figures even more enjoyable by making sets of matching blonde and brunette hairpieces for the boxers. The way Digby played it, the winner didn't knock the other's block off, but his wig. His brothers refused to play with him after a couple of times. "What fun is knocking each other's wig off?" they asked with a shake of their heads. Digby, on the other hand, saw it as the ultimate act of aggression. How could his brothers not see that?

The Lincoln Logs set proved a bust as well. After he opened the box, Digby asked Maynard to build a cabin for him. The construction of it held little appeal for Digby. He simply wanted to decorate it afterwards. The Lincoln Logs were sort of like getting a dollhouse, though he would have preferred something less rustic.

Model car kits were wasted money, as was his Little Mr. Fix-It Tool Set. Those things bored and confused him. What was the point? For Digby, play was about fantasy, glamour and above all, escapism. In Running Falls, it certainly didn't require toys or an imagination to see oneself working the line at the Band-Aid Factory, bent under the hood of a Plymouth at Smitson's Garage, or engaged in countless other blue collar jobs. Many folks in town grew into those roles without thinking. They went from toys to transmissions barely skipping a beat, but since Digby had to think about almost everything he did, he understood what was going on. For him, that lifetime of drudgery was a decision that held little appeal.

The Running Falls motto was supposed to read, "Work is My Salvation," but when the town was incorporated, the city elders got a bit full of themselves and tried to fancy things up by translating it into Latin. They should have run it by The Catholic Council for a grammar check, but they didn't. As a result, the motto actually read "Work is Your Saliva." No one noticed the error until it was too late, then no one wanted to come right out and admit the mistake, especially since it was an election year. Latin was a dead language anyway. No one used it except priests and nuns.

"We don't have to worry about any dead Latinos moving into town now do we?" laughed one of the town elders. They agreed to change the motto when they ran out of official stationery, but that coincided with the sewage problems and yet another election. Rather than change the phrase, the prevailing strategy was to embrace it, reasoning that "Work is Your Saliva" showed a real hunger for labor. Since no one mounted an organized movement to the contrary, the new stationery was ordered, and the motto stuck.

Salvation for Digby was something else entirely. He wanted acceptance, and as his world grew to include more people, he had more people to please. Now in addition to family and neighbors, he had to worry about the kids at school. Acceptance was no longer enough. Now he wanted to impress as well. Desperate to be one of the crowd, he was just as desperate to be above it. Given the fact that he was neither accepted nor especially impressive, this was no minor undertaking. After hours of earnest prayer, God answered with a solution. Digby heard a sovereign voice in his head that said he might make himself special by making the experiences and events around him special. How simple! Clearly deceit was the answer to his prayers. Feeling in many ways that he was carrying out God's will, Digby developed a knack for the enhancement and the very dramatic reinterpretation of events. No exaggeration was too outrageous and no embellishment too bold. The truth was only limited by the very vivid imagination that the good Lord had given him.

Though rather far on the Mason side of the Mason-Dixon line, Digby whispered that the Swank home had been Abolitionist headquarters. He claimed their root cellar was a collapsed section of the Underground Railroad. People had died there, and he'd seen ghosts. A figure in a hoop skirt and ringlets sometimes appeared, as did a bald man with elaborate whiskers. The anguished moans of those roaming the netherworld sometimes came from the stone walls behind the shelves of Lila's pickle preserves and homemade applesauce. Rog fermented wine down there as well, but Digby was not allowed to speak about that.

One day during class, Digby announced that the origin of the Mississippi River could be traced to a modest trickling stream on his Aunt Peg and Uncle Lou's farm. "You wouldn't think twice looking at it, but that's where it all begins." He claimed that with a good-sized stone, he could easily stop its flow, radically changing the topography of the country, causing barges and showboats to run aground, and seriously disrupting commerce in several states. Sister Kathleen told him to sit and explained how countless streams and creeks and rivers fed into the giant Mississippi, which emptied into the Gulf of Mexico. Since Digby was sometimes oblivious to subtlety and typically heard only those things that he wanted to hear, he thought her explanation was in support of his statement.

The following week in class, Sister Kathleen was not quite so circuitous in her response. With a cry of "Deus misereatur, (God have mercy)," Sister told Digby to take his seat. The boy had just announced during Show and Tell that one hundred and fifty years ago, his ancestors had invented tic-tac-toe in the midst of a Montana blizzard. He said they used the new game to determine whose turn it was to lose a toe or finger for the nourishment of the others. Telling the students to put their heads down and meditate on the virtue of honesty, Sister scribbled a note for Digby to take home. Digby put it in his back pocket. Lila discovered it two days later as an undecipherable lump in the laundry dryer filter.

Fortunately for Digby, Sister Kathleen had quite a lot on her mind and forgot the matter entirely. In the past few weeks, her dog had been the cause of quite an uproar in the parish by lifting his leg not on trees or fire hydrants or even lampposts, but on strollers. He particularly favored strollers with infants inside. More than a dozen babies had been marked by Sister's urinating hound. The Church elders gave her an ultimatum. She eventually taught him, some said by demonstration, to urinate on a pile of toddler clothes she kept in the convent courtyard.

Distracted by her canine woes, Sister Kathleen said nary a word about Digby's subsequent fabrications. Learning that he was born with a hernia, Digby reinvented the protrusion as the head and shoulders of a Siamese twin that had been cut from his side when he was but an infant. "There it was, he or me, a decision had to be made." Though Digby said the twin had bled to death under the surgeon's scalpel, he admitted that the ghost of the partial newborn still haunted him. He claimed this was the reason he needed extra room on the sidewalk. "Though I know my twin is gone, I can still feel his presence."

This portion of Digby's tale was modified from things he'd heard his grandfather say about his lost arm and Phantom Limb Syndrome. It's like pins and needles in the air. Digby felt the details added to the authenticity of his tale, but it was all a misperception. As usual, no one believed him, and this time Sister wasn't even listening. The only person he was fooling was himself, but he did that with such success that he wondered if he really was a Siamese twin. Maybe there was another entire person inside of him. It would explain a lot. Besides a tendency towards chubbiness, it would also explain why he was forever divided on matters both big and small. He always seemed to be right and left, this and that, alpha and omega, male and female. Since he was busy being both, in actuality he was neither. Being one but acting the other made him little more than a full-time impostor.

Sister Marianne took over for the rest of the term as Digby's second grade teacher after Sister Kathleen was injured in the big Dominican Nuns vs. The Sisters of St. Francis charity field hockey game. Some said that by worrying about her dog, she had left herself open to St. Francis' brutal defense. She lost her two front teeth, and broke her leg in three places during the match. The annual rivalry had a reputation for being fierce. Everyone thought God was on their side, especially the Sisters of St. Francis, who would pump their fists and chant "Deo dulce, ferro comitante," before each play. Roughly translated, this means With God as my leader and my sword as my companion. Afterward, Sister Kathleen and her dog, Bingo, moved to a convent upstate.

The new nun, Sister Marianne, chose to handle Digby in a different manner. "That Swank upstart had more than a touch of the blarney about him. We used to joke that it was easy to tell when he was lying because his lips moved. Oh, it was clearly a cry for attention. I understood that, but I also didn't really have the time or inclination to entertain such things. Mostly I just ignored him."

Digby's fibs were frequent, careless, and mostly petty. He never felt bad about it. His lies weren't really damnable; they just jazzed up the truth a bit. As a fellow creator, he assumed that God could appreciate that. Reality could be so blah. His exaggerations were always more interesting. He gave life a spin and made it more magical and mythical. His lies festooned the blasé. Lying was his power and his secret defiance. It was the only method of aggression he knew or used at the time, so he tended to use it as one would a blunt instrument, with no finesse and no subtlety. His sheer volume compensated for his lack of flair.

In third grade, a reading contest was held in the four weeks of October, which was declared National Reading Month. On the first of the month, Sister Catherine Claire revealed a bar graph on the wall at the head of the classroom. The names of Digby and his classmates edged the bottom border. Sister announced that a quarter inch would be given for every book they read in the coming weeks. Competition made Digby crazy, and when it was combined with publicly displayed results, things could get ugly. His reinterpretive skills shifted into overdrive. He had to win; his worth was on display. He counted chapters as books, and sometimes even exceptionally long paragraphs as volumes. Fictionalizing fiction seemed justified, as well as fitting. One evening, he claimed to have read fourteen books. In the end he won the prize for his grade, but the award presentation was tainted by Sister Catherine Claire's grim-faced lecture on the fate of liars. A blighted soul? A severed tongue? Digby was oblivious. His eyes were focused on the prize, and that glow-in-the-dark rosary was his! The second and third place students were given scapulars. Holy cards were also distributed.

The following week, Brad, one of his father's cronies at the phone company, came to class to demonstrate the proper use and function of the telephone. Digby was not impressed. A dial tone wasn't especially interesting. The bar for classroom speakers had not been set terribly high. The month before, the class speaker had been a representative from the Band-Aid factory, who came to discuss bandage use and various applications of the adhesive strips.

The phone company lecture was dull. Eager to add something memorable to the proceedings, Digby raised his hand. With some hesitation and the slight whistle of an exhalation, Sister Catherine Claire called on him. Standing beside his desk, Digby announced that once he'd dialed his own number and had heard himself talking, but from years ago.

Brad and Sister Catherine Claire exchanged looks.

"That is an impossibility," scoffed Sister.

"No," Digby replied, "It was a miracle."

His response brought punishment, of course. By claiming to have experienced a miracle, he mocked every saint and martyr blessed by God, and the Holy Father himself. With the snap of her bony fingers, Sister Catherine Claire banished him to the hallway, where he was instructed to kneel for the remainder of the day with his head bowed in humility. He was told to examine his conscience and beg forgiveness for his impudence. This was even more degrading than standing in the trash can for an hour, which was Sister's typical punishment for bad behavior.

Sister's nostrils flared like windsocks. "This will be going on your permanent record Mr. Swank." Sister Catherine Clare glowered, then added, "And I shouldn't be surprised if there were eternal consequences for this sort of behavior." With her broad shoulders, thin frame, and crisp habit, she resembled a stern playing card. Few would argue that the harsh-featured nun was one of Christ's most unfortunate looking brides. He heard her mutter something that sounded like "simpering oddkin" as she turned to walk away. Kneeling in the hall, he didn't repent or seek atonement, or examine his conscience or even bow his head. Digby spent the rest of the day asking God why He went to the trouble of giving him an imagination if He didn't want him to use it. With all due respect, Heavenly Father, wasn't that a waste of time?

Digby had his own thoughts on what constituted fact or fiction. To him, a lie became the truth when told long and earnestly enough, assuming a sort of squatter's rights over reality until truth became the intruder. Digby lost track time and again of what had exactly happened, what might have happened or how a happening was told. In the end, all that mattered was how it was remembered. Some may have called him a liar, but Digby preferred "discriminating realist," or at least he would have, had his vocabulary been more developed. His lies were simply part of God's plan, and intricate pieces of something we as mere mortals were unable to understand. In this light, Digby could easily reconcile being a good liar with being a good Catholic.

Digby's lying, his smirk, and his passive but contrary nature made him unpopular among both faculty and students. After a semester of reprimands and second chances following years of stern looks and exasperated sighs from the nuns of classrooms past, Sister Catherine Claire had little recourse but to send him to Mr. Cray, the school psychologist, during recess. "That boy is enough to send Jesus to a speakeasy," she silently seethed.

Sister Catherine Claire held little faith in psychology. She thought Digby's attitude was best served with the firm slap of a pious hand, or the whack of a metal ruler across the knuckles. Drawing blood had always been an effective deterrent. However, the thrill of a good thrashing was no longer an option. Education had gone soft. The thought of it made Sister sad and nostalgic. The ability to inflict corporal punishment was one of the things that had drawn her to teaching. Working with children and beating the grace of God into them used to bring her great satisfaction. Now even name-calling was frowned upon, though mockery and subtle forms of ridicule were still encouraged. She fingered the beads at her waist, and with a sigh of righteous indignation, signed the form to send Digby to the school counselor.

To Sister Catherine Claire, therapy was akin to exorcism, though the casting out of demons at least had a history with the Roman Catholic Church, unlike all this touchy-feely mumbo jumbo. In her eyes, psychology, or astrology, or whatever it was called, served no purpose but to gray the area between good and evil. "As if the world were not either/or," she scoffed with a shake of her head. She was not alone in her view. To most of the faculty, psychology was merely a newfangled form of quackery, a fad of modern times which would eventually pass. Clearly, issues were best addressed through prayer, answers from above being preferable to those that came from within. "Bring your issues with you on Judgement Day, and we'll see where it gets you," thought Sister Catherine Claire with a tight smile and the light caress of the crucifix about her neck. "There will be no mercy on the Dies Irae, the Day of Wrath."

Given such an uninviting environment, Mr. Cray was obsessed with justifying his worth. Like many therapists, he just wanted people to like him. He prided himself on being a good listener, mostly because he had so little to say. He meant well. He was a deeply concerned man with permed hair, and a permanent rut between his brows. Sadly, he possessed no intuition and scant imagination. A multicolored bar graph on the back of his door was evidence of the fact that he enjoyed categorizing the few students sent to him. The year Digby saw him, behavioral disorders were up a whopping fifteen percent among the Holy Martyrs student body. Mr. Cray's occupational bliss came from estimating behavioral patterns, calculating percentages, and almost every aspect of his job except dealing with the students.

He wasn't a people person, so naturally people avoided him as well. His office door was always open, but his threshold was rarely crossed. The colored paper around his doorframe gave his office the look of a diorama. He sat at his desk on display like a slow, blinking lizard upon a stone. Passing students stared inside, and when he looked up, they quickly scurried by. Mr. Cray remained at his desk clearing his throat and smiling, straightening his glasses and busying himself with the shuffling of papers and files, alternately trying to look occupied and available, depending upon his mood. He was not good with rejection.

When Mr. Cray received the note that Digby was assigned to visit him regularly, the counselor was thrilled and nervous. He circled 12:15 in his appointment book in several red loops. It was the only mark upon the page. In preparation for Digby's visit, Mr. Cray moved his stapler back and forth from the right to the left hand corner of the desk several times. He finally put it in a drawer.

Initially, Digby enjoyed his visits with Mr. Cray. That's what the counselor called their sessions. Digby enjoyed it primarily because he was scheduled to see Mr. Cray during recess. Free period on the playground had not been a pleasant experience. He often stood on the perimeter, watching the others and waiting for the half hour to be over. Sometimes the rotating playground moderators would force him to participate. He'd been pushed, shoved, kicked, teased, and picked on far too many times—and that was by the girls. As Mr. Cray said countless times with the same practiced gesture, "This office is a safe place for you, Digby."

Before each session, Mr. Cray would straighten his fingerprinted wire frames, and offer Digby a chipped tooth smile along with a stick of sugarless gum. Digby always accepted. Cray hoped the conspiratorial chewing, strictly forbidden at Holy Martyrs as a blatant indulgence of sensual gratification, would bond them. Mr. Cray carefully noted Digby's one hundred percent acceptance ratio, writing beside it in his notebook, Rebellious? Conciliatory? Orally fixated? I hope he likes me. Despite his community college counseling degree, he never realized Digby was skilled at reading upside down.

Mr. Cray sympathetically probed the boy for nearly half the school year, and was still baffled. Digby found it absurdly easy to second guess and manipulate the man, especially since Mr. Cray was so desperate to be accepted. Mr. Cray never suspected that a compulsive liar would lie to him as well. Perversely, Digby found that lying to someone who was trying to help him because of his lying brought him exceptional joy. Deceiving Mr. Cray was a bright red ribbon tied about his otherwise dismal school day. Digby never seriously considered confiding in him. He wasn't to be trusted. No one was, really. The only one he could trust was himself, and even that required an almost constant vigilance. Finally in frustration, and after several amended drafts, Mr. Cray sent a letter home with Digby.

Dear Mr. and Mrs. Swank,
I regret to inform you that your son Digby has been having difficulty functioning on a social level at Holy Martyrs. A firmly

embedded fear of rejection seems to lie at the core of Digby's neurosis. The boy is a compulsive liar, and although compulsive lying is not altogether irregular in a child of Digby's age, (roughly ten percent of the youngsters in America suffer from this problem, and at Holy Martyrs compulsive lying is somewhere in the three percent range) if the problem is not addressed and treated, there is a thirty-four percent chance that as an adult, your son will suffer severe emotional repercussions. To safeguard from such an occurrence, I suggest intensive family counseling and opening a dialogue as soon as possible. Please call me so we can begin this exciting journey towards healing.

Straightforwardly,

Ben Cray

Unsettled, confused by the letter and frustrated by already hectic schedules, Digby's parents chose to handle the matter differently. That night, Rog and Lila called him into the kitchen. "I'll open a goddamned dialogue," his father was saying as Digby entered the room. His parents were somber opposites. Lila was all disappointed resignation, while Rog was parental frustration incarnate. Rog raked a hand through his thinning crop of hair, and forbade Digby to ever lie again. "End of dialogue!" His mother sighed in agreement, and crushed out her cigarette. The family would be taking no journeys into healing. Digby apologized for any problems he'd caused, and said it had all been a misunderstanding. When Digby swore henceforth to be honest, he already knew he was lying. It had become a necessity. He had to lie to survive. Unsure about exactly which saint to petition for his cause, Digby lay in bed that night, and prayed to God for the strength to become a better liar in the future.

Digby now hated Mr. Cray for his blatant betrayal. They'd had a pact of sorts, and Cray had brought Digby's parents into the mess. It was unforgivable. Digby could have told him they wouldn't have time for all this. Digby had no place in his life for backstabbers, though he did prefer them to folks who said things right to his face. That safe place office spiel was just another trap, and although he'd shared close to nothing with Cray, he'd still been ensnared by it all.

Digby continued to go to Cray's office at the appointed time, but he no longer spoke to him with more than a simple "yes" or "no" or "fine." He sat silently and looked down at his swinging legs, or out the window. He never accepted another stick of gum. They only met two or three more times after that. During his final session, Digby read the upside down entry in his folder, "With the letter home, the bond was regretfully broken. Now I know Digby hates me." Digby looked up and met his eyes. In that instant, Cray realized Digby could read the entry, even if he probably didn't understand all of the words. Cray quickly closed the folder, and looked up. By then, Digby had already moved to the door. Cray called to him weakly, and repeated his name a second time. Digby kept walking. He left without a glance back or a goodbye.

What Digby or his parents thought of Mr. Cray made no difference in the end. Cray was the first casualty of budget cuts at Holy Martyrs near the end of the term. No one was terribly sorry to see him go. Most hardly noticed anything more than a closed office door where there'd once been a nervous looking man on display. Even Cray himself seemed a bit relieved when his post was terminated. A Catholic school was really no place for therapeutic guidance, much less emotional support. With his dismissal, Mr. Cray's small office was converted into a storage room. A year later, Digby was walking by, and looked in as the janitor retrieved the mop and vomit absorbent. He noticed that still taped to the back of the door was Mr. Cray's rainbow chart which read Be Happy, Be Free, Be Yourself! in magic marker colors.

8 – Low Grade Pain

Sometimes life in the Swank household confused Digby as much as his interactions in the outside world. A primary source of his perplexity was that he simply thought too much. Acts and deeds of no concern to most were of grave concern to Digby. He was constantly worried about things happening in other rooms, or just around the corner or downstairs or upstairs. He was sure some things happened simply so they could be kept from him. His fretting over secrets and deceptions at such a young age made it clear that he harbored many of his own. His paranoia made him a constant snoop, which often caused Digby and his family great embarrassment.

One evening, Digby was rummaging through the bathroom garbage and found a fist-sized bundle wrapped around and around in toilet paper. Opening this mysterious treasure, he gasped to discover a thick gauze pad heavy with blood. It was his sister's feminine napkin. Of course, he didn't know anything about this at the time. Digby wouldn't be privy to that sort of information for several years, when his cousin Tober divulged the details on a family camping trip. Even then it didn't seem quite believable. Blood? Eggs? The moon? The curse? He sat wide-eyed as Tober divulged the mystery of it all with a flashlight held beneath his chin for effect. Even without that added spooky touch, Digby felt as though he was hearing the plot of a Bela Lugosi film.

As fate would have it, the night he discovered his sister's Kotex was also the night for the unveiling of that highly anticipated hallmark of middle class arrival, the newly paneled rec room. His parents had gone all out on the remodeling, or at least as all out as they could go with a clear conscience. They even carpeted one wall in shag after reading that Sammy Davis Jr. had done the same thing. Rog and Lila felt terribly progressive doing that, since Sammy was a black Jew.

The Swanks were eager to impress Aunt Lucy and Uncle Willard, Bob and Ginny Van Camp, the Sterners, and all the rest of their circle. It was their moment to shine. Competitiveness padded their social fabric, and true satisfaction among their set required a coverlet of envy. Showing off to friends and neighbors provided the incentive to work, and subsequently, to flaunt the fruits of that labor. This wasn't just true of the Swanks and their circle, it was simply the way that things were done. Having more so you can dazzle others, inspire jealousy, and feel better about yourself was a cornerstone of what had made this country great. That's what The Pledge of Allegiance was all about. The rec room was proof that the Swanks were living the dream.

The rec room theme was nautical, with decorative netting draped in sweeping folds over the low ceiling beams. The bowed overhang above held starfish and maritime buoys, and a durable braid of rope wound around the two support poles from top to bottom in the middle of the room. The rattling boiler in the corner couldn't be disguised, so Rog had built a white paneled closet around it. An S.S. Meridian life preserver hung on the cabinet door. Blue shag carpeting covered the floor. A humming electric sign upon the wall announced that THE BAR IS OPEN.

An eclectic group of friends, family, neighbors, and business associates mingled amidst the converted surroundings that night. The Swanks had a vast number of people they wished to impress, but the two dozen in attendance were all that the space would allow. Rog and Lila were sure more parties would follow. This was merely the rec room's maiden voyage, a test to be sure it was sea worthy. Perry Como crooned on the hi-fi. His smooth sound mixed easily with the clinking of ice in cocktail glasses.

Still in a panic from his discovery, Digby bound down the blue carpeted stairs carrying the remnants of his sister's sloughed uterine bed in his cupped and trembling hands. Conversation dwindled to a full hush as the guests took notice of his entrance into the converted basement. All heads turned as he boldly confronted his parents. Displaying the bloody artifact he spoke. "Someone in this house is wounded and bleeding, and no one is telling me because I am the youngest."

Katie's mouth opened wide, her eyes glazing over. She dropped the hors d'oeuvres tray onto the bumper pool table, which had been converted into a food island for the party.

Turning redder than her nubile menstrual blood on display, she fled up the stairs with an anguished wail. "I could have just died," she would later exclaim.

Long moments passed in silence.

"What's going on?" whispered Aunt Lucy. She should have known the Swanks would be unable to successfully entertain on this scale. "It's really a skill, and you either have it or you don't," she thought with a small sip of her Manhattan.

The obese houseguest from Catholic Charities, Miss Doreen, cleared her throat and mopped a perpetually sweaty brow. "It looks like someone has communists in the summer house." Not realizing this was a euphemism for menstruation, Aunt Lucy just smiled and moved away under the guise of needing to freshen up her drink. Aunt Lucy considered all those Catholic Charity folks to be loony, and here was one talking right out in public about the Reds. It was no wonder they were outcasts. They may be a part of God's plan, but thank goodness that plan doesn't include me, thought Aunt Lucy with a shiver.

Rog attempted to shift the focus with an overly enthusiastic, "Who wants cheese fondue?"

Perry Como seemed unnaturally loud. The buzz of the electric bar sign droned.

Aunt Lucy caught Uncle Willard's eye. They always claimed they didn't want to say anything, but that was precisely what they liked to do. They'd discuss all this unseemliness on the car ride home, and from the looks of things, they'd need to take the scenic route to have enough time. Lucy and Willard only really talked when they were in the car. After twenty years of marriage, they found that facing forward and focusing on the road made talking much easier than facing and focusing on each other.

Wearing a painfully artificial hostess smile, which she wore so often it seemed as natural as an uncomfortable work uniform, Lila herded Digby upstairs and into the kitchen. Lighting a Pall Mall, she took an unnaturally deep drag, brushed the front of her burnt sienna pantsuit, and straightened the side knot of her matching patterned scarf. She looked at him for a long moment before telling him to go wash his hands. He could hear her heels tap on the linoleum as he did. She was thinking, Thank goodness Lizabeth is dead, or we'd never hear the end of this.

The sounds from the party downstairs started to swell once more. The damper of the feminine napkin had passed. Digby heard his mother sigh, and the refrigerator door open. He heard the added whoosh of the top-shelf freezer, and the clank of a bowl and spoon. Lila gave him a dish of chocolate fudge ice cream and explained nothing.

"Be a good boy, and go to your room and eat," she smiled.

Digby smiled and happily bound up the stairs to his room.

Carbs and sugar solved everything. In the proper combination, they even seemed to have magical properties that prevented some problems from occurring. Lila only wished she'd given him the ice cream sooner. Digby knew enough not to talk with his mouth full, so his mother filled his mouth a lot. Food made him forget all pressing questions. It softened edges and soothed nerves. His capacity to eat also brought him a sort of praise. Appetite was seen as a reflection of health and heartiness. However, there comes a point when appetite becomes indicative of something else entirely, but in those days stuffing things down was not yet seen as bad. Eating one's feelings seemed an entirely legitimate way of dealing with them. Under the poorly-patched Swank roof, as under many at the time, food was about pretty much everything except nutrition and sustenance.

The EAT response was representative of the Swank approach to conflict, discomfort, strong emotion, or any undesirable state that might arise. If the family was shipwrecked on a desert island, they weren't likely to need water. They'd need only food, silence, denial, liquor, and confession in order to survive. If they couldn't stuff it in, shove it down, turn away, chug it, or purge it to God, the results would not be pretty. Luckily, one of those survival tools always seemed to be at hand.

If confession was the chosen means of dealing with a slightly scandalous or potentially shameful problem, the best method would be to confess to something else entirely, and pray for a sort of blanket absolution. If the penitent was determined to confess something he actually did, driving to a different parish at an off time was a prudent move. If possible, choosing a visiting priest to act as the Angel of Penance was also wise, but not one who was hard of hearing. The priest behind the scrim may be deaf and bound to confidentiality by the Seal of the Confessional, but the naves had ears. Churches are typically built with an eye for grandeur and an ear for acoustics, and every parish seemed to harbor a network of wizened crones with the sharpened hearing of a wild dog. These members of Christ's coven lurked behind statuary, and crouched in pews outside confessional doors. Supposedly bent deep in prayer, these parishites were actually lying in wait to inadvertently catch a juicy transgression or two. They were rarely disappointed.

Longtime Holy Martyrs parishioner Mrs. Aileen Flaherty took deep offense to such comments. "How dare my motives for daily prayer be questioned! Is it my fault that some people confess in a full voice as if making boast of their trespasses? The good Lord gave me ears for a reason. Should I stick sausage links in each? Should I cut them off with a circumcision knife and stuff them in my coin purse to appease some brassy sinner who lacks the good sense to speak in a civilized voice?"

The Church was everything for so many of these people. Digby understood the attraction. The structure itself was impressive. Holy Martyrs clearly aspired to be a cathedral with its world of towers and belfries, gables and galleries, pinnacles and apsidioles. The church always seemed to be collecting for an addition or renovation, even though the labor and materials were usually donated. Holy Martyrs Church was one of the only places in Digby's lower middle class neighborhood where veined marble pillars, chandeliers, and red velvet runners were on display. Anywhere else, this lavishness would be considered showy and decadent, but the church considered such opulence divine. As Digby understood it, God was basically Liberace and

His pad was nothing short of a Vegas show palace. He didn't see God dressed in white robes carrying a staff, as He was so often depicted in paintings and religion books. After seeing several of His lavish homes, Digby instead pictured God in silk lounging pajamas with a monogrammed G. Digby imagined God napping on a king-size water bed, with a mirrored headboard and dozens of satiny throw pillows. A couple white Persian cats with glittery collars dozed nearby as one of Dean Martin's Golddiggers made His cocktail. God liked His martini neat.

All this grandeur and glitz appealed to Digby's flashy aesthetic, but he was equally attracted to the Catholic Church's dark side. In this respect, Holy Martyrs Church was as gothic and as terrifying as Catholicism itself.

Under that high, arched ceiling, every sound echoed, and each whisper was a roar. Prayer candles danced in the gloom, throwing medieval shadows across the high, irregular walls, the domed ceiling, and the flying buttresses. On the altar, Jesus writhed upon the cross with blood oozing from His wounds. Carved Stations of the Cross lined the perimeter. Tiny nooks of prayer were tucked in stone recesses which housed only a candle or two, a statue and a *prie dieu*. Saints lurked like teenage hoodlums in the corners amongst banks of deep red votives. Lighting a candle was a mere twenty-five cent donation. The fee gave added weight to one's petition to God, or to any of the saints. The nuns said that consistently lighting a votive candle could aid a soul in peril, and knock years off a person's time in Purgatory. Lighting a candle without paying the quarter brought damnation.

According to several adults in his world, the Church, and more specifically the mass, had once even been more grandiose and mysterious. Many adults felt the Church had been diminished in the "modern age" and the revamping that had occurred with the Second Vatican Council had pedestrianized the mass. Such talk awed Digby. He couldn't imagine Catholicism as more cryptic and mystical and removed from everyday reality than it already was.

Crouching on the stairs and eavesdropping on his mother's bridge club one night, Digby overheard Carolyn Evers loudly complain, "I am not one for all these newfangled changes. The priest used to say every bit of the mass in Latin and recite it, not just read it from a book. That always impressed me. I liked it when he said the mass while keeping his back to the congregation. It always seemed more sacred when it felt like the priest and God were mostly ignoring you."

"Now, I disagree," countered Sandy Treacle. "I didn't care for the way the mass was. With the Latin and the priest having his back to you, I felt like I was eavesdropping on a tourist making a telephone call."

Used to Sandy's contrariness, Carolyn continued, "Well now, standing up there facing the congregation with the chalice and the Bible propped open, the priest looks just like he's hosting a cooking show. And what with the way some folks carry on with that Sign of Peace, I half expect someone to start circulating with an hors d'oeuvres tray."

Even though several women nodded in polite agreement, most felt that Carolyn could use a bit more restraint of tongue. That kind of talk wasn't prudent for any number of reasons. Some supposed it was sacrilege and that she was jeopardizing her soul, but the other consequences of her chatter were more immediate. People who played cards with Carolyn only a couple of times noticed she only got to talking when she'd been dealt a losing hand. When she had the potential to take a few tricks, she shut up right away.

Digby recalled a period when his mother went to confession almost every other day. Digby never knew why. He knew from religion class that only mortal sins needed to be confessed in a timely fashion, so whatever she did was not a venial matter. In the confessional, Lila wisely lowered her voice after her introductory, "Bless me Father for I have sinned, it has been a day since my last confession..."

Digby wondered if she just needed someone to talk to. Lila had friends, but none of them could keep a secret to save their lives. On second thought, they weren't really friends, but mostly just women she tried to impress on a regular basis. During the period of her frequent confessions, Lila smoked a lot and drank coffee by the pot, and seemed even more worried than usual. And she usually dragged Digby along with her.

Digby noticed that a few elderly parishioners were always scattered about the pews, chanting desperately for sustained faith. Fearful of death, they gripped their rosaries as tightly as they gripped what remained of life. Digby assumed they worried they hadn't been quite good enough, or that maybe they had just been a bit too human. They played the odds in a big cosmic crapshoot. No one knew what to expect, but admitting to the uncertainty was the gravest trespass of them all. Digby imagined them approaching the gates to heaven, and St. Peter shrugging with a wince to explain, "I'm sorry, your request for entry has been denied—but you were so close. One more day of prayer, and you probably would have made it."

After Lila's confession, she always bought Digby an ice cream cone that he ate too quickly. Through the throb of his brain freeze, he watched Lila wipe her eyes and blow her nose. She always made sure to curse her allergies. He got the impression this was all to remain a secret between them, but the only time she came right out and said so was on one of the last of the weekday church visits. That day after confession, they turned the opposite direction when leaving the parking lot at Mr. Frosty's Ice Cream, and Lila went to see a psychic.

Madame Fortuna had a neon palm and the word READER in the window of her second floor walk-up. Digby had heard about gypsies and expected Madame to look the part, but she wore no bangles or beads and she didn't have a gold coin tucked in her navel. She looked just like a zaftig non-reader in her green slacks and yellow blouse. Reading his look of surprise, she said she only dressed up on weekends. Digby waited outside a heavy curtain while his mother went inside. Incense hung in a haze around the lights. He heard whispers and bells, but mostly he played with Madame's wiener dog, who somewhat ruined the ambiance with a squeaky toy. When his mother emerged from the curtain, she grabbed his hand. They quickly went down the stairs, around the corner, and onto the side street where she'd parked. "No one is to know about this ever. Is that clear?" clarified Lila once they were in the car. Digby didn't have to be a psychic to know that such things were sinful. Her hands gripped the wheel more tightly. "No one," she said. Digby nodded. "Ever." She bought him a second ice cream cone for the ride home.

Whatever the reason for those regular visits to church and the confessional, they ended just as abruptly as they had began. By the end of the year, Lila was once more a "Sundays only" girl.

During that stretch of time, Digby experienced a sudden epiphany or a vision. Or maybe he just had a good idea. Kneeling in the hallowed hollows of the church waiting for his mother to finish praying and confessing and seeking absolution yet again, he suddenly knew how he could make everyone proud of him. It had been staring him in the face all along. He could enter the clergy. It seemed a sure way to win admiration and much more. Maynard said they even got a free car. Maybe if he were a priest, then things would make sense. Maybe then he'd understand why He had taken Grandma Rose away. Maybe if he were really good, God would give him something to replace that loss. He felt liberated to discover his life goal at an age when most boys still had pipe dreams of becoming astronauts and firemen. That didn't bother him. Digby wasn't like most boys, and he found the things that most boys wanted were foolish anyway.

Religion gave him a sense of purpose as well as a good dose of awe, even if his beliefs were a bit skewed. He liked God better than Jesus, Mary more than her Son, and he never knew what to make of the Holy Spirit. Frankly, he was a bit leery of anyone depicted as a dancing tongue of fire or a bird aflame. What exactly was It? In every rendering he saw of that mysterious third wheel of the trinity, the Holy Spirit seemed to most resemble a biker logo. Digby would have definitely liked Him better if He was still called the Holy Ghost. Then he'd be like Casper.

Digby liked God best because He was in charge. The more the Divine Father flexed His miraculous muscles, the more Digby liked it. He especially enjoyed God in the Old Testament. That was His golden era. In those days, He let you know exactly where you stood. He intervened, was fickle, made crazy demands, cursed descendants, threw tantrums, and said precisely what needed to be done to win His love. Often, He was not easy to please. Sacrifice your son! Give me livestock! Go to Egypt! Circumcise that thing! God used to micromanage everything. His demands may have been compulsive and crazy, but they were clear. You'll do it because I told you to do it! In contrast, Digby felt that His sending Jesus to earth was a bad career move. It changed the God dynamic, diluting His bossy bravado. He grew soft, but even more disturbing, He became aloof and lackadaisical when it came to His flock. No longer a "hands on" deity, He spoke in riddles or through fisherman, and the middle management aspect made it all sort of screwy and vague. He no longer had His big divine nose all up in people's business. Things seemed to be going downhill. God needed a policy change. Digby hoped that as a servant of the Lord, he could be of some influence.

Digby thought about God so obsessively that he began to wonder if he might be The Second Coming. "Maybe this is all happening because I'm Him," thought Digby, staring at himself in the bathroom mirror. "That would be so cool!" He figured that the second incarnation of Jesus had to be someone. Even though he wasn't born to a virgin or in a barn or even on Christmas, he still wondered if he could possibly be Him. He might not be aware of it. Jesus didn't know who he was until later when he changed the water into wine, and the miracles started happening. The ability to perform that sort of magic was the answer, just like Bewitched, only deathly serious and more divine. Needing to know one way or the other, Digby made a numbered list of several miraculous tasks that might help determine his JQ, or Jesus Quotient.

When it came to performing miracles, things were not promising from the start. Walking on water was a complete bust, as was his attempt to feed six of his cousins with one peanut butter sandwich and a single glass of orange Kool-Aid. Sips and niblets did not satisfy as the fish and loaves had done at that gathering on the shore of the Sea of Galilee. He crossed both miracles off his list. Hoping to recreate the miracle of the wedding banquet in Cana, Digby focused on a half jug of wine on the kitchen counter, waved his hands about it, and prayed. Rog would have appreciated that miracle, but Digby could not produce even an additional ounce of liquor. Going down his miracle list, Digby frowned and put a line through catching a fish with a gold coin in its mouth. That hadn't happened in all his years of fishing, though he'd once reeled in a bra from the depths of Loaf Lake. He'd hooked the clasp with his lure. Maynard and Tom went into hysterics when the muddy bra, with a seaweed halo, came into view alongside the boat. When he finally stopped laughing, Maynard said that was amazing. Digby didn't think that counted as a miracle. Instead, he moved on to the next miraculous wonder and tried to raise a flattened squirrel from the dead. He only succeeded in scattering some of the flies.

Discouraged but not undone, Digby wondered if perhaps he could fill Jesus' sandals as a healer. That had been one of His specialties. Digby managed to stop his cousin Tober's nosebleed with a beatific smile, though that may have been a simple matter of clotting. Encouraged, Digby moved to the rest of Tober's face and tried to heal his acne, but that proved to be beyond his powers. To be fair, Tober's complexion was well beyond the power of any over-the-counter ointments. Digby was also unable to heal his mother's insomnia, or stop his father's drinking. He had wanted both of those miracles very much. Eventually, Digby accepted the fact that he probably wasn't Him unless Savior-dom, like armpit hair, was a secondary characteristic that didn't come until the onset of puberty. However, the entire holiness as hormonal angle seemed unlikely.

Despite his disappointment, Digby didn't mind compromising. He reasoned that even if he wasn't God's Son, he could still serve the Church in an upper management capacity. If the Savior slot wasn't available, then being Pope would be okay. His head was about the right size for that big white hat, which Digby considered to be almost as grand as the Miss Universe crown. However, he refused to go any lower than Pope. No velvet bishop vestment with towering mitre or crisp cardinal frock with tasseled belt would do. It was Pope or nothing. He would only give his life to God if he was allowed to remain in control. He respected the faith of others and was perfectly willing to have faith himself, so long as it didn't require blind allegiance. That just seemed foolhardy.

With stained-glass stars in his eyes, he begged to attend daily sunrise mass at Holy Martyrs. When he asked if he could go, his parents reluctantly agreed. What could they say? Forbidding a child to go to mass was bound to be a sin of some sort. Those hazy mornings when Digby walked to the church, he sat front row center and knelt on the cold marble floor until his knees ached.

He had learned in school that it was good to suffer. Redemption came through suffering. Other religions stressed being joyful; for Catholics, a wince was better than a smile. God loved Catholic people to be in pain. He loved when they were plagued by demons, crippled with anguish, and rife with disease. Being a victim was half the battle. Everyone knew the best way to become a saint was to be beaten or diseased or starved or sacrificed. Hardship was the road to redemption, and Digby would pay the price as long as there was something in it for him. Besides, he doubted the Pope had to suffer half as much as normal Catholics. He only really worked on Sundays, and Digby heard that he had a jacuzzi. The Pope didn't have one car, he had a fleet of them and a legion of chauffeurs at his disposal.

Never one for half measures, Digby became fully committed to his new goal. He silently mouthed both parts of the Stations of the Cross during car rides, and even sat in the car while it was in the garage and said it himself on a couple of occasions. He crossed himself until his arm ached, and tried to baptize the dog.

Donating a quarter and lighting a votive candle, he bent his head in prayer, "Please, please, oh please, make me the next Pope."

In a bold but unpopular move, he declined all Sunday chores to keep holy the Sabbath. This did not go over well with Rog and Lila. His mother chose to remain relatively silent on the matter. Lila worried that a rash censure of the boy might prompt Digby to mention her recent church visits, and heaven forbid, the trip to Madame Fortuna.

Rog, however, was unsympathetic as well as vocal about this keeping holy the Sabbath nonsense. "Absolutely not, young man!"

Digby offered a small nod of understanding. He'd expected as much. There is no blame, only acceptance. Digby had often heard the phrase used in reference to Catholicism, but had never known it to actually be practiced. Blame was a part of life, and denial was its echo. He needed to be above all that. Being Pope material meant taking the higher ground. With a sigh, he accepted their punishment. He said that in accordance with the Commandments he honored them, but that he now obeyed Canon law above parental authority. He said that he forgave them and realized they were only doing what they had to do. Digby considered his resulting punishment as dues invested in his eventual martyrdom. "This will certainly be in my Lives of the Saints bio," he reasoned, staring at the ceiling of his room after being grounded. In truth, it wasn't so bad. He thought of it as being cloistered. As an antisocial youngster, being banished to his room was no real hardship at all. Rog and Lila assumed that since Maynard, Katie, and Tom hated being grounded, Digby would as well. Keeping them all straight was tough sometimes.

During this period, Digby's clothes grew somber, and he wore his hair with bangs like a monk, or the Monkees. He turned his eyes either humbly to the ground or euphorically heavenward, which made him even clumsier than usual. Many folks didn't think that was possible. Digby spoke softly, and most surprisingly, he ate sparingly. He behaved better than he ever thought possible, and he waited. Patience was a virtue.

He prayed for the day when the golden halo above his head would appear. Surely as a future Pope he would get one! It would be the ultimate accessory, and it would also make going to the bathroom during the night and reading in bed so much easier. He'd be able to light up a room regardless of his mood. Digby waited, wondering if his halo would flip on like a light switch, or gradually brighten like a moonrise. Two weeks, nothing. Three weeks, nothing. Virtue or no virtue, he was getting antsy. When he closed his eyes at bedtime, he imagined a sacred illumination casting out the darkness. He hoped and hoped and prayed, and would quickly open his eyes, but the halo never appeared. Maybe that sign of saintliness was something only other people could see. Maybe it was like tickling yourself.

After a month of his holier than thou behavior, Rog and Lila had endured just about enough. The last straw was when he started listening to Sing! Sing! Sing!, a charity album featuring the local nun's choir, put together to help raise money for an eight foot cement crucifix in their courtyard. The sisters kept a list of all "donors" who had bought an album, and gave attitude to all who were not on the list. Rog would have just as soon handed them ten bucks. At the sound of the discordant warbles of They Call the Wind Maria, Rog and Lila could take no more. Rog snapped off the stereo. When Digby gave them a questioning look, they asked what all this religious nonsense was about. They would've asked earlier, but they thought Digby was just doing it for attention. "What's gotten into you young man?"

Digby grasped the hand of each of his parents, and confessed his intentions to become Pope. He couldn't contain his excitement. "I can't wait! Just you see, people will kiss my ring, and line the streets to see me and everything. I'm even going to make Grandma Rose a saint. You two can come live at the Vatican if you want. I hear they have a pool and tennis courts and masseurs." Rog and Lila exchanged looks not once but twice, and gave both of his hands a little squeeze. Lila offered an extended sigh, which, because of her cold, lapsed into a cough. When her hacking subsided, Rog said flat out that becoming Pope wasn't a career option.

"Rog and I didn't know quite what to say. Since we weren't Italian, it seemed impossible. That's all changed, of course. Poles, Germans—now it's anybody's game. Teaching kids how unfair life can be was more Rog's area of expertise. He was drinking pretty heavily at the time, and I suppose he could have been gentler, but that nun album always set him on edge. Even sober,

Rog was never one to mince words once you got him to open his mouth. He told Digby it was impossible for him to become Pope, and he told him exactly why. He said it didn't make sense, and that a lot of things don't make sense, especially when it comes to the Church. Rog added that being nonsensical didn't make it any less true. He said that was the test of a real Catholic, and that was why we needed faith. He said if it made sense, believing it would be easy. For the most part, Digby took the news the way we expected. He called us liars, and ran to his room. Eventually, we had to buy him a bike to snap him out of that Pope nonsense."

Not Italian! Digby scoffed at the lunacy of it through tears of frustration. None of this made sense. His father had to be either teasing, or delusional. Since his parents didn't typically tease, especially when it came to the Church, Digby supposed the latter to be the case. They had to be mistaken. He wondered if God was testing him. Surely the Catholic Church was above such pettiness and favoritism. Wasn't it?

Digby wasn't about to simply accept this nonsense. He needed a second opinion. The next day before the morning bell rang, he asked his acne-plagued teacher, Sister Marie Pierre about all this Pope/Italian business. With a loud slurp of her coffee and a forthright tilt of her wimple, she confirmed his parent's claim. "As Bishop of Rome, His Holiness is often of Italian descent." Though usually quite cranky, Sister was trying to be a bit more beatific since seeing a matinee of The Singing Nun the week before.

Dumbfounded and unsure of what to say, Digby asked about becoming a martyr or saint. With a slight shake of her covered head and a condescending chuckle, she said that would also be impossible. She said if he were going to be a martyr or saint, then she would certainly know. When he began to whine, her lips thinned. Singing Nun or no Singing Nun, Sister was through playing games. "Dei lucidium, (By the judgement of God) it is a sin to even think such a thing. Saints are chosen by God, and to attempt to negotiate or strategically attain sainthood or martyrdom is a sure sign of a putrified soul. That sort of behavior is a mockery of every saint's blessedness and suffering. You are adding another nail to the cross, Digby Timothy Swank. Go stand in the trash can and meditate on the vileness of your thoughts." Sister's anger subsided quickly, and soon she was merely perturbed. As he walked to the back corner of the room and stepped into the garbage can, Sister eyed the odd shape of the boy's skull and considered his oafish manner. She wondered if perhaps he'd been dropped on his head as an infant. That was still no excuse. When the rest of the class filed in and after the morning bell, prayer, and The Pledge of Allegiance, Sister announced just why Digby was standing in the trash. Heads turned, and students laughed. Sister suggested that if anyone had anything to clear out of their desks, now was the time to do so. "Being untidy can put a soul in peril," she added. His classmates lined up to throw the rubbish around Digby's feet. She made him stand there for a full hour, and told him that if one piece of paper fell out of the can when he stepped out of it, he would stand in there for an additional hour. Sister did not like being disturbed during her morning coffee.

Standing there gave Digby plenty of time to think. Being a bona fide saint or martyr was his second choice, anyway. The saintly devotion was okay, but martyrs always had such horrible deaths. The thought of being burned, impaled, raped, clubbed, drowned, starved, gouged, disemboweled, quartered, ripped, slashed, torn in two, clawed, crushed, mauled, decapitated, or hung on hooks was very unappealing, even if it did mean your own Holy Day, fan club, and scapular necklace. No, if he couldn't be Pope, he'd just as soon be a star of stage musicals.

Being Pope would have been perfect. He knew it, and God probably knew it, but God forbid the Church should know it. He still didn't have all his adult teeth, but he could see this entire thing was a big load of crap. Stepping out of the trash without any paper following him, Digby took his seat. He had been shamed, but more devastating than that had been the shock of having his dream so completely pulled from beneath his feet. Once again, the rules made no sense to him. He sat through mathematics in utter shock. Spelling was a dark night of the soul. At recess, he wandered onto the playground a directionless heathen, bitter and appalled at the Catholic Church's lunacy.

None of this made sense. Once his shock subsided and he followed that single thread of thought, the entire tapestry of his faith began to unravel. It was that way simply because it was that way. Ours is not to question why. Faith is the solution to all uncertainty. These were the supposedly acceptable answers? None of it made sense unless the purpose was not salvation, but manipulation. Digby was utterly dismayed by this abrupt glimpse into the twisted innards underlying the pageantry, the plush costumes, and the fabulous decor. At once those headdresses and fancy brocades became cloaks of deception, and shrouds of lunacy.

"Digby was a very spiritual boy," beamed Sister Marie Pierre. "He was quiet with a good heart, almost Christ-like in his innocence. The lad had fine penmanship, though he did have his problems in mathematics, if I recall correctly." Sister retrieved her grade book for that term. There was a photo of the Singing Nun clipped inside. With a smile, Sister continued, "Oddly, he understood division but not multiplication. I recall having to give him a Unsatisfactory on his progress report for that. It says here, 'He never played well with others or played much at all.' He used to make such a mess during art time that we eventually had to ban him from use of the Cray-Pas. I gave him a 'U' for that too. Digby was the boy who had all those problems in grammar early on. No matter where it was in a sentence, he would always capitalize the word Me. He just didn't understand the concept. Now we'd call it learning disabilities, I suppose. It could have had something to do with that ovoid shaped head of his. Here, I've made an odd-shaped circle next to his name to help remember him," she said, pointing to the book. "Oh, and he urinated in class on Ash Wednesday." With a furrow in her brow, Sister Marie Pierre turned the page in her teaching journal. Gasping, she reviewed her notes before continuing. "That's right. Digby Swank interrupted my morning coffee. He was the child Sister Catherine Claire sent to that fellow with the sunset and sailboat posters. Oh my! The more I think about it, Digby Swank wasn't

Christ-like at all, but I'm sure there was a Christ-like child in his class."

Sister's confusion is very telling. She only remembered the notations, not the boy himself. Without notes or seating charts or verbal reminders, teachers often denied knowing Digby, or spoke of him as someone else. They recalled him as a composite of non-Digby qualities, or called him Maynard or Tom, or even Katie. One teacher was certain he was not a student at all, but a restaurant off the highway. Another thought he was a style of shoe. With alarming regularity, people in Running Falls said they didn't recognize him or didn't notice him. In school, he was often marked absent when he was present, and vice versa. Twice he was sent more than one report card. Things of this sort happened with teachers, parents, neighbors, and even checkout clerks. It occurred with such frequency that Digby began to wonder if he sometimes became invisible, or shape-shifted or lacked distinct borders on his body. Maybe he walked between two worlds. That would explain a lot.

Although Digby accepted the bike as a holy bribe, he did not declare a truce. Catholicism had betrayed him. As the youngest, and often the lesser of four siblings, he was extremely sensitive to the issue of favoritism, things not being fair and being told he couldn't do something "just because." This Italians Only rule had struck a nerve, as well as opened his eyes. And lo, the blind shall see, Digby thought with a barely perceptible nod as he stood in the classroom trash can. Soon other cracks and faults became apparent in a faith so firmly planted upon the earth.

The Roman Catholic Church was not what it appeared. Good Catholics did not ask questions, or have reasonable expectations. If you had doubts and questions, it meant your faith was lacking, not that your mind was working. Catholicism was about doing and being what was expected. It was about giving generously, and donating a bit beyond your means, and beating your breast in gratitude to be just another sheep in the flock. Act this way, follow these rules, don't bleat too loudly, and the Good Shepherd just might watch over you. Nothing was guaranteed. It was all contingent on His mercy.

With his list of gripes growing and no answers forthcoming, Digby decided he'd had enough, though in truth, he opted for an extended pout rather than an outright rejection. Within the week, he began searching for a faith of his own. Maybe instead of a deity, God could be an exemplary human being. Choosing a role model made sense to him, so for an entire season his God became Marcus Welby, M.D.

Dr. Welby looked a little like the depiction of God on the cover of his religion book, only Welby was clean shaven and had better hair. Welby seemed like the pinnacle of saintliness. There would always be a place at His table. His intentions were honorable and ethical, and He was always deeply concerned. He never turned patients away because they weren't Italian. Digby had no doubt that Welby's soul was as pristine as His lab coat, which never seemed to get bloody, even when He was at the operating table. Digby dreamt of Welby's understanding crow's feet, and warm paternal smiles. That was how God was supposed to be.

However, faith did not come so easy the second time around. Digby's disillusionment with Catholicism had planted suspicions. Faith seemed a sucker's game, and Digby hated nothing more than being duped. Toward the end of the TV season, he saw Dr. Welby on a talk show, and the man joked about not really being a doctor. He said people asked Him for medical advice all the time, but that He had no idea what to say. He said He'd have no idea what to do with a scalpel. The thought of Him operating blindly caused Digby to tremble. What sort of madman would do such a thing, he thought, turning from The Mike Douglas Show. Overnight, Digby glimpsed a lunatic laughing behind the surgical mask, masquerading as God and saying things like, "Oh, I don't know—I'll just cut right here. I think this is what I'm supposed to be removing." Digby turned his back on Welby without further thought.

That very week, it rained steadily for two days straight,

which resulted in The Great Running Falls Flood of 1969. The downpour clogged sewers and overran gutters. Lawns became ponds. The feeder creeks swelled, and caused Loaf and Flounder Lakes to creep their banks and join as one. The rush of water toppled Doebbler House. Flooding ruined the Swank basement rec room, as well. Rog and Lila saved what they could, but they had water over a foot deep down there. Digby went to the bottom of the stairs, and saw the light shimmer on the black surface. It all stunk to high heaven. The insurance company said it was an act of God.

A week later, Rog suffered his first heart attack. Digby ran to his room, certain this was no coincidence. He trembled with worry that it was all his fault, quite possibly the wrath of God, or Welby, or even both. He feared locusts or boils would be next. He buried his head in his pillow. Life had become so complicated. He was a bed wetter, a tattletale, a girly boy, a liar, a left-handed smirker, and now a lightning rod for divine retribution as well.

Hearing the sniffles behind his closed door, his mother did the unthinkable, and gently knocked. She entered before he could answer. In her hand were four Twinkies artfully arranged on a green paper plate. Processed sugar will make it better. Glucose will absolve all. Digby bit into a cream-filled lard cake, and wept that this was all his doing.

Lila was frazzled, but gentle and assured him it wasn't his fault. "It's God's will."

Hearing her words he wept even harder. "Mother, it's His wrath…God's or Dr Welby's. Maybe both!"

"What?"

When he managed to catch his breath, he confessed everything between heaving sobs. Lila made him promise never to repeat his story. That afternoon, he could clearly see how much she loved him.

9 - Sweet Damnation

Digby was crushed to discover that basically many Gods were jerks with an agenda, and that they can be bossy, biased, petty, and jealous just like anyone. Weren't they supposed to be literally and figuratively above all that? He shook his head in disappointment. Only a short time before, he had a thirty-year plan to become Pope and/or a kindly surgeon with his own hit TV series. He swore that his disillusionment would not mean defeat. This wasn't the first time he'd been betrayed, or had something special taken from him. He'd lost Grandma Rose, and he'd survived. He'd survive the loss of God as well.

The first real sidestep in Digby's initial retreat from Catholicism occurred when he discovered confession. Unlike many other sacraments, confession, or Divine Reconciliation, really didn't disappoint. Thematically, penance was a perfect fit. It was bulimia for the soul. A nice purge after indulging. Even though Digby claimed he'd turned his back on it all and didn't really believe in God, he still believed in his own damnation. Grandma Swank had planted those seeds rather deep.

Kneeling in the darkened closet, confessing behind the scrim, and hearing the priest grumble his penance gave Digby hope. During penance, the priest acted in persona Christi, as a minister of Christ's mercy. With his ecclesiastical authority, he granted God's forgiveness and the absolution of Digby's sins by the Church.

Leaving the confessional, Digby felt pure. Whew! Damnation was a welcome burden to have off his back. In those moments, Digby liked God and the Church because he knew that if he was to die in that window of time, St. Peter would give a quick wink and wave him through the pearly gates. However, the feeling was regrettably brief. New sins would soon blotch his pristine soul like bugs on a bayou windshield. A bit of envy, a twinge of resentment, a fib or two, and in no time Digby was back where he started—destined for thousands of years in Purgatory, or headed straight to Hell. This meant another trip to the confessional.

Being pure of spirit was ridiculously time consuming. With no end to this eternal tail-chasing, Digby threw up his hands in a relatively graceful manner for a boy, and putting them on his hips, proclaimed, "Who has the time?" Digby decided that if worse came to worst, he would gamble on the final "I'm sorry," the Roman Catholic ace-in-the-hole, a perfect Act of Contrition.

Turning his back on the Catholic Church relieved him on many levels. All the Thou Shalts and Thou Shalt Nots would no longer directly dictate his behavior. That is not to say he was free of them altogether. God wasn't quite so easy to shake. Complete apostasy is almost impossible for any Catholic, especially one who was beaten with rosaries and who wanted to be Pope. Though he no longer felt compelled to obey the commandments and edicts and whatnot, those same rules would continue to subconsciously influence his behavior, warping his actions by undermining the fragile foundation of his self-esteem. It was the Catholic way. Blithely unaware of this enduring influence, Digby felt liberated. He'd been bearing a cross for years. He felt freed, no longer being obligated to be good or honor his father and mother by trying to be normal. He loved them, but he just couldn't be that someone who it seemed they might love a bit more.

Digby knew that, because of all this and more, he might well be careening headfirst into the fiery pit of Hell. That was a fear he'd deal with when the time came. For now, accepting that fact brought a rush of power. Knowing the worst was much less worrisome than dread. Some might say he gave himself over to sin or cast his lot with Satan, but Digby considered reclaiming his base humanity as being pro-active.

He made none of this known, of course. That would be foolhardy. He didn't want a bad reputation. Having the neighbors aware of your badness was far worse than the badness itself. He may have been a borderline sociopath, but he still wanted to be popular. Digby was such his parents' child.

He'd been pushed around by people and institutions and deities as far back as he could remember. He'd done his best to be who and what he was told to be, and all it had brought him was an overwhelming sense of failure. Now, he wanted to push back. For once, Digby thrilled to think he wasn't the person they all wanted him to be. The knowledge still brought shame, but also a sense of relief. Considering the possibilities was revelatory. Once he realized he had options, he knew that it was his turn to be God. It was his turn to judge and to punish.

The first people to feel Digby's sting were the fetid-breathed neighbors, Dolly and Lucas Sterner. As if to compensate for their name, their grim attitudes, or their odorous selves, the Sterner's double-lot backyard was heavy with greenery, and peppered with an array of frolicking and cavorting cement cherubs, some perched and some recumbent. As a result, their yard resembled a pedophile's version of paradise.

"I wanted a magical place, somewhere almost mythical," Dolly Sterner was often heard to say when people commented on her garden.

No one ever offered a contrary word, at least not to Dolly's face. However, most everyone found the Sterner's yard disturbing and downright pagan.

"That backlot is a shrine to Eros and the Greeks, and that sort of carrying on," Sandy Treacle said on more than one occasion. Sandy had studied art at Twin Oaks Community College, so she should know. "Those are not Christian cherubs, I can tell you that much. You can always tell by the set of the eyes and the poses. The Sterner statues are the ones that resemble angels, but are really drunkard, free-love babies. And to see that sort of thing alongside hallowed ground with the cemetery right there. Someone needs to file an ordinance on idolatry zoning."

But in Running Falls people preferred to cluck and stew, rather than cause a fuss in any official capacity.

The Sterners had earned a place on Digby's vengeance list after ratting on his graveyard visits, and recently for having the audacity to accuse him of putting globs of tar on the backside of a fat cupid strumming a lyre. Seeing the defacement, Dolly and Lucas sidled and minced like tiptoeing fiddler crabs over to the Swank home, and pressed a firm finger to the doorbell. With a yap, the new Swank puppy bound to the door. Semi-shouting over the dog, the Sterners wasted no time in complaining to Rog and Lila about "the seraphic incident." Digby's parents were aghast, deeply apologetic, and more than a little embarrassed that they didn't know the meaning of seraphic. This all reflected poorly on them. They swore to get to the bottom of it. After the Sterners left, Rog sprayed some air freshener, and Lila promptly looked up the definition of seraphic in the mostly ornamental pedestal dictionary in the hallway. The book would remain on that page for several months. Seraphic meant relating to an angel.

That evening at the dinner table, they confronted Digby with the Sterners' accusations. Despite the neighbor's claims, Digby kept a cool head, and denied all knowledge of the incident. He said he had no idea why anyone would want to do such a thing. After a pause and a carefully placed unless, he hinted that it could have been the work of Johnny Van Camp and his crowd. Digby had a score to settle with that jerk as well.

The truth was that Digby did do it, but he did it without really considering the consequences. He was just playing by absently rolling a stick over the fresh tar the city had used to patch the alley. Afterwards, when he was cutting through the Sterner's yard, he wanted to wipe off the stick. And that angel's ass had just sort of been there. Besides, whether Digby did it or not was immaterial. The Sterners had no proof. Their rancid accusations were all completely circumstantial.

Dolly was madder than a wet cat. "You didn't have to tell me Digby did it. I'd seen him poking a stick around in the tar that day after the road crew filled the potholes along the alley. It wasn't Johnny Van Camp. That sneaky little Digby can deny it until his vile, lying face turns blue, but that doesn't change the facts. Dealing with this sort of matter can be tricky, especially when it's a neighbor, but neighbor or not, I wanted to know what was going to be done about our cherub's backside. Who was going to pay for that? We couldn't have tar there. It looked like defecation, and everyone knows that angels don't go number two."

Filled with the self-righteous brand of indignation that only the genuinely guilty can muster, Digby vowed revenge. Opportunity came the following day when he noticed Lila baking a birthday cake for Maynard. Though decidedly "girly looking," cherry cake with pink frosting was still Maynard's favorite. The red food dye for the frosting was on the kitchen counter when Digby entered the room. Lila was watching one of her stories on television while the cake baked. Seeing no one around, Digby slipped the partially used vial into his pocket. This would come in very handy.

That night under the cloak of darkness, he crept into the Sterner's backyard. He heard nothing but the sound of the wind, the distant traffic, and the muffle of a television somewhere. During an especially loud laugh track outburst of what sounded like The Mothers-In-Law, Digby emptied the food coloring container into the Sterner's seashell-shaped birdbath, which was supported by the chubby upraised arms of three cavorting cherubs.

When Digby awoke the next morning, the birdbath incident was immediately in the forefront of his mind. He ran to the window to take stock of his handiwork. The results were better than he ever could have imagined. The Sterner yard had gone from tragedy to masterpiece overnight. While bathing, the birds had flapped their wings and sent food dye splashing over the basin rim. The red coloring trickled down the upraised arms of the cherubs below. After bathing, the birds shook their wet wings, covering the stone angel faces and splattering the torsos with red. Birds had even perched upon some of the other cherubs in the yard, leaving the marks of their scarlet talons as evidence. It looked like blood.

The neighbor across the street, Hattie Taylor, had squealed with excitement to see a red tinted goldfinch land on her back fence. Hattie was an avid birdwatcher, though some said those binoculars of hers had more to do with her being a busybody. "She likes to keep a close eye on things," was all Sandy Treacle would say on the subject.

The following day, a steady rain washed most of the red away, though a ghost of the tinting remained.

Since his retribution occurred one day after his mother used the now-missing food dye and two days after the Sterners first blustered into the Swank home with their foul-breathed accusations, the finger of guilt rested squarely upon Digby. However, the Sterners would soon have more to worry about than a backyard of temporarily bloodied cherubs.

Several weeks earlier, a young woman named Tawny had been hired at Lucas's firm. Tawny was a gum-cracking, hair-twirling pack of trouble in a push-up bra. She wore pointed high heels, and pencil skirts with thick vinyl belts. She all but came with her own jazz soundtrack. She was trouble with a capital T, which stood for tramp. She liked to hang out at Bobby's Pins, the bowling alley. Less than a week after the cherubic bloodbath, Lucas Sterner telephoned his wife. He said he was in love with Tawny, and was going away. He told Dolly she could keep the house. When Dolly looked in the closet, all his clothes and even his bowling ball were gone.

That night, Dolly's hairy knuckles came knocking. Bleary-eyed and bitter, she told Lila, and inadvertently the entire family and several neighbors, all about it.

Dolly smoothed back her thin brown hair. "Lucas has been unfaithful all this time, and with that girl with the crooked teeth and the bra straps. Tawny, that's her name, Tawny," she blubbered. "I should have known when he got the hair piece and started wearing turtlenecks. It turns my stomach, you know. It just turns my stomach. I knew she was trouble when he hired her, looking brazen as a strumpet strutting the streets of Babylon. I knew it. I felt it right here." So saying, Dolly laid a hand a bit too close to her genitals for Lila's comfort. Dolly was drunk and oblivious. "I should have gone with my gut," she added. Hearing her say "gut," Lila audibly sighed.

A week after Lucas moved out on Dolly, the Swanks were awakened at 2 a.m. by a piercing scream from next door. They met in the hall and exchanged cartoonish, open-mouthed and wide-eyed looks that went back and forth before they dragged their slippered feet to the window. In the moonlight, they could see Dolly drunkenly staggering about the yard in her nightgown. She was shouting profanities while chugging from a bottle of dark liquor. With a wail that made the peering Swanks back slightly away from the window, she beheaded each and every cherub with a croquet mallet.

Lila winced. "You think she's okay?"

"Oh, she's having the time of her life," replied Rog somewhat inexplicably.

The family watched in silence for another moment, before Lila turned from the window. "I never did like those things."

Katie said she thought they looked even more "classical" without the heads.

Staring at that headless grouping, Digby couldn't help but think how much more effective the cherubic damage would've been with the red dye still in place. Then it would have looked like outright carnage. Bloodbath on Olympus! Digby wasn't saddened to see Dolly so distraught. He considered it her karmic comeuppance. In his sociopathic mind, justice had been served. He smirked with purse-lipped satisfaction as she dropped the mallet, threw the bottle aside, and collapsed to her knees. Now she was forsaken. Now she knew how he felt. Seeing her shoulders shake as she cried in the moonlight, Digby felt a slight pang of remorse that was soon dwarfed by a walloping rush of power. Playing God was much more gratifying than worshipping him.

Following Dolly's screams, which many said could have peeled the paint off a red barn, lights went on all about the neighborhood. Soon, the police came to see what all the hullabaloo was about. Dolly collapsed on the officer when he came into the Sterner yard. She went with the police, and ended up staying with relatives for two weeks. A hauling company took the cherubs away two days later, then a landscaper came and seeded the yard. Everyone was relieved to have the cherubs gone once and for all, and most agreed that the Sterner yard looked twice its size that way. Room enough for a good-sized garden. The next time Dolly visited with Lila, she wore a serene smile and talked very slowly.

With Dolly Sterner brought down a notch, Digby had to trust that Lucas Sterner was getting his, as well. Gossip hinted that was indeed the case. "That Tawny is throwing his money all over town. They eat out at a restaurant every night of the week," whispered Lila. Some folks even went so far as to switch insurance providers, rather than give Lucas the business. Once she was done throwing about what money there was to be thrown, Tawny ended up leaving Lucas for a swarthy NASCAR mechanic six months later. No one was the least bit surprised. The week before, Tawny had been seen dancing with a stranger in the Bobby's Pins parking lot after closing. The car radio had been blasting the country station. The last anyone heard, Lucas had moved to Michigan, and was living in his widowed mother's garage. There weren't too many notches lower than that.

The Sterners were only the first of several names on Digby's list of resentments. He could hold a grudge for years, and he wasn't even ten. Some might find that surprising, but it's said the quieter ones tend to keep it all inside. That was certainly true with Digby. With the contented sigh of a job well done, he put a line through the Sterners. That score was settled. Next, he set his sights on that freckled incarnation of evil, Johnny Van Camp.

The Van Camps were the perpetually jolly clan that lived on the opposite side of the Swanks. Their son, Johnny, was Digby's age. Both sets of parents assumed the boys were friends because they were the same age, went to the same school, and lived next door to each other. The presumption was false and showed how little adults knew or paid attention. Johnny typically sneered in Digby's direction and was the first person to call him a fag. Johnny's light brown hair hung just so, and he had a habit of jerking his head to the side to keep his bangs out of his eyes. Digby knew Johnny did it because he considered the gesture cool, and by all measures of time and place, Johnny Van Camp was cool. Digby often fantasized what it must be like to be popular and effortlessly accepted. What if all it took to be accepted was to just be yourself? What if all it took was the just-right flip of your hair? Digby's hair didn't flip. It moved as a single unit like matronly hair, or the stretch wigs advertised in the back of the movie star magazines. Digby's hair was the opposite of cool.

Johnny and his cronies made a habit out of doing hateful things to Digby. No week at Holy Martyrs was complete without some form of aggression—snuggies, glue on his chair, notes on his back, name calling, spit balls—once, they cornered him in the lunch room and forced him to drink a big glass of hot dog water. Hot Dog Day had given him the shivers ever since. Another time, they pelted him with balloons filled with vinegar. Once, the group's lackeys held him down while Johnny peed on the back of his head. People laughed about that and pointed at him in the hallway for weeks afterwards.

Van Camp and his gang took great joy in pulverizing him in dodgeball, completely disregarding the No Hitting Above the Neck rule. Their gym teacher, Coach Crosby, just turned his big hog head the other way, which, since he didn't have a neck, actually meant turning his entire body. Crosby ignored it all. That's just what boys of that age do. That sort of aggression is natural. It's a way to toughen up the weaker ones. If they don't toughen up, well then they learn their place. Either way, they'll be grateful one day, thought Crosby with a scratch of his enormous head. Coach Crosby was on Digby's revenge list as well.

Another time, prior to receiving their ashes during Lenten assembly, Digby thought he heard Johnny say something to him. Against his better judgement Digby leaned close and whispered "What?" In a booming voice, Johnny replied, "No, I won't kiss you for a quarter!" Everyone turned to gawk. Digby reddened as Johnny flipped back his hair and laughed to his pals. The faculty members who overheard glared at Digby and not Johnny. "Making homosexual passes at a fellow student during the candle ceremony," he all but heard them sneer.

The final insult came the following school year, when Johnny slipped several sardines through the vents of Digby's locker the day before Christmas break. By the time they returned to school two weeks later, everything he owned smelled like the catch of the day. When Digby went to his locker, Johnny and his cronies pointed and laughed from beside the drinking fountains. Digby could see them from the corner of his eye, but he could feel their waves of ridicule even more clearly. Digby couldn't look that way. Acknowledging it seemed even more humiliating. He couldn't and wouldn't give them the satisfaction. His jaw tightened, and his fists clenched. He did his best to measure his breath. He was an expert at ignoring reality, at least on the outside. Inside, he was a suffocating fish flipping and flopping on the hot metal bottom of a boat. or on the inlaid tile of a grade school hallway.

Several feral cats followed Digby home from school that day, and as he heard their hungry feline howls, he decided that enough was enough. This sort of treatment was not going to continue without some sort of retaliation. The pee shampoo was bad, and the hot dog water was horrid. This fish thing might not have been the worst, but it was the last straw. He was through being the butt of every adolescent prank those jerks could devise. His rage bubbled over as he turned and hissed at the pack of cats behind him. Those strays scattered with their bellies low to the ground when they saw the size of Digby's fangs. Enough! Johnny Van Camp and his gang would soon fear his snarl, as well.

Two weeks later, Digby decided to take action. That afternoon, he was forced to go to the Van Camps after school because his mother had to work late at the office. His parents considered Digby too great a risk to leave home alone for two hours. Comfortable on his own turf and always eager to bully even without an audience, Johnny typically terrorized Digby on such occasions. Digby swore that today would be different. Today was payback time. This account balance was long over due.

Wearing his signature smirk, Digby took a ceramic bowl and held it over a candle until the bottom was blackened. Then he got an identical bowl from the Van Camp cupboard, and filled both with water. Johnny was in the living room watching afternoon reruns of Bonanza on TV. During a commercial break, Digby called him into the kitchen. He told him he had a trick for him.

"What are you going to do, turn into a fairy? Oh wait, you already did that."

Every word out of Johnny Van Camp's mouth was more evidence that he had this coming. Digby said he was going to hypnotize him. "Unless of course, you're afraid."

"I'm not afraid."

"No, I don't think you can handle it."

"Try me. Go on, hypnotize me."

Sometimes Digby shook his head at how easy it could be to manipulate others. "Okay, but I really don't think I'll have any problem hypnotizing you."

"Prove it," retorted Johnny, flipping his overhang back.

Gesturing for him to take a seat across the table, Digby explained that under no circumstances was he to break eye contact. "Now, hold the bowl in front of you and mirror my movements. Your thoughts are going around and around and down into a funnel as consciousness slowly leaves you. Deeper and deeper you go until there is nothing but the sound of my voice. Make a circle with your finger along the bottom of the bowl, and imagine all the while that your thoughts are spinning and mixing and growing lighter and lighter."

As he slowly moved his finger in circles, Digby said he was going to hypnotize Johnny into thinking he was a cat.

"Bullcrap."

"Shhh, focus." Digby told him to make a small circle on the tip of his nose and return his finger to the underside of the bowl.

Johnny did as he was told, just to prove that he couldn't be hypnotized.

"Your thoughts are going around and around and turning from human into feline as you make another circle on the smooth bottom of the bowl. Feel your fingers becoming as soft as a kitten's paws. Now make three lines from each side of your mouth out across your cheeks, these are your whiskers."

The doorbell rang. "This is stupid. I don't feel anything. This is just another one of your loser fembot games. What were you trying to do, hypnotize me into kissing you? That's Angela and Susan. We're gonna work on our social studies project together, so get lost."

Johnny put down the bowl and went to the door. When he opened it, the two girls burst out laughing, and then whispered back and forth as they giggled. Johnny flipped his hair back, which usually made the girls swoon, but their snickering continued. Their behavior wasn't that unusual. Susan and Angela giggled and whispered a lot, even for the average fourth grade girl.

Pulling the door closed behind them, Johnny looked down and saw his blackened fingertips. Puzzled, he looked into the Americana Liberty mirror in the Van Camp entry hall, and saw his little black nose and feline whiskers.

"Yeah smart ass, who's the pussy now?" asked Digby.

Storming back into the kitchen, Johnny rushed to the sink and wiped the soot from his face with a dishrag, which Digby had the foresight to saturate with pickle juice. "Shit!" Johnny shouted, throwing the rag aside and splashing water on his face. Angela and Susan continued to laugh. After he removed the majority of the soot, he turned to Digby. "I'll get you for this." The whiskers were gone, but he still smelled like a dill pickle.

He did get Digby back, several times over, but that wasn't really an issue. Johnny and his crowd would have tormented Digby anyway. Now at least Johnny knew there could be consequences. Digby had let them all know he had a spine, and that retaliation was a possibility.

10 - More Great Mysteries

Johnny Van Camp was a rarity in the neighborhood, and not because he treated Digby shabbily. That sort of thing happened every day. Johnny was a rarity because the homes surrounding the Swank residence on Aldo Boulevard had a serious shortage of children. Instead, the area contained a surplus of old people. The Van Camps, the Sterners, the Treacles, and the Swanks were the exceptions. The median age in the neighborhood had to have been in the late fifties. Some even joked that the cemetery drew the old folks like magnets.

Ancient widows, Mrs. Kerg and Mrs. Taylor, lived side by side across the street from the Swanks. Mrs. Taylor would often drop in to gossip with Lila about Edith Kerg's latest affront to common sense. "Loony is what she is," she'd say with a slight shake of her head.

Loony or not, Digby favored Mrs. Kerg. She had been a widow since 1940, when a runaway milk truck hit a telephone pole that fell right on Ralph Kerg's head, and pounded him into the ground like a wooden peg. As his widow, Edith Kerg got a handsome settlement and free dairy products for life. However, the most impressive thing about Mrs. Kerg was that she got a Christmas card from Barbara Hale. She knew Della Street! Her proximity to a genuine TV star represented the apex of glamour in Running Falls.

At that point in his life, the only secular celebrity of note Digby had ever seen in person was Franco Fantasia who hosted Hey Kids!, the children's Saturday morning program. As star of the show, Franco introduced cartoons and drew caricatures with a black marker on a big sketch pad. He sometimes shopped at the Piggly Wiggly. Each time Digby had seen him, Mr. Fantasia had asked the stock boys for various items in a booming voice, and then smiled and nodded his helmet of black hair when people recognized him. He always had his markers on him, and would gladly sign cereal boxes, grocery bags, or almost anything. Once he had even drew a caricature on a diaper and signed it. Mr.

Fantasia would then typically shake his head and smile, "I can't go anywhere without being recognized."

Barbara Hale was much more impressive.

Mrs. Kerg seemed to Digby like a dotty, dethroned countess with her French provincial furniture, a piano, dried flowers under glass, and little crystal things. Chimes told the time in her home, and all her furniture had tassels and fringe. Every photograph on her mantle was dominated by its frame. Mrs. Kerg would have Digby to tea now and then, and show him a box from the spare bedroom with the toys she had played with as a girl. Her dolls had delicate features and worn, chipped faces. They were made of cloth and porcelain, and one even had tiny teeth.

Mrs. Kerg also had a mean little dog that would often grab a doll from her memory box, as she called it, and run down the hallway, crazily shaking its head and giving the doll a good thrashing. One of her dolls had its face smashed on a doorframe in just such a manner. Her dog's behavior always seemed to confuse more than upset Mrs. Kerg. She'd usually have to give it a biscuit to get the doll back. The dog had bitten Mrs. Kerg so many times that after a while, she no longer seemed to care or even notice.

Years later, Lila, Tom, and Digby visited Mrs. Kerg at the Flamingo Lagoon Retirement Villa. The name made no sense, because The Flamingo Lagoon Retirement Villa had no body of water about or around it. It had no flamingoes, no birds, no real greenery or anything to suggest a villa of any sort. It was a dilapidated mess of cement block and aluminum siding. The inside smelled like it had been flooded by urine a decade ago.

The remnants of last week's Halloween crepe decorations hung in the lobby. An old man sat in a wheelchair turned toward a close-curtained window, as if awaiting an unveiling. On the other side of the room, another man sat repeatedly pursing his lips, and adjusting his dentures with a click as regular as the tick of a clock. A third resident sat blank faced with a magazine on the floor in front of her. The liveliest face in the room was on a cardboard skeleton that waved from the bulletin board, announcing the Halloween Gala from a week ago. His cryptic and inappropriate voice bubble said, "See you soon!"

Mother asked for Edith Kerg's room. After checking her clipboard, the nurse said the room number and stabbed a ballpoint pen toward the end of the hall. She lacked even the hint of a smile, which Digby understood. Given the environment, a smile would seem rather callous.

When they knocked and entered her room, Mrs. Kerg ignored the Swanks. At first she didn't realize they were there, or maybe since people seemed to come and go at random, she didn't pay attention to who entered her room. Fiddling with her wig, she looked out the window and kept repeating, "Mavis is coming to do my hair."

"That's nice," Lila smiled with a slow blink.

Mrs. Kerg abruptly turned to Tom. "You have a pretty girlfriend." She was looking directly at Digby. Tom laughed, and Digby reddened. She was calling him a girl! Digby could never separate her comment from his memories of her. Mrs. Kerg had the same sort of sweet acceptance that Grandma Rose had. She had let him do things that boys weren't supposed to do. Digby thought she had understood him. He thought she was a friend, but she'd betrayed him. He didn't understand her senility. For Digby, that was no excuse. How could she not know what she was saying, or who she was being?

He looked back at her staring out the window. Digby pitied her, and that was the opposite of love. Pity was disgust siphoned through Catholicism. Digby wished he'd changed the times on her chiming clocks. He wished he'd never listened to her tales of Barbara Hale, or looked at her dolls with their cracked skulls or silently defended her to Mrs. Taylor. He hated her for forgetting their afternoon teas, and evenings of watching gasoline price war searchlights scan the summertime clouds. Those happy times vanished in a moment, with a few simple words. How could she forget him so completely? She must not have cared, after all. When he heard of her death a couple of years later, he felt only a slight brush of sadness. For the most part, she was already dead to him.

Mrs. Taylor lived beside Mrs. Kerg. She'd never married, but the Swanks called her Mrs. nonetheless. The Swanks were trying to be kind. Like most folks, Rog and Lila felt that calling a woman Miss after a certain age mocked her spinster status. Unless a woman was a nun, the appeal of being thought of as virginal definitely had a "sell by" date.

Mrs Taylor had an oblong lot with two tall catalpa trees in her sprawling backyard. Giant sunflowers lined her back fence. Digby had been leery of sunflowers since watching a science fiction program on TV. He couldn't recall just what those sunflowers did on the episode, but it wasn't good. He didn't trust them. He saw sunflowers as alien beings, and with her big head atop that long neck, Digby saw Mrs. Taylor as basically a sunflower in support hose and practical shoes.

Hattie Taylor was haughty, wore cat eye glasses, and had pronounced elbows and knees, as well as an incredibly pragmatic air about her. To conserve electricity, she shut off the television during commercials. She washed and reused plastic utensils, clipped coupons, and used both ends of a toothpick. She resoled her own shoes, washed her clothes in rain water, and boasted that she'd never once taken a taxicab. Her home was as sparse and spotless as St. Patrick's soul. To Digby's recollection, she never travelled, yet Hattie Taylor lived by a wind-up travel clock which she never neglected to wind. She'd gotten it with S&H Green Stamps. "Those things are like money you know," she'd exclaimed.

Digby's parents greatly admired her common sense, and they held her up as a paragon of pragmatism. "That Hattie is a wise one," Rog or Lila might say, and the other would always agree. The allure of a woman who seemed passionate about all things banal was baffling to Digby, like glorifying a paper clip or tossing garlands before a standard hairnet. Like most "artistic types," he found practical frugality a deadening bore more closely aligned with shame than pride.

One week in March, the newspapers collected on Hattie's front stoop, so Rog went snooping. That wasn't like Hattie. Those papers had coupons in them, and reusable rubber bands holding them together. She didn't answer his knocking. Digby's father strained and craned to see through every window in her home to no avail. After scratching his head for a few moments, he decided to climb through her dining room window. He found Hattie Taylor dead in bed, and was amazed to discover that someone who always seemed to have no frills or fuss about her would have something like a rhinestone encrusted telephone in her bedroom.

"It was not regulation, I'll say that much," announced Rog.

Lila stopped her grieving long enough to add, "Can you imagine?"

Digby figured that the phone must have been the first thing Hattie Taylor saw every morning, and probably the last thing she saw at night. He understood. For once, Hattie Taylor didn't seem quite so alien to him, just understandably weird. According to his father, she died with the gaudy receiver clutched in her hand.

"I practically needed a nutcracker to get the handset free. She was holding onto it for dear life, so to speak. When I finally managed to wiggle it free, I phoned the police. When they came to officially declare her dead and bag the body and whatnot, the paramedics smiled when they saw the phone. I felt like saying 'Don't think of Hattie that way. She wasn't like that. Hattie was a level-headed woman.' When I came outside, Digby was right there swinging on the fence gate, singing Olive branch or Olive tree or some such. I never knew what that kid was doing, even when he was doing it right in front of me. He was always in his own world. It was a pity Hattie died with all her scrimped savings still sitting in the bank, but I guess you can't take it with you. Like my Uncle Mitch used to joke, 'There's no hitch on a hearse!' Hattie didn't leave a cent to the Church. She left every penny to some niece I had never even seen, which didn't seem quite right. That girl lived out east, and didn't even have the decency to come to the funeral. Where was her kin when things needed fixing? Not around, that's all I'll say. Far be it from me to expect a dime, but if the Church wasn't getting it, we sure could have used a windfall about then. After her place sold, the first thing the new owners did was rip out all those sunflowers, and throw them out in the alley. Hattie would have rolled over in her grave, if she hadn't been cremated."

In some ways, Digby's young life is a story of death. It's not a particularly sad tale since he didn't see death that way, except with Grandma Rose. The best kind of death came as a clean break from life, with no pussyfooting and lollygagging into the great beyond. A prolonged farewell could undermine a lifetime. That was what had happened to Mrs. Kerg. She'd simply had the misfortune of dying too long. Her soul had been trapped like a bird on a screened-in porch. In the end, few recalled its beauty, only the battering of its wings, and the guilty prayers that it would fly away and be gone. Fading from life was no way to die. It certainly never got the attention that a tragic death could bring. When done sensationally and with proper timing, the right sort of death could almost guarantee immortality. No one could ask for more than that.

Ignoring his parents, Digby kept visiting the Calvary Cemetery, though he tried to be less obvious about it. If anyone said anything, he could always say he was taking a short cut. As it turned out, no one said a word. By then, Dolly Sterner was too wrapped up in her post-marital mess and medications to pay attention. She kept her curtains closed. She even changed her religion out of spite. "What sort of God would let Lucas run off with Tawny?" she asked. Most folks thought it wasn't God to blame, but that push-up bra. Dolly called the Methodist God "a better fit" anyway. "He understands me. He's more like David Niven, and the Catholic God was always more Orson Welles." No one was too sorry that Dolly's bad breath wasn't stinking up morning mass at Holy Martyrs anymore.

"After getting a whiff of Dolly's breath, those Methodists won't be laughing about our liberal use of incense," cracked Sandy Treacle.

In Calvary Cemetery, Digby loved to stop at red marble monument erected in remembrance of a horrible parish tragedy that took place at Christmastime in 1897. Holy Martyrs school was holding their annual Christmas pageant, a group of seven-year-old girls spinning and dancing about the stage in lace angel costumes with feathered wings. Little Flora McDermott accidentally kicked a footlight. The glass shattered, and flames consumed her costume. The child screamed. Pandemonium ensued. Exits became blocked. And in the end, three angels perished in the blaze—or three legends were born, depending on how you looked at it. A nun who attempted to beat out the flames had to have her hands bandaged for a year. Mourned with beaten breasts, tears, and an honest to God monolith, those girls became mythical beings overnight. Each Catholic Church in town had a cry room named for one of them. Digby had heard about the legend before he even saw the marker. The story was often told at Running Falls sleepovers, with a warning that the girls still haunted the school. Supposedly, they stole pencils and homework assignments, clogged toilets, and even slammed desktops in the middle of class.

Sadly, Digby never saw any ghosts or demons or otherworldly visitations, but it wasn't from a lack of interest. Not a day went by when he didn't pray for those coy, incinerated angels to appear in a mirror, knock a crucifix from the wall, yank a nun's habit, emit an eerie moan, or write a cryptic message on a chalkboard. In the midst of one boring lesson or another, Digby would close his eyes and try to hear a whisper, feel a cold spot where there was no open window, catch a whiff of charred lace, or sense anything that might hint at a genuine haunting. Nothing. The dead were just as capable of disappointing as the living.

11 – Sacred Show Biz

Being both an altar boy as well as a borderline pantheist/atheist didn't seem the least bit contradictory to Digby. People did things like that all the time in his Roman Catholic world. Those who weren't the least bit hypocritical were labeled as crazy or fanatics, or holier-than-thou. They were widely suspected of having something serious to hide. Digby reasoned that if becoming an altar boy had been a purely religious decision, then it would have been disingenuous. But this wasn't about God. Like most things of dire importance to Digby, it was about him.

One spring day, psoriasis-plagued Father Dan came to Digby's class, and in a spray of spittle and skin flakes, asked if any boys were interested in serving God while serving the parish. "Laborare est orare," he spat. Work is prayer. Since they'd received Holy Communion a few months before, the boys were now eligible. Father Dan scanned the room. He wasn't surprised to see a lack of hands, and minimal eye contact. Altar boy recruitment was always a tough sell. He cleared his throat. "This is a position of great importance." Digby's ears cocked. Beforehand, Father Dan might as well have been speaking in tongues, but now he was talking Digby's language. Serving God held little appeal, and serving Holy Martyrs parish held even less. However, over the past year Digby had once again become desperate to win approval and gain recognition. With the promise of an improved reputation as well as a captive audience, his hand shot heavenward like the member of a Bob Fosse chorus. Finally, being technically a Roman Catholic had some benefit beyond getting off school on Good Friday, and The Feast of The Ascension.

"You have to know how to speak to boys of that age to get them interested. I guess I've always had a gift for that sort of thing," explained Father Dan while in the midst of serving his sixteen-month archdiocese suspension over four counts of sexual indiscretions with a minor. "Four months for each little soldier of the Lord," he smiled with a slight fingering of his rosary.

Digby approached his position of altar boy as more a matter of performance than piety. Each mass became a struggle to add some new dimension to his relatively static part. Digby was an integral part of creating the mood, and as such, he was determined to do that to the hilt.

From the moment he entered the stage/altar, he wore a beatific expression with an angelic "O" mouth, and eyes as round as communion wafers. Often, Digby would slightly blur his vision as if transfixed by some Greater Being, while simultaneously attempting to move with the utmost grace like the marionette of some divine Gepetto. His genuflections were low and somber. His bell ringing was flawlessly timed; with a flick of his wrist, he achieved ideal resonance. His lighting of the candles was something to behold. He'd light one taper, lift the hem of his white cossack like a busy Victorian lady, and turn brusquely to approach another candle. Generating such drama and pageantry over something so simple was hard to imagine, but overblown theatrics were Digby in a nutshell.

As an altar boy, Digby was hardly a team player, but that wasn't entirely his fault. In this case, Team God was full of losers. From the start of the first orientation meeting, Digby knew the other altar boys couldn't compare. The Murphy twins, Jim and Tim, Sam Deery, and Ralph Blumenfeld, whose family converted, were all utterly incompetent.

Robbie Compton was his only rival. He smelled like fried bologna and Fritos. Robbie's moderate popularity was purely the result of sympathy for his limp. He'd lost two toes to frostbite the previous winter. With every slow and cautious step, Robbie looked as though he might tip. This initially generated some suspense, especially when walking with a lighted candle, but the promised fall never happened, and his limp, and subsequent teetering, soon grew tiresome.

One Sunday, Augustina Donato, who always sat in the front pew, even claimed his constant swaying made her nauseous. The next Sunday, people weren't too surprised when she vomited into her pillbox hat during the consecration. Afterwards in the vestibule, she rose from her folding chair and remarked, "That boy is a menace." Mrs. Donato wasn't alone; Robbie's gait irritated and upset several parishioners. The thought of some partially lame child drawing out their weekly Catholic obligation by a few minutes was unforgivable. As parishes go, Holy Martyrs was known primarily for its speedy service.

Despite Digby's obvious superiority as top altar boy, he received no promotions, and no different hue of vestment to distinguish him as squad captain. Regardless of his consistently stellar performance, his primary duty was still to assist the priest. Father McLintock was neither handsome nor hideous, fat nor thin, pale nor ruddy, nor anything much at all. He spoke in a weak, mumbling monotone, and was middling in all ways except for his utter lack of charisma. Stained a shade of nicotine, his white hair hung in heavy disarray like a discarded mop.

Digby stewed. This was the headliner for Sunday mass? he thought. Couldn't this guy serve God in some other way? Life was profoundly unfair. Poor Digby—he was a true star relegated to going through the motions as a mere member of God's chorus line. This simply would not do. The notion of humility in service was completely lost on him. That first Sunday while still in the sacristy, Digby adjusted his frock and began thinking of ways to finagle more attention during mass. It wasn't difficult. Most people were bored senseless during McLintock's service much less his homilies which, despite being brief, were nonetheless tedious.

Poor Father McLintock might have been devout, but no one paid enough attention to care. It was only a matter of time before upper management realized it. Eventually, the Church elders recognized that some parishioners headed over to Our Lady of Perpetual Sorrows for Sunday service. The elders couldn't allow the flock to migrate. The higher ups knew that Sunday mass was an obligation best filled quickly and painlessly, and with a dash of pizzazz. In order to restore attendance at Sunday mass and thereby fill the coffers, some "reworking" of the service was necessary. The elders decided that they needed fresh blood.

Within weeks, Father McLintock had been reassigned to the dismal 6 a.m. Sunday mass. Dawn mass was an age-spotted wasteland, a hazy border between the living and the dead. The sparse crowd of supplicants were scattered over the expanse of the church like wilted garnishes from a banquet spread. They had little to give, so providing mass for them was more a service than a profitable endeavor, though they were often reminded of the blessings bestowed upon those who remembered the Church in their wills. Making God a beneficiary cannot guarantee salvation, but it can facilitate one's passage to Heaven. Dawn devotional mass was no place to be if you wanted to be seen, especially since half of the attendees were legally or mentally blind. The Blumenfeld kid was always assigned to that mass.

The reworking of the mass following McLintock's departure was anything but gradual. Overnight, services changed dramatically as a direct result of McLintock's dynamic replacement. Father Kenneth was a convertible-driving, Tiparillo-smoking, turtleneck-wearing priest of "today." In his dress slacks and mutton-chop sideburns, no one could deny that he was a stone fox of the 1970s. He had The Dry Look, splashed on Hai Karate and shopped at Chess King. He said his Stations of the Cross on a puka shell rosary. He was part Tony Orlando and part Englebert Humperdinck, and beneath his robes, the ladies of the parish imagined a Tom Jones sort of package. Is that a cross in your vestment or are you just happy to see me? Bless me Father for I am a naughty housewife with the fires of Hell burning in my loins!

Almost from the start, the women of Holy Martyrs vied for his attention. Arriving early to stake claim to the front pews, they teased their hair, showed their cleavage, and pushed their painted nails seductively into the red sponge of the holy water font. Various gestures during the service grew rife with suggestiveness. The blessings of the forehead, lips, and heart during the reading of the Gospel hinted at sexual promise. The beating of the penitent's breast during the Confiteor hinted at untapped ecstasy. Mea culpa! Mea culpa! Some flirted openly at the communion rail, and all but tossed their undies on the altar during his homily. The ladies of Holy Martyrs baked him cookies and pies, and even hams. They volunteered en masse to polish pews and candlesticks, tableware and floor tiles. They did his laundry, washed his car, and invited him to endless dinners. Father Kenneth was an undeniable stud, a temptation in suede, and a bona fide star. To many of the ladies of Holy Martyrs, he was the sweetest taboo.

Several church women were scandalized by the behavior of their fellow female parishioners. "I'd like to see her try and genuflect in that skirt," scoffed Harriet Cacciatore to her husband when she saw Patricia Matthews veer from the center aisle, and pause before entering one of the front pews. Seeing Patricia's right knee bend ever so slightly before she made the Sign of the Cross, Mrs. Cacciatore gave a self-satisfied click of her tongue. "I knew it. That looks more like a sausage skin than a dress, and pork sausage, from this angle." Mr. Cacciatore said nothing. The look on his face did not seem to be disapproving at all.

Father Kenneth always made an entrance. That first Sunday, he entered from the vestibule. Walking up the aisle, he shook hands, winked, and pistol-shot various members of the congregation like a Vatican approved version of Hugh Hefner. As he crossed the altar, he raised his arms to cue the free-spirited guitarist, Rainbeaux, whose crucifix necklace hung beside a peace symbol. Rainbeaux favored peasant blouses, and caused a scandal among the more conservative element at Holy Martyrs when she sang "He Ain't Heavy, He's My Brother," once at the Saturday evening service. She wore gauchos to mass the following week. It was rumored in the parish that she did not shave her armpits.

Rainbeaux's partner on the keyboard for Sunday morning mass was Miss Eugenia, an elderly organist with earlobes so long that they hung to her shoulders like exotic fruit. Her mountainous beehive, enhanced by her eccentric love of plumed hats, rivaled her height. Every so often, the weight of her head would snap her neck this way or that. Many thought that one day it would be the death of her. Miss Eugenia only missed mass when she went out of town to see Liberace in concert. She'd done so more than a dozen times, and always bought herself a wrist corsage for the occasion. She imagined them playing together. She was convinced Liberace had just never found the right girl. Miss Eugenia had played at the mass, as well as weddings for decades. She loved the feeling of her hands on that big organ as it trilled and swelled in the arches and apses of Holy Martyrs. An overpowering scent of mothballs and Aqua Net surrounded her.

Father Kenneth's arrival was a game changer. Having him as the new celebrant was an upsetting development in Digby's ongoing quest for parish recognition and social acceptance. The dreamy priest's sudden appearance robbed him of the few scant crumbs of attention he'd once had as McLintock's acolyte. It wasn't fair. Digby seethed at the upstart priest's apparent use of the Church to feed his own ego. Digby hated when people stooped to his level. He was down there first. Desperation was such an unappealing quality in others.

The Father Kenneth situation was unacceptable. Digby had no desire to be overlooked or to crawl out of bed every Sunday just to bask in his, or even His, presence. Simple service work and humility clashed with his true colors. If this was God's plan for him, then God had a lot to learn about omniscience.

Refusing to either quit or simply accept this regrettable new situation, the following week Digby began an aggressive upstaging campaign. Integrity of the mass be damned. He would shine in his own personal crusade. Just let the Holy Martyrs congregation try to ignore him.

The following Sunday, after presenting the offertory gifts, he attempted to show some spontaneous Christian joy by lifting his arms and spinning in a small excited circle on the return to his prie-dieu. During an especially poignant gospel reading later in the mass, he made a grand show of taking out a bright paisley hankie to wipe away a tear. Bold as these moves may have been, he barely registered a blip. The parishioners were far too focused on Father Kenneth, but Digby wasn't one to give up so easily. He was single-minded and shameless in his purpose.

The next Sunday in the sacristy, he removed his corduroys and slipped on a pair of gym shorts beneath his cossack. As he sat for the readings, he shifted his vestment and with a great show of nonchalance.He lifted the garment above his knees as he crossed his legs, offering a flash of his pre-teen legs to the front rows. The chorus of gasps and the two nods of approval pleased him. He'd finally broken the hypnotic grip Father Kenneth had maintained over this attentive flock. Be it good or bad or worthy of damnation, Digby had at least made an impression.

"I was shocked. In my day, a young lady wouldn't show her ankles on the street, much less flash her gams in The House of God. And here he was, a boy - and on the altar. If you ask me, that Digby Swank was just too saucy for his own good. Everyone was just scandalized," noted Miss Eugenia with a perilous tilt of her head.

Later in the mass, Digby flashed the gold paten to the crowd like a game show hostess. With an open mouthed smile and an arched brow, he played the bright circle of its reflected light across several faces in the congregation before bringing the shallow plate forward for communion.

Assisting in the serving of the Eucharist wafer was a curious affair. Digby was always intrigued by what it revealed. Before the "hand-or-mouth" days, it was a shuffling parade of congregants with eyes clamped shut, necks straining and gullets wide like chicks awaiting masticated worm-bits. Digby peered into every open mouth and noted who had nasty teeth, gold fillings, discolored fungal tongues, dentures, food residue, or atrocious breath. He discovered secrets about all of them. A few of the women who had their sights on Father Kenneth did outrageously suggestive things with their tongues and lips.

Communion itself was a mysterious sacrament that prompted more than a few questions from Digby. First and foremost, was the host truly the body of Christ? The nuns told him so. They said the oddly textured wafer was His flesh and blood, or more specifically, the presence of It due to the miracle of Transubstantiation. For this reason, the consecrated host was meant to dissolve on the penitent's tongue, and not be bitten. Chewing the host was a barbaric indignity. Suddenly, religion was simple. God was a lozenge.

Digby recalled his third-grade classmate, Ronald Gruber, asking what would happen if someone threw up right after they received Holy Communion. Right after, when they were walking back to the pew with it still on their tongue. Is even that holy? The question was a legitimate one, but Sister was not amused. Ronald had to stand in the garbage during recess for two days.

As evidence of the sacredness of it all, at the conclusion of the mass, the goblet, the paten, and the chalice that were used for the communion service were all washed in the sacrarium, which was sort of like a sink except the water drained directly into the ground, circumventing the sewage system lest any part of Our Lord's body or blood be on any of the utensils. The behind the scenes workings of the mass fascinated Digby.

After Father Kenneth had been at the parish six weeks, talk suddenly began to circulate about him. Digby had heard things before and even saw him wink at Mrs. Matthews during the presentation of the gifts. However, this new talk was sudden and incessant. People whispered in the vestibule, at the Piggly Wiggly, and at the Pick 'N Save that Father Kenneth was dating a waitress, and she was rumored to be a Lutheran. This was not Church policy. Digby couldn't imagine a juicier rumor. Evidently, Father Kenneth knew this waitress very biblically! Donna was a young "painted up" brunette with reportedly perky breasts, who wore a Scorpio zodiac pendant and served up more than hot lunches at Carol's Clam House, where this unholy union began.

The rumor mill churned as phone lines burned. Mrs. Huessin, the lunch lady whose dimpled butt and shadowy crack was always visible through her faded yellow stretch slacks, reportedly witnessed the duo in the parking lot behind the athletic field. The next week, various concerned members of the congregation, including an overly indignant Mrs. Matthews, went to witness the hash-slinging harlot who'd seduced Father Foxy. Midday business at Carol's Clam House soared, especially among Holy Martyrs parishioners. Clam House owner Carol increased the volume on the dining room music to cover the buzz and din of the chatty crowd.

"Donna was a fine waitress, and a bit of a tramp. Sometimes the two go hand and hand, if you know what I mean. That girl sure knew how to fill a section in the Clam House, or my name isn't Carol. Whatever she did to get those butts in the booths was fine by me. I crossed myself all the way to the bank. Sure, I'd seen the guy and watched them flirt back and forth, but I had no idea he was a man of God. I figured his being all in black was a Johnny Cash thing. Boy, but he was a fine looking fella. You couldn't help but notice the connection. There was more steam between those two than from a fresh plate of my breaded clam strips. I guess the signs that he was a priest were all there, but not being a follower, I sure didn't see it. Though I do remember thinking it strange when he brought her palm fronds one Sunday instead of flowers."

Lila Swank went to get a taste of the fishy doings at the Clam House first hand. She had the Crab Salad Supreme with coleslaw and a biscuit side, and left with her steely-eyed pronouncement. She didn't say a word to Digby, but he heard Lila talking with Sandy Treacle in the living room. "Oh, I couldn't believe my eyes. The service was quick enough, but she was cheap. Cheap, cheap, cheap. And I didn't leave one penny for the tip." His mother failed to see the irony in her statement.

Sandy went to the Clam House the following day and proclaimed, "There was not a bit of shame about her. You should have seen the way she wrote out the bill. All full of herself, just like a movie star signing an autograph."

The week was filled with whispered phone conversations, lingering chats, and guarded comments at the supermarket. New bits of information surfaced almost every day, though very few of them were true. Lila's bridge club that Wednesday lasted one full hour longer than usual due to so much chatter on the matter. Keeping track of points was close to impossible. Finally, they put the cards away altogether.

In the wake of the scandal, the grim-faced Church elders called Father Kenneth before them, their faces growing even grimmer at the prospect of a parish scandal, especially with Our

Lady of Perpetual Sorrows all but jumping from the bushes to steal congregants. They began by saying they had no choice. It was decided that this was the Catholic Church, and it was not for man to judge, but... whether the gossip had merit or not, an accused Lothario could not lead the flock. In biblical terms, the Church elders found it prudent to stone now and ask questions later.

The following week, Father Kenneth was reassigned to St. Veronica's Church in Winslow. Two hundred miles seemed a safe enough distance away. For the sake of damage control, the decision was called mutual. That very week, Donna shredded her Guest Pad, balled up her service apron, and quit the Clam House without giving proper notice.

Carol fumed. "She didn't even have the decency to quit in person. She wrote a note on a Guest Check, and put it under my wiper blade overnight. Can you beat that?"

Donna vacated her studio apartment at the Versailles Villa complex out near the Band-Aid factory, and left town the following day. Tongues continued to wag, and heads shook and nodded over the two of them all but leaving town together. Even with the remedial math skills of most Running Falls residents, folks knew enough to put two and two together. If the Church had permitted gambling, most of the Holy Martyrs' congregants would have bet a week's salary that Donna was slinging hash someplace in Winslow.

The episode was quite a to-do for a month or so, but it all died down as soon as the next scandal rocked the parish. The Father Kenneth episode became a juicy memory until years later when Digby came home from school, distraught with the social stigma of having failed Driver's Ed. Lila had Agnes Warner on the phone, and Digby could tell by the way she cupped the mouthpiece that she was privy to a choice piece of gossip.

Later on, he heard his mother mention to Rog that Agnes had updated her on the Father Kenneth saga. Agnes said Father Kenneth had left the order, married Donna, and fathered a mongoloid child. Though she wasn't one to judge, Agnes said she wasn't surprised. Though Agnes loathed making assumptions, and she swore she'd sooner get shingles than claim to know the ways of Our Lord, she said it was as if God reached right into Donna's womb and put a curse on the unborn child.

For all practical purposes, Father Kenneth's departure should've thrilled Digby, but when the popular priest departed, much of the challenge and sport of the mass left along with him. Digby's heart just wasn't in it anymore, and his eternal soul was more absent than ever. By then, he knew being an altar boy was never going to bring him the adoration and unconditional love he sought. Looking for that sort of thing in church was foolish.

The following Saturday, Digby called the rectory feigning illness. Planning to just say he was ill, he didn't know what to say when the church secretary, Mrs. Murphy, asked for details. Needing an explanation for his absence, he said he had a distended anus as the result of a spastic colon. He'd heard Sandy Treacle complain of the malady the last time Lila hosted bridge club. It sounded horrid. With a quick intake of air through her flat nose followed by a sharply clipped "Of course," Mrs. Murphy marked him as excused. Digby hung up the phone, and imagined Mrs. Murphy raising her impossibly arched brows even higher. He never went back, and was never asked to return. Maybe they'd grown tired of him. Maybe it was the distended anus issue. He had no real way of knowing. Nothing was ever said.

Resigning felt good to Digby. If only all of life's problems would vanish by uttering the magic words distended anus. Though it was a messy excuse, his quitting had a quiet dignity to it. He'd miss the ritual and show of being an altar boy as well as the attention, not to mention wearing something that flowed. No one had laughed at him when he was a part of the mass. It had all been very nice while it lasted.

That spring at the annual church bake sale, Lila answered "Umm, fine" when Mrs. Murphy inquired about the state of Digby's anus over a tin of peach cobbler.

She never asked Digby about it, but that night he heard his still perplexed mother relate the encounter to Rog, "That's rather odd, don't you think?"

Flipping the cap on a longneck, Rog turned with his back to the silverware drawer, pushed it shut with his butt, and grinned. "Well, Betty always did like sticking her nose where it didn't belong."

"Oh Rog!" Lila loved when he was clever, and smiled despite herself.

Lila tsked over that whole Betty Murphy business. Sure, Lila was pleasant to her and all, but Betty Murphy wasn't one of her favorite people. Though decidedly less juicy than the Father Kenneth story, another rumor made the rounds in the parish about Betty Murphy being unsound on the Virgin Birth. And with her working in the rectory.

Later on, he heard his parents laughing in the kitchen. That night, Digby thought it was very strange that his father put on his aftershave before going to bed. What was the sense in that? Digby had thought.

12 - The Den Of Shame

Camaraderie baffled Digby. Fellowship and the benefits of a group effort seemed contrary to his disposition. He worked best alone, and possessed an aversion to the trust and accountability that teams and collectives required. That hadn't changed with being the member of a congregation, or by being an altar boy. He found group projects at school and team sport activities in gym class loathsome. The tendency to not play well with others should've been only the first of many red flags to signal that Cub Scouts was not for him. In addition, he didn't enjoy doing boy things, had a disdain for scheduled activities, and resented being told what to do.

Digby was only a do-gooder when a clearly defined reward was involved. He was more a great mercenary than a Good Samaritan. Digby harbored no fantasies of rescuing cats from trees or assisting old ladies at crosswalks or harmonizing at campfire sing-alongs. He joined the Cub Scouts for a variety of reasons: his parent's desire for him to fit in among his peers as well as his own gender, a tendency to be impulsive, and the simple fact that the boy was partial to uniforms.

Digby's first inkling that life in the den was not all golden ascots and matching knee socks came that first afternoon in the radon-ridden basement of his troop den mother. The first order of business, after collecting dues, was for all Scouts to raise their hands in a two-fingered salute and recite the Scout oath:

On my honor I will do my best
To do my duty to God and my country
and to obey the Scout Law;
To help other people at all times;
To keep myself physically strong,
mentally awake, and morally straight.

Obey Scout law? Keep morally straight? Help others? He couldn't agree to this, but by the time it occurred to him, he'd already done just that. He lowered his hand in puzzlement. Thank goodness he'd only sworn on his honor. The level of allegiance required to be a Scout did not come naturally to him by any stretch of the imagination, but he would give it lip service for a cute outfit. Cub Scouts were supposed to be trustworthy, loyal, helpful, friendly, courteous, kind, obedient, cheerful, thrifty, brave, clean, and reverent. By Digby's count he was three for twelve, and those three often came with conditions. His personality was more accurately reflected in the Scout motto of Be Prepared. Those two simple words spoke volumes to his social dread, frequent bouts of paranoia, and control issues.

There were eight Scouts in his den. His den mother was a chain-smoking woman by the name of Mrs. Caine, whose skeletal torso was wedged right in the middle of a bitter divorce. Beyond unstable, her foundation teetered on worn heels. The woman was in an utter state of collapse. But despite her obvious issues, she assumed the role of scout mistress to be closer to her mouth-breathing son, Keith. Most of those aware of the situation agreed that Keith's adjustment period during the divorce would have been better served if his mother's top priority had been to seek alcohol counseling, or enroll in an anger management class. No one said a word, of course. It wasn't their place.

Listening to Mrs. Caine's coarse and blowsy diatribes should've earned the entire pack merit badges: the Slurring Eagle, the Gin Blossom, the Bitter Doe. After memorizing the Scout Oath, the next thing the boys learned was that men can't be trusted. Mrs. Caine gestured with her tinkling highball glass. "Not one damn bit. They'll cheat on you. The sons-of-bitches will cheat on you every chance they get, and lie right to your damn face."

Of course Digby liked her. A tragic and self-destructive female was definite gay bait, even if Digby didn't yet know that was what he was. If she sang, she could have been a superstar. Whether freshening her drink, wondering aloud where she put "that damn cigarette," or inappropriately displaying a bruise high on her upper thigh from when she "lost her footing," Mrs. Caine was infinitely more engaging than building a birdhouse, memorizing flag signals, or learning to tie assorted knots. "Tie the damn knot? Ha! I tied the knot. Boy did I ever. Only I didn't realize it was at the end of a noose. Let me set you straight. What they don't tell you in that damn book is that all knots can come undone. You hear me? I said every damn one of them. It doesn't matter what they call it or how much work you put into it."

More than once, she referred to the irony of her scout role. "Scout mistress. Now I'm the one who's the mistress. Mistress to a bunch of grade schoolers! Can you believe that?" If no one answered Mrs. Caine immediately after she posed a question, she had a tendency to suddenly turn and ask, "Well can you?" Eager to avoid such direct encounters, every scout in the den soon became members of her submissive wronged-woman chorus.

One Wednesday, Mrs. Caine trounced down the steps to the basement wearing an uncharacteristic smile. After straightening herself from a slight slip on the bottom runner, she told the boys that the night before she'd thrown gasoline on her ex's lawn. "That's something you should know as scouts—gas kills grass. You heard it right here, straight from your mistress. Mort was always so damn proud of his lawn. Hit him where it hurts, that's what I say. Know your enemy's weak spots. There's another lesson. I poured the gasoline out in his yard to spell Cheater, because everyone should know what that no-account did."

Curious to see her handiwork, the next day Digby rode past Mr. Caine's new place. There were indeed dead grass markings on his lawn. After climbing on a garbage can to get a better view, Digby thought the marking actually looked a bit more like "chedder" than "cheater," as though her ex was a misspelled cheese. From another angle, it looked like Chester. Either way, it looked mostly like a looping and odd-shaped patch of dead grass. If Digby didn't know what it supposedly said, he'd never even think it said anything. Since she'd been so proud of her handiwork, Digby never mentioned the fact to Mrs. Caine.

Digby was unsure just how long he stayed with the Scouts. The math is fuzzy. His estimates were somewhere between six and eight weeks, but it may have been half or twice or even three times that. The length of his membership was better than most in his family expected, but who could have predicted the inclusion of the sloppy, surly and sensational lioness who gave his den its edge? Divorce, adultery, and revenge were topics that interested him, and he couldn't have asked for a better teacher. Mrs. Caine made him actually enjoy scout life until that final week.

Tom Swank was one of those surprised by Digby's apparent commitment to the Scouts. "I thought he'd run home crying that first day. He was like that. He'd curl up like an armadillo if something rubbed him the wrong way. Most times, all it took was for someone to look at him cross-eyed before he came bawling to Mom. I don't quite know how it was even possible, but over the years, it sure seemed that kid quit more things than he ever started."

The first big event on the Scout Land social calendar was the annual Pinewood Derby. This tradition consisted of each Scout shaping a five-ounce block of pine into a car, attaching wheels, and racing it during a testosterone fueled evening of good spirited competition. "Good spirited competition" was a contradiction in terms, as far as Digby was concerned. There were winners and there were losers; one group was envied, and the other humiliated. No middle ground. Digby was determined to risk it and participate. There was no logical reason for him to think this would be a success. Many would even call him delusional to assume such a thing. It was all very unfamiliar turf. The project was designed to bring fathers and sons together for hours of car design and tool-usage, supposed male bonding stuff.

Mrs. Caine was having none of it. "Screw that." She said she'd be damned if she was going to leave Keith alone with his father for five minutes, much less an evening or two. "If I did that, what do you think Mort would do?" She turned to notorious crayon-eater, Nathan Altgeld, who was nibbling a pencil eraser at the time. "What do you think my ex would do?" Unsure of what to do or say, Nathan swallowed whatever eraser bits he had in his mouth and shrugged. Mrs. Caine sighed. "I'll tell you what he'll do. That bastard will bad mouth me and make excuses. They all do. It'll be, 'Ida was a nag,' or 'Ida drove me away.' Drove him away? Ha. At the end I wanted to chase that no-good bastard out with a pick axe." She threw her head back and laughed before pouring herself another drink. She never cared about the effect all of this venomous insanity would have on impressionable young boys, much less her own son.

"She is magnificent" Digby said, smiling.

The few hours Digby and Rog spent working on their car showed that neither one of them was a master craftsman, or very good at male things. Maybe they lacked the gene. Whatever it was, the guy bonding stuff just wasn't their style. If they had been more open, they could have bonded over their inabilities in the area.

Rog tended to be better at crafts. Digby fondly recalled the previous Thanksgiving, when he and his father had made place setting "turkeys" out of pine cones. Orange pipe cleaners became the legs. They glued bobble-eyes on the flat end of the cone, and placed a name card for every guest in the woody bract wings of the torso. They spent hours together in the basement, making the fourteen settings. His father had called him "son" that day, and let him have a glass of beer. Sometimes love was just that simple.

Things were very different when they crafted the Pinewood Derby car. For one thing, time was a factor. They didn't get around to making the car until the night before the event, and by seven o'clock on a weeknight, Rog was a bit drunk. After assuring Digby he'd done this a hundred times, he promptly sliced his thumb with the coping saw.

"Now you try," he said, handing Digby the saw and wrapping a reddening rag around his thumb.

"Are you sure we…"

"Of course I'm sure. Just saw," said Rog as he climbed the stairs, leaving a trail of blood drops that the dog eagerly lapped up.

Digby gulped uncomfortably and picked up the coping saw, used primarily for cutting curves in thin wood. He wanted his car to have a sloped hood like the sports car he'd seen Ann-Margret drive in a late night movie. He imagined his little soapbox car with a petite driver wearing a sheer scarf, white sunglasses, and frosted lipstick. Male bonding wasn't quite Digby's style.

He did the best he could at carving his car, but his best was still woefully inept. Digby hoped adding wheels would make it look more like a vehicle and less like a pinewood potato, but that was not to be. Wheels merely made it look like a mutilated block of wood on wheels. He tried to improve things with a nice salmon shade of paint, which did nothing to help matters.

Fortified with two more highballs, Rog staggered back down the stairs with a huge gauze bandage on his thumb. He plopped onto the stool beside Digby, and grabbed the paintbrush in his non-bandaged hand. He tried to add a racing stripe to the car, but bourbon made walking, much less painting, a straight line all but impossible. Rather than interfere, Digby sat back in resignation. By then, he was beyond caring. The veil of delusion had lifted, and he was fairly sure which group he'd be in tomorrow night at the Pinewood Derby.

When he went downstairs the next morning, Tom and Maynard laughed at his creation. When they finally caught their breath, Maynard pointed at Digby's roadster and said, "It looks like a dick."

At first Digby didn't see what his brothers were talking about, then unfortunately, he did. The sloping hood gave his longish car a general phallic shape, a resemblance enhanced by the salmon paint job. Rog's uneven blue racing stripe looked a great deal like, well, a vein. His entry looked more like some pervy sex toy at a clothing optional crafts fair than a Pinewood Derby car. Digby reddened and trembled and bit his lip until it bled, then just kept biting. In a desperate attempt to disguise all penile resemblance, he put an "8" decal on the hood. The fact that it was five inches but labeled with an "8" made it seem even more phallic.

He didn't have time for any more last minute changes. The

derby was that night, and he had to participate. If he didn't enter a car, he'd be howled right out of the pack. He didn't want to disappoint Mrs. Caine. Plus, the Pinewood Derby patch was a must-have Scout accessory. He would have preferred some sort of brooch, but Digby liked the way the checkered flags and roadster emblem really popped on the navy blue of the uniform.

Throughout the school day, Digby mulled and debated, and desperately tried to decide upon the best course of action. Listing his options for the umpteenth time, he stared at the paper:

Go with car.

Go without car and claim theft.

Don't go.

Feign contagious disease and/or kidnapping.

Distended anus again?

Like a discount girdle in the one-size-fits-all bin, he was yanked in every possible direction. In the end, he opted to go. He'd get the patch just for entering a car. That was what he really wanted. However, if he was going to participate and enter this thing, he'd do it alone. Things of this sort were always worse when one of his parents was around to witness his social ineptitude. It made him feel like their crown of thorns. He still fondly recalled his father calling him "son," and didn't want to do anything to shatter that illusion.

After a hasty meal, he told his father the event had been cancelled due to a flash fire on the premises.

"At the church?" his mother gasped, dropping the spatula and turning abruptly from the waffle iron with a hand splayed upon her chest.

"Uh, yeah, four are dead. Two were burned beyond recognition. I heard they're checking dental records. I'm going to go play."

Digby left his parents stunned and open-mouthed at the kitchen table. Running out the front door, he went alone to the

Pinewood Derby with his entry in a brown paper bag. When he got to Holy Martyrs, he stopped and sat on the steps leading down to the church basement. Fear made him hesitate. "I can do this. I've been mocked before, and by better packs of people. I'm a survivor. I'm a Cub Scout," he said, tightly closing his eyes as testimony to his determination. With a deep breath, he threw out both his chest and chin, and descended the cracked cement stairs to the double doors.

The church basement was festooned in gold and navy. Pennants waved, whistles blew, and fruit juice flowed freely as fathers and sons stood either awkwardly arm in arm or uncomfortably apart. This event supposedly celebrated something natural, but no one seemed too comfortable with this whole male bonding thing. Digby felt a glimmer of hope. Maybe this wouldn't be so bad after all. Maybe everyone else felt the same way.

He caught a whiff of gin and cheap perfume, and at the same time heard the scrape of high heels. A defiant Ida Caine was present at the all-male event. Look out fathers and sons, there's five feet two inches of 40 proof estrogen in the house.

She waved and yelled "Hey" at the same time a whistle blew.

The emcee for the evening was Hector Hastings, an excessively enthusiastic man with a tragic comb-over that swept about his head with wispy coverage. Hector took a hit off his asthma inhaler and clapped his hands, which caused his belly folds to jiggle. With a wide smile that seemed to meet somewhere behind his ears, he welcomed one and all before shouting, "Let the race begin!"

Despite Hector's declaration, the race itself did not begin until later. First off, lots were drawn to select the racing order. During that portion of the evening, Digby's name was incorrectly read as Dogby, which prompted several scattered snickers. Letting it slide was easier than correcting it. He was in the seventh heat. Hoping to see lots of poorly constructed and non-functional cars, Digby was disappointed to see that the entries fell into groupings of great, good and mostly not-so-good. In his eyes, none were laughable or disastrous except for his. As the seventh heat approached, his knees knocked and his body shook. His lips twitched like an out-of-pitch tuning fork.

"Okay, number sevens," wheezed Mr. Hastings, who seemed already exhausted by his own enthusiasm.

Digby placed his entry on the track, eliciting a fresh round of snickers. He breathed and he breathed, and he tried to think of nothing but his breath. He could feel the stares. They looked down at him like they always did, and like it seemed they always would. He felt the eyes on his back, and judgement in their gaze. It burned holes in him. Waiting. Waiting. Breathing. "Just blow the goddamn whistle already. Let it be over," he prayed.

The whistle blew.

His humiliation was blessedly brief. The gate lifted. After only a few inches, the right front wheel wobbled and rolled from his car. The whistle blew again. Hastings eliminated him with a dramatic "you're-outta-here" gesture that seemed unnecessary, since his car had already spun to a halt. However, the errant wheel did cross the finish line in third place.

As the boys in the eighth heat readied their cars, Mrs. Caine approached Digby. In a thick whisper that was clearly audible to all those nearby, she asked where his father was. Digby said he was working late. Mrs. Caine exhaled and rocked on her heels. "Oh ho, is he now?" she said, crossing her arms and pursing her messy lips.

Digby looked down at his loser car. Someone had already thrown the fourth wheel away. He turned number "8" over in his hands. The life lesson here at the Pinewood Derby was not the one promoted in the CSA booklet. He never learned the things he was supposed to learn about father/son time. He'd learned that lesson last Thanksgiving. The Pinewood Derby didn't teach him about craftsmanship or sportsmanship or the satisfaction of a job well done. Those things would continue to elude him for years to come. Digby's lesson was the clear realization that he was meant to be chauffeured about, and/or drive luxury cars. It certainly wasn't his life goal to build them, much less fashion them out of wood. If that made him a snob, then maybe being a snob was his life calling.

No stranger to disappointment herself, Mrs. Caine raked his hair. "So you lost a race, big deal. Just be grateful your man didn't cheat on you." Digby wasn't quite sure what she meant by the comment, and truthfully, neither did she.

Unsure of how to respond, Digby excused himself and approached the long table at the other end of the track. He gave his name. With a very precise check, Mr. Lister, the diabetic fainter who owned the drugstore, marked his name from the list and gave Digby his Pinewood Derby patch. Like many of life's rewards, it looked better in the manual.

As the evening drew to a close after the finalist heat, the heavy outer double doors to the church basement burst open. On the threshold stood Lila, balancing two foil-covered casseroles and a basket of dinner rolls. Digby should've seen his mother's Catholic disaster relief coming. To Lila, nothing could soothe third degree burns or untold grief like Mac and Cheese with Weenies, or Tuna-Bean-N-Noodle Delight. Circumstances such as flash fire fatalities beckoned for a meal that all but clogged arteries in a matter of moments.

His mother's nostrils flared, trying to catch a whiff of singed flesh. She scanned the room looking for weeping survivors, black shrouds, the food table, or at least someone swathed in bandages. The mild disappointment some of the fathers and sons displayed following the Pinewood Derby could hardly be mistaken for the deep grief expected in the aftermath of such a catastrophic tragedy.

Lila did another quick scan of the church basement before focusing on Digby. Uh-oh. Her lips narrowed. She did the slow blink, and when her eyes opened the second time, they narrowed dramatically. Digby was thankful her hands were full, and they were in a crowded room on church property. He couldn't tell whether she or the Tuna-Bean-N-Noodle Delight gave off more steam.

He had some serious explaining to do, but defending himself or his actions would be too complex and simply too degrading.

She'd never understand about the car and the group, and how he just didn't want to be "that kid" again. She wouldn't understand that he didn't want to be the outsider, and even worse, that he didn't want to be seen as the outsider by his own father. He knew he'd be a laughingstock to the other scouts; he just didn't want to see the impact of all that ridicule reflected on his father's face. Shame always worsened when shared, because then it included guilt as well. At those times, he was not only shamed, but shameful. That was too much. Being a disappointment never got easier. This time, he wanted to spare his father and limit the collateral damage.

Digby reasoned that accepting his punishment was more dignified, than to try and explain all of this. Better to be seen as mischievous. Then his behavior would be in question, not him. He'd survive this. Lila wouldn't hit him in the church basement or in front of another adult, even a drunk divorcee. That wouldn't happen until they got in the car, or maybe after they got home.

As they were leaving the church basement, Ida Caine told his mother to keep an eye on her husband. Giving her most insincere smile, Lila nodded. "Okay, thanks, have a good night, we'll see you soon." By the sugary tone, Digby could tell he was a dead man.

"Boozehound," he heard his mother mutter as she pushed through the church basement door.

To those present, the scene looked innocent enough. In some ways, the apparent normalcy made it all the more frightening. It was like anticipating the force of an erupting geyser. It was the hushed retreat of water before the rush of a tsunami. Digby figured his punishment would be proportional to the size of what was being contained. His mother waved to some people as they approached the car. She even exchanged chit-chat with a passerby while putting the casseroles and dinner rolls in the trunk. Giving the impression that everything was just fine and was part of the illusion. Once the car door clicked closed, she turned to him.

"Lock it."

She was still somewhat smiling, but her lips trembled in an

unsettling manner. Digby gulped. Locking the door was not a good sign.

When he turned back, she grabbed his arm. "What is wrong with you? Why did you lie and tell a story like this? A flash fire? Fellow parishioners burned beyond recognition? Thank goodness I was too busy cooking to activate the Holy Martyrs Ladies' Relief phone tree. Can you imagine what would have happened if I'd have done that? Can you imagine how many casseroles there would have been? Dozens! As it was, I made two casseroles! Two!" She squeezed his arm twice to emphasize the number.

In truth, Lila didn't activate the phone tree not because she was busy cooking, but because she wanted to be the first on the scene with comfort food. She could be very competitive that way.

"You made me look like a fool," she continued.

In her eyes, few things were worse than being made to look like a fool. It showed a lack of consideration and respect, and most importantly, an utter disregard for the opinion of others. What would the neighbors think? What would people who heard about it from the neighbors think? His behavior made absolutely no sense given the warped physics of the Swank universe, where the more distant a person or object was, the greater its impact and influence. Digby knew how his mother hated looking foolish. He hated doing it. He'd tried not to, but it happened nonetheless. The Pinewood Derby was a prime example of how he tried not to make them look bad, and it ended up worse than he ever could have imagined. He couldn't seem to help it. Humiliating his mother, his family, and especially himself seemed to be one of the few things he did exceptionally well, and without the slightest effort.

Simmering, Lila started the ignition. She rolled down her window. "Give me that damn thing." She grabbed the remnants of Digby's pinewood car, and hurled it into some bushes behind the church. An orange tabby yowled and dashed from the hedge. Things were already getting scary, and they weren't even out of the parking lot.

Digby didn't care that she tossed his car out the window.

He was about to throw it in the dumpster downstairs when Lila arrived, so instead he'd gripped it tighter. That car had already been five ounces of sheer hell. He would need no reminders of tonight's humiliation. The memory would stay with him just fine.

Fortunately, Sandy Treacle pulled out of the IGA at the corner. She honked and gave his mother a tinkling wave. It brought Lila back. Sandy was a PTA official, and a member of Lila's bridge club. Sandy had big ears, huge eyes, and the wide, whiskered mouth of a catfish. She loved to gossip. Her sentences tended to end only when she ran out of oxygen. Digby all but heard the pop of a thought bubble emerge from his mother's head. "Sandy will notice. Sandy will talk. Others could be watching." Lila took a few rapid mouth breaths and talked herself down. "Relax Lila, just relax."

In a moment she resumed the chastisement, but her tone had changed. It wouldn't get physical. He'd get spanked once they got home, but his butt had ample padding. Much worse was the stern lecture. Lila had already begun her heavy, disappointed sighs. He became the cross to bear once more.

Digby simply wanted to be invisible when things like this happened. Since he was already adept at being overlooked, invisibility seemed a mere matter of degree. He imagined a chalk outline surrounding his body, and envisioned himself shrinking deep within that border until he was no more than the emptiness where a crime had occurred. He tried to imagine his mother's words hitting his white homicide line and bouncing off. He tried to pretend her sighs and silences were only ricocheting about him. He failed at that as well. Despite his wish, Digby was still very much there. He held the merit patch in his fist, and heard the same tone in his mother's voice that he had heard time and again. It carried the same disappointment, the same rhetorical questions, and the same weariness. He knew that tone represented more than him, but he also knew he was a part of it. He hated adding to her bigger hardship and bigger pain, and complicating the bigger game she had to play day in and day out. He heard the strange echo of his repeated apologies. He promised to be more considerate and to think first and to be good and never to do

- 144 -

this or that again. At this point in his life, "sorry" was his most frequently used word.

Lila fished a cigarette from her coat pocket and lit it. After exhaling, she said "And don't tell your father about this," with a nod towards her smoke. She needn't have worried. Digby was a genius at keeping secrets.

13 – Near Death Experiences

Loaf Lake was the best lake for swimming in Running Falls. Flounder Lake wasn't any less scenic; in fact, it had a sandier bottom than the rock lined basin of Loaf Lake. But because of winds and a slight drainage problem, a dip in Flounder Lake left swimmers smelling like adhesive Band-Aids for days afterwards. Sometimes getting the bandage stink out of a thick head of hair took a full bar of soap. Flounder Lake was okay for fishing, but even then the catch tended to have an unsavory tang. Instead, the public beach and attached parking lot at Flounder Lake became the spot where most of the bastard babies in the county were conceived.

With Flounder Lake ruled out by most residents as undesirable, the beach at Loaf Lake became a popular spot for most of Running Falls families to escape during the summertime heat. Over euchre and longnecks one Thursday night in August, the Van Camps and the Swanks planned a combined family outing that coming Sunday. Ginny Van Camp enthused, "Let's go to Big Loaf Beach at the Loaf Lake Forest Preserve." The idea seemed grand. The weather reports all said that Sunday was going to be a scorcher.

"It'll be one for the record books," said the bony-faced weather girl on the ten o'clock news, as if joining in on their conversation.

When Bob Van Camp heard that, he suggested they stake out a place early on Sunday morning "right after church." They decided to bring lunch to the beach and make a real day of it.

"It will be a blessing not to cook in that heat," said Lila.

"If it's going to be as hot as they say it's supposed to be, I am going nowhere near the stove," Ginny added.

"We can go straight from mass and change at the Shower House," offered Bob.

Rog nodded. "Well if we're doing that, it's probably best to leave church right after communion so we can be the first ones out of the parking lot and beat anybody else to the beach who has the same idea."

"Amen to that."

"Oh, Bob," Ginny gushed with a giggle.

On the day of the record scorcher's estimated arrival, the dreaded warm front dipped south. As a result, the day was a good fifteen degrees cooler than had been predicted. However, the coolers were full, the lunch baskets packed, and a case of beer on ice. Calling off the outing on account of the weather would have been foolish. Despite the fact that there was now no crowd to beat to the beach, both families went up to the altar for Holy Communion, received the host on their tongues, and kept on walking right out the back doors of Holy Martyrs. The body of Christ hadn't even dissolved in their mouths by the time they pulled out of the parking lot.

As it turned out, they had the beach to themselves. By eleven that morning, the adults were already drinking. Bob Van Camp announced they weren't going to start the charcoal for another hour. Hearing this, all the kids ran into the water. After some splashing and dunking and frolicking, Maynard suggested a game of King of the Raft. The idea was met with shouts of approval, and boasts over who would ultimately be victorious.

The Running Falls version of King of the Raft was played on a wooden raft held afloat by six hollow oil drums beneath. The Loaf Lake public swimming area had three such rafts, each equidistant between the six identical piers. The kids chose the closest raft. The object of the game was simple: to push all your opponents into the water by whatever means necessary, and become the only one on the raft at any given time. Once that occurred, the person was to raise his arms and shout, "I'm King of the Raft." This contest of supremacy had no other rules. Weapons would have been permitted if they were handy. King of the Raft had a way of bringing out the beast in everyone.

Playing in the game that Sunday were Digby, his brothers Maynard and Tom, Johnny Van Camp, and his sunburned cousin, Dawn, who resembled a bursting bud in her tight orange swimsuit and petaled bathing cap. Maynard had the hots for Dawn because she had boobs.

The battle for raft supremacy was especially fierce that day. Maynard showed off for Dawn, who in turn tried to prove she was as strong as any boy. Tom Swank had a good time as he did when participating in all boyish things, and Johnny Van Camp was an asshole as usual, which meant flipping his hair back, and calling Digby a wimp. When he called him that a second time, Maynard called Johnny "a dirty butt-wipe" and gave him an especially brutal shove. Johnny fell belly first into the water. Though Johnny called Digby a wimp, the youngest Swank proved to be quite the opposite. Digby clawed and kicked and pulled hair, and was a formidable combatant for King of the Raft. The game triggered his survival instinct. It did in all the kids. There were screams and shouts, as well as bites and a good deal of scratching.

On the beach, Bob Van Camp sat up and set down his beer. He stood, rubbed his enormous belly, and yelled at the kids to "Cool it!" His reprimand caused the children to stop for a moment and look his direction, but his breath was wasted. The game soon reached its former intensity, and moments later grew even more brutal. Dawn, three years Digby's senior and easily 25 pounds heavier even without her boobs, ran from the opposite end of the raft and body slammed Digby. It was like being hit by an overstuffed couch. Digby grabbed hold of a couple of petals from her cap, which tore off in his hand as he fell. Rather than falling directly into the water, Digby's feet slipped back beneath him, and his chin hit the corner of the wooden raft with a resounding crunch. His eyes rolled back in his head as he flopped backwards into the lake. His hands opened, and the two rubber petals in his grip fell upon the waves.

Digby felt the splash as a slow motion parting and subsequent regrouping of the water. The lake had opened and closed to swallow him. Everything grew fuzzy. Sound muffled. The world seemed to move behind a frosted glass wall. As he sank, he floated down through the water, and watched the rays of sunlight through the surface. The dance of light reached for him with rolling arms. The light felt peaceful, like Grandma Rose's embrace. Bubbles trickled from the corners of his mouth as he smiled. He sensed a complete and utter silence as more bubbles rose around him. Nothing mattered but the light, and the quiet and the cool sense of sinking. Maybe he was finally floating, like he had in his dreams. Maybe this was the bliss he'd tried so hard to find. Maybe heaven was down here instead of up there. Maybe he was going to see Grandma Rose instead of having her come to him.

After the occurrence, Digby wondered if what he saw was really sunlight, or the purported "tunnel of light" that ushers the deceased into the underworld. If that was true, he was both comforted and unsettled to discover he'd only been truly happy with life at the moment of transition into something else. If that was the experience of death, it felt like letting go of everything, and realizing that all the opinions and goals and things that seemed important really didn't matter. In the end, only the memory of love made him feel free and secure. There's no way of knowing if he died or dreamed or simply sank that day. Memory, especially combined with a concussion, can be as murky as the August waters of Loaf Lake. Some larger questions baffle even narrators.

Dawn dove in and yanked him to the surface. Wrapping a hefty arm about his neck, she dragged him to shore. He stared into the colorful rubber bouquet of her bathing cap. With his head against her chest, he could feel the deep reverberation of her screaming. Her hysterics must have snapped him from his euphoric coma. Once he reached the beach, he staggered about covered in strands of seaweed and crying, "I've seen it." No one knew exactly what he meant. When Rog and Lila asked, he looked at them blankly. Maynard and Tom thought he meant one of Dawn's boobs. Bob Van Camp declared Digby to be "really out of it," and judging by the number of empty Pabst cans around the picnic table, he wasn't the only one.

Though tipsy at the time of the incident, Rog recalled the day quite well. "We heard that heavyset girl yelling, and then saw her dragging Digby to shore. He was covered in blood. Dawn was screaming and carrying on so that Ginny finally slapped her, and told her to take off her bathing cap and the damn earplugs. Being able to hear things quieted her down. I asked Digby how many fingers I was holding up, and Bob Van Camp was being showy and asked him the capital of Missouri. Digby just stared at us. Bob and I took him to the Loaf Lake Shower House to get him cleaned up. Once the blood was gone he seemed right as rain, or at least as right as Digby ever seemed."

For Digby, the day was no more than a mosaic of bits and pieces composed primarily of things he was later told rather than things he remembered. After the accident, the first thing he actually recalled was looking into a strange pair of eyes, and seeing the blood flow from both nostrils and mouth. The sight caused his eyes to widen. The creature did the same. That was when he realized he was looking into a mirror.

"He's fine," said Rog.

"Way to be a man," added Bob.

Digby had experienced not recognizing himself lots of times. In fact, his outsides rarely matched his insides. He never seemed to be the person in the mirror, but it had never happened to that degree. Maybe this was God's way of giving him a clean slate, or an altogether different one. Maybe now he could be who he'd always wanted to be, or who the school or the Church or the neighbors down the street had wanted him to be. Maybe now he could assemble those overlying "proper" pieces, and become something acceptable rather than whatever it was he'd been.

Digby didn't go back in the water that day to play Marco Polo or any of the other games the kids were playing. He spent the rest of the afternoon sitting at the picnic table, watching the adults get drunk.

"If you ask me, Dawn may have done him a favor," said Ginny Van Camp with a quick pat of her sausage curls. "As Digby was sitting there, after they cleaned him up that day, it looked to me as though that whack on the head might have helped push that misshapen skull of his into a more acceptable shape. You know, a big city doctor would charge a good amount of money for exactly the same thing, though he would probably go about doing it differently."

From that day onward, whenever Digby wiped the fog from the bathroom mirror he liked to imagine wiping himself away as well. One swipe and he'd be gone, quickly replaced by some new expectation or reflection. His game became a necessity. Often, he couldn't stand being himself and whatever and whoever that someone was. All he knew was that he couldn't be him any longer. He couldn't be that bundle of disappointment, that dismal heap of "less than." At those times, he'd imagine all his ugliness and foibles coming to the surface, ready to be wiped away with the brush of a magician's hand. In a swipe, he'd be transformed. He'd become more than just acceptable. He'd become the most beautiful, the most popular, the most desired, and the most wanted. "Most" joined "sorry" and "I" as yet another verbal pillar.

A favorite fantasy of his was to wrap a beach towel about his waist like a terrycloth sarong and parade up and down one of the six public docks on Loaf Lake, pretending to be various beauty pageant contestants. Life would be so much easier if he could only wear a crown and wield a scepter. Digby walked, turned, ran his tongue across his lips, and smiled hugely to imagined applause, flashbulbs, and general adoration. The piers were his catwalks. But his fantasies always had a tragic twist. To truly resonate, being superior required an ample dose of humility. His Roman Catholic upbringing made wanting anything a potentially sinful experience. As a result, winning required something more. This usually took the form of tragic sympathy.

In his beauty queen scenario, a broken heel would result in tragedy. With flailing arms and a squeal, he'd slip from the runway and plunge into the lake. The crowd would gasp. Some would rise from their seats. He'd struggle to break the surface, but his form-fitting evening gown would drag him down like a beaded albatross. In his playtime tragedy, he'd sink to the sandy bottom, lie for a moment in lifeless suspension, and imagine his luxurious hair in a swirling cloud about his face. He often wondered if, by doing so, he was attempting to recreate the quiet glory of his near death experience.

In his pretend pageant world, his arch rival, Miss Florida, would ignore his cries for help with an indifference that rendered her dream of making the world a better place by teaching religion to refugee orphans with polio suspicious at best. Pageant play absorbed him, taking him into a zone of oblivion that blinded him to the response his gender-bending behavior might have. By being himself while being someone else, he was unaware that he was once again an embarrassment to his family and his sex.

Though no one came right out and said anything, a boy screaming, "Help me Bert Parks! Miss Florida, please help! Dr. Joyce Brothers, I can't swim in this gown!" was bound to attract attention. Though frequently unseen, eyes in Running Falls often peered through parted curtains and gaps in sickly hedges, and sometimes even through binoculars. Since he was never directly confronted, Digby assumed his playtime behavior went unnoticed. He should have known better. People noticed, but no one knew quite what to say. However, they found more than ample words to discuss the matter when talking amongst themselves.

"He was strutting to and fro, wrapped up all fancy in a busy beach towel," offered Eli Thatch. "I was down a ways walking by the public landing with my metal detector. Someone found an engagement ring down around there a while back. Anyways, I was there minding my own business when I seen Digby Swank out the corner of my eye, prancing about. Not a minute later, I seen him stumble in the lake. Then he popped up sputtering and splashing and carrying on that his hair was caught on something, and his sash was looped around his neck. Well, everybody knows the water there ain't but shoulder deep, so I couldn't understand what the commotion was about. Still, after another couple sweeps with my detecting device, I turned to go over there. By that time he was walking to shore just like nothing had happened. That one has always been a queer duck if you ask me."

Digby's beauty pageant antics were not relegated to the waterfront. The lady-contest game could be effortlessly adapted to many venues. He could strut, pose, and die almost anywhere. One variation took place standing before his bedroom mirror. Here he'd pose with a lady-hair towel over his head, flipping his terrycloth mane side to side and tucking it behind an ear as he gazed into the looking glass.

Since his bedroom was too small for a proper catwalk or stage, he would pretend to be competing in a different category of the overall contest. Staring into his bedroom mirror, he made believe he was in a soundproof booth awaiting his turn for the final question. The air crackled with excitement. Scores from the interview portion often decided the winner. Suddenly, the sliding door of the booth would malfunction. Smoke would billow into the booth from the ceiling. What's happening? Oh my God! He'd sputter and cough. More smoke. The deadly fumes would fill the plexiglass chamber. Determined to perish with poise, he'd straighten his shoulders and lift his chin. Tears would cloud his eyes as he turned to the audience and waved. With mascara running down his cheeks, he'd stifle a cough, manage his biggest smile, and blow a kiss before collapsing to the floor. Henceforth the contest and title would be renamed in his/her honor.

The last time he partook in his "lady mirror" posing routine, he remembered the dog watching with a cocked eye from the foot of the bed. As usual, he was posing, pouting, smiling, and then just starting to panic and choke in the smoke-filled chamber when he heard the crunch of gravel outside. In the corner of the mirror, he saw his parents and the Van Camps watching him through the window. The bubble about his fantasy world exploded. When he turned, all five erupted into laughter. Johnny Van Camp was with them. His pageant composure vanished. He couldn't believe his parents were party to this ambush.

Thoughts pounded in his head. Why for God's sake had they chosen now to stop being ashamed of his girlish behavior? Was this a misguided lesson, a sort of last ditch shock treatment fueled by alcohol? By their laughter he could tell they'd all been drinking, all except Johnny, of course. Digby felt stunned, naked, guilty, betrayed, and most of all, in utter shock. Everything seemed shattered beyond repair, and the shrapnel from the blast would remain a part of him, covered in time perhaps, but still inside. Still able to cause a stab of pain or a spasm of shame.

To be safe, he'd have to live deeper beneath the silvery scars. Subcutaneous was not enough. He'd need another layer or two or three, or a thicker crust or a calcified shell. He wondered if he could ever go deep enough to really feel secure.

Bob slapped his knee and guffawed to recall that night. "There was Digby, turning this way and that, smiling like a real girl. It was the last thing you expected to see, but at the same time it made perfect sense. He was wackier than Paul Lynde. Even today, every once and a while when Ginny or I take a shower, one of us will come out with a towel on our head and give a certain look, and whenever we do, that night comes right back. We've cracked up over that for years."

Caught red-handed and limp-wristed, Digby had no excuse for his mirror posing or for the terrycloth towel atop his head. He may have even been wearing a pair of Lila's clip-on earrings. He usually did, but suddenly nothing was clear. The minutiae of the moment blistered and burned beside the catastrophic impact this would have upon his life. He had no explanation. Nothing to say. He never imagined a level of social ruin beyond hopeless, and yet he had found it. His wide-eyed gasp and "Oh," with a covering of his chest, and then a quick hand to the side of the terrycloth turban made it all so achingly clear.

He fled to the bathroom, the only room in the Swank house with a means of preventing free entry. Hooking the door, he pulled down his pants and squatted on the toilet. He cursed his situation. He'd been stupid and careless. He should've closed the curtains, anticipating humiliation and expecting betrayal. He was an idiot to feel secure, even on the playground of his own imagination. His thoughts were not to be trusted. He should always imagine that what he was doing was degrading and wrong and therefore, he should take proper precautions. Now it was too late. People didn't forget things like that. Now every time the Van Camps saw him, they'd recall that ridiculous nancy boy before the mirror. That's who he'd always be to them. A person never outlived a thing like that. Ever.

Digby fell asleep on the toilet that night. When his parents knocked on the door a couple of hours later, he awoke with a start. He could smell the stale beer, and didn't want to hear whatever it was they had to say. He ran through the thick of them to his room, and buried himself beneath the covers. In the morning, all three acted as though nothing had occurred.

The Van Camps were a different matter. Digby dreaded what Johnny would say in school, but thankfully there were still a few weeks left of summer vacation. Digby planned on living the remainder of his break like Anne Frank, hidden in a darkened room in the midst of a grim and threatening social climate. It seemed little more than the prolonging of the inevitable, but prolonging was certainly preferable to confronting.

Then out of nowhere, a miracle occurred. The Van Camp home, which had apparently been on the market for years, suddenly sold and the buyer wanted to move in as soon as possible.

Ginny swore with a chortle that the prompt sale was due to burying a St. Joseph statue upside down in their backyard. "We had tried most everything else, but not forty-eight hours after I shoveled the dirt on top of the earthly father of our Lord Jesus Christ, St. Joseph came through. Out of the blue, we got a call from Matt Reed Fickerson, that realtor who wears those awful hats, the one whose wife had the two hysterical pregnancies, or maybe it was just the one hysterical pregnancy with twins. Anyway, he called to say he had a client who wanted to make an offer."

Whatever the reason, the results were a blessing. Bob and Ginny and their bang-flipping son Johnny were out of the olive green two bedroom ranch home, and on their way to Duluth in mere weeks.

"I'll sure miss them," said Lila. All Swanks stood at the end of the drive and waved at the flat rectangular back of the big green moving van. Digby's parents and his siblings murmured regrets. Katie cried a bit, but her tears were more the result of being randomly sentimental than over any great sadness to see the Van Camps go. She thought Johnny was a brat.

Digby said nothing. He was still too afraid to assume anything. It wasn't until the van eventually disappeared from view that he let out an enormous sigh. Rog put a hand on his shoulder. "Let's go, son," Rog thought Digby was sad that his pal Johnny was moving. Inwardly, Digby smiled. The Van Camps were really gone. Maybe God had been saving His miracle and waiting to play His ace all along.

14 - Acceptance Moves In

But He had been holding a pair of aces. In only a few weeks' time, the Van Camp family was gone, and the Manns had moved in. What made this mere change of ownership so dramatic and miraculous was that Doug Mann quickly became Digby's best friend. Digby had never had one before, or at least never one that existed in time and space. He'd had dead friends and imaginary friends, friends who were ancient or things or animals, but never a genuine flesh and blood same generation and same species best friend. The experience changed him profoundly.

The boys connected from the first day. Doug rolled his eyes and pursed his lips in Digby's direction when Doug's father, Norbert Mann, shouted at the moving men to step it up because they were being paid by the hour. "God rewards the industrious," Mr. Mann had warned, prompting sneers from all three of the movers, who were more familiar with the rewards of leisurely work at an hourly wage.

In response, Digby had nodded towards Rog, who was sweeping the unpaved Swank driveway in a transparent effort to check out the new neighbors. "I can't just stand out there with my hands on my hips and a pair of binoculars around my neck," he had said to Lila when grabbing the broom earlier. Doug and Digby's eyes connected. Both understood that dads could be so embarrassing.

The following week, class began for both the parochial and public schools. Digby had just gotten home from Holy Martyrs, when the public school bus stopped at the end of the Mann drive. A ball of paper and an apple core hit Doug on the head as he came down the bus steps. Digby heard the laughter and the names the kids were yelling from the windows. He saw the look on Doug's face. Digby was familiar with that horrible feeling of shame and pain. He asked Doug if he wanted to play.

In no time, Doug and Digby proved to be kindred spirits in a world that seemed to be constantly and aggressively unlike them. Neither boy had seen himself reflected the way they were in one another. For the first time, each realized they were not a singular species, not the only one. Not a mutant. As a result, they both felt a little less like flamboyant unicorns. It made them aware that a larger unicorn herd must be out there somewhere. If there was Doug and there was Digby, then there must be others, even if they weren't sure quite sure what that other label meant. The connection they felt and the realization there must be a tribe changed them. They were not alone.

Less than a week after moving in, Doug and Digby were spending long afternoons together after school. Lila had finally allowed Digby to be home alone during that two-hour gap time, especially if he had a friend over. "But no roughhousing," she had warned. She knew as soon as she said it that she needn't worry, not about their roughhousing anyway. They amused themselves in other ways.

Their favorite pastime on most of those afternoons was making prank phone calls. In the era before caller ID, automatic call back, answering machines and voicemail, the field for pranking was fertile ground, and the boys were eager young plough men. They spent hours perfecting their phone shenanigans. Much of it was rather raunchy, since they were at the age when the existence and utterance of all things regarding genitalia and sex were terribly hilarious.

They'd call, and amidst snickers and snorts, ask for Mike Hunt or Hugh G. Rection or Buster Hymen. They'd call one taxidermist and ask how much it would cost to stuff a large beaver, then call another to ask how much they would charge to mount a forty pound sturgeon. They'd dial the Greyhound station and ask the cost of a ticket to Bangor. Another favorite was to go into a department store, call the service desk from one of the interior pay phones, and ask for Norma Stitz. They'd almost pee themselves to hear the page, "Attention shoppers, if there's a Norma Stitz in the store, could they please come to the service desk?"

Most of those on the receiving end were not amused.

"Yes, I was unfortunate enough to receive one of those disgusting and disturbing prank telephone calls. I was in the middle of doing laundry when I heard the phone ring. I ran all the way upstairs with my bad knees and breathing problems to answer. The caller asked if they were speaking to Lou Bass. When I replied "I'm sorry, there's no Lou Bass on this end," I heard laughter, and was then asked if that meant I sometimes chafed. Well, as a Christian woman who has experienced a good amount of digestive problems, you can be sure that didn't sit well with me. That filthy-minded humor is the sort of thing that happens when you take prayer out of the schools, and start teaching sex education."

During those hours of pranking when Lila was still bent over her steno pad at the office, no prank was too crass or crude.

Brrrng.

"Brace Hardware."

"Yes, I am looking for some black caulk."

"We have black caulk."

"Oh, that's great. And that caulk is for filling holes and crevices?"

"Ummm, yes. We have a large and small size."

"Great, would you mind holding a large black caulk for me at the front counter?"

If they'd managed to carry the prank this far, they'd inevitably start tittering. On the other end, there'd be a gasp or "Humphff," followed by an indignant click. Eventually they ran out of hardware stores in their area code. Dialing over seven numbers was unthinkable. Long distance calls would surely be noticed when the bill arrived. Bleary-eyed or not, Rog always noticed any extra charges.

Though predominantly crude, the spectrum of their pranking was somewhat broader. They did all the school kid standards:

"Is your refrigerator running? Better go catch it" and "Do you have Janitor in a Drum?/Prince Edward in a can? Better let him out." They also did prank calls that promised a delayed gotcha moment, like when they'd call a local restaurant and make dinner reservations. "I need a table for four, last name Knight, first name Tamara." If the reservation was taken, they'd snicker and imagine the staff awaiting the party at the specified time, waiting and waiting until someone at the restaurant would eventually look at the name and realize the joke. "Hey this reservation is for Tamara Knight!"

Though obnoxious, these small, anonymous acts of aggression also gave Doug and Digby a voice. Empowerment was a new and exciting thing for them. Both boys had been beaten down, silenced and stifled. Their worlds had made them fearful of speaking up. Now doing so was easier, especially since it wasn't face-to-face. For once, they were the ones doing the laughing. Together they seemed fearless, or at least much less fearful than either of them had been apart. Their pranks soon expanded beyond the telephone.

Doug and Digby did not typically practice their shenanigans on people they knew. Most of their trickery was done at random, with the butt of the joke usually being a stranger. They meant these people no harm. Those folks were just in the wrong place at the right time for Doug and Digby's amusement. Cruelty was something others did. Doug and Digby weren't technically being cruel, since no specific maliciousness was intended for those particular individuals. These patsies were a necessity, a tool, the means to an enjoyable end. The boys were only having fun, and it wouldn't be half as funny if no one suffered.

It was all a mad spin of destiny's wheel as to who was on the other side of the door when they snuck into local motels and ran through the halls flipping the Do Not Disturb signs to Please Clean Room. It was nothing more than rotten luck when it came to who had the maple syrup dribbled on their bike seat or the grape jelly smeared on their handlebars or the lunch bag of dog poop slipped through a mail slot.

Another favorite random prank the boys enjoyed took place

in a department or grocery store. For victims, they sought people who were alone and browsing in a specific aisle. The optimal patsy was shy, meek, and most importantly, someone who probably couldn't catch them if they ran.

Taking note of the chosen's attire and the area in which they were shopping, one of the boys would go a row or so over and crouch low. When all was ready, the other gave the go-ahead with a clearing of his throat. At this point the crouching member of the duo would shout, "Hey everybody, look at me! Here I am. I'm over here in the red sweater, looking at hairspray. Would you be my friend? I'm a lonely soul who needs love so badly. Oh please be my friend! Please, please be my friend."

Hearing this, other shoppers would immediately look up and gawk in annoyance, curiosity, or outright pity at the unsuspecting victim, who was of course the shopper in the red sweater looking at hairspray. Ordinarily, the person didn't immediately realize he or she was the supposed source of the needy plea. At such times there would always be a delicious light bulb moment. "Hey, I'm wearing a red sweater AND looking at the hairspray!"

Though Doug and Digby preyed upon the meek and the weak, it's still surprising they were never beaten up. In Running Falls, violence was an accepted form of social discourse, interaction, and resolution. In retrospect, Digby supposed they were spared because fighting them would've made their attacker seem more feminine. Girl fight! Girl fight! This theory didn't work for females, of course, but thankfully, no women kicked their asses. Most able-bodied local ladies would've had no problem doing so. Running Falls broads are a dangerous breed known to tuck razors in their hair, wield bargain bin stilettos, and show they mean business with an economy-size can of Aqua Net and a Zippo lighter.

As seasoned jokesters, the boys soon realized that they would also need a backup plan, just in case things didn't go well. So whenever things got threatening or they found themselves in a sticky situation, they would act retarded. They could think of no easier way to escape all forms of punishment. Even in Running Falls, beating up retarded kids was taboo, unless you were drunk or they made a homosexual pass at you or something. Mental retardation seemed like the ultimate Get Out of Jail Free card. Doug and Digby were very believable as disabled youngsters, and were not at all above exploiting this skill to escape censure and culpability.

Once, the boys rode the elevator up and down and down and up and between the floors in Running Falls' tallest building, the twelve-storied retiree residence, Coronation Towers. The Crown of the Running Falls Skyline! When the doors of the building's single elevator parted after a half hour of their antics, the boys were confronted by the fissure-faced manager, Flavio Slather. Mr. Slather stood akimbo with one shoe tapping testily. The mismatched pupils of his eyes made his glare all the more alarming. Spread out like a gray, wrinkled sheet on either side of Flavio was an elderly mob of disgruntled tenants. Rather than attempt an explanation or mumble an apology, Doug followed Digby's lead.

They cooed and drooled as they pawed at the pretty flashing numbers on the control panel. Several of the elderly exchanged looks. Slather bowed his greasy-haired head and backed away. The crowd parted, embarrassed they'd been so quick to anger when the cause of all the commotion had been two unfortunates. Smiling politely, they made a wide arc around the boys while gingerly entering the elevator. No one wanted to be exposed to a fit, get groped, or be party to any other socially unacceptable behavior commonly associated with the mentally challenged. Some folks continued to stare over their spectacles or above their newspapers as Digby and Doug crossed the lobby. For added effect, the boys continued to snort-laugh while going around and around in the revolving door leading outside. Everyone breathed a sigh of relief when the two finally moved onto the sidewalk.

"Yes, that is true. Sometimes the differently-challenged or inconceivably-abled do wander into the building without chaperones or proper guidance. However, we have tried to safeguard our residents from such mishaps by installing reflective glass on the outside windows, since those types often flee at their own reflection or become so mesmerized by the sight of it that they don't think to come inside. Unfortunately, if they do make it through the revolving doors and into our lobby, the ping and flash of the elevator seems to have an almost magnetic effect, and then we sometimes have problems," sighed Slather.

Sometimes, even being retarded wasn't enough, and the boys needed an alternative back-up plan. Doug and Digby's other option was called the Neptune Factor, conceived and christened in the desperate moments following a gag gone awry. The prank itself was nothing unusual. They'd done it several times. It was another brand of hijinks almost impossible today, given the nature of the cineplex and the multiplex, and the sad disappearance of the good old-fashioned movie palaces.

The two old theaters in town were magnificent. The decor of both the Dakota and the Carolina had the power to transport Digby from the plywood, cinder block and aluminum siding contours of Running Falls into some tastelessly opulent castle or brothel in a gaudy faraway land. This frippery extraordinaire was escapism of the highest order.

When they were being tricksters at the movies, they'd sit in the front row of the balcony. During the show, one or the other would take an eraser and stick a pin through it so only a bit more than the tip broke the surface, then they would drop it on some unsuspecting patron. The sharp prick would cause the movie-goer to jump or cry out at the most inopportune times: a death or sex scene, the naming of a killer, a sweeping panorama shot—any unnaturally quiet time would do. Their antics enlivened more than a few dry 1970s films. Digby and Doug even considered the act somewhat noble. They were giving people a bit more entertainment for their $2.50.

The most memorable execution of this bit of japery occurred during a matinee of The Neptune Factor at the Carolina Theater. They were there the first Saturday. Purchasing their tickets, popcorn, candy, and soda, they climbed the red carpeted stairs with the regal gold fleur de lis pattern, to their seats in the extremely rococo balcony. Scanning the audience below, they moved a few seats until they were above an unsuspecting teen couple. Doug and Digby exchanged genuine smirks. After the lights on the teardrop chandeliers dimmed, Digby pulled the pre-assembled eraser/pin from the pocket of his down vest. They'd found their mark, but timing was everything. For optimal effect, the intended victim needed to be fully immersed in the movie. Rash behavior could ruin it all. Patience was a virtue, even if their ends proved less than virtuous. They sat back, munched popcorn and waited.

The Neptune Factor was no classic, so plenty of segments could have benefitted from a good jolt. Eventually they chose an especially tedious scene with Yvette Mimieux and Walter Pidgeon. After exchanging a look, Doug and Digby did a quick security glance before moving into launch position. Aiming for her shoulder, they mouthed "bombs away" and released the eraser. At that very moment, the boy reached around the girl to snuggle or go "draping for a tit" or whatever. The eraser was a direct hit, pricking him squarely on the arm.

"Ouch, goddamn it, holy fuck!" he shouted, yanking his arm abruptly away and inadvertently smacking his girlfriend on the back of the head.

Unfortunately for him, domestic abuse had just begun to gain issue awareness among junior high females in Running Falls. Many women in town were physically abused. Some thought it was simply part of being a woman, and just another trickle down repercussion for the transgression of Eve. But those notions were changing. This newfangled idea that abuse was inappropriate and neither a right of ownership nor an aspect of love was revolutionary. Many of the younger women were becoming militant about standing up for themselves.

The girl turned toward him, and stared in disbelief before leaping from her seat. "Goddamn you, Jimmy! This is not acceptable! That'll be the last time you hit me, or I'll cut off your nuts," she hissed, tossing a jumbo Coke in his lap and storming up the aisle with a jingling of earrings and a jangling of bracelets. All heads that hadn't turned at his initial outcry did so at this point, movie goers whispering and shifting restlessly. Necks craned. It seemed as though even Walter Pidgeon and Yvette Mimieux stopped their mundane on-screen conversation to peer into the audience. Dumbstruck from the prick as well as her indignant response, Jimmy got his bearings, wiped the ice off his crotch, and charged up the aisle in pursuit. "Steph wait, Steph."

Moments later, the dejected beau returned alone. Evidently, Steph was having none of it. Fumbling for his seat in the dark, Jimmy inadvertently sat one place over from where he'd previously been sitting. Unfortunately, that was where the eraser/ pin had landed after poking him in the forearm. Plopping down in defeat, Jimmy got a solid prick on the butt, and leapt to his feet. "My ass. Goddamn it!" A stern looking gentleman several rows over turned and shushed him. He'd had quite enough of the disruptions from Row NN.

Jimmy reached down and found the eraser/pin, which had fallen to the floor after being briefly embedded in his butt. At this inopportune moment, Doug snickered. Digby saw the giggle start with a crinkling at the corner of his eyes. He knew it was coming and tried to shush him, but he was too late. Jimmy looked up. The boys gasped before covering their mouths in unison. Jimmy drew back and hurled the eraser towards them. To their dismay, Jimmy looked like he probably started smoking at the age of four, lost his virginity at eight, had a homemade tattoo at nine, and could break two buffoons into four with no problem.

"You little fuckers! I'll pulverize you," he shouted.

By this point, even the shusher was fully engaged in the drama. Jimmy stormed up the aisle. Doug screamed. Hearing this, several people turned back to the movie, thinking the high-pitched shriek had to be Yvette Mimieux. They were perplexed to see only Ernest Borgnine on screen.

Doug and Digby heard Jimmy's big, booted feet clomping up the plush balcony stairs two at a time. The boys needed to do something fast, confronted yet again with that eternal question:

hide or act retarded? This seemed to be one of those rare situations where they'd be beaten up even if they were retarded. They'd need something like stage 4 cancer to get away with this.

They crouched low, scrambling up the balcony rows and looking desperately for a place to hide. Circling around, they went out balcony entrance A, as Jimmy entered through entrance D. The overdone hallway of red flocked wallpaper, crested chairs, and gilded mirrors offered little in the way of camouflage. Wearing matching blue down vests, the two chubby boys had scant hope of blending into surroundings better suited for a sequined cape or feathered headdress. They were desperate. Digby stooped to muttering Hail Marys.

Luckily, Doug was no stranger to desperation; in fact, he functioned best in these situations. Digby suspected it was a skill honed by living in a crazy born-yet-again Christian home. With split-second timing, Doug leapt into action—or rather leapt, fell, frothed and rolled down two flights of balcony stairs. Thank goodness for the down vest and plush carpet! He was feigning an epileptic fit. Doug had witnessed several of Alvin Fong's episodes on the neighborhood playground. The only thing missing was that Alvin usually wet himself.

Hearing the ruckus, the blustery manager waddled from his office, chafing his inner thighs in haste. He hiked up his plaid pants, mopped his head, and with a worried glance asked, "What's the problem here? There wasn't glass in the ice again, was there?" His eyebrows lifted, then shifted from side to side like a drawbridge.

Even with his adrenaline pumping and all this craziness unfolding, Digby still recalled looking at Doug writhing on the floor, and thinking, "glass in the ice again!"

By now, several moviegoers had gathered in the lobby. Just then, an enormous woman in a crocheted poncho rushed from the ladies room with her arms raised in a panic. Her girth shifted right, and then left, and back again with such momentum that it continued for several cycles after she stopped running. As her poundage settled, she shrieked the obvious. "Oh my God, he's having a fit!"

"Are you a nurse?" asked the manager.

The woman shook her head. "No, but I watch a lot of medical shows."

The manager nodded, and took a step back. At least someone qualified was on the scene.

Digby assumed a look of competent concern. Imagining himself a missionary nurse, he crouched beside Doug. Turning to the onlookers, he spoke. "Sometimes fear or excitement brings on an episode. It's best to just keep him calm. I know how to deal with this." Inspired by a recent episode of Medical Center, which he hoped poncho lady hadn't seen, he used his finger to fish inside Doug's slobbery mouth, and anchor his tongue. Doug's "fit" was even more disturbing and believable, since his tongue was blackened by the box of licorice he'd eaten only moments before. Seeing this, the crowd looked more than willing to let Digby take charge. Everyone was curious, but no one wanted to get involved, especially if involvement entailed fingering Doug's unnaturally blackened orifice.

Jimmy took a step back before fading into the crowd and pushing through the front doors of the theater. He was still pissed, but evidently he wanted no part of this craziness. Whaling on a guy having a seizure was even less cool than beating up a retard. Seeing Jimmy turn and leave the scene, Doug's fit began to dissipate. "He's been spared," Digby said, looking heavenward and trying to muster up some tears. Turning to the patrons who hadn't already returned to the movie, he added, "praise His mercy."

Hearing that Doug's fit had passed, the manager sighed so heavily that an explosive fart erupted from him and faded into a long sputtering release. There was no mistaking the sound. The rrrrppppttt and then phhhhhhhhhhhh caused Doug to start laughing. Several onlookers made sour faces, but said nothing. Sometimes there are no suitable words. Even in Running Falls, passing gas loudly in public was frowned upon, unless of course it was part of a contest or the passer of gas was quick enough to ignite the fart with a lighter. If the latter happened, the passing of gas was considered a bon mot, and downright witty. Hoping to distance himself from the social crime scene, the rapidly reddening manager returned to his office, leaving a trail of stink in his wake.

Doug was on his feet seconds later, and a second after that, the boys fled. Leaving the theater, they tentatively looked around. They sighed to see that Jimmy wasn't lurking outside, having a smoke and waiting to kick their asses. They were on top of the world. Giddy with relief, energized by adventure and impressed once again by their resourcefulness, they joined hands, jumped up and down, and in a high pitched chorus of squeals, spun in a celebratory circle. Behaving unlike a boy was much more fun with a friend.

Though retardation and epilepsy got the boys out of more than a few predicaments, in some situations mimicking those afflictions simply didn't work. The obvious glitch was that neither of those strategies worked with people they knew, and it especially didn't work with their families.

The most memorable of these inexcusable situations happened over Christmas break. Doug and Digby were playing Deadly Darts in the garage. Deadly Darts was a game they created to vent some of their prepubescent aggressions. The boys drew an array of heads and bodies on several sheets of paper, and labeled them as people they loathed from Doug's public school, Digby's class, the faculty at Holy Martyrs, or around the neighborhood. Then they tacked the images one at a time to the dartboard, and took aim. They imagined it as a sort of voodoo. It was perverse and empowering.

They squealed with the thrill of imagining Marion Greenspoon dropping to her knees outside the Orange Julius at the mall with a mysterious fountain of blood issuing from her belly; giggled to consider Reese O'Reilly convulsing in pain outside the Sinclair gas station; and gasped to imagine the horror as Don Clapper's eye was suddenly and inexplicably poked in while he sat at home watching Kung Fu. The boys played Deadly Darts for hours on end. They loved playing God by doling out judgement, and anonymously inflicting debilitating punishments.

On that last afternoon, they'd been tossing darts so long that their arms were achy. Rather than simply deciding to do something else, they opted to shake things up by throwing the darts in a variety of ways: over their shoulders, with their eyes closed, with the opposite hand, in the midst of a swoon, holding a hand mirror, and almost any other way they could imagine.

During this freestyle session, one of Digby's under the leg shots missed the board entirely, and barreled into a shelf of odds and ends. The forcefully thrown dart struck a can of gray spray paint that wobbled before falling from the shelf. Upon hitting the cement floor, the dart dislodged from the can. Before they could scream "Caution: Contents under Pressure," a gray geyser spewed from the puncture hole. The spray was forceful enough to propel the can to roll forward –thwump thwump, thwump thwump. The revolutions increased in speed. As the can rolled towards them, Doug and Digby screamed, and attempted to cover themselves like modest coeds seen in revealing lingerie. The only door out of the garage was on the opposite side of the room, on the other side of the car.

"Oh my God! The car!"

Digby gasped and gasped again before gasping yet a third time. With trepidation, he saw that the paint shooting from the rolling aerosol can was also shooting a fountain of gray all along the side of the relatively new, for the Swanks anyway, red Buick. The now empty can slightly rocked to and fro before coming to a standstill.

In the aftermath, a deafening and utterly terrifying silence filled the air. It was the silence of death, a state not terribly hard to imagine, given the circumstances. Doug and Digby were frozen, paralyzed in their attempts to process the surreal chain of events that had just occurred. It was beyond bad, and beyond tragic. It was catastrophic. When the moment passed, Doug ran home without turning or saying a word. Digby couldn't blame him.

Given the circumstances, flight was a means of survival rather than an act of desertion. He would have been crazy to remain.

Digby wasn't so fortunate. Leaving the scene wasn't really an option. He had no easy out. He couldn't lie or deny knowledge of the incident. The same paint dripping from the car also coated his trousers and arms, and was even beneath his chin.

In his post-traumatic state, he attempted to wipe the paint off of the car with an oily rag, a rag soaked in turpentine, a dry rag, and finally, a wet, soapy rag. It was no use. If anything, the damning gray spots and streaks seemed to grow and multiply and darken. "It is just like sin on my soul," thought Digby with downcast eyes.

He considered blaming the incident on Doug. That's what friends were for. He could say Doug took some sort of pill given to him by a seventh grader from the public school, went insane, and graffitied the Buick. "He really scared me. I tried to stop him and in my struggle to protect our property, the paint got all over me. I was only trying to help." A lie of that magnitude wasn't beneath Digby, but he doubted the story would hold up under closer scrutiny. Even worse, if they did believe the story, his parents might forbid him to remain friends with Doug. That wouldn't be worth it. Without Doug in his life, Digby would be right back where he'd started, and being alone again was certainly nowhere he wanted to be.

Digby ran to the bathroom, and tried to scour the evidence from his skin. It was useless. He contemplated using the potato peeler or the cheese grater, but thought better of it. Clasping his hands and dropping to his knees, he made a silent petition to the heavens. Sure, he had all but turned his back on God, but he was really desperate. Technically, he was the one being a Christian. He was giving God a chance to redeem Himself after dicking him around with all that Pope nonsense. He owes me. Digby promised anything and everything. He swore chastity, piety, service work, and a heavily tithed allowance. He tried to have unshakeable faith, and imagine the hand of God reaching down with a scrub brush and Savior-strength cleanser to remove the paint. He squeezed his eyes tighter and prayed so hard, he almost shit himself. A minute or so later, he checked on the effectiveness of his foxhole prayers. The paint was still there. Thanks for nothing, God. Is divine intervention another special privilege reserved only for Italians?, he thought.

At a complete loss of what to do or say, Digby said and did nothing. Sometimes nothing can be done. Powerlessness sucked. Hopefully before anyone discovered the defacing, there'd be a sudden death in the immediate family, a house fire, nuclear war, or some catastrophe to make this mishap pale in comparison. "Oh please God, let The Apocalypse descend upon mankind and specifically upon Running Falls this afternoon," he prayed. It seemed unlikely, but he could always hope.

Behind the closed door of his bedroom, he curled into a fetal position on his bed with the dog at his feet, and awaited the inevitable. Hail Marys were said. Digby briefly imagined his own funeral, a small affair followed by a shameful burial. The cortege would probably only consist of the hearse. His parents would probably be no-shows. "After what he did to that car," they'd scoff. He doubted he'd even be buried on hallowed ground. Just leave his body at the dump. Doug would be forbidden to attend. Being mostly ignored in life made it easy to imagine being snubbed in death.

Later that afternoon, Lila called upstairs that she was heading to get her hair done. Digby heard a jingle as she lifted her keys from the dining room table, and then the methodical click of her heels as she crossed the linoleum. He winced to hear the opening of the door to the garage. There was a pause, and then a gasp so large, the back draft of it jiggled his bedroom door. Almost at once, Digby heard a muffled wail that trailed into a guttural moan, before swelling into a screech.

"DIGBY TIMOTHY SWANK!"

She'd noticed.

At this point, everything became a chaotic blur of red-faced shouting, curses, tears, shaken fists, and random threats of no allowance, no TV ever again, and "You're grounded until you're eighteen." Digby recalled hearing the words "reform school," as well as grandiose general pronouncements like "This is the worst thing that has ever happened to us or anyone we have ever known," and "It's all been leading up to this." All Digby could recall saying in his defense were some weak verbal side-steps, like "But I..." "I'm sorry..." and "I didn't mean to..."

Since he remembered so little beyond that initial torrent of anger, his punishment may well have been capable of causing a partial mental block, a minor concussion, or both. Surprisingly, he wasn't grounded. On the contrary, as a result of the mishap, he found himself virtually exiled.

The family drove that Buick for another decade without any attempt to touch up the damage, which would cost "an arm and a leg." If anyone mentioned the gray paint, and at some point most everyone did, either one or both of his parents exhaled dramatically, and scowled in his direction. That aspect of the punishment lasted for years. Inexplicably, it was even referred to time and again as "proof" that Digby was a bad driver.

Netty Mann, Doug's mother, had something to say about all this. Her opinion mirrored that of her husband, since as a reborn-yet-again Christian, she vowed to worship her husband as God's form on Earth. "We thought that car was a bit too flashy for the neighborhood, anyways. It was bright red. The very hue and shade of sin, and with children around! Those Swanks seemed like respectable folks, at least on the surface. But we didn't expect much of them, since at the end of the day they were still misguided idolaters who did not follow The True Word. To each his own, we suppose. My husband, Norbert, tells me that Catholics have their own special place in Hell, right beside livestock and the Jews and the Arabs."

Though he was certainly no paragon of Roman Catholicism, Digby still resented having his religious heritage besmirched. The Manns made no secret of their disdain for papists. Digby contented himself with knowing that the Manns would shit fishes and loaves, and maybe even a crown of thorns if they knew the

Van Camps had sold the house to them after burying a St. Joseph statue upside down in the backyard. He was always tempted to divulge the truth, but Digby would never intentionally do something to threaten his relationship with Doug. Besides, he never conversed with Doug's parents. No one did really. The Manns were people of few words, and most of those were quoted scripture with one finger raised to Heaven. You couldn't talk to that.

The actual event that most involved parties blamed for the break in Doug and Digby's friendship occurred not long after the incident in the garage. It was soon enough that Digby still had flecks of gray on his hands and cheek.

On the Saturday of the incident, Doug and Digby were downtown killing time prior to yet another matinee. In their boredom, they wandered into the Goodwill store. It was so stinky and depressing that even squalid seemed too flashy a word to describe it. The secondhand shop was one of those places where five dollars could practically buy a dining room set. The boys browsed through the books and records. Digby had a Do the Cha Cha LP with a racy cover in his hand when they drifted into the toys and games section.

Partial games were the rule here. Random dice, game cards, and colorful plastic chips lay discarded on the bent metal shelving units alongside the boxed remains of Don't Break The Ice with only one mallet, Tip It, Sorry!, a dented Chinese Checkers board, Ants in the Pants minus half the colony, Toss Across with a couple suspiciously stained bean bags, and Headache with a cracked Pop-O-Matic. They'd seen variations of all these many times, and were almost ready to turn around when something caught Digby's eye. Light gleamed off the plastic wrap as he saw, at the farthest end of the bottom shelf, a Ouija board still in the shrink-wrap. Better still, this "window to the other side" was a mere dollar and a half. Digby squealed. Doug saw the reason for the excitement, and shrieked. Both were tittering and aflutter as they headed the checkout line seconds later.

Unable to postpone the dark promise of the Ouija, the boys skipped the movie, and went back to Doug's house. They carefully concealed their "mystical portal to the beyond" in a grocery bag, along with a candle for atmosphere. The brown paper bag was a necessity. Their session had to be kept secret. As Bible-thumping fundamentalists, Doug's parents would not approve, to say the least. As it was, the Manns weren't thrilled to have their son socializing with someone outside of their fold, The Advent of the Seventh Day of Pentecostal Tribulations Church. They probably would've forbidden it, but Doug needed a friend.

Doug confused the Manns. He was never quite what they expected. He was mostly good and dutiful, but had a lingering sadness about him. That melancholia had begun to fade when they moved to Running Falls. Digby made him happy, and that pleased the Manns, at least as much as they registered pleasure. They'd prayed on it, and since they didn't receive a definite "No" from the Lord, they figured it must not rankle Him that much. They made allowances. A boy that age needed a playmate, and it was Digby or nothing. They would simply have to keep watch, and make sure this young papist wasn't a corruptive influence.

That afternoon, in the privacy of Doug's bedroom, the boys unwrapped the Ouija box and lit the candle. They began to summon the deceased. As adolescents with what some might term "the gay homosome," they first called on the spirit of Judy Garland. After keeping them waiting a good amount of time, the planchette weaved across the board. The message was indistinct. If it was Judy, she was having an off night. Both boys thought it was the other pushing the planchette around.

Digby considered asking to speak to Grandma Rose, but that would've been too revealing. He'd learned to keep painful things to himself. Doug knew nothing of her, and despite their closeness, Digby had no intention of telling him. His friendship with Doug wasn't about important things or painful things, or really anything other than fun and games. By that age, both boys had been betrayed by reality a bit too often to open up even to each other. It was the same reason Doug never discussed his scrapes and bruises, or his displaced shoulder. So instead of Grandma Rose, Digby suggested Abraham Lincoln. Nothing.

Marilyn Monroe. Nothing.

Diane Linkletter. Nothing.

Jim Croce. Nothing.

Shawn Schlummer, the boy who choked on the peanuts and Coke cocktail. Nothing.

Doug called on the spirit of Lazarus. When Digby asked Doug why he wanted to talk to someone from The Bible, Doug said that he always wondered what it would be like to be dead and have your Final Judgement, and then suddenly be pulled away from it all and wake up staring into the face of Jesus.

"He may have been in Purgatory," offered Digby.

Doug looked at him. "What's that?"

Digby couldn't believe he hadn't heard about this place. It was huge. "You know, it's the kind of in between place when your soul is in aveum."

"What sort of room?"

"No, in aveum. It means outside of time. You can be there for a thousand years, but a thousand years can be the blink of an eye, or the blink of an eye might be eternity. It all depends on atonement, and what prayers were being offered up for you and the number of votive candles in your parish and the money sent to missions and stuff like that. Hardly anyone goes straight to Heaven."

Doug paused a moment. "Well, we don't have any of that. We have Heaven and Hell."

Digby continued. "Well, and if Lazarus wasn't baptized, he might have even been in Limbo. That's where all the unbaptized folks go who don't know any better, like babies and non-Christians."

Doug shook his head. "We don't have that either."

Digby never figured that Purgatory and Limbo were just Catholic things. If the priests read The Bible, and Doug's parents were Bible thumpers who quoted the good book half the time they opened their mouths, then how could all this be so different? It made no sense. After all, it was the same book. Digby wondered if maybe Purgatory and Limbo were created for a reason. If you just had Heaven and Hell, things were very threatening, but either/or left little room for negotiation.

It seemed like Limbo was created to explain some things, and answer some simple questions and logistics regarding the hereafter.

The creation of Purgatory, however, seemed different. Purgatory created hope. Cynics might even say that having an in between place made it possible for the Church to bilk the living by holding their deceased loved ones hostage. Purgatory was a bargaining chip. Having parishioners pay off a relative's eternal debts, as well as their own, was not very Christian, but it was very Catholic.

Digby himself had often heard it said, "Offerings to the Church can take years off a loved one's time in Purgatory," which was followed by "Wouldn't you like to see them in God's arms?" Digby had seen charts with specific calculations of service rendered, and the subsequent time subtracted. He'd been given story problems in mathematics in which he'd had to calculate a penitent's period of atonement prior to entering the pearly gates. "For those of you who think arithmetic is not applicable in real life, take note," Sister had warned as she passed out the Purgatory math quiz. "And be sure to show your work."

Theology was strange and somewhat intriguing, but certainly not as thrilling as the spirit world. Turning back to the Ouija board, Doug once more called on the spirit of Lazarus.

After some thought, Digby could see the attraction of the Lazarus story. As he focused on the planchette and the lettered and numbered board beyond, he thought about sinking in the lake, and the sunlight through the surface, and feeling the spirit of Grandma Rose. He wondered if that was like what Lazarus had felt. Maybe that warmth and acceptance was the pure spiritual experience, and all the rest of it was just religious nonsense. Maybe he was a fool for turning his back on God when it had been the Church's lunacy all along. They were two very different things.

The planchette remained stationary. When it came to the

Ouija, Lazarus refused to rise. Perhaps he was in a better place, and didn't want to be disturbed yet again. Perhaps all the dead they'd tried to summon were in a better place.

After upwards of an hour, the boys got loopy. They couldn't stop giggling. Contrary to popular belief, attempting to contact those in the afterlife was proving to be hilarious. They eventually reasoned that no self-respecting spirit was going to take them seriously and permit a glimpse into the hereafter unless they curtailed their laughter. As a solution, they decided—actually Digby decided but Doug agreed—that whoever laughed from that point on had to remove an item of clothing.

It seemed like a good idea at the time. However, playing gay strip Ouija in the home of people who waved a Confederate flag, hung their coats and hats from an antler rack, and threatened to remove Doug from school after a teacher mentioned evolution, was not terribly wise. The boys, however, were in the moment. If anything, the element of danger made it all the more exciting. Nothing was quite as thrilling as that which was forbidden. Doing all this in the Mann house was beyond taboo.

As fate would have it, Digby had just stripped to his skivvies when they heard a creak. With surprised expressions and breathy gasps, the boys turned as Mr. Mann burst through the door.

Mr Mann recalled the day with shame in his voice. "I was just passing by in my own hallway, thinking on godly thoughts, when I heard a voice say, 'Come to us on this day from your place in the underworld.' I knew right then something was not right. But despite my fears, I sure as hell did not expect to find my son in nothing but his underpants alongside a half-naked Papist, calling on spirits in the candlelight. A man just doesn't expect something like that coming right under his own roof. Things don't get much more unholy than that."

Mr. Mann reacted in an oddly cartoonish manner, and did sort of a ya-ya-ya double-take. His jaw dropped, he began to quiver, and his eyes all but bugged out of his head and went ahooooga, ahooooga. Digby and Doug leapt to their feet just as his eyes settled back in their sockets. Mr. Mann had turned a bright shade of red by the time he managed to speak, "Did I hear right? Are you conjuring?"

Hearing the hubbub, Netty Mann rushed in behind her husband. Without turning, he snarled, "Get back to the kitchen, woman. This is none of your concern." At his reprimand, Mrs. Mann turned her gaze downward and with a whimpering "Yes sir," slithered away. She called her husband sir? Digby couldn't believe it. He half expected her to piddle on the floor, or roll to expose her belly. If Rog had dared to use that tone with Lila, who was basically a dutiful Irish-Catholic wife, he would've had a spatula shoved a good foot up his ass.

Mr. Mann had gone from red to eggplant. Sweat beaded his upper lip. Digby had heard that when they get reborn the second or third time, they get really crazy. Mr. Mann took a step forward, picked up the planchette, and threw it at Digby. Digby was too shocked to duck, and the plastic tool to the netherworld hit him squarely on the head. Digby was mostly surprised because Mr. Mann threw like a big girl, or like he and Doug did. Mr. Mann then slapped his son once, and then backhanded him, swung him around by the arm, and locked him in the bathroom. Digby stood wide-eyed. That is so not what Jesus would do, he thought. Now Digby squared off against Mr. Mann. The air crackled with the elemental clash of good vs. evil. Digby wasn't quite sure which of the two he represented; he only knew he wasn't the crazy one. He dressed quickly while Mr. Mann commenced quoting verse and casting out demons.

Mann raised his fist. "Don't never set foot back in this house again, you hear?"

Digby raced from the room. He wanted to say something smart and sassy like, "I am so tempted to come back and bask in your hospitality," but he fled in silence. Confrontation was not his style, not actual confrontation anyway. He confronted in his mind and behind people's backs all the time. Digby crossed the intersecting plastic runners dissecting the Mann living room, and ran out the side door.

He'd hoped the hoopla would all cool down, but it didn't. He hoped that he and Doug could meet on the sly, but they didn't. He couldn't imagine anything worse, and it was happening. He'd gone from the nothingness of Purgatory to Heaven. Losing what he had with Doug cast him straight into Hell. That year had been everything to him, and for it all to be over because of a somewhat innocent game of strip Ouija was just madness, especially when they had been having a religious conversation only a few moments before. Within a month, the Mann house was sold. The family moved away soon after.

For the duration of their stay, Doug was a prisoner. Digby would see him going to school and coming home, his head always down. One day, he was wearing a sling. That day Digby called him on the telephone. "Doug, it's me."

"Please don't..."

"But how are you?"

"Just, please..." Doug hung up.

When Digby called other times, Doug said he couldn't talk. Finally, Doug told him that the time would never be right. "Not on the phone. Not in person. Never."

Digby didn't know if Doug was being watched, or being honest. Maybe Doug had seen the face of the Devil. Maybe he'd awakened in Hell every day since the incident. Digby didn't know what to do, or whom he could possibly tell. The Gods in both their worlds seemed to think they deserved all this, anyway. Besides, he'd never want to make things any worse for his friend. He'd already done enough. Digby knew he was the latest excuse for the sling and the bruises and the downcast eyes. The situation wasn't fair, but no one seemed to care. If they did, they would have noticed.

"Digby and his playmate, Doug were all but joined at the hip," recalled Katie. "They were always giggling and up to something. They even had their own language. People said they acted like two little schoolgirls. The main thing was that for the time that weirdo family lived next door, Digby was happy. He'd always been so melancholy, especially since the death of Grandma Rose. It was nice to see him smile and not be such a loner. But it all ended as suddenly as it began."

Supposedly, the Mann's relocation was on account of work, but Digby knew better. He knew so many things that he could never tell anyone. He felt abandoned again, but the guilt he felt by causing such hardship for Doug was much worse than any loss. His love could do horrible things.

Running Falls wouldn't miss The Manns, but Digby would. Doug would be the best friend Digby had ever had. This time when the moving van drove away, Digby was the only Swank at the end of the drive. He watched from behind a sycamore tree as the truck disappeared. He ached so badly. It had all been a big prank gone terribly awry. Mea culpa. He beat his breast, and then the sides of his head. He only stopped when he felt too hollow to have any Devil left inside of him. He stared at the road. There was nothing there. He felt raw, as though he'd been peeled and a protective coat of laughter and camaraderie was gone.

Netty Mann wished to clarify the reasons for the family's relocation. "Well, it was nothing like what's been said. Our boy would never do anything like that. Truth was, Norbert got himself a job working out at the power plant back home, so we jumped at the chance to head back to Burnfield. That's where our home church was, and where our souls found Christ and where our people were from. We never really left it behind. It was still in our blood. The Manns weren't meant to roam too far from the homestead, and for good reason. The entrance to Heaven is a narrow passage. Hell isn't just down below; it's out there as well. Satan's realm stretches from city to suburbs, and all the way to Running Falls. The Lord had good reason to teach us that lesson, and we learned it the hard way. At least that's what Norbert tells me we learned, and how it was we learned it."

Digby ran to the graveyard and collapsed on the ground. He

lay on a grave and wished himself dead, crying until his eyes were red and swollen. Rolling onto his back, he looked up into the arching tree greenery and tried to feel himself floating down. The tree swayed and two swifts flew by, but he felt only stillness. For a while, things had been different. The loneliness had gone away, or was held at bay. Now it was back as before, only now he knew what he was missing. Now it was a lack, instead of an absence. He had no one but himself to blame. He had undermined his own salvation by his actions and his hope.

At some point that day, his sadness became a role. Digby could see himself apart from what he was being. Sadness had become a game of pretend, an activity he was doing rather than something he was feeling. Pain was always easier when he could see it that way.

The guilt over Doug took a bit longer to subside. He hated feeling responsible for Doug's pain. A couple of weeks later, he received a short letter that proved to be a tremendous relief. In it Doug wrote:

"Dear Digby,

How are you? I am fine. Hope you are well. Last year was the most fun I ever had. Things are better for me now. I am trying to think of all this as that place you called Purgatory. I am hoping that someday I will be moving on to something better. Maybe I will see you again, but even if I don't, I will never forget you.

Always,

Doug."

Digby looked at the envelope. There was no return address, but in the sender spot, Doug had written the name Hugh Janus. Digby smiled. The letter was the last that Digby ever heard from Doug.

In the aftermath, Digby started taking an interest in church again. He'd stop by Holy Martyrs sometimes after school, light a votive candle, kneel at the prie-dieu, and pray for his favorite soul in Purgatory. Digby would never forget his cohort, his soulmate, his fey partner-in-crime. Sometimes as he knelt in prayer, the memories of that year with Doug would make him smile. Sometimes they even made him laugh aloud, which was met with a clucking tongue or an unwavering glare by the afternoon zealots. Laughter was never appreciated in Holy Martyrs Church unless it was in direct response to a priest's corny joke, and even then a person typically gave only the slightest hint of a polite chuckle. Joy and frivolity were best left at the vestibule.

Kneeling before the votives, Digby often said a small prayer of appreciation. He was not quite sure if it was God's doing or not, but because of Doug, he felt that for a while he'd been known, accepted and understood. More importantly, for that year, Digby knew what it was like to give those things in return. Digby crossed himself, "Thank you for putting him in my path and showing me those things. I appreciated that."

15 - Scandal

As a result of the overzealousness of the Mann clan, Digby discovered a newfound appreciation for his own family. In no way is that meant to suggest that his family was perfect, normal, or even terribly easy to appreciate. The Swanks had all the typical, as well as some not-so-typical, forms of dysfunction combined with selective doses and overdoses of Catholicism to warp things. They may have been freaks, but they had the good sense to try to disguise the fact. So, despite their sometimes skewed interactions, the Swanks were what many would consider "within the spectrum of normalcy." Even when they periodically strayed outside those bounds, at least they aspired to being inside the line.

Most rules of modern etiquette were upheld by the Swanks, at least in theory. They usually said Please and Thank You. They held doors, respected most elders, and were desperately polite to house guests. Gender roles and rules certainly existed, but not to the point of lunacy. Lila didn't call Rog "sir" or bow her head in his presence.

Catholicism was mostly kept in its place. Since Grandma Swank's passing, the Bible was merely something to have on hand. The last time it was opened was to press autumnal leaves. The Swanks showed up for church every Sunday, and the kids got smacked if they laughed or misbehaved by "going limp" in the pew, which rarely happened, given the brevity of the service. Mass at Holy Martyrs was over in under forty-five minutes, unlike those all day affairs and rebirthings and in-the-spirit shenanigans Doug endured at The Advent of the Seventh Day of Pentecostal Tribulations Church.

Digby's newfound appreciation for his kin percolated outside his immediate family to include extended relatives, as well as their spouses. Not everyone in his family tree was quite so accepting. They had an aversion to anything scandalous, but the criteria of what constituted a scandal were fuzzy and arbitrary. An unwed pregnant cousin might not be an issue, but being seen at a Runnings Falls singles bar like Swallows might result in weeks of being ostracized. Getting drunk at a baby shower and peeing in the play pool might be seen as just having fun, or it might result in stony silences for a year. It was all completely subjective, and depended on who the offender and the offended were, along with when the incident happened, and what else was going on concurrently. The only rule was that when Catholic Church doctrine was invoked, the situation always worsened, and became all the more righteous. A religious scepter was a handy tool for stirring the pot.

When Grandpa Vint remarried a good five years after the death of Grandma Rose, there were squawks and chatter and several eggs laid in various branches of the family tree. Grandpa's new wife-to-be, Leonora, was a divorcee. In the eyes of Lila and her sister Lucy, she may as well have been a golden cow, a Jewess, or another man. It was wrong. The Church and the Pope and The Bible said so. In the eyes of the Lord, she was still a married woman. This, of course, was a convenient excuse to use for two women who simply did not want a new mother. Their brother, Lionel, didn't give a good goddamn, but then again he married a Methodist, ate meat every day of the year, and didn't bat an eye to skip his Sunday obligation. "Lionel never gave up a thing for Lent his entire life, unless you count being a good Catholic," sneered Lucy. Lionel was considered fallen.

Digby had nothing against Leonora. She was a tall and willowy "redhead" with a back as straight as an ironing board at an age when many of her peers were shuffling about like white-tufted question marks. Leonora was often described as a handsome woman. The description was certainly apt. It conveyed her slightly mannish air, and forthright manner. There was little fuss about her, and it was said that Leonora's toothy smile could light up a room. To flaunt her top quality dentures, Leonora typically curled back her lips when smiling, giving her a decidedly horsey quality. In pictures, she often looked as if she was tempted by a sugar cube just out of frame.

Leonora was of Hungarian descent. "Like the Gabors..." added Aunt Lucy with a cocked brow and a voice pregnant with meaning. Lucy had been to Europe the year before, so she claimed to know how that sort of woman could be. "In those parts of the world, they teach them the art of being a femme fatale right along with reading and writing." Lucy had toured the continent in five days with her son, Ted, after Uncle Willard had died. Mostly they got on a plane, took a long scenic bus ride that sometimes ended up at their American chain hotel, and sometimes circled around and headed back to the airport. That's how they saw Paris, Rome, Florence, Venice, Munich, Stockholm, Zurich, Brussels, and Madrid in less than a week. On the way over, they even stopped to refuel in Iceland. Given her breadth of experience, if there was one thing Aunt Lucy knew, it was Europe.

Lila shook her head, "But Leonora is Catholic."

"And also a divorcee, so I don't know just how Catholic you would consider her. Even Lucifer was once an angel."

When Aunt Lucy saw the engagement ring on "that dirty gold-digger's finger," she fainted straight into the Please Wait To Be Seated sign, which toppled the Buddha from the hostess desk at the Mandarin Room. Lionel stepped out of the way. Grandpa Vint tried to catch Lucy in the midst of her swoon, but that was difficult for an elderly gentleman with only one arm, and it had become downright impossible with the extra weight Lucy had put on after she went through "the change" and Uncle Willard's passing.

Lila didn't faint. Her sturdy build did not lend itself to constitutional delicacy. She looked to be more the sort of woman to hike up her skirts and give birth in a potato field, before clamping the babe to her bosom and promptly going back to pulling the plow. Lila's response to this unsettling news was the slow blink, and an almost audible grinding of her teeth. After the moment passed, she became so frosty that reportedly folks two booths on either side asked their waitress to please turn down the air conditioning. Some even swore a thin layer of ice formed on the serenity pond.

Lionel shook his father's hand, and said congratulations. The sisters saw that sort of well-wishing as a sign of betrayal, and a clear indication of how little he cared about this family. "There's a Methodist for you," Lucy whispered. She tapped her teacup furiously when Lionel agreed to be the best man.

The sisters had been blindsided by the news. Lila and Lucy had no idea that things were serious with Leonora and their father, or that their father was romantically involved at all. They'd heard him mention Leonora a couple times. Lila shared with Aunt Lucy that Grandpa Vint had blushed a bit when he commented on Leonora's tightly packed trash bags, which "were always filled to capacity." But aside from that, they'd thought little of his mentions of her, though later both recalled a slight discomfort when he'd mentioned her "flaming red hair." However, they had ignored it since it had been unpleasant.

"Let him socialize," each had thought with a shrug. They'd cajoled him into moving to Woodland Manor so he could meet people. The senior's residence purported to have all the modern conveniences, but what the sisters really wanted was for their father to socialize with men his own age.

They hoped he'd find a buddy for checkers or fishing, and bond with a band of cronies who would love nothing more than to chat about the good old days of ten-mile uphill walks both to and from school, five-cent bottles of milk, Great Wars, the decline of morals, today's gas prices, prunes, mashed bananas, and all things elderly. They certainly didn't anticipate that he would find a girlfriend. Knowing that their actions played a large part in this unpleasant development made the situation even worse. Both felt they had somehow been deceived by the Woodland Manor housing brochure, as well as the hospitality coordinator. Henceforth, both women spoke of Woodland Manor in hushed voices of utter disdain, as though their father had met Leonora at some key party hook-up at the senior's complex.

Leonora was Vint's neighbor across the hall.

"She got just what she wanted, another man to add to her collection."

Lila nodded. "If Dad would have found himself a nice Catholic widow, I would be the happiest woman in the world, except for you of course. But that Leonora woman is still married in the eyes of the Catholic Church."

"There's no question about it. She's already got herself a husband. That makes her a polygapuss, an adulteress. That's the way they are on The Continent, with the morals of an alley cat."

The scenario was all very skewed and dysfunctional. It was okay for the sisters to disapprove of Leonora on religious grounds, but not okay for Lila and Lucy to admit they were upset because their father wanted to get remarried. That would seem too juvenile, too selfish, and much too revealing. That could get messy and downright emotional, and no one wanted that. Why confront the real issue, when all that personal unpleasantness could be avoided with the invocation of dogma? We'd love for you to be happy and we'd love to give you our support, but the Church says no. Such high-buttoned moralizing was extremely Irish-Catholic.

"This is about the Church; it has absolutely nothing to do with us," said Aunt Lucy with a tug at the tight waistband of her skirt.

"The Pope does not approve..."

"And heaven forbid Saint Peter should need more consideration before opening the gates of Heaven to Dad."

"Yeah, and who is he going to go with on Judgement Day, mom or her?"

Aunt Lucy was not really a crackpot, but more of a Crock-Pot because she had a habit of stewing for quite some time. She used to have Uncle Willard as a sounding board, but then he'd up and had a heart attack sitting in the Impala at a stoplight. Folks said that cars honked for a good five minutes before anyone thought to get out and look. By then, he was already stiff as a frozen fish stick behind the wheel. His cigarette had burned right down to his fingers.

Though older, Lucy's son, Ted, did not fulfill that sounding board role. Ted had inherited his father's sense of humor, but neither his patience nor his understanding ears. Ted did not like to have things bounced off of him. He did not enjoy the "glorious" six magical days/five magnificent nights tour of The Continent with his mother. As part of his own passive-aggressive nature, he intentionally blurred all their sightseeing pictures. He told her it was probably the result of the X-ray machines at the airport. "Those things retard development," he'd said while looking his mother straight in the eye.

With Lila just as upset as her sister, the entire situation continued to mushroom and deteriorate and warp over the coming week. Finally, Aunt Lucy burst into Grandpa Vint's senior's studio apartment by using her pass key. Grandpa Vint was on the couch with Leonora. They were holding hands, and Gershwin was on the hi-fi. Only one of the three hooded bulbs on the tree light floor lamp was illuminated. It was shocking. Aunt Lucy gasped, and brought a gloved hand to her mouth.

"Serves you right, Nosey Parker," scolded Grandpa Vint.

Recovering from her shock, Aunt Lucy thrust out her chin—no simple task given that her chin typically nestled in a series of wider and larger chins. Aunt Lucy placed her hands on her hips, and gave her father the "her or me" ultimatum. Her spunky father stunned her anew when he slung his remaining arm over Leonora's shoulder, pursed his lips, and answered, "Her!"

Dumbfounded, Aunt Lucy backed out of the room step-by-step in time to Rhapsody in Blue. Too shaken to even sob, she opened and closed her mouth like a flabbergasted fish when she relayed the story to Lila. "Choosing her over me is a sin, or at least a trespass. Isn't it?" she asked while suckling the very air about her.

Given the circumstances, Digby wondered if Grandpa Vint truly felt that way. The one-armed former saxophonist could be terribly stubborn. Digby wouldn't be surprised if he choose his bride-to-be over his own daughter out of spite. His relatives did things like that all the time. Irish stubbornness and pride to the point of lunacy were in their blood. A gun pointing at one's own foot, or the phrase, "You're not the boss of me" would've been part of his mother's family crest, had they been well-heeled enough to have one. As it was, they were little more than lace-curtain Irish. Given that branch's bullheadedness, it made perfect sense to Digby that someone might get married and disown a daughter as a result of being in a snit, or simply to prove a point.

Lila learned from Lucy's example. She didn't want to cut ties with her father. That wasn't Christian, even when it was done for supposedly sound Catholic reasons. It was unseemly. Estranged was such a tawdry word. If her father wanted to jeopardize his place at the side of his true wife in Heaven, then so be it. Hers was not to judge. Oddly, Lila found great satisfaction by "not judging." It allowed her to silently, but clearly, proclaim her superiority.

Rather than ban her father and his bride-to-be from the Swank home, Lila swallowed her accusations of bigamy. With the pained sigh Digby knew so well, she soldiered on with upraised chin and a formula smile. Many said Lila compensated for the sordid state of affairs with Lucy by being nicer to Leonora than she had been to her own mother. Digby understood the confusion. His mother's conscious, rather than genuine politeness, could seem rather extreme. Some may have seen her behavior as artificial, but for the most part it was authentic, albeit with an agenda.

Sibling rivalry was also a factor in Lila's benevolence towards Leonora. Lila's brother, Lionel had been fine with the news. He'd served as best man at the nuptials, then went back to his scandalous Methodist life in Nashville. As for Lucy, she had been rubbing things in Lila's face for years. Lucy never failed to mention her travels here and there, or the fact that she had two mink coats and color-coordinated appliances, which included a dishwasher with the three different settings. Lucy even had two full shoe trees, and a standing manicure appointment.

Practically the whole county heard about Lucy having dimmer switches installed in every room of her house. Lila seethed to hear Lucy add, "Dimmer switches are essential for setting the mood, and that's so important for any serious hostess." Joan Kennedy had said the same thing in Family Circle magazine. Lucy was the chairwoman of the Ladies Committee at St. Boniface, and the monsignor there had dinner three times at her house. She had called Lila every time and asked, "What should I make for the monsignor?" Lila said meat loaf, pork chops, and shepherd's pie. Each time, Lucy had just laughed and said, "I can't serve His Grace that!" She served duck and veal and swordfish instead, and included vegetables that Lila had never even heard of.

Lucy was always the sister in the spotlight, and the one at the center of every holiday photo. Lila had no way of competing with all that. Until now. The truth was, Lila was thrilled to be her father's favorite daughter after so many years as second best. One rarely outgrows that desire.

Leonora was hardly the evil force Aunt Lucy purported her to be. She was slightly vain, but Digby didn't consider that a character defect. Vain people always looked better, or at least tended to be well-groomed and took greater care in putting themselves together. Digby even considered divorce glamorous. After all, everyone did it in Hollywood. The most inexplicable and misguided of all Aunt Lucy's accusations was her claim that Leonora was a gold-digger. If Leonora was looking to land a rich husband, she was either sadly misled or a serious underachiever. Grandfather Vint had little money to speak of, aside from his humble pension. Leonora was the one with the French provincial furniture and supposed five-figure divorce settlement.

Within a few weeks of the modest civil ceremony, people came around. Within two month's time, even Aunt Lucy resolved to make the best of it. The general consensus came to be that Leonora's most unappealing quality wasn't her divorcee status or her pride or materialism or horsey smile or even anything to do with her past or present behavior. Leonora's main handicap was her family—specifically her unhinged, unfiltered, and often present sister, Edna.

In a family that refrained from any hint of a scene or controversy, Aunt Edna wielded great power. Not because she was intelligent or rich or beautiful, but because she was borderline insane. Prone to wearing large bows in her cotton-candy hair and covering her mouth during coquettish bursts of laughter, sometimes she seemed to have the brain of a lusty, dim-witted adolescent, and sometimes that of an old racist nun. Edna wore dresses cut above the knee to display a spotted pair of emaciated legs that appeared to puddle at her thick ankles. Edna always thought men were being fresh with her. The Swank relations on both sides were terrified of her. The seventy-something unmarried sister of a divorcee rumored to use pool chalk as eyeshadow and wear two sets of false eyelashes at once is a real wild card.

After Grandpa's remarriage and the brouhaha it caused, Lila attempted to make peace by inviting Edna to gatherings in order to help Leonora feel more at ease. After Edna was invited to several family functions, she no longer considered an invitation necessary. If she discovered more than four or five people gathered in the Swank home for any reason, be it a bridge club, a simple evening with neighbors, or even a slumber party, Edna would show up under the guise of "just popping by."

Introducing Edna always put Lila in an awkward position. Her voice routinely stumbled throughout. "Edna this is Franklin, he works with Rog. Franklin, this is Edna, my stepmother's sister." The shame in Lila's eyes was apparent. My Stepmother's Sister sounded like the title of some lurid dime store paperback with the cover graphic of a .45 tucked in a black lace garter. Every time she said it, Lila felt she was announcing her father's questionable love life to the world.

Though introducing Edna could be awkward and perhaps unsavory, the real embarrassment was Edna herself. Whenever Edna stepped foot in the Swank home, the dog bounded to shove her nose in Edna's crotch and butt. Once she got a whiff, the dog could not be deterred. The usually obedient black lab had to be dragged by the collar to the basement, howling as she was being pulled away. Digby never discovered the fascination with Edna's private areas. Rather than be embarrassed by the dog's attachment, Edna either ignored it or drew attention to the impropriety by joking about it. "What's in there for you, huh? What's in there?" she'd tease, making everyone present deeply uncomfortable.

Edna was not the least bit shy around others. Without a moment's hesitation, she would cross one scrawny leg over another and spout the most outrageous and inappropriate things. She did not understand what was said to her in confidence, and what was not. She was like a drunken parrot in support hose. When she asked Lila's friend Jane how long she'd had her yeast infection, Jane was understandably mortified. Digby remembered being utterly perplexed at the time. Yeast? Edna asked Rosemary, the woman who lived down the block and never cleaned her gutters, where to buy her shade of hair color, adding, "I'm on a budget, and it certainly looks affordable."

Hearing their neighbor Trudy, who had moved into the Mann house, was going by train to see her sister, Edna tottered out the door and confronted Trudy in the yard. Raising a finger, Edna warned against sleeper cars. "Why, a girl could go to bed at night on one of those trains, and a man could part that curtain, sneak in, have his way with her, and she would be none the wiser until months later when the doctor told her she was pregnant."

"I think I'd notice a man having his way with me," replied Trudy with a puzzled look.

"Well, not everyone is a light sleeper."

Trudy thanked her for the advice, made an excuse, and went inside. Trudy recounted the conversation verbatim to a very embarrassed Lila the following day.

"She's on medication," was Lila's common explanation. When that excuse grew stale, Digby heard his mother use "brain tumor" and even "wet brain" as reasons for Edna's behavior.

Edna loved to talk about herself. At the drop of a hat, she would tell the story of how she was born in a horse trough, and that a chestnut mare had licked her clean. "Just like I was her own foal," she'd add. Edna claimed that she'd once seen The Virgin Mary hovering above the pumps at a Texaco gas station, "just like she was strung up on a wire," and later that night, a fire burned it to the ground. Edna swore that as a girl she'd had an ice skating goat, and that she won two dance marathons. Leonora would neither support or deny the stories. No one could blame her for not wanting to get involved. Edna also claimed that Al Capone had winked at her right on the street. This latter sort of memory would always prompt Edna to add some delusional comment like, "I'm just fortunate that I never lost my looks." One of these asides would always bring about a long and uncomfortable silence.

Her tales seemed endless. One of Edna's friends had once sneezed while tying his shoelaces, and supposedly whacked his nose so hard on his knee that it was shoved into his brain and he died. Therefore Edna would sometimes go into near hysterics whenever anyone with a cold was wearing shoes with laces. "When you have a cold, you should always wear slip-ons. If not, you might as well be wearing the suit you want to be buried in," she was known to say.

Edna also claimed that she could write two different letters at the same time, one with each hand, but when asked to demonstrate this unique skill, she could never quite perform the task because her "arthritis was acting up." She said she wrote her beau, Miles McDonald a letter every day when he went overseas during World War I. Edna sighed, "He went over to France to fight whoever it was that was causing all the problems there. It was so dangerous that he stopped writing me after a couple of months. He didn't die in action, I checked. After it was all over he and his best buddy from the service went off to Italy before coming home to the States. That was the last anyone heard." At this point if Leonora was present she would often change the subject.

Given the volumes Edna spoke, it's not surprising that every once and a while she could be rather profound, like the time she turned to Digby and said, "The people who want to protect you will hurt you most of all." The way she said it with her unfocused and penetrating gaze sent a chill down his spine; almost as though she was channeling something or someone. Digby didn't quite understand what she meant at first, but in the months and years to come, he understood exactly what she'd been talking about.

Rog summed up Edna's periodic wisdom best when he said, "Even a broken clock is right a couple times every day."

Obviously Edna was nuts. Usually Digby enjoyed this sort of behavior, in the same way he fancied the thought of a car losing control and crashing through the front window of their home. It was dangerous and thrilling, and typically he was an avid supporter of anything that even briefly lifted the shroud of monotony that draped and muffled their drab, lower middle-class world. However, there were exceptions.

Not counting Mrs. Kerg's senile "You have a pretty girlfriend" comment, Edna was the first person to mistake Digby for a girl. When he came down the stairs one Sunday for dinner, she eyed him head to toe, tugged at a ribbon in her pinkish cloud of hair, and right in front of everyone said, "And who is this chubby young lady?" She had brought Digby down with one dead-on shot, its accuracy making it particularly horrid. Nothing can cause greater embarrassment and pain than an unspoken truth finally spoken. In one second, his not-so secret shame had been ripped from him and thrown into the center of the room.

There was a long silent moment before all the adults laughed, but only with their mouths. Their eyes revealed volumes of underlying shame. The too hard laugher covered all the not-so-funny thoughts that had suddenly been laid bare. Digby knew what Aunt Edna was saying. Everyone in that room knew. It was something they'd avoided and talked around, but never about. Digby had no idea if it was an honest mistake, or if Edna was using her typically twisted means to comment on his effeminacy.

Ever since Digby could walk or talk or had the good fortune to stumble upon his mother's clip-on earrings, he knew that being feminine was bad. Being girly made him feel guilty, but in a different way. This shame was caused simply by being himself. He was born into it, like a personalized form of Original Sin. He thought time might numb him to the disgrace of this ongoing stigma, but Edna and his very red face made it clear that was not the case.

The morning after Edna's "mistake," Lila marched him down to the barbershop. Digby was being changed, disguised and, in effect, punished for the unspeakable crime of being himself. Edna had been right. The people who want to protect you can hurt you the most.

The downward spiral of the barber's pole outside Mr. Abernathy's door seemed apropos. A replay of yesterday wasn't about to happen anytime soon. When Digby climbed in the chair, Lila raised a finger to silence him. He wasn't going to say anything. He wore his barber's cape like a monastic robe, and with it came a vow of silence. The gauze neck band was his collar. Lila gave Mr. Abernathy a smile and said, "Give him a buzz cut," before taking a seat and flipping through a copy of Look magazine.

Mr. Abernathy assumed a flamenco dancer's pose, and clicked his scissors and thinning shears as if holding a pair of castanets. Mr. Abernathy always tried to be entertaining. Some thought he was a frustrated actor and some considered him a frustrated comic, but everyone agreed that he was frustrated in some way, given his behavior and the theatrical curl of his mustache. His brandishing of scissors that day was all for show. Seeing he wasn't going to get a laugh or even much of a response, he decided to get down to business. Mr. Abernathy pumped the rear pedal to raise the chair, and reached for his electric clippers. Digby gulped to hear the low hum. He closed his eyes and tried to think of it as a lullaby. A crew cut was social suicide in the 1970s, but given his less than popular status, social suicide for Digby was akin to desecrating a grave.

With a few broad strokes and several subsequent clips, it was all over. In a cloud of talcum powder and a grand arm gesture that said, "Behold," Mr. Abernathy spun the chair around while simultaneously yanking the cape away. Lila looked up and offered a smile which had more to do with reading in Look about Liz and Dick getting back together than it did with Digby's new haircut. "They are one of the great love stories, just like Cleopatra and Marc Antony," she sighed.

Digby looked this way and that in the mirror while Mr. Abernathy swept his shoulders with a tiny broom. He offered a hand mirror so Digby could have a rear view, and spun him fully around for Lila's benefit. The crew cut was different, but it did little good. The issue was much larger than his no-longer luxurious hair. The crew cut enhanced his cheekbones and full lips, which made him look more like a chubby ingenue than any sailor Digby had ever seen. Regrettably, the bristle cut also accentuated his grossly misshapen head.

Lila made sure Digby got a follow-up crew cut from Mr.

Abernathy before the next major family gathering. She needn't have bothered. Digby could have worn a pineapple skirt and espadrilles, and still not been the focus of Edna's unsolicited attentions that holiday.

16 – A Grim Feast

Despite all the pressures and frustrations that befell her as the Swank matriarch, Lila tried in her heart to do good. Presumedly, she had much to be grateful for. Not to share in that bounty was a sign of avarice, and therefore, a transgression. Lila genuinely enjoyed helping others. It made her feel like she didn't need to be told she was deserving. When she did good things, the truth of her worthiness came from within. Though being a host family for Catholic Charities had been a horrible experience, helping others was still a priority to her.

The solution was offering reasonable and selective assistance to others. Generosity in deed as well as spirit was the right thing to do. In addition to making her feel good, it helped atone for some of her former occasions of sin: the malefactions, the misdeeds, and trespasses she'd rather not recall. It could all be very tricky. Sometimes those sins and blatant acts of human imperfection were done unknowingly, picked up along life's path like cockleburs or gum on a Christian's sandal. Obliviousness made them no less sinful.

Lila's call to generosity and bigheartedness was intermittent throughout the year, but that yearning began a steady and consistent ascension around the holidays. It was the season of giving, and a time for shows of brotherly love. Alongside the forty days of Lent leading up to Easter, the period between Thanksgiving and New Year's was the time of year for true Christians to shine, or at least polish things up a bit. Although Lila's attempts at being a Good Samaritan had been undermined time and again, she continued to persevere with the childlike hope that things would be different, and would work out splendidly.

That was certainly the case the year she invited Susie for Thanksgiving dinner. Susie worked with Lila at the office. Hearing the church bells peal down the street, Lila stopped her typing, turned to Susie, and asked her to join the Swanks for their holiday dinner. It was a sweet and hospitable gesture, but one that made many wonder just what she'd been thinking. Granted, she had a lot on her mind, what with the ongoing Swank money woes and Rog and his drinking, and Katie starting to date and Maynard's poor school grades. Lila also worried about her thinning hair, and felt guilty that she had impulsively spent some of the Swank emergency fund on two wigs, The Frosted Gala and Autumnal Sensation. Less than a week after her purchase, she chanced upon Digby modeling the latter in her bedroom.

Being overwhelmed and exhausted, she sometimes didn't see things too clearly. Less than a week after happening upon Digby in Autumnal Sensation, she told him they would be having Susie over for Thanksgiving. Hearing the news, Digby's eyes widened. He'd met Susie, and was shocked that his mother would be foolish enough to invite a shy albino to any function attended by Aunt Edna. And since it was Thanksgiving, Edna would definitely be present.

"We had a real nice girl temping with us. Susie was just a gem, like a friendly white pearl. She had come to Running Falls all the way from Lincoln, Nebraska," explained Lila. "With no family in town, the poor thing didn't have anywhere to go on Thanksgiving Day. It didn't seem right for her to be sitting home all alone. I wanted to do the right thing, so I told her to come over and wrote down our address then and there. She accepted, and gave me a big smile. Then, just as I was leaving to head to the break room, I remembered Edna."

That blustery Thanksgiving Day, Susie showed up with rosy cheeks and a pumpkin pie. When the redness faded, Digby was amazed. Susie was so white and unlined, she almost seemed to be drawn on a sheet of plain stationary. She was an ethereal snowflake, with fake blue contact lenses and a navy blue sweater. Susie was the unassuming type, but it took little effort for an albino to draw attention when perched upon the Swank's busy patterned couch. The poor girl was promptly scrutinized by several tactfully gawking relatives, as though a unicorn in a blue jumper had wandered into the room.

Oddly, the single exception to all the staring was Edna. She was preoccupied with shooing the dog from beneath the hang of her skirt while prattling on about a building north of downtown that was being torn down. "It was a brothel. No decent woman would even cast her eyes upon the place." Edna was in a state because Grandpa Vint had driven her and Leonora past the demolition site on the way over. "Imagine treating your wife and her sister that way," she crowed at Digby abruptly. "You can't imagine it can you? That is because it is unthinkable!" Fearing another sting from Edna's castrating tongue, Digby nodded as boyishly as possible and ran a hand over his reassuring crewcut bristle. He was baffled by her rage, but grateful that her venom was directed elsewhere. To Edna, the mere rubble of such an establishment could shame a decent woman.

Despite her show of being scandalized, Edna's foothold on decency was nary a toehold. Though this phrase is meant to convey precariousness, in truth Edna had toenails as long as a brown-throated sloth. Digby had seen her in sandals, and once even heard the clicking as she walked barefoot across the linoleum of their kitchen floor. As to her toehold on decency, Digby had overheard Rog and Lila whispering phrases like "slow dancing with a married man" and "cocktail lounge," which were accompanied by a clicking tongue, pursed lips, or a lifted brow. When pressed for details, his parents kept silent. "She did some running around in her day," was the most they would say.

That Thanksgiving Day when the doorbell rang, the dog raised her head from Edna's crotch and barked a single time before burying her snout back between Edna's thighs. More people arrived. Voices and laughter echoed down the hallway. It was Aunt Lucy and Cousin Ted. She'd settled matters with her father and Leonora. All that unpleasantness was now coated with a thick lilting layer of Irish civility. Tom and Maynard took their coats. "That's real mink," said Lucy, handing her wrap to Tom.

Maynard rolled his eyes when Cousin Ted said, "Thanks my good man," and tipped him. Cousin Ted was quite the card. "The joker of the deck," as he liked to say. Cousin Ted had a reputation among the relatives for his sense of humor, the bathroom of his bachelor apartment being a perfect showcase for his wit. Ted had a roll of toilet paper that looked like fake money. It hung on a talking dispenser that said wacky things like "This stuff doesn't grow on trees ya know," "P-U!" and "Leave some for the rest of us!" As an added accent to the décor, Ted also had a clear toilet seat with coins suspended inside the Lucite. "That's where all our money goes, right down the crapper," he liked to guffaw.

A moment later Katie's boyfriend, Wes, arrived with a sparse and slightly drooping bouquet. This was another first, and runner-up for insane invitation of the day. Katie had never invited a beau home, much less on a holiday. Wes's anxious-to-please attitude only added fuel to the already flammable contents of the Swank celebration. When Wes came in, Tom did his corny act of pretending to be deaf. With a shake of his head and an arm on Tom's shoulder, Maynard told Wes that this strain of deafness was hereditary. "Be sure and speak really loud when talking to our parents."

A moment later, Digby heard them laughing when Wes shouted, "So nice to finally meet you," to Rog, who smiled in a good natured way. He was already buzzed. When Wes saw Katie, he walked up to her and kissed her on the mouth. Lila saw it, blinked slowly, and shook her head as though clearing the screen of an Etch A Sketch. Now was not the time. She was a hostess overwhelmed. Her lipstick was already caking at the sides of her mouth from her ultra-wide smile. She straightened the line of her Frosted Gala wig, and took a deep sigh.

Somehow amidst the entire fracas, Aunt Edna was allowed to plop down on the couch beside Susie. Crossing one bony leg over the other, she turned and extended a hand. "Hello, I'm Edna."

"I'm Susie. Very pleased to meet you, Edna."

"Isn't this nice?" Edna leaned back and eyed Susie more closely while attempting to keep the dog at bay with her free hand. "Do you happen to have a brother or cousin named Ross?"

Susie shook her head. "No, I don't."

"Really? Now I find that odd. I used to know a man named Ross something or other. He wasn't a Catholic, but he could have been your twin."

"Well, I'm not Catholic either."

Edna gasped, and bent closer with a conspiratorial giggle. "Oh really? How exotic. What's it like?"

"What do you mean?"

"You know, not being Catholic."

"I don't know, I've never not been anything else," uttered Susie with an uncomfortable slurp of cider.

"I see. Well, being Catholic is what you would expect, or at least it's what I've always expected." With a smile, Edna reached for a deviled egg before adding, "And you know, being non-Catholics, you could very well be related to that Ross." Edna's sense of the world and its demographics were a bit askew. For the past few decades, the Church had been her social hub, so most everyone she knew, met, and even gossiped about without actually knowing, was a Roman Catholic. "This young man, Ross had your coloring. That pale skin. Why you're white as a geisha. You're not one of those Oriental hostesses are you?"

Susie blushed. "No, I'm an albino."

"Well, as I said, I can't recall that pale young man's last name, but his first name was Ross. Very nice for a non-Catholic too, not as much debauchery as you might expect."

Susie shook her head and blanched, which made her vascular system almost visible from across the room. Witnessing the events as they unfolded, Digby was surprised to see that albinos can indeed grow paler. He imagined it possible only in extreme circumstances like hypothermia, severe blood loss, or conversing with Aunt Edna. "No, I mean...."

Edna giggled and placed a hand on Susie's arm. "How silly of me, I didn't know what you meant at first. I think he was an American. That's right, he was from Michigan. I'm not sure about his people."

Seeing the twosome on the couch, Lila crossed the room nervously, her smile now twitching at the edges. Those muscles were becoming very strained. Her wig wasn't the only thing that was frosted. Once they were within earshot, Lila overheard Edna say, "You must never get out in the sun, and it's a good thing you don't, you would burn like a fornicating pagan in Hell." Mortified, Lila snatched the hors d'oeuvres tray from Katie, and leapt into action, "Crackers?"

"So is this Albinoland where you're from, is it a part of Europe up by Sweden?"

Susie looked at Lila and smiled stiffly.

"Maynard, come get the dog," called Mrs. Swank.

Maynard yanked the whimpering pup from Edna's crotch, and dragged her by the collar toward the basement.

"Boy, that dog sure loves you," laughed Lila.

Maynard snickered. "Well, she loves…"

His comment was cut short by the combination of his mother's slow blink and her frightening frozen smile. If she'd have upped the intensity a mere notch, he'd have burst into flames on the spot.

Edna took a summer sausage on a Ritz, and three cheddar cubes. Cellophane-adorned toothpicks were the defining detail of special occasions in the Swank household. "Susie and I were just talking."

Noticing the desperation in Susie's fake-blue eyes, Lila asked her to come meet Ted. "He's hilarious," smiled Lila.

For reasons unknown, Lila actually thought they would be a good match. Ted was the most eligible bachelor on her side of the family, which actually said more about the lack of available men in her family tree than it did about Ted. He was a thirty-something unmarried city worker with a good pension. The phrase was used so consistently to describe him, that "with a good pension" could have well been his surname.

Susie seemed eager to meet him, though Digby suspected her eagerness actually masked an understandable desperation to flee Edna. "How-dee-do," said Ted, shaking Susie's hand so vigorously he appeared to be pumping water. Later he told Maynard that her hand felt just like a sweaty tube sock full of Jell-O. "No bones, and slimy."

Ted liked spunky women with dirt beneath their nails. "Manly women," was how Aunt Lucy often referred to Ted's firm-footed and broad-shouldered dating pool. "I'm glad he dates, but he has the oddest taste. Why, one of the girls he brought home had a mustache as thick as your Uncle Sherman's, and another cracked her knuckles and picked her teeth all through dinner. To each his own, I suppose. Still, it's a pity. I'm not just saying this because he's my son, but he could have almost any young lady he wanted with his sense of humor and a pension like that."

Having no facial hair to speak of and fetchingly buffed fingernails, Susie stood little chance of charming Cousin Ted. Nevertheless, Lila tried to fan the flames of romance by seating Ted and Susie beside one another at dinner. The arrangement was ill conceived. Susie was left-handed. For all practical purposes, she should have been seated on an end if she didn't want to spend the meal bumping elbows.

With a bit of beet juice dribbling down her chin, Aunt Edna fingered one wiry pigtail, leaned across the table, and cocked her head toward Ted and Susie. "Hey Leonora, what do you think? I doubt he'll want to be with her. If there were white sheets on the bed, he'd never find her." The tasteless comment was a prime example of Edna's tendency to go from prude to crude in a heartbeat.

Leonora shushed her, but the concept was lost on Edna, who when shushed would usually respond with, "I was just saying that…"

Susie left almost immediately after dessert. Actually, during dessert. She got up from the table and carried her plate with a slice of pumpkin pie to the door, eating it in large forkfuls as she walked. She swallowed the final mouthful as she was pulling on her coat. "I have to get home and call my folks and wish them a happy Thanksgiving, or they'll never forgive me. Thanks for such a memorable day."

It wasn't terribly clever or believable in the least, but Digby could hardly blame her. Flight seemed a natural response. He imagined her scuttling into the first open liquor store and buying a jug of wine before running home, bolting the door behind her, and unscrewing the cap for a long swig. Holidays with the Swank family often made folks appreciate their solitude, and even embrace loneliness.

The other casualty that Thanksgiving was Wes. When Lila was bringing the dessert plates back and forth from the kitchen, Wes kept rising and sitting and rising and sitting each time she approached and left the table. Cute and somewhat gallant at first, it rapidly began to grate on everyone's nerves. Finally, Maynard slipped his piece of pumpkin pie onto Wes's chair when he rose for the umpteenth time. Just as he was about to sit, Katie saw the pie and reached to snatch it away. She was too late. Wes sat directly on her hand. Katie screamed. Wes screamed. Katie yanked her hand away and Wes bolted upright, bumping the table and tipping over more than one glass of wine. Edna screamed when a glass of merlot landed squarely in her lap.

"What is that boy's problem?" she screeched.

Maynard and Tom burst out laughing. Katie ended up with two broken fingers, and had to retake typing class the next year since she could not take the final. Sister Helen gave the same test every year, which consisted of typing line after line of O's and X's and semi-colons, creating the perfect face of Our Savior at the finish. "One blemish on the complexion of Christ, and you fail," Sister Helen warned with a stern look over her bifocals.

After breaking Katie's fingers, poor Wes excused himself to go to the bathroom and didn't come back. Those in attendance heard the toilet flush, and then footsteps. They heard the door to the front closet open and close, then the whoosh of the larger front door open before straining to hear it lightly click shut. Wes had left without saying a word.

"Thanks for ruining my entire life," cried Katie as she heard him leave. It was hard to gauge how upset she was over Wes, since she was already crying from her broken fingers. Wes never visited the Swank home again. Katie did not have another boyfriend for over two years, and she still hears a slight clicking when she bends those two fingers.

17 - Public School Boy

Swank family gatherings were rarely joyous or even pleasant occasions for Digby. He viewed them with dreaded resignation. Even the excitement of his birthday was typically marred by underlying anxiety. He enjoyed receiving gifts and eating cake, but as the center of attention, he often felt like he was wearing a bull's-eye. The thought was especially unsettling for someone with a history of being an easy target. The presents, the cake, and the serving of his favorite meal sometimes seemed compensation for whatever embarrassments he was expected to endure. That was how it had always been. Only one childhood birthday broke the mold, and that was his surprise eleventh.

In typical surprise party situations, the guest of honor is led somewhere under false pretenses. Upon his arrival, friends, family and others shout "Surprise," which ideally stuns the unsuspecting guest of honor. Hopefully, he looks presentable and wasn't bad-mouthing one of hidden guests. Often, the duped honoree is brought to tears by the thoughtfulness. Digby's surprise party was different. Instead of Digby, his parents were the ones taken off guard. They were not reduced to tears of gratitude.

That year had been difficult for Digby. Early that spring, the family dog died after darting in front of a car to bite its tires. Digby saw it all. He heard the thud and the yelp, and saw the dog's staggering daze before it simply stiffened and fell. It was a horrible series of images, more like a gruesome filmstrip than reality. The only thing missing was the beep between frames.

Katie took Digby back in the house, and tried to cheer him up. Though she was several years his senior and typically frowned to consider playing with him, she asked if he wanted to play Mary, Queen of the May. That had worked in the past. The game was fashioned after the slightly pagan parochial school pageant and parade honoring The Virgin Mary. Katie said they could use one of mom's wigs and a bed sheet as a garment. Katie said he could hold the highest honor, presenting the virgin's flowered crown upon the rocking chair cushion. Five or even three years ago, the prospect would have thrilled Digby, but not anymore. Though cross-dressing games were tolerated if they involved the Church, he'd grown decidedly more guarded of that part of himself.

After the grim experience of seeing the dog die, he simply wanted to be alone. He remembered the sadness he'd felt in the aftermath of Doug's moving away, and how being aware of his sorrow had made it a separate thing. With the dog's death, he did something similar. He gazed at his reflection in the bathroom mirror and examined his bereavement. He grew conscious of it as a thing. This is me grieving. This is grief I see in the mirror. It has watery eyes and skin with splotches of red, and a blubbery mouth. Its shoulders sometimes shake. The grief is in the mirror, I am turning away from the mirror and therefore I am turning away from grief. I am no longer grieving. It is not a part of me. Now I am merely sad. Sadness passes much more quickly. Sadness is experiencing a cloud; grief is being overcast. By the time he left the bathroom, he felt much better.

Digby had made pain an imaginary game for over half his life. When Grandma Swank would wield the rosary, he imagined himself as Jesus, and she was a Roman soldier in a housedress. That was only one example. Removing himself from pain by whatever means necessary seemed natural to him.

Dealing with unpleasant emotions was not a Swank strong suit. In the case of the dead dog, the family worked through their grief by walking around it. After a day of not talking about anything, the entire clan consumed a gluttonous dinner with two entrees and two desserts, and the next day they adopted a new puppy. They went to Animal Cruelty. The barking in the cavernous kennel quickly gave Rog a headache, so they chose a mostly schnauzer puppy in one of the cages nearest the door. Rog went to the car while Lila filled out the paperwork. In less than twenty-four hours, it was as if their previous dog had never existed.

Replaced and quickly forgotten, the dog's death was nevertheless not the primary reason for Digby's difficult year. The most stressful change in his life at that time was undoubtedly having to change schools mid-term. Rog was starting to slip at work after years of drinking, or maybe given the fiscal concerns at the company, the higher-ups had just started to notice or care about his slippage. For years he'd managed to keep all the pieces in place, but heavy drinkers are rarely capable of keeping the plates spinning for long.

He was "called upstairs," censured and put on probation. "Perilous probation," they assured, though Rog was too nervous and afraid to ask just what perilous probation might mean. It was very simple. It meant last chance. He came home and cried at the kitchen table with the yellow pieces of paper spread out in triplicate before him. Digby lay on the living room carpet just around the corner and listened to the mumblings of his parents. Rog slid forward and buried his head in the crook of his arm. Lila patted his forearm and picked up the yellow sheets of paper. Finally she said, "They want you to sign at the bottom."

That night, the entire family prayed while kneeling on the living room floor. None of the Swank offspring except for Digby knew quite why they were praying, but the apparent gravity of whatever was going on prevented them from questioning or complaining.

Lila was beside herself, but since that was where she often stood, she knew there was nothing to be gained by panic. The situation called for assessment and action. Prayer was a good start, but that final Amen signaled a time for more practical measures. God helped those who helped themselves.

They had no savings to speak of. Lila cursed her most recent lapse in frugality. Her wigs sat on their styrofoam heads, and moved farther and farther back in her closet as though huddling in shame. They had become symbols of indulgence, something the Swanks could no longer afford. Lucy had some money set aside, but Lila could never go to her.

Proactive steps had to be taken regarding finances. The first order of business was budgeting, and a plan to tighten the already cinched family belt. The next morning when Digby went out the back door on the way to school, he noticed a stack of beer cases alongside the garbage cans. He'd seen the bottles there before. In the past, it had always meant no more drinking for now. It was always "just until things straighten themselves out."

As a budgetary consideration, the "value" of a Catholic education no longer seemed quite so valuable, and Digby was promptly taken from Holy Martyrs and enrolled in public school. Truthfully, Digby had never understood why his Catholic school education had been valued in the first place.

His parents had been paying good money for his parochial school tuition, and the cost necessitated payment in monthly installments. Every month on the final day the bill was due, Digby had to hand deliver the check to the main office. It was always too late to be mailed. The three ladies in the office would often exchange a look or make some remark when he brought in the envelope marked Payment. They thought they were being clever, and would say things like "We're going to send your folks a calendar next year." or "Let's see, check for the Swanks. Due on the first of the month, received on the fifth." They were so snide and superior acting. Digby knew what they were really saying, and he hated them for it. He called them the iceberg ladies. They were cold and pale and, when seated, they appeared normal-sized. However, when the iceberg ladies rose to lurch and waddle about the office, he saw that a good two-thirds of them had been hidden from view. It would be a relief not to deal with them anymore.

As bad as his Catholic school experience had been, Digby had heard about public school since first grade. The nuns said those schools were run by gangs and juvenile delinquents. "It is like West Side Story without the songs and dancing," sneered Sister Anthony. Godless administrators downstate decided the curriculum. As a result, there was no morning prayer or drive to save the "pagan babies," or commitment to the Maryknoll mission or even any religious instruction whatsoever. They didn't sell candy bars for a cause. In public school, you could chew gum and talk in both the bathrooms and the hallways. They had no school uniform. Blue jeans and charm bracelets were permitted, and they even allowed pierced ears. Desks were often untidy since in public school, one's belongings were not an extension or reflection of one's soul.

Other nuns swore that many of those students went right from eighth grade into prison. They said the majority of girls ended up at halfway houses, and that most were eventually condemned to eternity in Hell. "Purgatory is too good for the majority of the public school cases," warned Sister Clementine. The nuns claimed that not only the "occasion for sin," but the reality of it permeated the air. They said public school abortions were common, and that young men's hair often hung well beyond the collar. That sort of thing was expected when you didn't have the proper education, and a good amount of spiritual guidance.

Last July, public school students got blamed for changing the outdoor sign at Holy Martyrs School, which said, 'See You In The Fall'. It was a reminder of the upcoming parochial school term. Removing the 'T' as well as the 'Fa', the hooligans altered the sign to say 'See You In hell!'

Common knowledge also held that public school hooligans were behind the vandalism of the outdoor manger scene at Holy Martyrs. Betty Murphy, the rectory secretary, hyperventilated when she drove into the church lot and almost ran over the head of one of the Three Wise Men. Betty fainted dead away when she laid eyes on the rest of the desecration. In addition to the headless Wise Man, someone had put a ball cap on The Virgin Mary, and a rotten pumpkin had been switched with the Baby Jesus. The next day, The Morning Star headline blazed, CHRIST CHILD STOLEN! WISE MAN BEHEADED! MARY IN CARDINALS CAP! The story went on to describe the scattered straw of the "manger massacre" site, and the littering of beer bottles and cigarette butts. The Christ child was found the next day on a bus stop bench.

With this brand of violence and sacrilege as the foundation of his public school knowledge, Digby was terrified. If public school kids did that to Jesus, who knew what they'd do to him? Jesus was the Son of God; Rog was nowhere near as powerful, even before the perilous probation. The night before his first day of class, Digby couldn't fall asleep. Like most insecure folks, he didn't do well with new social situations or radical change. The unknown was always good reason for an overwhelming sense of dread. He supposed he would be met by a new band of bullies. Tormentors were always on the lookout for fresh meat.

Perhaps unprecedented horrors awaited him in public school, though he was hard pressed to imagine what that untapped source of harassment might be. Parochial school was mostly a nightmare, and never better than tedious. The other students didn't like him, and the nuns thought him cheeky. He was considered a bad influence, and frequently punished for lying, as well as asking inappropriate or disruptive questions. It had started in first grade, when Sister Anthony spread news among the order to keep an eye on that Swank youngster. Digby had asked her why she had a man's name and if she was really a boy-nun. "Is that why you have a mustache?" With an outstretched arm, she pointed to the corner and commanded him to stand in the trash can with the rest of the garbage. The next day, he asked if our Guardian Angels were always with us, at our desk and on the playground, "Did they come in the bathroom with us too? Did my Guardian Angel have to stand with me in the trashcan yesterday?" Even though Digby wasn't trying to be fresh, Sister took it as such. She was not amused. "Dei ludicium (By the judgement of God), Digby Timothy Swank. You so try the patience of even a Guardian Angel, that I imagine by that point even He might have abandoned you," sneered Sister.

Not two weeks later, during Lent, he asked her why everyone sat on one side of the table at The Last Supper. Sister Anthony scowled. "Forsan et haec olim meminisse iuvabit," she muttered. Perhaps one day it will be enjoyable to remember even this. She'd had quite enough of this impertinence. She strode towards his desk so quickly her habit fanned out behind her in the breeze. Towering above him, she told Digby that his every word, every thought, and every deed was only adding another brick on his roadway to Hell. He knew from Sister's description in class that Hell began with the sinner's eyes being gouged out, and his tongue split with a razor. This agony was followed by skinning the body of the damned, whose agony was then compounded by being forced to roll back and forth in pits of sharpened salt for all eternity. She said they never get used to it. "The pain is constant and everlasting." When she discovered that her description had given Digby and several of his classmates nightmares, Sister snapped, "Good. That was the point." The parents agreed that Sister was right. Questioning her methods was unthinkable. Confronting nuns and priests about their teaching skills was sinful. It challenged God's word.

Digby had been pegged since the start—branded, exiled, and labeled as trash. Things at Holy Martyrs had not improved since. If anything, the situation had deteriorated with his every infraction. He had spent many hours standing in garbage. The more Digby considered it, leaving Holy Martyrs School didn't seem like such an altogether horrible thing. Sure, it was the Hell he knew, but it was still Hell. Maybe instead of a bad thing, a school outside of God's jurisdiction would be an opportunity for a fresh start.

Digby was smarter now, more worldly than he had been when his bad reputation and history of ridicule had begun. Maybe coming into the situation as a savvy sixth grader would make things different. As far as he was aware, no one knew him at this new school. He was arriving with a clean slate. The possibilities may not have been endless, but at least possibilities existed. In order to become the new person he wanted to be, he first needed to coerce, manipulate, and trick people into liking him. He'd lied plenty of times before and with great gusto, but never with such a clear purpose. This time, he would lie and lie big.

Maybe he could even be more than simply accepted. Despite his fears, Digby still craved acceptance, but more than that, he wanted to be recognized and envied. Standing alongside his peers was nowhere near as attractive as standing above them. Being a teen icon on a pedestal sounded sublime. Adore me from afar. Love what I represent. Love the concept of me. That sort of distance flattered him. Distance was actually his best angle. When Digby eventually drifted off to sleep that night before his first day of school, he did so with a plan in mind, and a smile upon his face.

His new future began with the proper shedding of his past.

He lied about his popularity at his former school, his parent's income, and most everything else. Lies rolled from his lips with the skill and agility of a campaigning politician, a serial adulterer, or someone in the witness protection program. He even said witness protection was the reason he'd changed schools. Looking in either direction, Digby lowered his voice. His audience bent closer with widened eyes. "My sister Katie saw a gangland killing," he whispered. Creating an entirely new biography was so easy. His life sounded infinitely better when he wasn't shackled by the truth.

Digby met Walter on his first day at Doblyn Elementary. They both had Mrs. Hyde, a sad, beige woman with long limbs. Her thin hair was kept in a thin braid with the end bit choked by a thin beige rubber band. Terribly paranoid, Mrs. Hyde constantly accused the class of whispering and passing notes, unaware that her teary-eyed accusations encouraged the behavior. During composition, Digby introduced himself and Walter told him his name. "It's not my birth name. I made Robert and Jennifer change it." Walter called his parents by their first names. "I was born Sidney. Can you imagine? What were they thinking?"

"What's all the chatter about back there?"

Walter looked at Mrs. Hyde and in an unwavering voice said, "It's really none of your concern. Carry on, you're doing fine."

The flustered Mrs. Hyde emitted a semi-choked peep, and turned back to the board with an exasperated flip of her braid.

This was certainly different than being taught by a snarling pack of nuns. When Walter saw Digby's look of surprise, he smiled. "What? This is a public school. We pay the taxes that pay her meager wages, or at least our parents do. That woman is working for us. Why, she's no more than a servant girl in polyester drip-dry."

Mrs. Hyde's chalk paused at the board for a moment before continuing on its sad squeaky course. Her shoulders peaked and then slowly sagged, and even her thin braid seemed to droop a bit. Digby had little doubt she'd heard him.

Blatantly ridiculing a teacher. Calling his parents by their first names and making them change his. Digby was in awe and, as a seasoned Catholic, he didn't experience awe too easily. In less than an hour, Walter had become his pre-teen idol. Walter was an outsider like Digby, but he was an outsider with a difference. He was intimidating. Rather than simply being socially acceptable, Walter seemed to define what was socially acceptable at Doblyn Elementary. Witty, urbane, and slightly aloof, he was above it all, just like Digby wanted to be. Walter chose his outsider status. He danced. He dressed. He had class and an air of superiority. He was the Noel Coward of the tween set. He would've worn a smoking jacket and cravat to class if it struck his fancy. His opinion of the school play was the one that mattered. He held court during recess. The girls loved and confided in him. They sought his advice on anything and everything. Boys feared his acerbic tongue. Even at eleven, he was that kind of gay.

As a neurotic newcomer with social ambitions, Digby quickly grasped the importance of befriending Walter, and aping and modeling his behavior. Over the next week, he morphed into his clone. Walter never mentioned Digby's transformation directly, so Digby wasn't sure if he was oblivious, too tactful to broach the subject, or merely flattered.

"Of course I knew. I could hardly blame the misguided waif. It was natural, given his lack of substance. He really was a formless lump of clay in husky corduroys and a western shirt... with snaps. Can you imagine? I knew he was a kindred soul, and I knew from the start that he was telling lies. Others knew as well. Running Falls is not that big of a town. It's not New York or Paris, or even Lexington, Kentucky, for god's sake. Those who knew the truth about Holy Martyrs kept quiet and went along with the entire charade because of me, and I went along with it...because it was all so terribly sad, I suppose.

"Naturally, his choice to mold himself in my image was both wise and flattering. It always is. He was a promising experiment for a while, but there was no happy ending to that Digby story, if I remember correctly. In the end, he stopped being me and foolishly regressed back into being himself. He was such a

Catholic. It was a pity really," confided Walter over a martini and finger nibbles on the veranda of his chic Holmby Hills home.

Walter was the first to explain to Digby in no uncertain terms the ins and outs of male/female intercourse. The thought of Rog and Lila actually engaging in such shenanigans was preposterous. He may as well have told him that in order for him to be conceived, his parents had to dance a jig with a goose, which would be especially preposterous since Lila had a nervous dread of live fowl. Sex as Walter explained it simply couldn't be. Digby laughed. "Well, maybe your parents have done that sort of thing, but mine never would."

"Well, they did, or you wouldn't be here."

Walter's emphatic claim haunted Digby. Walter was so worldly and knowledgeable, and he wasn't really the joking sort. Digby wondered if this lurid behavior had been going on all along. Throughout the week, he couldn't look at his parents without imagining them sneaking off to do some variation of that unspeakable deed. He recalled those aftershave-at-night evenings and the overheard giggles, and he shuddered. That week, he lurked outside their bedroom door in the hope/horror of hearing them carrying on. This couldn't be true. Intercourse! There had to be some other way, something they could do fully clothed and in the dark without touching, like some secret Catholic fertility handshake or maybe a special prayer with an offering, a few votive candles, and a precisely rung bell.

Digby learned all sorts of things at public school. Even if it was a bit behind Holy Martyrs academically, it more than made up for things in street smarts and real-world knowledge. Coming from Holy Martyrs, he felt in many ways as though he'd been schooled in a much darker version of Oz.

Before he knew it, Digby had been at Doblyn a full month. The following week was his birthday. As a boy unencumbered by a past, this birthday was especially powerful. It could be anything. There was only one problem. His parents already had a family celebration scheduled, the same family celebration that was always scheduled. For Digby, nothing enunciated the word loser quite so clearly as having elderly relatives and immediate family members at a birthday party. This asinine Swank tradition would ruin everything he'd worked, or at least lied, so hard to create. Digby swore that his transformation, his new outlook, and his fresh identity would not be compromised. "I have not done all this in vain," he vowed.

The morning of his birthday, he voiced his complaints to Walter. Digby moaned that although it was his birthday, his parents were still dictating the day. He whined that they would give him crappy gifts. "They will sabotage it. They will turn my day into a nightmare. My grandparents will be over, and my brothers and sister. It will be boring and meaningless without my friends." Of course, Digby neglected to mention that his friendless birthday was due primarily to his glaring lack of friends, but that detail wasn't part of his fabulous new mythology. Walter was sympathetic. "That's just wrong. It's ridiculously authoritarian. It's your birthday. Own your day. Simply tell them their intrusive party ideas and pedestrian plans are not to your liking. Your celebration should be your business, free from all their meddling whether it's well-intentioned or not. You can't go on living your life as though you were nothing more than their son, because if you do, that's all you will be." Walter made everything all sound so simple.

Digby continued to bemoan the unfairness of never being allowed to do what he wanted. He was laying it on rather thick. "I have a curfew and chores. It's barbaric. It's like being a prisoner of war for eighteen years, or something."

"Let's focus on the birthday. If direct confrontation isn't an option, then perhaps you should counter their invitations with some invitations of your own. You should invite some friends."

"I should, but I don't know if my parents will let me."

Walter exhaled.

"I'm sorry I just…"

Walter raised a hand to pause Digby in mid-sentence, while he adjusted the cuffs of his royal blue dress shirt. When all was perfect, or even more perfect, he looked Digby in the eye. "Because they won't permit you? Digby, you're missing the point. Listen to yourself. Grow up. You're eleven now. You are officially a pre-teen. It's time to rebel and stand up for yourself. You're a human being, not some house pet. You have rights. Don't disgrace the age."

"You're right."

"Of course I am," Walter laughed, as though the serious consideration of any alternative was absurd. "Just because they're older doesn't make them wiser, especially when the details of your soirée are none of their affair."

"Yeah."

"This is your day. The way you choose to live it will dictate how they're going to treat you for the rest of the year, perhaps even until you're in high school. They've behaved unforgivably for long enough. It's not entirely their fault. They've been misguided and poorly trained. They need to be corrected, and for that to happen, you need to take charge. Greatness only comes when you take the reins of your own destiny. Don't let them continue to call the shots. I wouldn't dream of letting Robert and Jennifer treat me in that manner."

Walter was completely convincing, especially since so much of what he said was exactly what Digby wanted to hear. "You're right. It's my birthday, and I should celebrate how and with whom I want."

Walter pursed his lips. The wheels of thought were in motion. "Let me handle it."

"What are you going to do?"

"I'm going to give you a party."

Digby's jaw slackened, widened, and then nearly smacked the checkerboard floor of Doblyn Elementary. He felt like the luckiest kid on the face of the earth. This sort of thing was unprecedented in his life. All his bitching and moaning had blossomed into something more. He was taking a stand, or at least stepping aside and letting someone else take a stand for him.

It was empowering in a passive way. Walter explained that it was about more than just him or his birthday. "This is about human decency, free will, and the rights of the unseen masses," Walter intoned. Digby suddenly found himself as poster child for Kid's Lib.

Throwing a party meant inviting people. Watching Walter bestow or deny invitations was to see him in his element. He ended up asking about a dozen classmates to Digby's house that evening. "For an unforgettable evening, be there at seven. We're having a select group over." If the would-be guests voiced any hesitance about "the new kid," Walter brushed away their worries with the assurance that this would be the party of the season. "It's about all of us, but if you want to miss it all to watch Adam 12 or some such nonsense, no one is stopping you. In fact, go ahead. If that's what you'd rather do just say the word, I'll keep it in mind and won't burden you with any more invitations in the future."

Digby was beyond amazed. His birthday was being touted as the party of the year. An event not to be missed. The concept was almost inconceivable. Last year, the highlight of the evening had been when Aunt Lucy hooked the brace wires of her dentures on an ear of corn, and ran about the table flapping her arms and mumbling "Help!" with the cob still wedged in her mouth. She swore afterward she'd only eat corn out of the can. Since then, Lila always had it as a side dish whenever Lucy came over. It was Lila's way of being outwardly thoughtful, while simultaneously reminding her sister of the humiliating incident. That was just the way they were.

Aunt Lucy running around like a dog with an ear of corn in her mouth was then. This was now. Digby smiled. This year, the sky was the limit. The golden door to popularity was finally opening, and Digby was about to be granted entrance. Over that threshold was almost everything he'd ever hoped for: to be accepted, to be envied, to be wanted.

Digby rushed home from school, giddy with excitement. His enthusiasm dissipated in a matter of seconds when he saw his mother cooking his birthday meal of spaghetti. Her broad legged stance told him she was in a mood. She stared into the bubbling cauldron of Bolognese sauce, and said things he couldn't quite hear. Money woes and family problems were taking their toll. Making demands about tonight's plans and telling her he'd added a few more people to the guest list would have been especially foolhardy and masochistic just then. That sort of thing was best addressed in front of others. Besides, it was an easy conversation to postpone. He would cross that bridge when he came to it. He quietly backed out of the kitchen, thankful that his mother hadn't seen him.

Grandpa Vint and Leonora arrived about five o'clock with a wrapped gift. Digby wanted to wait, but they pestered him until he finally opened it then and there. It was a gyroscope. This was better than the usual handkerchiefs, shoehorn, clippers/brush/shears set, or other geriatric male gifts they usually gave. A device that maintained its balance and orientation anywhere it was placed seemed oddly appropriate, given Digby's recent adaptation to public school and his fabulous new lifestyle. Though the gyroscope may have been apt, he still didn't like or really understand it. He ended up hanging it on a string in his bedroom window.

As expected, they also brought Edna. The puppy ran to the basement of her own accord. Unlike their previous dog, the schnauzer mix had sniffed Edna's crotch only once, and subsequently yelped and scurried to her bed with her tail between her legs. Even before taking off her coat, Edna teetered on her spindly legs into the kitchen and said, "That spaghetti looks good enough to eat." Supposedly, Edna was trying to be nice. Whenever she was in a good mood, Edna used lipstick liberally, and that night multi-colored Saturnian rings encircled her mouth. Lila looked up, and offered a smile that looked haphazardly tacked upon her otherwise grim face. The slow blink betrayed her annoyance.

Edna hovered at the linoleum border of the kitchen, and ran a finger along the top of the refrigerator. "Oh, what's in the sauce?"

Lila tried to maintain her smile, but the strain showed. Every day and every week, she was expected to endure more and more. Rog was doing fine for now, but who knew what next week might bring? Perilous probation was serious business. She was able to take on some extra shifts at work, but that only added the smallest of financial cushions. There was no money set aside for the college funds, much less for any sort of emergency.

"I said what's in the sauce?" repeated Edna.

Lila's smile curled into a snarl. "It's beef."

Edna's eyes narrowed. "Are you sure?"

Fortunately, Leonora came in and dragged her sister back into the living room.

At five past seven, the doorbell rang. The dog ran up from the basement, and began barking. Digby uncharacteristically got up from a full plate of cake. Opening the door, he took a deep breath. Hello newfound status! Welcome pre-teen popularity! Walter looked stylish in a tailored denim leisure suit with white contrast stitching. He was surrounded by his fawning entourage: Connie, Nancy and Marie. A couple of other schoolmates walked up the sidewalk behind them. Digby was thrilled, until he felt his mother's hot breath on the back of his neck. She was standing directly behind him. He could feel the heat emanating from the smile he knew she was wearing. With a swallow, Digby turned. "I've invited some of the kids from my new school over," he managed with a trembling smile. Of course it was manipulative. He was hardly above exploiting that I'm the new kid in class and my life is in shambles angle for all it was worth, especially in matters of survival. His mother may have been in a mood and near the breaking point, but she was still a Catholic. Tapping into her deep Holy Water reservoir of perpetual guilt was Digby's ace in the hole.

Rather than slap him and tell his friends to go straight to Hell, his mother told Tom and Maynard to go to the store and get a case of Coke and some chips. It wasn't until she said this that Digby finally exhaled. As mentioned, the Swanks were usually quite polite to strangers. Lila sighed. They'd just have to cut corners elsewhere in that week's budget.

Altogether, ten classmates showed up. The kids played 45s,

screeched, ran about, and basically wreaked pre-teen havoc. Julie and Connie looked at one another before turning to Digby's sister, Katie. "Oh my God, what's it like to see a man shot point blank in the face?" Digby put a finger to his lips to shush them, but he was too late. Katie's perplexed reply of, "I don't know what you're talking about" sounded just like something someone in the witness protection program would say when their cover was blown. When Katie excused herself a moment later, Digby told Julie and Connie that she had to play ignorant. "After all, the mob is still after her. There's a price on her head."

Connie nibbled a chip, and tried to sound nonchalant. "So, I'm curious. How much is the price on her head? Like, does the mob pay cash for information? I mean, is there like some anonymous toll-free number to call, or something?" Her unsettling line of questioning was followed by an awkward silence.

Walter wagged a finger at her. "Now hush, Miss Scarlett." Walter told Connie he called her Miss Scarlett because her dark hair and spirited nature reminded him of Scarlett O'Hara from Gone with the Wind. Digby knew for a fact that was not the case. He told Digby the real reason he had called her Miss Scarlett was because she reminded him of someone who would do it in a ballroom with a candlestick. "Or even in the conservatory with a lead pipe, for that matter," Walter had added.

An hour later, Miss Scarlett and Julie locked themselves in the upstairs half-bath. With squeals of "No, stay out," and "Oh my God!" and "You'd better not," they basically challenged Stuart to imitate Mannix, and shoulder butt the door in. Piercing screams followed the splintering of the door frame.

Downstairs, Edna leapt from her seat. In full neurotic mode, she accused Digby's parents of inviting rapists into their home. After all, that was a public school boy who was causing all the screaming. "Is this a home, or some sort of outpost for teen love?" Her hand pointed to the ceiling. "There are young girls upstairs being sodomized at this very moment."

"No one is being..."

"Don't tell me you can't hear it." Edna considered all public school boys, even those in sixth grade, to be rapists. "I know what they teach there."

Leonora eventually managed to calm Edna by slapping her hard across the face, pausing a moment, and then asking about her bursitis. It was an interesting tactic that had clearly worked before, though none of the Swanks had actually seen it.

Lila looked down at her hands. A small smile betrayed her apparent yearning to try this approach on Edna herself sometime, just to help the poor dear to re-focus.

With shouts of sodomy, doors breaking, gangland witnesses, and today's top hits blaring on the hi-fi, Digby's party was the talk of Doblyn Elementary the next day. As host of the "happening frolic," his name was whispered, and accompanied by nods of approval. He's all right, that new kid. He has got it going on. His place is the place to party. People looked his way and smiled. Not laughed, but just smiled pleasantly. They waved him over, and not away. So this was what it was like to have his friendship coveted. He heard a couple girls had crushes on him. This was status. It made Digby feel more important than he'd ever felt, even as an altar boy. It made him feel like he mattered. The air about him felt charged. It was a heady concoction.

Given the minimal number of things in his life that had brought the slightest bit of pleasure, he was immediately addicted. Digby wanted more, much more. He wanted it bigger and faster and stronger and longer. The world beyond acceptance was new and thrilling terrain. Needing to feel more and to go farther, he did the unthinkable.

Before he could clamp his hands over his mouth, he boldly announced that he was having another party that night. Stupid. Stupid. Stupid. News of the second Swank bash spread quickly around school, as quickly as herpes had spread the previous summer at the Derby Downs Drive-In. Digby had been spared his mother's wrath last night. After all, yesterday had been his birthday. That had cut him a good amount of slack. Today was not his birthday, and Digby would bet money, lots and lots of money, that a surprise party was not going to be tolerated a second time.

As the day passed, his dread mounted.

Lila accidentally encountered the first arrival upon her return from walking the dog. She was surprised to see Darcie McDuff on the sidewalk in a crocheted vest, carrying a 45s case covered in Flower Power decals. Darcie was very hip. That ginger-haired trendsetter drew peace symbols on her sneakers, and pentagrams on her jeans. She was the first girl at Doblyn to wear, and then promptly burn, her bra, declaring, "If you love something, set it free." She had "future groupie" written all over her, a promise that was eventually realized the summer before her eighteenth birthday.

Darcie smiled. "I'm here for the party."

Lila's mouth grew small. No hint of the Swank hospitality was apparent. "There is no party here tonight."

"But Digby said...and my ride just dropped me off."

Lila's mouth pursed to the size of a pinhead before she hissed, "I said there is NO party here tonight." Ironically, it was only her being leashed to the dog that kept Lila from a full-fledged attack. "And Digby is grounded for lying."

Digby's mother ended up giving Darcie a ride home, along with a couple of other kids who had arrived a bit later. The tires squealed as Lila pulled from the driveway. The wait for her return seemed both too short and interminable. Digby heard the keys hit the dining room table, the sound of hangers falling as she hung her coat, and the slam of the closet door. Her footfalls boomed in the stairwell, and down the hallway. It was the gait of a woman who meant business. Each step matched the anxious pounding of his heart. The puppy whimpered, and crawled beneath his bed. Lila opened the door to his room with such a fury, that the knob was embedded into the plaster wall. "You are never having another party again... ever." Turning, she added, "And next month it's back to Catholic school. You're going to Holy Martyrs. I don't care if we have to sell every stick of furniture in this goddamn house to get the money."

"But..." said Digby. At his one-word utterance, Lila turned.

Her face began to twitch. A strong survival instinct silenced him from any further protest.

Lately, Digby found it tough to keep his mouth shut. At eleven, he was developing a pre-teen attitude. He was more likely to rebel, and not just in his mind. He'd never really been a wiseacre before. He wondered if this new trait was a public school thing. The nuns had warned that walking through those doors was like lighting a fuse. They said that public schools were "occasions for sin in every way imaginable, and in some ways, even beyond mortal comprehension." They maintained that sins were like yeast, and public schools were an oven. Was that all true? Maybe God and persistent threats of damnation had kept some of his badness in check. Given Digby's long history of consistently doing things that good Catholics simply did not do, that theory seemed unlikely. Besides, he hadn't left religion behind. He still went to church, and unfortunately, God was still in the curriculum. Every Wednesday afternoon, Digby had been forced to attend the after school nightmare of CCD, the Confraternity of Christian Doctrine.

Catechism was a system of bringing religious education to Roman Catholics who were not quite holy enough to send their kids to Catholic school. It was considered necessary if Rog and Lila were going to show their faces at Holy Martyrs Church. Digby considered it an expensive and ridiculous waste of time. Of all the times his parents chose to splurge. They considered CCD especially important for Digby, because his confirmation was coming up, and apparently his eternal soul needed additional tutelage.

Confirmation was a sacrament, and yet another Catholic right of passage. It supposedly made him a part of God's legion by reaffirming all the things he'd already unknowingly agreed to when he was baptized as an infant.

In truth, Digby had no more choice in being confirmed than he did in being baptized. And this time, he had to memorize precise answers to all the religious questions he might possibly be asked. In every parish's Confirmation class, Bishop McNamara was known to fire off at least a few questions at the children, reducing several from each Confirmation group to tears. You answered the bishop without hesitation, without thoughtful deliberation, and without ad-libbing.

One of Digby's memorized answers was: The character of Confirmation is a spiritual and indelible sign that marks the Christian a soldier in the army of Christ. As he memorized the sentence, Digby had to wonder if God actually wanted soldiers who were forcibly drafted into his army on Earth. Besides, wasn't he omnipotent? If he was all powerful, why did he even need an army? It seemed excessive to Digby, but all his complaints, eye-rolling, and caterwauling meant nothing. Lila had ended his carrying on with a look. He was signed up to go to catechism, his name was on the roster to be confirmed, and, by God, he was going to go to CCD and be confirmed. Digby tried to find consolation in the fact that he would be able to choose a confirmation name. As might be expected, he was terribly indecisive on the matter, and only chose Michael because the boy in front of him had chosen it. If he'd had a different seat, his Confirmation name might well have been Felix or Eligius.

Catechism was little more than two hours of dogma bombardment via a tedious series of overhead transparencies, and mimeographed sheets. It was all up in the ether. They never studied the really cool Catholic stuff like exorcisms or spontaneous stigmata, or the gory details of martyrdom. Aside from the Confirmation specifics, CCD was mostly another avenue of revenue for the Church. He recalled very little from those Wednesday afternoon classes, though the answers from his Confirmation questions still came to mind as unfelt reflexive responses.

What is a sacrament? A sacrament is an outward sign instituted by Christ to give grace.

What is grace? Grace is a supernatural gift of God bestowed on us through the merits of Jesus Christ for our salvation.

What does the Bishop say in anointing the person he confirms? The Bishop says, "Be sealed with the Holy Spirit." The accepted response is, "Amen."

What is Holy Chrism? Holy Chrism is a mixture of olive oil and balm blessed by the Bishop on Holy Thursday, or any other day during Holy Week.

What does anointing the forehead of each person being confirmed with Chrism in the form of a cross mean? Anointing the forehead of each person to be confirmed with Chrism in the form of a cross means that the person being confirmed must openly profess and practice their faith, never be ashamed of it, and rather die than deny it.

Blah. Blah. Blah. There were a couple dozen possible questions with the tidy answers in the opposite margin. Digby tried to think of it as nothing more than a word game. He pretended that Confirmation was a sort of Catholic Quiz Bowl! Imagining a buzzer in front of him helped him to memorize.

He liked to show up early to catechism, and wander the halls or set aside extra time to go through the desk of whoever sat at his CCD seat the rest of time. The blackboard always had a note scrawled on it reminding the CCD students to respect the belongings and property of the daytime students and the school. Some of the regular students even set desk traps with paper clips and rubber bands. Supposedly, people had been stealing supplies and food as well as homework. Digby had the feeling the CCD kids got blamed for a lot of things.

His most vivid memories from those afternoon classes were of his teacher, a heavy-lidded floor-gazer named Miss DeForest. Digby recalled her array of dirty V-neck sweaters and yarn-tied pigtails, as well as the Jesus-on-the-Cross necklace that she claimed had been personally blessed by the Pope.

Most Wednesdays, Digby would sit in class with his butt as numb as his brain. Miss DeForest would drone and mumble the same drivel Digby had heard as long as he could remember, though the nuns delivered the goods with greater gusto and menace. God was perfect. He was not. He was in a state of mortal sin. He would always be in a state of mortal sin. He needed forgiveness. He needed mercy. How often did he need to hear he was not worthy? How often did he need to be reminded that if he managed to somehow avoid Hell, he'd probably be sent to Purgatory until enough prayers were offered up for him that he could enter the Kingdom of Heaven? Miss DeForest said he should offer prayers to the poor souls in Purgatory, so that someone might do the same for him one day. She also said that was a good reason to have a big family. Surviving family members were more likely to offer prayers to relatives than to complete strangers. "I want to have a big family," Miss DeForest added in a voice of such transparent desperation that it embarrassed her, as well as the fraction of the class who was actually listening.

Borderline catatonic, Digby often stared at Miss DeForest's jelly-stained sweaters, which often included clusters of toast crumbs. He was hypnotized by watching Our Savior hanging helpless and pointy-toed above the cavernous hollow between her breasts. It never failed to give him chills, like the further adventures of Dashboard Jesus.

Though catechism was an attempt to sustain and strengthen his spiritual self, it accomplished just the opposite. Digby was AWOL in spirit, and sat every Wednesday afternoon at his desk, a tabernacle of flesh housing an overflowing chalice of resentment. Rather than aid in his spiritual and moral redemption, those two dreadful hours actually fed his dark, rebellious side. It could even be argued that his weekly catechism class ultimately caused him to break the earthly law, even though he'd apparently been breaking spiritual and natural laws for years.

Few things are as humiliating as being busted for shoplifting, especially shoplifting an age-inappropriate toy when the item is inappropriately young. Digby's life of crime began one Thursday afternoon, as he and Walter contemplated the candy at Ben Franklin Five and Dime. Walter pulled him from the sweets. He was dieting. "Processed sugar makes me balloon and summer is just around the corner." Around an end cap from the candy and chocolates were the toys. Amongst the toy cars, cheap dolls, bouncing balls, Slinkys, bubble wands, and giant plastic poodle banks, Digby spied a bin of miniature Looney Tunes bendy characters. "Cool," he cried. It wasn't quite the right word. They were cute, but kind of dorky even for a seven year old, and Digby was eleven. When he squealed and ran to them, Walter followed. Digby couldn't tell whether he liked them too, or if Walter was just humoring him. Digby usually would've been more guarded, but he was really excited.

"Aren't you a little old for that?" The question stopped him dead in his tracks, but it wasn't posed by Walter. It had come from within, the voice of rebellion fueled by preteen testosterone, and catechismal resentment. That emerging part of Digby was disagreeable and moody, and loathed all things good and cute. It hated being told what to do or not to do. His dark side was reactionary and primal at the same time. When provoked, his internal voice would refuse to be silenced. It always had an opinion. His dark side would allow Digby to have those bendy Looney Tunes characters on one condition: They had to be stolen.

Looking around, Digby took the package holding Elmer Fudd, and ripped it open before shoving Fudd into his down vest pocket. Walter did the same with the Road Runner, thereby accepting the unspoken challenge. Moments later, they boisterously and blatantly ripped open packages, adding the entire Warner Bros. cartoon gang to their pocketfuls of booty.

Once outside, around the corner, down the block, and at the end of a deserted alley, the boys pulled Tweety, Wile E. Coyote, Sylvester, Daffy Duck, and Yosemite Sam, along with Fudd and the Roadrunner, from their pockets. Digby's personal hero had always been Bugs Bunny. What wasn't to love about a wisecracking, cross-dressing rabbit? He dug deeper into his pockets. He remembered the rush of taking it, but Bugs was missing.

"It fell out of your pocket when we were walking out."

"What?"

"That figure fell out of your pocket when you reached for

the door."

"But Bugs was the one I really wanted," Digby said with an undeniable whine.

Walter gave him a strange look. Before he had the chance to speak, the five o'clock whistle blew, which heralded the end of the workday at the Band-Aid factory. It was time for both boys to head home for dinner. Walter was always irked that his parents didn't eat at a more respectable, European hour like seven or eight. "Five thirty is so working class. And dinner with Robert and Jennifer is always some strictly meat and potatoes affair."

Digby waved goodbye, and headed over the bridge toward home. This would all have to wait for the time being, but tomorrow, the bendy Bugs would be his.

When they returned to Ben Franklin the following day, Digby felt uneasy. His gut churned, and something inside told him "no," but he'd grown accustomed to ignoring his instincts. Instead of abandoning the plan, Digby made sure to be extremely cautious. He peered around corners, checked the rounded security mirrors, and scanned the creaky wooden floors for the sales ladies in their light peach smocks.

Walter gave a nod.

Seeing the signal, Digby tore another Bugs figurine from the cardboard and plastic package, shoved him in his pocket, and with a premature smile, turned and stepped on the flat, sensible shoes of Fern, an assistant manager. Digby nearly screamed, and leapt backwards. Fern stood akimbo, looking as tough as a two-dollar steak. Her tight perm was the orange-pink shade of a cheap perfume package, and the irregular planes of her face were caulked in autumnal concealer. Fern cocked a penciled brow, and held out her moist palm. Trying to recover his composure, Digby gave her a trembling smile, and a wide-eyed look. He tried to project innocence. He probably shrugged and perhaps even smirked. Fern was having none of it. She jiggled her outstretched hand. The gesture was a silent command, and a bit of an ultimatum.

With a shaking hand, Digby pulled Bugs from the pocket of his down jacket, and promptly burst into tears. This was so not cool.

"We had a lot of these things stolen yesterday." She furrowed her brow. "I would have thought that the thief was someone at least four or five years younger."

Through his tears, Digby blurted, "But I, this is the first thing I've ever stolen. I swear to God. And it wasn't even for me. I was stealing it for my girl cousin, who's in kindergarten."

Fern crossed her arms over her formidable chest. She wasn't buying it. She'd held the position of assistant manager for years, and wore the plastic smock badge with honor. Fern prided herself on being nobody's fool. She could smell a thief downwind of a landfill, and two towns over. "You can tell a thief by the squeak of the floorboards," she was known to say. And the Ben Franklin floorboards squeaked a lot.

Digby continued to blubber and sputter, and spit things like "Oh God, I am so sorry. I am so sorry, oh God," and "I will never, never, never steal again, ever." Pride was entirely absent from his display. Even groveling seemed too dignified a description of the level his begging soon assumed. It was unpleasant by any standard.

Walter stood slightly apart from the goings on with his arms folded across his chest. He pursed his lips, and turned his chin upward as if to avoid an unpleasant stench. Digby recalled Walter's referring to Connie as Miss Scarlett, his parents as the Kramdens, and their teacher Mrs. Hyde as Esmerelda with a scullery maid's braid. At that moment, Digby wondered what unpleasant cultural icon he had become in Walter's eyes. Was he the quivering Barney Fife or fellow Mayberry resident, Floyd the barber? Perhaps he'd become Mr. Whipple, the milquetoast tissue fondler? Digby could see it all unfolding. He knew Walter was thinking, "That Digby is such a blubbering baby, such a hopeless case and such a loser." Any social standing Digby had managed to achieve at Doblyn Elementary had been reduced to rubble right there on the Ben Franklin floor in the shadow of Fern.

Walter addressed the incident with more than a hint of

irritation. "I abhor when words are put into my mouth, when thoughts are placed in my head, or when feelings are blindly attributed to me. I was not thinking he was being a baby, nor was I concocting a disparaging nickname, not at that moment, anyway. At first I was shocked at his being caught. That was such idiocy! I signaled to him that some horror in a hairnet was lurking about, but he blithely opened the package nonetheless. And look where it got him, humiliated right in the middle of a five and dime store. He should have known better. As to my response, initially it was a shock, then I grew embarrassed by the hand-wringing apology, and finally numbed into boredom by the repetitiveness of his pleas. That discount store drama seemed interminable. It was actually just the last in a long line of disappointments I had with him."

Fern had never seen shoplifter's remorse to such a degree. She loved kids, and especially loved putting the screws to them, but even seven- or eight-year-olds rarely grew this weepy. Digby positively crumbled. Fern put her hands behind her back, and inhaled the heady scent of her dime store power. It was the sort of thing that made her go into retail in the first place. "Young man..."

"Digby."

"Digby."

"Hi."

"Hi," replied Fern, a bit irked. Fern had her duty to do, but she could also see that the last thing this kid needed was another problem. Though several neighborhood children and a couple of her co-workers might beg to differ, Fern was only human. "Digby, I want you to turn on your heel, march out that door, and never step foot inside this store again. Do you hear me?"

"Yes sir."

At his response, Walter snickered. Fern gasped, and leaned back before making a shooing motion with her puffy, liver-spotted hands.

Digby walked across the worn dime store floor toward the entrance with his eyes dead ahead. He was saying Hail Marys, praying to be suspended in a bubble and carried away from all this. He didn't want to see Walter, or think of Walter seeing all this. He didn't want Fern to change her mind or have anyone in the store recognize him. It was all too much to process. Mostly, he just didn't want this to be happening. His recurring fantasy of having the power to disappear was never stronger. When they got outside the double glass doors, he was still shaking.

Walter sighed and popped a sugar-free mint into his mouth. "Well, thank God that's over." He paused a moment before adding, "And why in heaven's name did you give her your real name?"

It was certainly a valid question. Digby had panicked, showing little control or recall of what he'd said or done. "It just seemed polite."

Walter shrugged "Well, if etiquette was such a concern, it would've certainly been more gallant to address her as ma'am instead of sir." Digby thought at first this was just some of Walter's good-natured teasing, but the tone of his barb was slightly off, and the comment wasn't followed by a cocked brow or pursed lips. He wasn't joking. It was blatant bitchcraft. When Walter turned, Digby heard the click of his tongue.

In that instant, Digby knew the bubble had burst. Digby wasn't sure whether Walter was bored by his adoration, or bored because Digby was not a perfect copy. Maybe he simply deemed him no longer worthy. Digby thought they were friends. His assumption had been wrong. This wasn't friendship. They had no mutual respect, no equality, and no sharing. He'd been a member of Walter's entourage, an easily replaced ear for his witticisms, and just another source of adoration. On one level, the sudden clarity shocked Digby, but on a deeper level, it hardly surprised him. In retrospect, it all made perfect sense. He was a misfit, and a sad impostor. All the lies in the world couldn't change that. Part of him knew that something like this would happen once Walter discovered the real Digby, and the real Digby had just put on quite a show amidst the clearance bins at Ben Franklin. "I'll never be able to shop there again."

Walter turned his way, but didn't meet Digby's eyes. "You'll survive. There are worse things than being banned from that bargain barn. Consider it the guiding hand of a tasteful God." Walter was quiet for a long moment. "Listen, I just remembered something I have to do at home."

Digby was no fool. In fact, when it came to recognizing rejection, many would consider him an intuitive genius. Walter's abrupt goodbye had more to do with their past-tense friendship than any urgency at home. Digby was being dismissed. Walter was saying goodbye instead of merely so long.

Digby couldn't do a great deal about it. Even he had more pride than that. He'd already groveled enough for one day. His well of remorse had run dry. "You're right, Walter. There are a lot worse things. I'll see you, okay?"

Walter's "bye" sounded even briefer than it looks in print.

Other than a nod in the hallway and pleasantries in class, Digby was doubtful he'd see much of Walter again. Those instincts were dead-on. It didn't matter as much as it might have. He was only a student at Doblyn Elementary for one more week.

18 – Teachers Can Be So Gay

Returning to Holy Martyrs meant returning to the hell he had known. Doblyn had been but a brief reprieve from the torment of school, and even that had ended painfully. In the few short months he'd been gone, some changes had occurred at Holy Martyrs. One of Digby's former teachers, Sister Anthony, had reportedly died in her sleep after feeling "gassy" the night before. Her very close friend, the sixth grade teacher Sister Anastasia, promptly went on sabbatical.

Sister Anastasia had been the most compassionate nun at Holy Martyrs. She reportedly did not enjoy punishing students, an almost unheard of trait among the order. During recess, Sister Anastasia frequently asked the quieter students to help her feed the birds from the bag of crusts that always appeared from beneath her habit. Some students said if she wanted to, she could have one of the swallows perch upon her fingertip. Sister Anastasia also jangled her rosary when approaching the classroom as a warning to any students who might be misbehaving. The other nuns usually softened their approach, creeping towards the doorway in eagerness to catch any transgression—rough-housing, talking, and sin-of-sins, mimicking a nun. Sister Anastasia had done none of that. Supposedly she even told students that they were all the children of a kind and benevolent God, a God of mercy, and a God of joy. It was whispered that her saying such things was a clear warning sign of her eventual breakdown.

With two sisters down and no available nuns to pick up the teaching slack, Holy Martyrs took a leap of faith and hired two additional "lay" teachers as replacements. Non-ecclesiastic teachers were considered a last resort. Teachers outside of the order were expected to perform all sorts of side duties, and were treated more like servants by the nuns than faculty peers. They played the roles of lunch monitors and playground monitors, and some even assisted Mr. O'Moynohan in light custodial chores. These janitorial duties encouraged the nuns to hire another man. As a result, when Digby returned to parochial school in the latter part of sixth grade, his teacher was a "progressive" and grossly underpaid man named Mr. Beloni.

Digby did not like the sound of progressive teaching. Unconventional meant untrustworthy and unexpected, and Digby found no pleasure in being exposed to new things. Though guilty of inflicting mental anguish on a regular basis, the draconian methods of most of the Holy Martyrs nuns had suited him just fine. They had been severe but predictable. Beloni was fond of telling his pupils to throw all their ideas of what an education should or shouldn't be out the window. A chill ran down Digby's spine when Beloni winked and said, "a classroom has no walls" and that he wanted to "erase the blackboard jungle." Catholic school was no place for such talk. Classrooms should have walls. Structure was essential. It offered protection. Without structure, Digby feared even greater torment. He had no Walter to protect him here.

As an unbridled libertine, Mr. Beloni allowed open seating in his classroom. He didn't believe in the demerit system, and he'd been seen attending movies that received the "C" (condemned) and/or "O" (morally offensive) ratings from the Catholic Office for Motion Pictures, which most folks still called the Legion of Decency. "Midnight Cowboy of all things," whispered the iceberg ladies in the office.

Digby waited for some sort of censure or action to be taken by the parish as it had with Father Kenneth, but none happened. Where were the zealots when you really needed them? It was all quite inexplicable. From what had been pummeled into him about Catholicism, Digby figured that surely an open-minded teacher could be just as scandalous and threatening as a fornicating priest.

Digby's indignation grew with each passing day as Mr. Beloni became "one of the guys." All the girls had crushes on him, and those who said they didn't had the biggest crushes of all. They all gushed and fawned and mewled whenever he was about. Beloni was everybody's pal. He drove a Volkswagen Beetle, and wore desert boots and was generally considered "cool." This annoyed Digby to no end. Being considered cool in this environment was not terribly impressive. It was a Catholic grade school. It didn't take much to out-cool mustachioed Sister Marie Pierre, touchy-feely Father Andrew with Bell's palsy, sweaty Brother Bob with all the ingrown hairs, or Miss Tusslesnatch—the grotesquely wrinkled librarian with a head so disproportionately large, it seemed part of a child's collage.

Friday afternoons were always primetime for Beloni's "newer than new" teaching methods. He called Friday afternoons "free your mind" time. One Friday less than a month after Digby returned to Holy Martyrs, Beloni instructed the class to write a few sentences on a scrap sheet of paper and pass it to the front of the room without signing it.

"What should we write?"

"Be creative. Write anything you want."

"Anything," his bolder fans joshed. Digby rolled his eyes. This was the overly familiar yuk-yuk brand of humor he endured daily in Beloni's class. The camaraderie never failed to perturb him. He was a stranger to that sort of behavior, and the annoyance he felt was little more than envy. Closeness in others made him feel all the more apart.

After hearing the assignment that day, Digby was suspicious, but he dutifully followed the instructions despite his qualms. In the classroom, he always wanted things to run as smoothly as possible. His dream of invisibility was stronger than ever. Digby scribbled some nonsense on the paper. The content was unimportant.

Once the papers had been collected, Beloni introduced a pal of his, Mr. something-or-other, who flashed a smile and said to call him Ben. First name usage! Digby's mind sputtered at the audacity of it all. This was surely in violation of some Holy Martyr rule. Ben worked with the police department as a handwriting analysis expert. A couple of the kids in class muttered "cool." Digby was not impressed. The literacy rate in Running Falls hovered around forty percent. If a writing example existed at all, the suspect was in the minority, and if the message was written instead of spray painted on someone's garage, the list of probable offenders was even shorter. If it was grammatically correct and lacked profanities, the possible suspects dropped to under ten percent. If the note was on stationery, the culprit was clearly an out-of-towner, and probably a homosexual.

Mr. Beloni folded the pupil's papers and dropped them into a cowboy hat he pulled from a side drawer in his desk. Seeing the Stetson, a couple of the guys chuckled. Digby could read their minds. They were thinking, "How cool is that?" The entire episode was manipulative, and thoroughly transparent. Beloni and his open-air classroom were thick with that kind of calculated behavior. Digby recognized acting for effect. He'd been doing it his entire life. He sat silent and sour, cocooned in resentment over the fact that Mr. Beloni was so undeniably successful at manipulation.

Ben fished in, picked a slip of paper, and read it aloud. The sentences were a boring hodgepodge just shy of gibberish. This writer was only marginally within that fortieth percentile range. Finishing, Ben closed his eyes and lifted the sheet to his temple like a cheesy psychic. More guffaws from the class. "This boy is a sports enthusiast, and a little hard to keep in line. He likes to laugh." It was Eddie Hooten. Ben was dead on. Eddie was all those things, but Ben neglected to mention that eclipsing all those qualities was Eddie's tendency to be a complete jerk. He liked to laugh all right, often at Digby's expense.

He'd been one of Johnny Van Camp's loathsome crowd, and had inherited Johnny's role as the Pontius Pilate to Digby's Jesus after the Van Camps relocated. Eddie found great joy in teasing, taunting, and torturing Digby, and as a result, made his schooldays all the more hellish. Eddie had taken even greater delight in doing this since Digby's return to Holy Martyrs. A cousin had told him about some of the tall tales Digby had been telling at Doblyn. Eddie made sure everyone at Holy Martyrs heard about it too. "You're going to really need a protection program to survive now, you little creep," was the first thing Eddie had said to Digby upon his return. Digby never understood why Eddie took such pleasure in all this. He figured assholes behaved that way mostly because they could. Assholes usually don't need a reason. It was just their natural state of being.

Edward Hooten felt compelled to respond. "I am hardly illiterate. I am currently a blogger with a bent on humor. I have over one thousand followers. The American public knows what's funny. We are a smart nationality, and I think my daily writings are a bare witness to my literal ability. As to the claims of my being a jerk, I was simply enforcing the social order in school. That's what young men do, but Digby wouldn't know about that. Pubessence aggression is a true fact of life in the real world. Bullying toughens people up for adulthood. Sadly, Mr. Swank has yet to move on."

Ben chose another writing sample from the hat. "This young lady is outgoing and likes to organize." Blah. Blah. Blah. Kimberly Bennett. Digby rolled his eyes. Though still in a state of panic, Digby found these character assessments dull. Ben needed to take the profiles up a notch if he was really going to describe the people. Digby wondered if Kimberly's handwriting sample also revealed that she was the first girl in his class to have a full bush, and that she liked to get finger-fucked behind the equipment shed on the athletic field. Digby had even seen her getting fingered by a high school guy behind a tombstone in Calvary Cemetery. He knew it was her. He saw that big bush from three grave rows over before he even saw her face. It was all common knowledge at Holy Martyrs, so much so that whenever the word "finger" or even "digit" was mentioned in class, someone would giggle, or if they were particularly bold, turn and look at Kimberly.

Every time Ben reached into the hat, a wave of panic rushed over Digby. He prayed not to have his selection chosen, but recognized his paper the second it emerged from the box. Thanks again God! What's next in your divine plan for me, boils or locusts? Ben held up Digby's writing sample and cocked his head. "This is a very intelligent young lady but a bit on the shy side. She likes everything to be neat and tidy." The room grew silent. Digby wanted to liquefy, evaporate, rain down upon the soil, and be eaten by worms. Moments passed. Heads swiveled this way and that like brainless whirly gigs, all heads except Digby's that is. Silence. Long, pin-drop silence. Someone was mowing the lawn a block away silence. No one claimed ownership. Rather than recognize that this person wished to remain anonymous, Beloni turned the paper towards the class. "Anyone?"

Marsha Grunwald, an orthodontics horror with a freakish overbite unclamped her reptilian jaw. "Mr. Beloni, that's Digby's paper, I saw it when we passed our sheets up the aisle." After speaking, Marsha blushed. She was one of the girls with the biggest Beloni crush. She even had his initials and hers inside an arrowed heart on the back of her notebook. After a moment, everyone laughed. Ben grinned. "You stumped me, Digby." He may as well have added, "You big old nancy boy!"

This indignity was an absolute nightmare. New names catapulted to the top of Digby's vengeance list. Though years had passed since he began it, Digby had been very consistent and thorough in its upkeep. By this time, his shit list had evolved. It now included categories, levels, bullet points, and a complex system for exacting justice. Nature had punished Marsha Grunwald far more effectively than he ever could. Marsha's teeth protruded so markedly from her protracted jaw that with only a slight tilt of her head, it was rumored she could eat an apple through a picket fence.

Digby vowed that Beloni was going to pay dearly for this day. He'd made a grave mistake with this latest abasement. I have my own progressive ways of teaching. I have my own unconventional lesson plans, thought Digby, feeling slightly villainous, despite his humiliation. All he needed was a plan. He wasn't worried. He naturally excelled at vengeance.

Wilson Beloni's address was easy to find. He was listed in the white pages. Digby scoffed to see he had the audacity to choose bold typeface for his listing. So proud. So eager to catch the eye. Digby casually rode his bike by the residence a few times to become familiar with the area. Exercising a great deal of patience, for Digby anyway, he spent the next few weeks formulating a fitting plan of action. His retaliation would take time. It would be calculated for optimal devastation.

One cold, moonless night, he knew the time had come. He

gathered the necessary materials, put them in his bike basket, and sped to the address. Lowering his three-speed (with the glittery green banana seat) into the bushes, Digby crept around the back of the building. He scanned the area. No witnesses. The darkness beyond the sliding patio doors was matched only by the darkness of his intent. This was the perfect occasion for sin. He opened his bag and fished out the Luncheon Meat Fiesta Pack, and two tubes of Superglue; this was his recipe for justice. He'd give Beloni an education all right!

Seething from the humiliations he'd endured in that stupid "progressive" class ever since his return, Digby glued a random spread of spiced luncheon loaf, cotto salami, and all-beef bologna to the glass door. Instead of throwing all he'd learned about school out the window, he was retaliating by sticking it to the glass. He adhered one slab, then another and another and before he knew it, the package was empty. Payback came so effortlessly. He took a step back to inspect the buffet of his retribution. His smirk was never smirkier. "Open seating," he scoffed, "First name usage." Satisfied that his hunger for justice had been served, Digby retreated to the shadows.

Rounding the building, he noticed light flickering from another patio door. Mr. Beloni and Ben reclined in the glow of a television screen on a tasteful avocado couch with their arms and legs entwined. Digby cocked his head. His smirk faded. This was very curious. Digby seriously doubted that Ben and Beloni were watching a ballgame with dates, and the chicks were just in the bathroom. Digby may have been relatively naive about the particulars of sex, but he wasn't a complete oaf. He was certainly worldly enough to know that snuggling on a tasteful couch was not typical straight guy behavior, especially in Running Falls. They might as well have been drinking beer out of a glass.

In retrospect, Digby shouldn't have been so shocked. Beloni was a progressive teacher and a well-groomed, fashionable dresser who championed an open-minded approach to the world, kept a Stetson hat in his desk drawer, and saw Midnight Cowboy at the theater. It all made such perfect sense. Seen in this new light, Beloni may as well have pulled those writing samples from a leather jockstrap. Digby raised a hand to his mouth to stifle a gasp when he saw Beloni bend down to kiss Ben in the shaded blues of the television's light.

Then it struck Digby. If they were watching TV here, then who lived in the place he'd just vandalized? He turned around and saw a gigantic bra and girdle on the clothesline, and farther down, a dingy pair of men's underpants. He gasped yet again. He wasn't expecting a duplex. What –to –do? What –to –do? Panicked, he ran about in a tight, confused circle before hopping on his bike to skedaddle home. Though upset by the mix-up, once out of the cul-de-sac he found himself more aroused than anything. The rest of the evening was dominated by vague adolescent fantasies. He recalled the "blue kiss" and remembered Walter's description of sex. Digby wondered how that would work for two men, and how his teacher and Ben might play hide the Beloni. He put on his sister's Carole King Tapestry album, and imagined himself with Beloni and Ben on that avocado couch. It was an orgy of white wine, macramé, throw pillows, and diffused sunlight. He felt the earth move.

He awakened after a troubled sleep dominated by the sinfulness of his vandalism, the vileness of his fantasies, and his disgraceful dry humping of his mattress. He offered up a couple of Our Fathers, and a few Hail Marys. He added a couple psalms for the victims of his meat pasting binge. Unfortunately for that innocent third party, his prayers were not enough. Temperatures in Running Falls plunged below freezing the night before. Digby wasn't aware of it, but once meat freezes on glass, a molecular transformation occurs, and the two actually meld into one. Removing that luncheon meat selection from the glass would pretty much mean replacing the door.

One agonizing week passed s-l-o-w-l-y before a morbid curiosity about the door and a carnal curiosity about Mr. Beloni motivated his return to the crime scene. The meat was still there. The pinkish hues had gone gray. It was rotting. Even in the cold, the rear of the duplex smelled. The residents had tried to remove the cold cuts. The rounded edges of several slices of bologna and salami had been chipped and scraped with little success. In another week, the door was replaced.

Digby snuck back several times afterwards in hopes of seeing some sort of guy-on-guy sexual behavior. As for Mr. Beloni, this new discovery made Digby see him in a very different light. He still hated him, but now he also wanted to have sex with him. Rather than cause a conflict, these seemingly opposing forces would prove a fairly common theme in Digby's future relationships. Jerky behavior was a heady aphrodisiac. Loathsomeness was so sexy, that sometimes he almost considered it foreplay. For his gay Catholic conscience, it was a form of multi-tasking. It made hating himself, along with what he was doing and who he was doing it with, all very simple. For years to come, most men on Digby's to-do list were bastards.

Having a gay teacher wasn't unusual. After all, Digby was taught by a lot of priests. However, in the influx of lay hirings, Digby had to wonder who conducted the job interviews, and just what was being discussed. The following year, in seventh grade, Digby strongly suspected his English teacher, Mr. Roth, "played for the team." Those strong suspicions solidified into absolute certainty following the school's short story contest.

Eager to promote writing among the students, the Holy Martyrs composition teachers decided to hold a school competition for the seventh and eighth graders. To ensure upstanding moral content, the students were instructed to write a short story of any length that thematically depicted one of The Ten Commandments. In truth, this rule did not insure upstanding moral content at all, but only some form of categorical Christian depravity.

The three upper level English teachers—Sister Frances Kildare, Miss Mavis, and Mr. Roth—raised a good number of eyebrows among the school instructors when they stepped forward and named themselves as "clearly the most competent judges among the school faculty." As incentive, the three lucky winners of the story contest would receive a complimentary dinner for two at AnnaMaria's Italian Restaurant. Supper Club!

Banquet Facilities! Private Parties! AnnaMaria's boasted authentic Italian cuisine, and in Running Falls, the accepted pronunciation of that cuisine was EYE-tal-yun. AnnaMaria's was a dim cavern of "old world charm" defined by checkered tablecloths, garlic bread with every entree, gondola-shaped serving dishes, and a red candle shoved in a Chianti bottle. Instead of the radio, they played a recorded mix of violin music, Sinatra, Tony Bennett, Dean Martin and even some Connie Francis. They had mints in a dish at the hostess desk, enormous amber ashtrays at every table, and crushed ice in the urinals.

Digby embraced the assignment wholeheartedly. He was wildly competitive, especially when he could compete without having to actively engage with others. He had a wonderful time writing his short story. His entry was definitely unique, most notably for capturing the smeared lipstick soul of tawdriness. His lurid tale, BARBRA CORDAIR: ADULTRESS! was a smoldering ten page potboiler that caused quite a stir at school. His narrative ability and writing talent could not be disputed. The boy was passionate about telling a tale. It was the content that caused the controversy.

Dashing investment banker Paul Davis was trapped in a loveless marriage to society matron Claudia. They lived in a spacious colonial mansion with white pillars and a wrap around porch on a corner lot at the right address. Claudia's daddy, Beauregard, had bought it for them as a wedding present. Paul and Claudia were invited to all the right parties and had impeccable manners. People considered them the ideal couple. It was everything they were supposed to want, and yet something was lacking. It was all just a show. Both were afraid to end the charade. Ending it was much harder than the mild everyday pain of living a lie. The only light in the Davis household was their five- year-old daughter Penny.

One evening Paul was working late at the office "breaking in a new secretary." (The secretary was NOT the adulteress! Yet Digby specifically recalls using that phrase. At that early stage of his literary career, he used a lot of phrases with no concern as to meaning.)

After work Paul wandered into a cheap twenty-four-hour diner to get some pie before heading home. There he spied Barbra, applying her makeup in the dingy reflection of the napkin dispenser. She saw Paul in the reflection and cocked a brow. "You enjoying the view?"

"Oh, I'm sorry."

"Don't apologize. I wouldn't be painting the merchandise if I didn't want fellas looking over the goods."

Paul blushed.

Barbra laughed and poised the lipstick tube at her slightly parted lips. "So, shy boy, what brings you into this joint?"

"Oh, I just came for some pie after work."

"Well, you came to the right place buddy. The pie here is the freshest in town."

One thing led to another. There were batted lashes, the tense twist of a wedding band, a loosened tie, the flick of a tongue across moistened lips...

Paul picked up the tab for Barbra's danish and coffee. It began raining outside. Barbra was on foot. "Oh darn, and I just bought these shoes!" she said, running a hand down the back seam of her stockings towards the black pumps.

Paul smiled and offered to give her a lift.

"I wouldn't want to inconvenience you."

Paul replied that it was no trouble.

"Brother, I don't think you would recognize trouble if it came up and clocked you in the puss."

Paul laughed.

As they neared her rented room, Barbra spoke."Listen Romeo, I owe you one, and I hate owing folks. I'm a gal who pays her own way. There's a quiet little juke joint on the corner. What do you say? Let me buy you a nightcap."

Paul smiled. "Sold!"

The two wound up having not one but seven nightcaps

and then went dancing at a bohemian club where the patrons practiced "free love." (Another phrase used with reckless abandon and minimal comprehension).

The lust in Paul's heart spread like leprosy to his loins. He tasted of the forbidden fruit and like the serpent's apple, one taste was not enough. The tryst continued. They met the next night and the next night and the night after that as well. Dinner, theater, bowling, after hours clubs, miniature golf...

Paul was smitten. Barbra was incredible, just like Jayne Mansfield - except with a head.

It wasn't too long after that when Claudia, Paul's wife, discovered the infidelity: a lipstick stain, a whiff of perfume, a swizzle stick and a tiny scoring pencil from Razz-Ma-Tazz Lanes. The evidence and her intuition told her in no uncertain terms that there was another woman. She raised a fist to her mouth when she realized that her husband was having an extramarital affair! "Commandment number seven," she moaned, "Thou Shalt Not Commit Adultery."

Distraught by his betrayal, the former debutant took a tube of lipstick and slashed her reflection in the bathroom mirror. "It's all ugly. It's all ugly and damned to hell!" Trembling, Claudia opened a bottle of pills and washed down a handful of dolls with a tumbler of whiskey. "Bastard!" she screamed time and time again until she staggered from the bathroom and collapsed upon the divan in the living room like a boozed up bag of potatoes.

Coming home from an evening of unbridled passion with Barbra and smelling of cigarettes and liquor, Paul discovered Claudia's slumped form. Pulling her to her feet, he shouted, "What have you done, you mad little fool?" He shook her until she eventually vomited the barbiturates onto the white shag carpet.

Hearing the ruckus, little Penny toddled into the room, wiping the sleep from her eyes. "Daddy, why is Mommy sick? Is Mommy sad and pukey because of me?" she asked with a trembling lisp, holding her teddy bear closer.

Paul grabbed Penny and looked into her wide eyes. With an

anguished wail he turned heavenward. "Oh Penny, my darling, Mommy is fine and she loves you more than all her jewels. It's Daddy who's the sick one! It's Daddy who's violated one of God's ten laws." So saying, Paul raised a fist to the heavens and ran out into the night, leaving the front door ajar in his wake.

He drove like a maniac across town - through stop signs and stoplights, swerving lane to lane and crossing the train tracks just ahead of the lowering bar. It had begun to storm and the wiper blades pounded along with his rapidly beating adulterous heart. He came to a screeching halt and leapt from the car. In a flash of lighting, he pounded on Barbra's door. She lived in a motel!

Barbra answered the door in a teddy and heels and holding a bottle of champagne. "Back for more, tiger?"

Paul grabbed and kissed her before back-handing her hard across the face. The blow sent her sprawling across the bed.

"You're like some beautiful poison."

Barbra wiped her bloody lip. "And buddy you've been bitten...with both fangs" was her hard-as-nails reply.

Light from the flickering V C NCY sign shone through the four-paned window of Barbra's room. The illumination formed a flashing cross upon the dirty wallpaper. Paul saw it and remembered his truth and his God. He remembered all God had done, how He had sent His only Begotten Son to save mankind. Paul recalled all that Jesus had sacrificed for His people. For a brief moment, Paul thought he heard the weeping of angels… or was it merely rain upon the windowpane? Covering his ears, he wailed in remorse before his fingernails clawed at his cheeks. With a mournful cry, his hands reached out to encircle Barbra's throat. "If I can't escape your grasp, you shan't escape mine, you harlot, you Jezebel!"

Barbra struggled to free herself and knocked over an ashtray. Their two lit cigarettes fell onto the tangle of blankets. The struggle continued as smoke began to rise. Fire spread from the sheets and bedspread to the mattress and finally the bed board and the wall behind it. Hell itself had come to The Traveler's Inn. The modern oil painting began to bubble and curl. Barbra broke free and threw her flute of champagne onto the fire. The flames leapt even higher.

Grabbing her from behind, Paul began to recite the Our Father.

Barbra struggled. "Shut up with all that hooey, I tell you, shut the hell up!"

Paul continued "...thy kingdom come, thy will be done..." He wrestled her back onto the burning bed. Just as he concluded The Lord's Prayer with a solemn "Amen," they were consumed by fire.

When the fireman arrived, Barbra was dead, her polyester teddy had melted onto her still firm but lifeless thighs. Paul was still breathing, though by that point the former "golden boy" was a much crisper shade of red. Though little more than an oozing blob of raw flesh, Paul still managed to linger for two final words, "Forgive me."

One fireman turned to the other. "What did that poor sap say?"

The other shrugged. "I don't know, it was too late to tell and too hard to understand! He couldn't form the words without lips!"

"Well whatever he said, I hope at least God heard him."

Finis!

Curtain!

The End!

As might be expected, BARBRA CORDAIR: ADULTRESS! was chosen as one of the finalists for the top entries. A special note was delivered to Digby's geography class. He was to report immediately to the school library to discuss his work. Digby sat on a small orange plastic chair, and the panel of judges sat at a long table opposite. Sister Frances sat wide-eyed and winded, looking, as always, to be a mere moment from the grave. Sister was shocked by the mature content of his piece, but respected his "passion." Miss Mavis, whose hair was twisted into an extremely tight bun, focused on petty details. She said things like "People don't live in motels," "Seven drinks is not a nightcap" and "Barbra is spelled B-A-R-B-A-R-A."

All her criticisms were promptly addressed. In the Swank house, seven drinks was oftentimes a nightcap, though since bringing his father's monthly liquor bill to Show and Tell in second grade, Digby had been forbidden to discuss the issue with outsiders. His mother had called doing such things "a sin of etiquette." Digby agreed to adjust the number of nightcaps to three. As to her second point, he told Miss Mavis that transient hotels were full of residents.

She conceded that point, and tapped her red pen upon his story before continuing. "Now about the spelling of Barbra..."

And then it came. The gay moment. A comment so telling, that even as a gay egg still to-be-hatched, Digby splayed a hand across his chest and gasped. At her comment, Mr. Roth clucked his tongue, got busy with his hands, and squealed, "That's how Streisand spells hers. She dropped the "a" of the second syllable after high school, when she moved from Brooklyn to Manhattan to break into stage work on Broadway. That was such a defining period for her. That's when she really became Barbra Streisand." His response was not even remotely heterosexual. Mr. Roth's comment ended all discussion, as well as Digby's interview.

In the end, Digby's story was chosen as one of the top three entries in The Ten Commandments writing contest, and he was awarded the dinner for two. But even that authentic Italian dining experience came at a cost. In order to get the meal voucher, Digby had to read his winning story at a special assembly during parent/ teacher night, which was mostly a ruse to raise funds for another series of renovations to the convent.

"Next they are going to be building tennis courts over there," fumed Rog.

Lila shushed him, and said she would go.

Digby rolled his eyes. This "free" meal was coming at quite a price.

The night of the assembly, Digby's sin-slathered selection

was read last, following two comparatively wholesome tales—one of coveting goods, and the other of bearing false witness.

Digby took the podium. He'd never been at a microphone before. With an audible gulp, he read his selection amidst a couple gasps and scattered snickers, and ultimately a round of hesitant but polite applause. His story made everyone uneasy, especially his mother. Looking up twice whilst reading, Digby couldn't miss Lila's ashen face, unfocused eyes, and mouth open wide enough for him to see most of her fillings all the way from the stage. Digby knew that expression quite well. Not again was all but spray-painted on her forehead. Once she realized that people might be watching her, Lila quickly closed her mouth and assumed the frozen smile Digby knew even better. She nodded periodically for good measure. Digby found it somewhat surprising that his mother didn't expect this sort of thing from him. After all, he had a good idea of what to expect from her.

He'd only tried to do his best, but once again, his best had disappointed. Even though his best had been declared as one of the best, it had been an embarrassment. Lila wasn't angry, just unsettled. She had dread in her eyes, not shame. This wasn't about him. He was old enough to see that now. It was about holding it all together. Situations like this frightened her because any and all revelations posed a threat. She feared at any moment people might leap from their seats, point their accusatory fingers her direction and shout "Aha! I knew there was something going on in that house!" His best was not the problem. It was that his best and his being were usually too revealing. And that was very threatening.

"As soon as he read that title, I thought, 'Oh boy, here we go.' I was proud of Digby, and pleased he was getting some recognition. He always needed that sort of thing. That boy had a quiet way about him. He held back too much, so that when he did do something, it always seemed bigger than what was called for. Like, if the normal or expected was here," she explained with the placement of her hand, "then he was all the way out there," she gestured with an overhead pointing of her hand. "There was no real halfway about him, and halfway was about as far as folks went in Running Falls."

"It was nice that Digby was appreciated now and again, but it always seemed to come at such a price. Why couldn't he have written a nice story about a fine, upstanding Catholic family with sound values? Not my Digby. The things he put in that story! And the tone he took reading it! And then when he imitated the adulteress and read that part in a woman's voice! Heaven help us!

"I could hardly believe my ears when that Miss Mavis called it an essay! An essay! The way she spoke, people would have thought it was a true story. We sure got a good share of stares when we left the auditorium that night. That was fine. Nobody was going to stare us down. Digby gave the coupon for AnnaMaria's to his Father and me for our anniversary. We were excited to use it. The gift certificate was only good for thirty days, so we went the following Friday. It still turned out to be an expensive evening. It was too bad that gift certificate didn't include the bar tab. Still, I was humming Come-On-A-My House for a week."

19 - Never-Zippy

Though Digby frequently embarrassed one or both of his parents, the tendency for shaming was by no means a one-way street. In fact, for the Swanks, shame was frequently a major thoroughfare. Family members routinely disgraced one another, because almost all of them harbored hopes of being something more or something less, or simply something other than what they were. Shame was mostly a slap back to reality, and a reminder as to the true state of affairs. For the most part, degradation was never the goal, only the common result.

When Maynard farted during mass, the stench was so sour that the usher rushed to open a side door, causing a whoosh of February wind to blow the floral-crowned cake hat right off Miss Eugenia's head. The gust and subsequent loss of her hat caused the elderly organist to squeal right in the middle of the Homily. After regaining her composure, she glared at the pew from her musical perch. Neither Miss Eugenia nor any of the congregants knew which one of the Swanks was responsible for the offense, but all knew that one of "that brood" was at fault.

Luckily, there was an almost immediate diversion. Mr. Lister, the willowy pharmacist, had fainted yet again. He did that a lot during services. Diabetes was no excuse to neglect the three-hour fasting period prior to mass. The Lord would protect His chosen, though He seemed to be waffling when it came to Mr. Lister, who'd been in two comas already that year. Things used to be much worse. Prior to the Second Vatican Council, the rule had been no food or water after midnight the night before. Back then on Sundays, the diabetics had dropped like flies.

The week before, Digby was mortified when Rog had sent him to the pharmacy to ask Mr. Lister if he had anything for diarrhea. "Tell him my bowels have been loose for three days," instructed Rog, "And that my stool feels lumpy." The store was crowded. Digby couldn't bring himself to approach the counter. He lingered in the back of the drugstore by the gum and trinket machines for an hour, and watched Lister flit about. When Lister finally put his hands on his hips and asked Digby if he needed anything, the boy said he was just browsing. He finally went home and told his father that Mr. Lister said just to rest and drink water.

Swank degradation took other forms, as well. It often masqueraded as "a surprise." Sometimes Lila, whose taste was questionable at best, would surprise Digby with a new outfit that she picked up on sale. She often couldn't believe how cheap something was but, given the item, it was usually not too surprising. She'd tell Digby to try on the clothing, and would then have him walk around the block, presumably to "break in the cloth." Truthfully, she did it to show the neighbors that a Swank had new clothes. His siblings were forced into similar wardrobe parades. Sometimes they were all told to circle the block as a group, after Running Falls had their big Summer Sidewalk Days specials. The practice became somewhat common. The week after the sidewalk sales, it was not unusual to see all the children in the nearby neighborhoods meandering about in new outfits, some even wearing new coats and hats despite the August heat.

Sometimes Rog and Lila even coerced Digby into situations in which he'd cause himself certain embarrassment, like a form of assisted social suicide. That was the case with the annual Running Falls Thanksgiving Day Parade. Rog worked for the electric company, and every year he'd happily volunteer one of his sons to dress as the electric company mascot, Zippy Megawatt. Maynard and Tom had paid their dues. Now, it was Digby's turn.

For unknown reasons, Rog always assumed the experience would be fun. He considered it an honor. "Not many kids can say they've done that." Technically his statement was true, but it was followed by a huge leap of logic that equated the rarity of an experience with it being desirable. That was hardly a rule. Sometimes lots of people don't do things for a very good reason.

Though still desperate for attention, dressing as Zippy Megawatt was not the sort of notoriety Digby craved. He wanted people to be envious of him, desirous of his company, and think about him in good ways. It was not his fantasy to be gawked at as though he were a two-headed calf at the county fair. He'd already experienced plenty of that sort of attention.

Zippy Megawatt, the bug-eyed electricity icon, was initially created to make electricity "fun." Zippy had a round light bulb head, a light bulb nose, and bushy brows over lidless, bulging eyes. He wore a tiny beret and had a wide, gap-toothed smile beneath a pencil-thin mustache. Inexplicably, a pair of red horns sprouted from his forehead. Zippy had red lightning bolts for limbs, white gloved hands, and the wide, flat feet of an albino duck.

As a modestly-budgeted company costume, Zippy Megawatt was recreated as red lightning bolts ironed onto a black unitard. The costume featured a giant Styrofoam head with a small beret stapled on top, as well as enormous white mitt-hands, and white flippers for feet. The outfit was impractical for any sort of movement, and was almost impossible for marching. The only real upside of the costume was that the Styrofoam head completely covered the wearer's face.

Dressing as Zippy was cruel and unusual punishment for obvious reasons, as well as for some reasons that might not be readily apparent. Though not ridiculous in and of itself, a sheer leotard was a nightmare for Digby. He gasped to see his fleshy boy-breasts and nipples through the fabric. Rog told him he could wear a t-shirt and bathing suit underneath the unitard if he'd like. Digby nodded vigorously, though the t-shirt and swimsuit option did nothing to qualm the pudgy preteen's fears. Like spandex, thongs, and rubber fetish wear, sensitive, pudgy folks should refrain from wearing certain things. Unitards are high on that list, especially when that unitard is part of a costume to be worn while marching down a city street in broad daylight.

It was cold and snowy the year Digby donned the Zippy-wear. The bitter irony of calling it a Thanksgiving Day Parade was not lost on him. The body costume provided minimal coverage, while the headpiece proved to be stifling. Hearing his own breathing inside that styrofoam head added to the claustrophobic feeling, rankling Digby's nerves and resulting in his perspiring in spite of the cold. Looking through the headpiece mouth hole, Digby gulped to see himself in the reflective glass along either side of the drugstore entrance. The unitard assumed an unsettling transparency when wet.

Despite wearing his swimsuit beneath the unitard, wolf whistles and howls rose from the sidewalks. He couldn't see much from the mouth opening of the headpiece. The crowd could've been shouting for any number of reasons, but Digby doubted any of them were the least bit positive. He tried to breathe deeply, keep in step, and hold his Styrofoam head high. It wasn't easy. The ridiculous flipper shoes lacked adequate traction. Every time he would briefly take the focus off his steps, he'd hit an icy patch, and slip or slide. It required almost continuous vigilance. Nevertheless, he waved mechanically and tried to focus on Miss Running Falls, Lornalee Lincoln, before him, and the lurching progression of accident victims representing the Band-Aid factory behind.

Lornalee flicked her cigarette from the float, stuck two fingers in her mouth, and whistled to her boyfriend. "I love you Joshua," she screamed.

If Digby's headpiece hadn't blocked all peripheral vision, he might have seen Joshua bolt from the curb. With a sinister guffaw, he shoulder-slammed Digby, raised his fist in a pumping "whoop whoop" victory cheer, and joined his laughing cronies on the opposite curb. Digby's big, white-gloved hands flew into the air. His legs jack-knifed as he slid, spun, and stumbled into the filthy, slush-clogged gutter. The head shifted. He couldn't see. He'd become a big blind light bulb wearing a tiny beret. The awkward weight of the Zippy-head made him top-heavy. He couldn't push himself up with the puffy hand mitts, or get his footing with the floppy tractionless footwear. He only managed to rise to his knees before losing his balance, and sprawling face first into the curbside snowbank.

With muffled cries, he pleaded for help. Rather than lift a finger to offer assistance, the onlookers laughed. Apparently, ridiculing someone who was screaming while wearing a unitard with a light bulb for a head was more entertaining than watching the March of Dimes band, or the staggering drunk hired to be Mr. Peanut.

Digby finally regained his footing. He saw Lornalee turn around and yell something from her yellow and pink throne of tissue paper and chicken wire. She was laughing. He was just reclaiming some measure of composure when a snowball smacked the back of his head, and knocked him, big Styrofoam face first, into the snow. In his fall the head turned backwards, which apparently added to the hilarity. Despite the debilitating handicap of the Zippy-head, Digby refused to remove it. He merely spun it around. He wasn't about to show his face. This was an ideal time to remain anonymous. If he kept the headpiece in place, he could almost believe they were laughing at Zippy, and not at him.

The crowd moved simultaneously, as if sharing one tiny reptilian mind. If one snowball was funny, then lots of snowballs would be hilarious, overkill being a cornerstone of Running Falls humor. Bystanders eagerly packed snowballs for their perfect target. Digby was a bull's eye in a see-through unitard. He heard his own gasp of realization inside the head chamber before he was pummeled on all sides. He imagined himself as part of a Biblical stoning. Snowballs stung his thighs, back and buttocks. Some even aimed for his genitals. And some pelted him so forcefully that the Styrofoam head was dented.

"Score," he heard someone cheer when he felt another whack, and saw the beret knocked to the ground.

Only Harriet Schlummer deferred from the Zippy attack, throwing her snowballs instead at the Mr. Peanut with shouts of, "That bastard killed my son!" Mr. Peanut was oblivious, by now openly taking swigs from a brown paper bag and weaving his way to the opposite curb.

In the onslaught, one of Zippy's ears, which was actually an off-white nightlight, fell to the ground beside the beret. Reaching to retrieve them, Digby lost his footing, and hit the ice yet again. Pushed beyond the absolute brink, something inside of him snapped. Or maybe a switch was flipped. This was intolerable. He was through with being a martyr, especially for a major utility company. Rising to his knees, Digby emitted a monstrous wail, amplified by the hollowness of the headpiece. Raising a whitemitted fist to the sky he cried, "So help me God, you'll all pay dearly for this!"

That was only the start of his tirade. Parents gasped at the threats and foul curses coming from Zippy's big Styrofoam head. Digby vowed vengeance, hurling curses like lightning bolts. He called them sinners and swine, Pharisees and Sadducees, whores, morons, and inbred butt-faces. He swore that he'd leap from sockets and burn them beneath their electric blankets. He'd infiltrate hair dryers and curling irons, sabotage glue guns and stereo systems, and reduce their mobile homes to cinders.

"There will be nowhere to hide," he screamed before making a grim guarantee that they would all burn alive. "If not here, then in the eternal fires of Hell!" Some children turned to hide in the folds of their parent's overcoats. Even a good share of the adults were justifiably fearful of the raging figure in the see-through unitard. In his current state, the electricity icon seemed capable of almost anything.

Finally, the initial shock and fear of the crowd gave way to indignation. Digby, as Zippy, was resoundingly booed and flipped off, and pelted with more snowballs for lack of sportsmanship. He didn't care. This public appearance was over. He ran blindly through the throngs, knocking down the elderly and causing a couple of pregnant teens to drop their cigarettes. He cut down one alley and then another, before dropping to his knees in weeping defeat. He was an outcast and a freak. Overheated and sickened by the entire experience, as well as the three hot dogs he'd had for lunch, he unceremoniously heaved. Unfortunately, the wave of nausea came upon him so suddenly that he didn't have time to remove the head.

Witness Jodi Lynn Blatherby had this to say. "We was all having fun, just throwing snowballs and such. It was all in good humor, so there was no reason to do what he went and did, and on a holiday, too. It was unconstitutional, and we were all sick over it. I'll tell you this much, I'll never buy another light bulb! You hear me! Never. I'll unscrew them from the gas station bathroom or take them from under the sink at work or whatever. The where don't matter. But personally speaking, I'd sooner live my life in the dark than give a penny to that creature and his kind. Thanksgiving Day, my ass! After that, my kids was having nightmares for weeks, and when I would go in and turn on the light to try and calm them down, they would see the bulb and scream all the more! It was a viscous circle."

Arriving home, Digby ran to his room and slammed the door. After a few minutes, Lila brought him a plate of four Twinkies, and since this seemed especially bad, she added a pack of Suzie Q's. A snack from Hostess was sure to help. Digby was on his bed, and turned toward the wall. She brushed the hair back from his forehead with her hand, and kissed his cheek. "I know," was all she said. After a few moments, she left without saying another word.

Having made an ass of himself, and possibly jeopardizing his father's already perilous place at the company, Digby felt shame and guilt in equal measure. He thought his life was over, and feared he was taking the family down with him, but as had happened so frequently, he survived something that seemed unbearable. In the end, the incident taught Digby an important life lesson: perspective was everything. Digby was more surprised than anyone to discover that dismal Thanksgiving Day Parade experience had a silver lining.

His tirade resulted in several letters to the editor in The Morning Star. The commentary included a stern note from the alderman, and a blistering diatribe from Miss Running Falls herself, Lornalee Lincoln. The incident generated enough negative press and PR problems that the company opted to refrain from all future participation in the Running Falls Thanksgiving Parade. Evidently, Digby's behavior as Zippy Megawatt was not in line with the company's image as "the friendly power conglomerate."

As a result, Digby felt a bit like the martyr he'd always wanted to be, and being pelted by snowballs was better than being hung, burned or disemboweled. The experience had been awful, but due to his hardship, future sons would be spared the shame of wearing the unitard and the Zippy head. The thought made him feel exceptionally good. Self-sacrifice was a wonderful ego boost, bringing him a warm sense of self-satisfaction. Perhaps it all really was part of God's inexplicable plan.

The following week, Digby smirked over the snap, crackle, pop of his Rice Krispies to hear Katie whisper that Lornalee Lincoln had been stripped of her Miss Running Falls title when someone discovered she had been married twice, and had a three-year-old toddler.

Most folks in town agreed that Lornalee did always seem a bit too experienced to wear the crown. Then again, the sash did say Miss Running Falls, which all but translated into I blew three of the five judges. Maynard wasn't surprised at all by the disclosure. He said that when Lornalee started driving a couple of years before, the vanity plates on her white Camaro read JL BAIT.

20 - Alone Again, Naturally

Given the circumstances of his life and his often fragile disposition, it became second nature for Digby to go to his room and shut the door on the world's insanity. If he could have locked it, he would have. Out there could just be too crazy. His room was a sanctuary. That closed door gave him a sense of security, and a feeling of peace. This was his. Having learned his lesson years ago, Digby hung thick curtains to guard against prying eyes. Behind that door and within those four walls, he dreamed of massive successes to come. He performed rituals to ensure his desires. Power, wealth and fame would be his. He practiced paparazzi smiles, and motorcade waves. He pretended to be a guest star on The Mike Douglas Show and Dinah's Place. In his room, he was universally loved, admired, and accepted for who he was. People clamored for his company, hung on his every word, and adored him for being so genuinely and irresistibly himself.

With the onset of puberty, the safety Digby found in his room was more important than ever. Being at "that awkward age" caused him to grow even more secretive and self-conscious than he had been before. He was desperate to hide almost everything he was, because almost anything could be used against him. All truths seemed potential weapons, and possible sources of degradation. As a walking spiritual and social transgression, he was forever on the defensive. It was best to reveal nothing. Being neutral and neutered was his game plan; when he strayed from this, disaster would strike.

That's what happened on Digby's twelfth birthday. After the sensation of his eleventh birthday, his twelfth was a return to sad routine. Lila cooked spaghetti, opened the canned corn, made garlic bread, and mixed a cake. Rog hung some crepe paper above the dining room table, and taped five balloons to the back of Digby's chair. He gave him a special Birthday Boy hat to wear. The scenario hadn't changed since he was five. It was all very sweet, but Digby was twelve, so he rolled his eyes and dragged his feet, and considered it all horrid torture. The guest list for that evening was no surprise. It was the usual cast of characters—the immediate family, plus Grandpa and Leonora, Aunt Lucy and Cousin Ted. Edna was also there, though she'd suffered a stroke the previous winter.

The stroke had happened when Edna was being fitted for footwear. When she slumped forward, Mr. Hackett thought she was just bending to get a better look at the lacing on her saddle shoes. Mr. Hackett had worked with her before, and was well aware of her peculiarities. Her request for saddle shoes didn't cause him to bat an eye. "If the shoe fits...," he liked to shrug into the mirror when he went in the stock room to search the back bins. He considered the cliché to be clever, understanding, and indicative of a keen business sense. Mr. Hackett prided himself on being all three. He even used the phrase at various gatherings, and despite the number of times it was heard, "if the shoe fits" always generated polite laughter.

Edna's eventual drooling on the low-heeled Oxford alerted Mr. Hackett that something was amiss. She didn't usually dribble on shoes. When the paramedics lifted her head, they found a large lipstick print on one kneecap. They took her away by ambulance, and she didn't come home from the hospital until ten days later.

By Digby's birthday, Edna had recovered for the most part. She was mobile, though she still had trouble controlling half of her mouth, as well as her right arm. Though tragic and unsightly at mealtime, Edna was much more socially acceptable as a result of the stroke. She had a harder time offending, since she was now almost impossible to understand.

The first part of Digby's birthday evening went smoothly enough. No apparent physical or emotional scarring occurred during dinner, or the off-key rendition of Happy Birthday, or the presentation of the cake. Perhaps that was the reason Digby felt a false sense of security when it came time to open the presents. He had discovered that when receiving gifts from his family, it was best to expect the worst. Since Digby was not blessed with a poker face and had not yet mastered his mother's plastered-on smile, when opening gifts he found it wise to complain of a stomach ache to explain his lingering sour expression. "The gift is great, it's just this stomach acid." Digestive issues excused almost anything.

Aunt Lucy and Cousin Ted gave him a Bread album. "We were going to get you a hula skirt and lei, but they didn't have them in husky," said Lucy with a smirk. Digby let the comment slide, even though he found it terribly annoying. He wanted to tell her to give it a rest. He'd been a child when all that happened. The incident had been a staple of her repertoire for years, and it had never been funny. Sometimes he thought Lucy only brought it up to remind Lila of that embarrassing evening. The thought angered Digby even more. Though he typically turned the other cheek, Digby swore that if they were still eating, he would have asked if she was sure she didn't want more canned corn.

Digby thanked them for the Bread album, and moved on to opening the rest of his presents. He smiled through a polyester shirt, a polyester sweater with a geometric snowflake motif, white dress shoes, and a shaving kit. The latter brought big chortles from the adults. Digby shaving! Hah! Digby gritted his teeth. Their laughter bothered him. If it was so absurd, why had they given it to him in the first place? Sometimes adults made no sense.

Finally, only one present remained. Rog waved the poster tube before Digby. "Woo hoo, woo hoo." This was an especially tough period for Rog. His work evaluation had not gone well. The company didn't fire him, but they made it clear they were not pleased with his performance. Perilous probation had not been the kick in the butt that many had hoped it would be. His superiors let him know they were doing him a favor by keeping him on. There would be no raise, and certainly no bonus. Rich Crain, who Rog had trained, was his new superior. Rog had gone back to drinking that night. He'd been off and on the wagon so many times by then that Digby couldn't remember which meant sober.

Rog took another gulp of his highball. At least he wasn't drinking from the plastic cup yet. That would probably come with his next cocktail.

He waved the poster tube again and almost knocked over

the coffee pot. "Are you curious?" His chuckle was followed by a slightly slurred, "It's a poster of your favorite movie star. Guess?"

Given that Rog was a father eager to stay in the dark regarding his son's budding homosexuality, "Guess your favorite movie star" was not a wise question to ask. If he was sober, Rog would have realized that asking his probably gay son his favorite movie star was almost the equivalent of injecting Digby with sodium pentothal.

Red faced and laughing, Rog repeated, "C'mon, it's your favorite movie star."

For unknown reasons that Digby could only attribute to elevated blood sugar levels brought on by the cake, ice cream, and soda, he answered honestly. "Ummm—Judy...Marilyn," he gushed, hands all aflutter. His response was so blatantly gay, that he even refrained from using surnames. It was Judy or Marilyn. It seemed that even at the tender age of twelve, he was a martini-swilling, ascot-wearing, Live at the Palace sort of homosexual.

Being stereotypical unnerved Digby. How did it happen? How had he become so keenly representative of this larger whole without extended exposure to it, aside from his friendships with Doug and Walter? The inexplicable mystery of it was unsettling. All along he'd been sashaying down life's path towards a predictable array of tendencies. Suddenly he became part of a different world, where an appreciation for All About Eve, haute couture, bitchy banter and Greco/Roman wrestling bubbled from him in a geyser of gayness. He hated being predictable, and as the youngest child, he had an aversion to being led, but he'd somehow been drawn to it all like a flaming moth.

At his whispery utterance of "Judy...Marilyn," his father should have seen the big, girly writing on the wall with open circles crowning the I's. That didn't happen. Liquor can cloud a mind already reluctant to see the truth, and Rog did not want to consider the possibility that his son, flesh of his flesh and fruit of his loins, might be that way. Rog had a tough time absorbing things, and around that time, he especially had trouble with things that weren't fermented. He cocked his head and replied,

"No, it's The Fonz," followed by a beyond embarrassing thumb raised version of Fonzie's signature "Ayyyy."

Digby gasped and reddened. He wanted the earth to part, and swallow his wide-hipped homosexual self. Tom and Maynard snickered. Katie cleared her throat uncomfortably. Edna mumbled something that thankfully no one understood, or asked her to repeat. In addition to a difficulty with enunciation since her stroke, Edna's mutterings no longer seemed to match her lips. Now, for all practical purposes, when she spoke she seemed not only incomprehensible, but also poorly dubbed.

Digby was mortified by what he'd revealed, and also irked that an undeniable television star had been referred to as a movie star. Any homosexual will be quick to explain that the two are very different. Besides, The Fonz was not his favorite TV star. Given the era and his level of gayness, his favorite television star was obviously Cher.

Katie recalled the incident quite well. "When father told me he bought that Fonzie poster, I said "Oh really," but in a way that was meant to hint that I didn't think Digby would necessarily like it. I guess I should have been a bit more forthright. Father didn't pick up on many hints. After Digby guessed and Father unrolled the poster, it got so quiet that you could hear the coffee pot brewing, and that was about it. No one knew what to say. Most everything on the subject had already been said, or at least actively neglected at one time or another. Edna did say something in her post-stroke mumble that no one could quite make out. The dog plopped down in her bed. In a moment, mother clapped her hands and offered everyone more ice cream and cake."

The occurrence was certainly humiliating, but that was nothing unusual. Digby was not immune to the pain of embarrassing situations, but they no longer surprised him. What hurt him most about this specific incident was the depth of misperception that was so apparent. It pained Digby that his father's idea of who he was and who he wanted him to be were so vastly different from reality. For once, being thought of as "son" hurt. He wanted to be thought of as "Digby." Rog saw the boy as typical, and to some extent that was true, only Digby was typical of something quite different from what his father had in mind. Alcohol had cocooned, or pickled, Rog that way.

Rog was a kind and gentle man. He loved animals, and left the farming life in which he'd been raised because butchering cows and slaughtering pigs and wringing the necks of chickens deeply upset him. Once he was of age, he escaped to join the army. The thought that he might have to kill in the military never occurred to him. Fortunately, he was assigned clerical work and was never stationed outside of his time zone.

In the army, he learned how to type, learned to love the taste of coffee, and drank liquor for the first time. Getting drunk was a great way for him to make friends. He could be awfully shy without alcohol. After his term of service, Rog went to school on the G.I. Bill. Lila was a townie who liked to dance, and squealed whenever she was dipped. Rog dipped her a lot. They went driving most weekends, and Lila loved to stick her head out the window when they sped down the country roads around Running Falls.

When people asked just what they intended to do with this budding romance, they both blushed and figured they ought to do something. The Church didn't approve of young folks not having some sort of plan. One Sunday after a day of driving, Rog kissed Lila goodbye and said, "I'll call you tomorrow after class. With this test out of the way, I should be ready to ask you to marry me." Lila wasn't sure if she should squeal, or say yes, or just wait until tomorrow. When Rog was drinking less, that roundabout approach was just his way of doing things.

They were married at Holy Martyrs, and they both cried at the wedding. The party afterward was held in Aunt Mildred's backyard. "You'll be doing me a favor," laughed Mildred with a wave of her hand. "All those high heeled shoes are just going to help aerate the soil." She was right, too. Her lawn looked better than ever that summer. Lila had always been Mildred's favorite niece. "That girl has a head on her shoulders," was what Mildred would say with a wink. "She's going to make something of herself."

Rog and Lila weren't expecting a gift from Mildred aside from hosting the reception, but she gave them the wooden wall cross with the sliding front for Holy Water and a candle for a wedding present. "You never know when you'll need one for Last Rites," said Mildred, who'd become quite concerned with preparing for the hereafter in the past couple of years.

Once the kids came along, life promptly became a whirl of work, bills, church, and diapers. It was easy to get distracted from who they were. Every once in awhile, they would remind themselves. Years later, after saying the rosary in the car, Rog and Lila would look at each another and take the long way home. If the kids weren't in the back seat, Lila would stick her head out the window, and sometimes even squeal. Rog would smile, and in that moment, everything that had happened in the twenty years since they met made sense.

Rog loved his wife and his children. Although he loved Digby, he never quite understood him. They were alike in many ways. Digby was a sensitive loner who loved animals, and ached for something different. By the time those tendencies had become apparent in his son, however, Rog had forgotten many of those things about himself. Instead, he loved Digby deeply for being his son, rather than for being himself. For years, that thought made Digby's heart ache, and sometimes awakened him during the night. He mourned the possibilities. If only he'd been more himself and Rog had been less of a drunk, things might have been different.

The lack of understanding wasn't Rog's fault. Alcoholism was a disease, and to Digby's way of thinking, it was a perfectly understandable affliction given that, for all practical purposes, his parents were trapped in that miserable town. They couldn't afford to move, or even vacation outside of the county. Rog knew he would probably be buried there. Drinking seemed the best option. Being sober in Running Falls was almost more unfortunate than being a hopeless drunk, or a drug addict. Sometimes people choose to escape for good reason.

The Chamber of Commerce billboards along the main roads at the town limits read, Thanks for Visiting Running Falls, Please Take Us with You! The sign was meant to express gratitude to visitors for shopping in the city, but the not-so-hidden message was clear. The exclamation point at the end of the sentence revealed the common desperation. The slogan seemed little more than the plea of a wild-eyed hostage. Please Take Us With You! Those who weren't desperate to leave Running Falls were part of the problem.

As a result, the classrooms were basically holding tanks for yokel offspring. Holy Martyrs was the same, only instead of docile stupidity, the parochial school system rewarded docile obedience. In both cases, the norm was the ideal, and Digby was outside the acceptable boundaries of that norm in almost every way.

His presence alone seemed to baffle the school system. Holy Martyrs was about religious adherence and gender identity. Digby was atypical in both categories. Boys were supposed to excel in science, math, and maybe religion, if an angel had spoken to them on Vocation Day. In every one of those subjects, including religion, Digby placed at the very bottom of the student rankings, and that included Special Education.

In arithmetic, he never worked with flashcards, and always went down in the first round of the math bowl. He didn't seem destined to be an accountant, or even run a cash register. Once he moved beyond simple addition and subtraction, he became even more hopeless, and had to do extra credit work in order to pass his math classes. He was consistently given D's, primarily because no teacher ever wanted to have him a second time. Each of his instructors felt that once had been quite enough of a cross to bear.

"At first, it was maddening," fumed Sister Clementine, reddening at the memory of having Digby in class. "His inability to grasp even the simplest work with fractions and decimals would try the patience of His Holiness himself. It seemed Our Savior was testing me the year I had him for mathematics. By the end of the term, if Saint Veronica had taken a shroud to my face, she'd have seen the true image of suffering. As it turned out, He, in His infinite wisdom, was merely working in a divine and mysterious way. The sisters in the math department bonded over Digby Swank's deficiencies. He became a sort of "hot potato" between us, and we used to roll our eyes and call him 'the null set.' We found it deeply ironic that boy couldn't understand the concept of the lowest common denominator. 'Look in the mirror,' we were always daring one another to say."

Gym class was a predictable nightmare for Digby. Coach Crosby had his own way of conducting class. He didn't mollycoddle or show support, or promote sportsmanship or do much of anything other than shout indecipherable gibberish for long stretches of time, and blow his whistle. He was so confusing, that most of the class only knew what they were doing by seeing the sports equipment that was presented.

Whatever the game, gym class always involved choosing teams. A student's rank on the roster was as much a sign of social standing as it was of athletic prowess. As a clumsy and uncoordinated outcast, Digby couldn't remember having ever heard his name called when picking teams. He was simply the one who remained, the student who drifted over to join the grumbling team who had to take him. His teammates usually encouraged him to "just stay out of the way," and Digby was happy to oblige. The end of class was signaled by an especially loud blast from Crosby's whistle, followed a double clap of his paw-like hands. He did not socialize with the other teachers, and even ate lunch in his truck. His wife was a Lutheran.

Science proved an even greater challenge for Digby. Though he did quite well when learning about nature and animals, his skill and interest abruptly ended when his studies crossed the border into such areas as basic electricity, simple microscopic biology, or beginning chemistry. He never scored higher than ten percent on any exam in those areas, and managed to botch every in-class experiment. Though he was accused of "endangering the class" several times during lab, non-participation was not an option.

The favorites in Sister Cordoba's class could be discerned by their distance from Digby and his bunsen burner. Assigning students to be his lab partner was often used as a disciplinary tool. Each time it happened, it was accompanied with Sister's grim pronouncement, "Deus tecum." May God be with you. When he was called on by Sister during lectures, Digby would either answer incorrectly or stare in vacant-eyed silence. "That head is thicker than the Earth's crust," Sister Cordoba might say. Other times, with a sigh of exasperation, she might add, "Crux mihi ancora," (The cross is my anchor) before turning to another student for an answer. Digby was an exceptionally poor student, whose pitiful classroom performance was coupled with a complete inability to apply that knowledge in the outside world.

After spending an entire week learning about electricity, Digby went with his parents to his Aunt Peg and Uncle Lou's dairy farm for the day. He loved it there. The land was green and rolling, the sky was clear, and the air was free of the Band-Aid and leather stink. It was like the Land of Plenty from the Bible. His aunt and uncle had an inbred sheep dog that they kept chained in the yard. The dog routinely worked herself into a frenzy watching the laundry flap in the breeze, and would run maniacally around the pole, shortening her chain until she inevitably collided with the metal pole and stunned herself. Digby never tired of watching her do it.

That Sunday, he was playing with his cousin Cora down near the stream that ran across their farm. He could hear the grasses and reeds in the breeze. Crossing a marshy area leading to the creek itself, they needed to go below the electric cattle fence. Rather than touch the live wires, which Digby may have done before studying electricity in Sister Cordoba's science class, he picked up a tin coffee can from the muck, stood in the water, and touched the can to the fence to see if the current was on. In that instant, he thought The Rapture had arrived. The next thing he knew, he was lying on the day bed on Peg and Lou's back porch, half covered in mud.

Cora recalled that Sunday. "Hell yeah, I remember that. It

was one of the few times he was over that Digby didn't want to play Mystery Date the whole time. I tried to stop him from touching that fence. I knew better than to do something like that, and I was three years younger and got held back a year in school. Digby was always a few sandwiches short of a picnic. He had no common sense. The instant he touched the wire I heard ZZZZ and he flew through the air. He landed ten yards away, flat on his back in the marsh slop! I ran to the house and called the folks from their game of euchre. They carried him back to the porch draped over a fresh case of beer. Dad said he wouldn't be surprised if the whole thing scrambled his fool brain even more."

21 – In Heat

Digby had to at least partially agree with Uncle Lou. His brain did feel scrambled, or at least like it had stopped doing the thinking. The new control center for his body was decidedly lower on his anatomy.

Ever since Digby could remember, he'd had puppy-dog crushes on boys and men, saints, and sometimes the dead. Digby Swank + Saint Sebastian = True Love 4 Ever! He'd absently drawn hearts featuring their interlocked initials on notebooks and wooden rulers, in plates of food, bubble baths, and across steamy windows. Then, with a blush at what he'd been doodling, he'd quickly destroy the evidence. His behavior had been embarrassing, but quite innocent. However, that "higher love" innocence had coarsened and changed. He'd been blindsided by hormones. Mooning gave way to indecent obsessions. That puppy dog became a bitch in heat overnight, and thoughts of sex became an around the clock affair.

None of this gay stuff pleased him. It pleasured him, but it didn't please him. He hoped that being girly had been just a phase, and that playing with dolls and dressing up and making Bugles corn chips into glamorous fingernails had been nothing other than imaginative childhood play. Maybe he'd shown unusual cunning. Perhaps it had all been some ingenious way of learning how to understand women. How many straight men knew how hard it was to run in heels, or the optimal places to apply perfume, or the proper way to wrap a turban? Maybe by knowing these things, he would somehow be more attractive to women.

The idea that this was about women and not about his being a bona fide girly boy was delusional. The fantasies he had every night and every other waking hour had to do with men and boys, and didn't waffle in the least. It was all penis, all the time. Not a vagina or set of boobs in sight. The idea that he was just a big old homo scared him, because he felt that if that was the case, his life might never change. He didn't want to always be invisible, or an outsider, or a shushed secret. He wanted his life reflected in pop songs, TV romances, and silver screen coupledom. He wanted to be a part of those things, but being a part of any of that stuff seemed to mean being heterosexual.

He accepted long ago that he'd be damned to Hell or maybe Purgatory, unless of course he said a perfect Act of Contrition on his deathbed. However, going to Hell for being a selfish liar or a non-believer was at least socially acceptable. At twelve years old, Digby could only imagine gay life as filled with endless teasing and hassles, and he assumed Hell would be more of the same. He could already hear the demonic cackling. Hey, check out the flamer! Hell would probably be an awful lot like gym class in August for countless lifetimes: an eternity of never being chosen, an eternity of incomprehensible barks and commands, and an eternity of dreading additional miseries. Only an Irish Catholic could be condemned to eternal Hell, and still worry that life would get worse.

From pulpit to playground to prime time, Digby had constantly heard that homosexuality was a sin and an abomination, a joke and punchline, a diseased gene, and a mental illness. Though it was called unspeakable, "homosexuality" was always said with great precision, the speaker often adding an extra syllable as though it were being held at a distance and dissected in mid-air. It was something to snuffed out, or converted, or contained at any cost. Don't do this. Don't be this. Don't fantasize about this. At every turn, and with every mention of the word came a resounding and unwavering DON'T.

It didn't matter in the end. Digby couldn't stop being who he was. He felt guilty about it, but he'd always felt guilty about something. Shame was certainly nothing new. In many ways, being forbidden had backfired. Defiance could be very enticing. DON'T had a tendency to heighten his eagerness to DO. Experience had shown that when something was that forbidden, it was well worth the transgression. When he was in this frame of mind, the Catholic Code of Unacceptable Behavior became a sort of double-dog-dare to-do list. This sex thing and the homosexual thing were so wrong, that it had the potential to be really great despite the consequences.

At other times he didn't feel as defiant, and he thought of it as a terrible burden. He struggled with what it all meant. Why had he been made this way, and given this cross to bear? Sometimes he felt like a freak, and sometimes the words they used echoed in his head: fag, travesty, femme, sodomite, queer, sinner. He struggled and waffled on the issue, but rarely reached any conclusions. Even when he did, they were of little consequence. The matter had been decided. He didn't choose this; it had chosen him. It was what he was. There was no not being it, there were only levels of acceptance or denial.

Pretending not to be gay was certainly one of his options. He'd been hiding who he was for as long as he could remember. Puberty brought that ongoing masquerade to a different level. Containment had suddenly become messier, and he had much more to hide. Digby could lie and deny his way through the years and live a double life of quick gratification and self-loathing. Many in Running Falls did just that.

For years, Digby had heard rumors about Mr. Lister, the pharmacist with the unfortunate lisp who owned the drugstore, and lived two blocks over with his wife. Mr. Lister wore short shorts when he mowed the lawn or pruned his rosebushes in the summertime. In the winter, Mr. Lister's gloves always matched his shoes and scarf. He collected souvenir spoons and bells. People often confused Mr. and Mrs. Lister when they phoned the Lister home. The click of Mr. Lister's platform shoes always announced his entrance Sunday mornings at Holy Martyrs. Even after he was given permission from the bishop to eat something before mass on account of his diabetes, Mr. Lister continued to fast. Many thought this was because every time he fainted, he was carried from the nave to the foyer in the arms of some strapping congregant.

Mr. Donnelly was a "confirmed bachelor" who sold insurance, and always toyed with his collar as though fingering a string of pearls. He crossed his long legs at the knee, and sometimes even wrapped the top leg beneath again to hook at the ankle. He won the Holy Martyrs benefit talent show for two years running with renditions of "Too Darn Hot" and "Steam Heat." The third year he competed, many raised their eyebrows when Mr. Donnelly came out in a full saloon gal getup and performed "See What The Boys in the Back Room Will Have."

Several folks felt that crossed the line, even if proceeds from the show were going directly to the Maryknoll mission in Africa. "This is a church basement after all," scoffed Betty Murphy, who'd come in second to Mr. Donnelly the previous two years. That was the last year Mr. Donnelly competed. When he lost, he clucked his tongue, turned on his heel and stomped up the church steps, still wearing his skirt and corset. His feather boa was found tossed over a hedge outside the rectory the next day. Eventually, he moved to Baltimore.

Folks also whispered about Mr. Castallucci, the successful owner of AnnaMaria's who dressed in a tuxedo and kept the lighting of his restaurant dim enough to hide his concealer. He bleached his teeth, and was rather extreme when shaping his eyebrows. The whispering intensified when Castallucci hired Randy as head waiter. Randy was a slender gent from out of town, who confused everyone when he said he'd been a gypsy. Some thought it meant he used to tell fortunes, and others supposed that he used to travel about in a caravan. No one in Running Falls, except perhaps Mr. Lister and Mr. Donnelly, had ever heard the word used to describe a dancer in the chorus of shows.

There were plenty of other gay men in town. Straight priests were more the exception than the rule in the diocese. To most men of the cloth, celibacy was little more than an eight-letter word for discretion, which was a synonym for forest preserve. Some folks thought that parish cars in the park district lot meant the priests were merely getting out into nature to collect their thoughts and get in touch with God, but many folks knew better. The topic was never discussed. A priest seen tricking was seen as a trick of perception. The Devil was causing doubts by planting seeds in a filthy mind. Priests simply did not do what it seemed they were doing, even when they were seen doing it.

Living that sort of secretive life held little appeal. Digby didn't want his life to become one long game of hiding or make-believe.

If he was going to do that, what was the point of becoming an adult? There were other ways. Digby could just be gay, and let the chips fall where they may. He couldn't imagine making such a bold declaration, especially now, and certainly not in Running Falls. Doing so was almost unimaginable, until Digby recalled Mr. Beloni and his friend Ben on that terribly tasteful couch. Maybe with independence and prudence, that sort of life would be okay. Digby knew a decision like that would come with compromise. It probably meant living quietly, but Digby wasn't sure living quietly was something he wanted to do.

He wondered if it would be better to disappear in the blend of a big city populace, or even find a community there. The idea occurred to him after he found a copy of After Dark magazine in the parking lot behind the grocery store. He was flabbergasted to think that someone would be bold enough to read something like that right in the Piggly Wiggly lot. Digby was too afraid to keep the issue, but after running into an adjoining alley, he scanned every page front to back and back to front, with wide-eyed wonder. The images were emblazoned on his memory. There seemed to be a whole urban world out there, a place where underground meant cool and accepted, and something other than dead. That full-body immersion into glamour was what he really wanted, but all that San Francisco/New York/L.A./Chicago debauchery was a world away from Running Falls.

In the span of a few short months, his two simple options for how to be gay had suddenly become several points along a seemingly infinite spectrum. This gay thing was really whatever he wanted it to be, and however much of his life he wanted it to be. Some hid it, some fit it, and some made it a career and lived it twenty-four-seven. It was just a card that a person was dealt; how they played the hand was up to them.

All Digby knew was that he was not going to let this awkward stage last a lifetime. He'd find a special someone, or maybe a few at one of those fancy big city discotheques. That was the sort of thing he fantasized about his life becoming. But what he really wanted, even more than the sex, was just to feel that sense of belonging in someone's arms. He'd known that special something once in his life. All else had paled in comparison. It seemed he'd been looking for unconditional love since Grandma Rose was taken from him. Her hugs were everything Heaven could be. More than anything, he wanted to replace that loss.

Doug had brought him a wonderful kinship, but it was too guarded. Walter had opened doors, but Digby had entered with a fake I.D. His parents loved him as well, but they wanted him to be a certain way. Maybe the right beau would make him feel wanted and complete. Sex would just be the icing on the cake. Maybe then, when he looked into his beloved's eyes and was held in his beloved's arms, he'd finally be enough just as he was. Maybe then there would be nothing left to hide, and nothing more to be. That sounded like Heaven, and it seemed worth any hardship.

Until true love or even true sex came along, there was masturbation. Since he was still inexperienced, despite looking through an After Dark magazine, Digby's overactive imagination went to work. He didn't necessarily envision a variety of scenarios, but he certainly created a revolving door of participants for his male-only nasty thoughts. There were some constants in his masturbatory lineup, while others came and went. His legion of hazy dreamtime lovers grew with every new bag boy at Piggly Wiggly, and each high school football hero. They came from the pages of After Dark, and the Sears catalogue. Whenever Digby bought the latest issue of Tiger Beat, he'd wait until he was the sole customer near the checkout at the drugstore, and then rush to the counter. Mr. Lister would always clear his throat and say, "Well... um" and adjust his glasses. Digby typically hid the magazine amidst everything from candy bars to construction paper. Neither of them ever said anything regarding the magazine, but a silent knowing passed between them. Digby never fantasized about Mr. Lister, though he did sometimes think about men outside of his age bracket.

One of his adult fantasy men was his grumpy, hog-headed gym teacher, Coach Crosby. The attraction somewhat embarrassed Digby, but he seemed helpless in Crosby's presence. It wasn't the way Crosby's indecipherable bark emerged from beneath his walrus mustache that attracted Digby, or the way his huge head opened on its clam-like hinge to issue those commands. Crosby was mainly on Digby's list for his beyond hirsute pelt. For Digby, body hair equalled virility. It was the epitome of manliness. Hair covered Coach Crosby's arms and legs with an unusual thickness. His chest hair spilled over the collar of his sweatshirt like an exotic moss. With no neck to speak of, Coach Crosby's head sat like a stone atop a tuft of prairie grass.

Another local crush of Digby's was the guy at the Sunoco gas station named Norm, if his attendant smock was to be believed. Digby had once seen Norm grab his crotch while Rog was getting a fill-up. Digby stared openmouthed from the passenger window. It looked nonchalant, but this was only days after finding the copy of After Dark. In the magazine, "the crotch grope" had been number three in a photo bank piece about "the fundamentals of cruising." Smitten, Digby ignored the fact that Norm was oblivious to him and for weeks afterwards Digby wandered in the field behind the Sunoco. He'd sit near the railroad tracks and petal pick flowers (He-Loves-Me/He-Loves-Me-Not) and hope Norm would notice him. In Digby's fantasy, once Norm saw him, he'd drop his wrench and approach in his greasy jumpsuit. Norm would wrap him in his arms, hold Digby tight and say something like, "I must have you."

For the most part, Digby was operating without guidelines. Most heterosexual kids his age had peers, parents, and the streets for learning all this stuff. Aside from his quick study of the world according to After Dark magazine, Digby had nothing. There was no mentor or feedback. Sometimes there were "very special episodes" on TV, but Digby would never risk suspicion by actually watching them. Most of them were too vague to be of much help, anyway. The truth of the matter was that when it came to sex, he was on his own. As might be expected, being bombarded by hormones and bereft of advice, Digby made some terribly humiliating choices.

Being Catholic, ritual was in his bones, so each of his crushes was the subject of secret love spells. His hexes often involved going to extreme measures to obtain personal items from his intended. He searched through dumpsters, and even lurked in shadows waiting for a beloved to discard a Kleenex or flick a cigarette butt. Anything "infused" with their energy would do: discarded assignments, gloves, hair, a green paint footprint on butcher paper, and even a scab became powerful talismans. He kept the items in a bejeweled shoebox.

Amidst candles, he donned one of Mother's colorful caftans, played an LP called Authentic Tribal Beats, and intoned sacred sounding incantations to the love gods. He burned poems and incense, writing the initials of his crushes in blood, and in one case, the poop from a crush's dog. It was all an intense form of foreplay, especially since most of his rituals culminated in masturbation. He knew he was on the right track with his attempts, and certainly enjoyed the efforts. Digby was sure that eventually he'd discover the proper magical spell for romantic success. When he broke the code, endless love would be his.

He was an adolescent obsessed, and he'd often go to demoralizing lengths to fulfill a mere fragment of his teen fantasies. Once he hid beneath the bed in the Swank guest room to see his cousin Tober and Uncle Mort peel off their swim trunks. Acne spread across Tober's big ass like cloves on a ham. Even though Mort and Tober's nearly identical man-parts looked like two field mice in a tangle of weeds, Digby found it all quite thrilling. An excited inhalation caused the fringe on the bedspread to tickle his nose. A sudden sneeze gave him away. Caught and desperate, Digby quickly blurted an excuse about falling asleep.

"Under the bed?" asked Uncle Mort, scratching his bald, freckled head.

"Um yeah, I didn't want to mess up the covers." Digby scrambled to his feet and angled out the door. Mort and Tober merely shrugged and finished changing. Fortunately, people were used to Digby doing strange nonsensical things.

This sort of thing was more the rule than the exception. Digby's inner drive to catch a glimpse of those enthralling male appendages overruled almost any consideration. At the time, he didn't necessarily want to do anything with those penises; he merely wanted to see them. He wanted to note their size, heft, and potential. This motivated him to such a degree, that he wondered sometimes if the person was incidental to his member. Maybe it was the penis, and not who it was attached to that would bring unconditional love. Maybe the security and satisfaction he was seeking didn't come from any one penis, but from a hundred or ten thousand.

Digby was mystified that puberty was so confusing, and at the same time so utterly and undeniably simple. In many cultures, rituals help define this puzzling juncture in life: the bar and bat mitzvah, the debutante ball, and Aboriginal front tooth evulsion are but a few. Without traditional rites, this transition from child to adult can come too soon or linger too long, leaving one in adolescent limbo.

The Catholic Church was no help. When Digby asked Father Andrew during confession, he was told, "You're an adult when you're an adult in the eyes of the Lord, and if you have to ask, it is not yet your time." The priest then asked if he masturbated. He said no, and in a feisty act of dismissal, left the confessional without even waiting to hear his penance.

The issue of adulthood continued to bother Digby. How would he know when he had gone from becoming an adult to actually being one? He found innumerable answers. The law called it eighteen, but some considered it coming from the DMV with license in hand. Others swore on a full pubic bush, a lowered voice, or other hormonal factors. Some said you really understood the meaning of the word "adult" when you started earning your own way in the world. Other sources believed adulthood came with marriage, or becoming a parent. That reasoning made no sense to Digby. What about those who never married, or those who remained childless? After considering the options, Digby decided that his transition to adulthood would only occur as the result of actual bona fide sex.

Though unsure about exactly what sex was, or rather what all it entailed, Digby was very sure about what it wasn't. Sex wasn't masturbation or imagined doings with toothy Sears underwear guys or the teen idols from Tiger Beat. It wasn't nocturnal emission, or humping a pillow, or French kissing a photograph. It was something even greater than all three of those things combined. For Digby, sex would be an orgasm with someone else in the room, and parts of their anatomy actually touching. He knew that when "it" happened that "it" would change everything.

Love was something else entirely. It was the Holy Grail. That sort of sacred journey could wait. Digby reasoned that before he went on the crusade, he'd have to learn how to mount a horse. Sex was his new goal. He'd practiced masturbation to the point of perfection, and was ready for more. By then, many of the kids in his class were doing "it," or at least several versions of "it."

Then the absolutely unthinkable happened. In another Catholic case of too little too late, Holy Martyrs was pressed to have a marital relations class for all eighth graders. The state government had deemed it mandatory for all institutions of learning. In the administrative offices at Holy Martyrs, there was a good deal of grumbling about "those godless legislators downstate and their liberal agenda."

On the day of the seminar, the boys and the girls broke up into separate groups. The girls were taught by Father Andrew, whose speech impediment was especially pronounced that week due to a flare-up of his Bell's palsy. Father Andrew was chosen to teach the girls since he wanted to be involved in the "adult relations" talk, but even the administration recognized having him teach the boys was unwise.

The boys were taught by Sister Mary Patrick, whose broad stance, sturdy gait, and thick neck made her what would be an imposing figure on any defensive line, much less in a classroom. Sister Mary Patrick moved like a claymation dinosaur. One strong leg shot forward, turning her body slightly to one side as the rear leg swung ahead of the first, turning her body slightly in the other direction. Given her menacing gait, she always seemed primed at any moment to attack a papier-mache fishing village.

Everyone considered Sister Mary Patrick an odd choice as a sex education instructor. She was about as far removed from marital relations as humanly possible. The class taught the boys next to nothing. If anything, the nuts and bolts of sex became even more confusing as the day progressed. Perhaps that was the point. One thing the class did make abundantly clear time and again, was that all manner of sexual conduct was base, evil and bad.

Abstinence was the bottom line. "After all," said Sister Mary Patrick, as her furry uni-brow scanned the room, "it's hardly worth damnation." Did she know? She smacked her pointer upon the board, where the word SIN was written in the hitherto unused red chalk. As she continued to tap the word, she continued, "The cost of a moment's pleasure is eternity in Hell. Even the thought of a moment's pleasure is eternity in Hell. Wanting, considering, and doing are all occasions for sin."

Digby shifted in his seat. He never understood how thought and action resulted in an equal punishment. That was so stupid. Where in the world besides in the Roman Catholic Church was that true? It seemed a part of human nature, and of normal brain function to automatically think of something when told not to. If a person actually believed that what the Church taught was true, why would anyone only think about doing something when actually doing it had the same repercussions? He'd been in Catholic school long enough to know that questioning the logic of such things would bring only sneering judgement, probable chastisement, and an hour or two standing in the garbage can. Valid points were often explained as clever tactics of the Devil. Responses such as, "You may question the truth but rest assured, there will be no debate on your personal Judgement Day," typically put an end to such discussions.

"That includes touching yourself." She spat the words syllable by syllable while slowly lurching up and down the aisles, as if her flaring nostrils could sniff out those among them who'd touched themselves, or had even thought of doing so. "That is a sin, a horrible horrible sin. Onanism is a mockery of God's creative love...and if such a sin occurs, know that the Virgin Mary, as well as her cousin, Saint Elizabeth, will be watching and weeping. Let prudence be your watchword. Do not invite an occasion for sin. Keep your hands atop the covers at night," she warned. The only sounds were her strained breathing, her leaden-footed advance, and the jangle of the heavy rosary about her waist. "Nocturnal emissions hint at daytime depravity." Click. Clomp. Wheeze. Click. Clomp. Wheeze. "Kissing in an unchaste manner is repulsive to all God-fearing people." She paused, as if daring any one of the boys to snicker or show the slightest sign of disagreement. "Bundling with intent is a sin. Canoodling is a sin. Frottage is a sin. As are all other forms of carnal pleasure too vile to bear mentioning." Digby noticed a couple perplexed looks. Onanism? Bundling with intent? Canoodling? Frottage?

According to Sister, even close dancing was evil. She maintained that all couples should keep their torsos a minimum of one foot apart at all times, "…with only a slight bend to the elbows, making certain there is enough room for the Holy Spirit between you and your partner. And the hips should remain stationary at all times, as if cemented in their sockets," she added with another swing of the rosary about her waist. Digby cowered. Swinging rosaries always brought Grandma Swank to mind.

Sister returned to the front of the classroom before continuing. The "answer" amidst all this murk of the flesh was evident. To avoid damnation, the boys needed to remain celibate or only have relations after marriage, and not even think about sex in the meantime. If they found themselves tempted, they were to drop to their knees and offer up prayers to the poor souls in Purgatory until such sinful feelings had passed. Even after a man and woman exchanged their wedding vows, "the act" was not to be enjoyed.

"Sexual relations of any kind are the burden of Original Sin, and are as removed from pleasure as the savoring of one's food is from the simple act of digestion. Bestial acts are done for the sole purpose of having children and strengthening God's kingdom on Earth. Is that clear?" Her question was not a question at all, but the clarification of a command. Her pointer hit the board again. "Wearing a condom is a sin." She pronounced it as con-DOME. She smirked, and was quick to remark at how much it sounded like condemn. "There's a good reason for that. Likewise, the IUD may well stand for I Utilize Demonology. The so-called birth control pill is a tool of the Devil, and by swallowing it, a woman is inviting Satan inside of her. Each pill is the equivalent of years in Purgatory." By this point, Sister had turned beet red, and noticeably dewy. Her breath had become a pant. "And those who perform, support, or have an abortion should be cut from this earth and cast into Hell as surely as they cut the miracle of life from the womb." By the end of the sentence, she was breathless and shouting at the same time. In a moment, Sister crossed herself and mumbled, "Dabit Deus his quoque finem. Di meliora." God will bring an end to this. Heaven send us better times.

By this point, none of the boys took her seriously. Digby supposed that very few in the marital relations class ever did, but by now it was hard to understand even half of what she was talking about. Sister continued, "A baby is the fruit of God's love between a Church-wedded man and woman. When the two express their love in a chaste fashion, a council of angels meets to determine the authenticity of their faith. If the union is deemed godly, a covenant of creation is made, and an infant springs from the junction of a woman's nether limbs. Deo gratias." Digby scratched his head. Granted, he was a horrible student in science, but there were so many loopholes in this explanation. Did Sister Mary Patrick actually believe this stuff, or was it all just another ruse of the Catholic Church?

Even then, Digby suspected Sister Mary Patrick played for "the girl's team." She was almost always accompanied by Sister Bernadette, who moved and hovered about her like a slender mustachioed moon. They always seemed bent in secret confidences, whispering like coy tulips joined at the stem. The following year, the two released a book about serving our Lord by teaching in a parochial school. With Caissons and Crucifixes received glowing reviews in the diocese newsletter. Copies of it sat in the vestibule of all Catholic Churches in the area. The suggested donation was ten dollars.

On the day of the martial relations class, when Sister began talking about conception being decided by a council of angels, the boys still listening looked at one another incredulously. What the hell was she talking about? Is there some other sex besides the usual fingering, oral, and intercourse stuff? Maybe there were two kinds of sex—Catholic sex and normal sex. Maybe we are a different species. If all this was to be believed, that seemed the only feasible explanation.

Supposedly, on that day Father Andrew had told the girls that their bodies were the temples of the Holy Ghost, and that boys would do almost anything to "invade their temple and soil their tabernacle." They were told that when the torso of a boy touched them, that the young man was often using them as "a masturbatory tool." Many of the girls eyed the boys very strangely for the remainder of the week. By Monday, all was back to normal.

22 - The Real Deal

When sex finally happened, it couldn't have come at a better time. Digby was horribly down. He had been displaying every symptom of clinical depression except for weight loss. His first real sexual experience was the result of an unlikely chain of events. Cousin Ted, that prankster with a pension, sent shock waves through the family tree when he announced his engagement. Aunt Lucy was beside herself with excitement, and actually choked on a bit of beef jerky when she called Lila to share the good news. Lila was not surprised in the least when Aunt Lucy also revealed that she'd broken out in hives seconds after hearing the news. Most figured she'd be a complete mess by the wedding day.

Ted's intended was the manliest of all his conquests, with the ill-fitting name of Monique. Aunt Lucy gave the entire extended family the privilege of meeting "the lucky lady" at a backyard luau, complete with a pig on a spit and leis. As was befitting Aunt Lucy, it was quite an elaborate affair that served both as an engagement party, as well as an opportunity for her to show off the new AstroTurf on the patio. The newfangled marvel promised to positively transform outdoor entertaining.

"All the society hostesses throw parties with themes," she'd said to Lila when speaking of the Hawaiian theme. A luau made perfect sense, given Aunt Lucy's drooling adoration of society hostesses. As an egotist with low self-esteem, Digby frequently felt he was the piece of shit that the Earth revolved around. As such, he wondered if this entire shindig was yet another snide reference to his hula from years ago. That was not the case. In fact, the luau was one of the few times he saw Aunt Lucy that she didn't mention his hula. She didn't really have time. The entire afternoon and evening she flitted and fluttered about in her bright caftan, which she called a sarong. She was on a new sort of diet pill to try and take off some of the weight before the wedding. Even without those little white tablets, Aunt Lucy had always been a drain. Hosting her only son's engagement party,

Lucy drove everyone crazy by trying to make everything perfect. She'd approach a guest, laugh and ask small talk questions, then buzz off before they had a chance to answer.

"She was wild-eyed, like Little Orphan Annie with the whites blackened and the pupils big as her eye sockets. She was hopping about her green AstroTurf like a half-crazed kangaroo in that busy bed sheet she was wearing," joked local butcher Cyrus Burden, a man who never was one for parties to begin with. After a couple of drinks, he told anyone who would listen that it was his pig on the spit.

Despite Aunt Lucy's lofty aspirations and eagerness to put on airs, most parties she hosted only bordered on being socially acceptable. The luau was no exception.

No sooner was Cyrus' pig rotating on the spit than Cousin Christine staggered to the window box, broke off a couple of geranium stems, and shoved them in her beehive. She'd had a few. With loose gestures and a firm jaw, she ordered Tom and Maynard to hold a lawn rake horizontally. "I'll show you how the natives do it," she said, beginning her drunken limbo approach. Almost at once, her back gave out and Christine twisted awkwardly, reopening her appendectomy wound from weeks earlier. She screamed, collapsed, and bled all over the AstroTurf in that order. After a few moments of general pandemonium, which resulted in one side of the pig getting significantly burned, Rog offered to drive her to the emergency room. Lila gave the keys to Katie, and told her to drive instead. Christine may have had a few, but Rog had had a few more.

Aunt Lucy shook her head to recall the incident. "I told her to take it easy, but you know how Christine can be when she's around fresh flowers, and has had a few. Once she gets something in her head, there's no talking to her. All Willard's side was that way. That fool woman claimed she was limber enough to get under that garden rake, and said that she didn't take those yoga lessons at the YWCA two years ago for nothing. Thankfully, her bleeding and such didn't ruin what was really the party of the season. It required some serious Christian forgiveness to forget her behavior, but luckily for her, I am high-minded. She sent a hanging plant, and offered up a mass for Ted and Monique as a way of apology. One thing I will say, that new AstroTurf didn't disappoint. It really resisted the blood stains."

The Swanks had a fine time, and Rog and Lila resoundingly agreed that Monique Williams was a nice girl. She seemed outgoing, with a very easy and likable way about her. This tendency was even more pronounced alongside Aunt Lucy's fussy bustling. Those diet pills made her jittery and emotional. The two times that Lucy managed to pause in one place for more than two minutes, she burst into tears, saying it pained her that Willard hadn't lived to see the day.

Monique had a wide face, an irregularly bleached mustache, a firm grip, and a quick, infectious laugh. Aunt Lucy pointed out several times that Monique came from money. Her father was Walt "The Wizard" Williams, the legendary tri-state used car dealer who "refused to be undersold." With her family's money and Ted's good pension, people were certain the couple would do just fine financially. Everyone seemed to think Monique's folks would give them a top-notch used car as a wedding gift.

Ted thought the world of Monique, and she did seem like a lot of fun. Ted and Monique were both big and boisterous, and loved to clown. Combining their households would mean more than one rubber hand and squirting corsage.

Monique had chortled when Ted pulled a pair of slinky eyeglasses from his pocket during their pre-Cana class with Father Cedric. The priest was not amused, though his wincing sneer could be attributed to soreness. Father Cedric was such a religious man that it was whispered on good account that he was part of the Opus Dei. After having his wine each night, he knelt in prayer in his cell at the rectory and begged for the Lord's mercy with a bit of self-flagellation from a leather cattail of knotted cords called a discipline. As he wept and asked God's forgiveness, he liked to swing the instrument in progressively stronger loops over one shoulder and then the other, until he finally collapsed with a scream before his personal altar. His religious devotion brought great satisfaction, and a good number of welts.

Monique was from just across state line, and her family was mostly from around those parts. They decided that the nuptials would take place at St. Gregory's Church in Odessa with Father Cedric presiding, and a reception with an open bar following at the big nightclub in Odessa, Chez Pandemonium. Digby's parents were thrilled. This would be some party.

Odessa was a mere forty miles from Running Falls, but given an open bar reception and the recent crackdown on DUIs, driving home afterward would not be wise. They print those people's names in the paper for God and the world to see! Digby didn't want to quibble, but being omniscient, didn't God already know about the DUIs? Even if he didn't, did God actually read The Morning Star? Rather than worry, his parents decided to rent a motel room in Odessa.

None of Digby's siblings would be able to attend the wedding. Katie had a job at Carson's Pancake House, and was out the door every morning at five in her brown polyester jumper with tan trim, and an oversized Carson's Breakfast Special button that said, "Ask Me Why I'm Smiling!" Unless it was Wednesday. On Wednesdays, she wore a large blue ribbon that said, "Quiz Me About Our Big Stack Supreme!" Despite her buttons and ribbons, the most common question Katie was asked was why Carson's was called an all-night pancake house when they closed at midnight. In true Swank fashion, she ignored their question, smiled, and served them food.

Katie hated the job, but she was eager to add items to her hope chest. Sadly, her bridal box was just a few plastic milk crates in the basement that contained some old towels, four soup spoons, a quilt, a travel iron, and a crock pot. After work at Carson's, she planned to spend the night at a girlfriend's house. At least that's what she told Lila and Rog. In truth, she'd be having pre-marital relations with her new beau, Amos. She may have been going to

Hell, but at least she was going there with clear skin and an even disposition.

Maynard was out the door early in the day, as well. He was working at the Spit N' Shine Car Wash, saving money to buy his own set of wheels. Rog and Lila liked to see him determined and working towards something. "A young man needs direction," they both agreed. Maynard said he had to work double shifts all weekend, which was not quite true, though the boss had asked him to be prepared to stay two extra hours on Saturday. Maynard was more than happy to miss the wedding. He hated dressing up, and anything that required polished shoes.

The weekend of the wedding, Tom still going to be out of state for three weeks at baseball camp. Digby's parents glowed when he was called "promising" by the local papers, as well as his coach. No Swank had ever been called that before! The 'Swank Shows Promise' clipping from The Morning Star went directly into the Swank family scrapbook, which was mostly funeral cards and wedding announcements. The only other "news" pieces were two more The Morning Star articles, one on the Holy Martyrs' Youth Group that mentioned Katie. The other was a 'Christmas Season Heats Up for Shoppers' photo, also from The Morning Star, which showed a blurred but nonetheless perturbed Lila amidst the packed checkout lines during Hampton's Holidaze Sale-a-thon. The Swank scrapbook was only partially filled, and really no bigger than the meagre diocese missalette.

With all his siblings occupied, Rog and Lila had a problem. What were they going to do about Digby? Maynard was enough of a worry on his own without putting him in charge of watching someone else. Maynard had a wild streak, and Lila was sure that if Digby was left in his care that both boys would be in jail by Sunday night. Only two weeks earlier, Lila had caught Maynard sneaking a six-pack of beer inside the house. He'd hidden it outside in the bushes, and tried to bring it inside after he thought Lila had gone to bed. His mother heard the creak of the front door, and was right there with a baseball bat. She made Maynard give it to Rog as a gift. Rog was confused as to the occasion, but was grateful nonetheless. "It's just my size," he joked, popping the cap from the first bottle.

Despite Digby's protests that he was old enough to stay and take care of himself, Rog and Lila would not hear of it. His parents weren't totally daft. The suggestion was met with an unwavering chorus of, "Absolutely not young man!" They brought up the Buick again, and they didn't debate the matter. He would be accompanying them.

To complicate matters, the wedding was a "no children" affair. The relatives grumbled and made some snide asides, but Ted and Monique remained firm. Some of the family, like Cousin Noreen and her husband Will, resented the rule, and even went so far as to deduct the cost of a sitter from how much they spent on the wedding gift. Noreen and Will even showed the deduction on the attached wedding card, and circled the new amount with a red pen. At Noreen's urging, Will also told this directly to Ted, just in case there was any confusion. Slapping Will on the shoulder, Ted just laughed, took out his slinky eye glasses, which he never left home without, and pretended to check the math. He and Monique didn't care. It was their day.

Digby was far from distraught to learn he was banned from the nuptials, especially since it wasn't personal. Ted and Monique actually seemed to like him, but rules were rules, and at fifteen, he was too young to attend. Eighteen was the cutoff. Ted and Monique chose that age partly so they didn't have to worry about underage drinking, and partly so cousin Tober wouldn't be invited.

Cousin Tober was the surly sixteen-year-old with flat features and acne whom Digby had hidden under the bed to see nude. Tober was a suspected casualty of inbreeding, a suspicion given added credibility what with his mouth-breathing, his third nipple, and his lack of an "edit" button. Tober called Monique a man right to her face. Digby paled when he heard this. He knew just how Monique probably felt. That was just plain rude. Insulting someone directly was not how things were done in this family, even in the farthest hillbilly branches of the family tree. They took pride in being raised properly where things of that nature were discussed the right way—either behind a person's back, or prefaced with, "I'm not saying this to be mean but..."

Digby would be staying alone at the motel almost the entire day, and well into the wee hours. It was even better than staying home alone. Better still, the Swanks weren't staying at any old Motel 6 or Red Roof Inn. His parents were actually being extravagant, at least extravagant for them, which meant they weren't being outlandishly cheap. To impress Aunt Lucy and Monique's father, Walt "The Wizard" Williams, they booked reservations at the Solaridome Motel.

The Solaridome had a common central area covered by an opaque fiberglass dome. It featured color TV, Magic Fingers on every bed, free parking, a coffee shop, and air conditioning. Best of all, was the dome itself. Beneath that plexiglas canopy, amidst the plethora of greenery was a heated pool, a sauna, a changing area, a mini pinball arcade, a pair of pool tables, an air hockey table, and a shuffleboard court.

While Rog signed the register and collected the keys, Lila and Digby waited in the car. Thinking this was about the most glamorous place he'd ever been, Digby scanned the lot for possible celebrities visiting Odessa, but saw no one famous. He was so thrilled at the prospect of all the ritzy fun, that Lila chastised him for fogging the windows. "You're panting like a porch dog in August." Despite her remark, Lila was excited as well. Since she was a little girl, she'd dreamed of fancy places like this, and being one of the well-to-do folks. She sat up a bit straighter in the car, and lifted her chin just enough that Digby knew what she was thinking. Now she had a little taste of what it must be like to be Aunt Lucy.

Once in the room, Digby begged for a quarter and tried the Magic Fingers, which was a serious letdown. After shoving the soap, note pads, pens, and matches into his small suitcase as souvenirs, he was far too excited to relax. While his parents dressed for the wedding, he changed into cutoffs, grabbed a white motel towel, and made a beeline for the recreation area. Rog and Lila were glad to have him out of the room. It was a little small for two adults getting ready for a wedding, much less with a hyperactive teen bouncing off the earth-toned walls.

Digby scanned the array of additional souvenirs as he passed the maid cart in the hallway. The Solaridome itself was just ahead. He smelled the chlorine immediately after entering the double glass doors. Scanning the world beneath the plexiglass dome, he couldn't help but wonder if this was what the Garden of Eden was like before Adam and Eve ruined it for everyone. Top Forty radio blared from a bank of speakers suspended along the dome supports. The excitement Digby felt to be there was even better when accompanied by current hits from Jigsaw, Jim Croce and Olivia Newton-John. Surprisingly, only one other person was enjoying this splendor, a trim blonde in a Speedo doing laps in the pool.

Digby coyly approached. The swimmer was gorgeous, with a superb physique. Digby had always mooned over guys with athletic torsos. They seemed a different species. They were brick shit houses, when the building Digby's body most resembled at that time was a slightly sagging and somewhat lopsided A-frame. He gawked as the young swimmer cut through the water in his form-fitting suit. He stopped after a turn, flipped the hair back from his eyes, finger pinched his nose, and flashed a ready smile. "Hey, my name is Roland. Come on in."

Digby looked around to make sure he was the one being addressed, and even did the finger-to-chest gesture. Roland smiled and nodded. This made no sense, and Digby feared it was some sort of prank, but his suspicions were fleeting or at least secondary to his desire. With a coy smile and an audible gulp, he jumped in the pool, but what he was really jumping into was something else all together. He would've gladly dove into a pool of cat urine for this, even though he was still unsure as to what exactly this was. His gut and his groin cried Onward!

Roland and Digby frolicked a bit—racing, dunking, and bobbing while serenaded by Firefall, John Denver, and Seals & Crofts. Digby felt weightless and carefree, and the big, continuous smile on his face guaranteed that he got more than one mouthful of water.

After a half hour or so, his parents burst through the double doors of the glass pool area in an explosion of big collars, fussy bows, pastels, wide belts, and assorted plaids. At first glance they looked like two couples, or maybe prom chaperones in Dogpatch. Digby swallowed his budding gay aesthetic and said, "You guys look great." Those matching smiles made him wonder if they'd already started the party. They announced they were taking off, and would be back late. His mother blew a kiss and left a lipstick print on her palm that Digby could see from the pool. The party was definitely underway. Digby asked them to leave the key on his towel. He was told he could order room service that night. Yet another first!

Roland and Digby treaded water in silence, and watched his folks go back through the glass doors and around the side of the building. The parking lot was visible through one glass wall of the dome. His mother got in the car slowly, guarding the shellacked shape of her hairdo from potential denting.

Roland looked puzzled. "What are those gray marks along the side of your family car?"

Digby splashed him. "Never mind."

Once the car pulled from the lot, Roland grew even more attentive. He grabbed and tickled Digby until he couldn't breathe. "Stop," Digby managed weakly. In this case "Stop" meant "Go" and "No" definitely meant "Yes." Harassment never felt so good. Digby felt Roland's firm Speedo bulge brush against him. Is that what I think it is? He felt it again, then Roland ground it decidedly into Digby's thigh. Digby sputtered and reddened, and that was his version of playing it cool. Oh my God! A cute 16-year-old guy's boner! And it was touching him!

They both knew where this was heading. At least, Digby liked to think he knew. He kind of knew what was coming, but had no idea what exactly it entailed. He was as naive about the actual doings of sex as a shy Edwardian bride. Imagining two guys doing something sexy on a couch or Norm the mechanic carrying you off was one thing, engaging in actual sex was another. The air was thick. Digby trembled as Roland leaned forward. Digby could smell his breath. Maple syrup? Sausage links? Tang? He asked if Digby wanted to go take a sauna, which at that moment sounded like the dirtiest and most delicious thing imaginable. Of course he wanted to. He'd never been in a sauna before. At the mere suggestion, Digby's teeth chattered. He was too nervous to reply, so he merely nodded.

With a coy covering of the bulge in his cutoffs, Digby climbed from the pool. Roland offered him a stick of Juicy Fruit with a smile. Digby accepted, and slipped it quickly into his mouth to avoid being bitten by his still-chattering teeth. He then followed Roland down AstroTurf stairs to the lower level. AstroTurf was everywhere that year. Below were the showers, the changing area, and the sauna. No one else was around. Digby said a small prayer; to what God, he hadn't a clue. This hardly seemed Catholic God turf. Dear God, please let me score some gay sex!

Roland slipped off his suit, and hung it on the hook outside the sauna before wrapping his towel around his trim waist. Digby stared. Roland was so beautiful and perfect. It was hard to believe he was only one year older. Digby tried to mimic him, but his foot got hooked on the leg of his cut-offs. He hopped, falling against and through the sauna door as he inadvertently swallowed his gum. Roland was already inside. Once Digby's choking cough subsided, he said "Hi" for no apparent reason. Gathering a smidgen of composure, he removed the cut offs, reached out and hung them on the hook outside. After wrapping a towel about himself, he had a seat. They sat on the bleached wooden benches in silence. Digby's heart was beating so hard that it might have actually been visible, at least as a slight quivering through his chest flab.

The situation and the atmosphere were incredibly tense. With no food nearby to stuff in his mouth, Digby's need to speak grew unbearable. "Is it hot in here, or is it just me?"

Roland chuckled. "Well, this is a sauna."

"Oh, right." Stupid! Stupid! Stupid! Digby was already being such a goof that it seemed absurd that he could actually reach new levels of awkwardness. "Well, then..."

Roland leaned forward. "You have some sweat on your cheek."

"Oh do I?"

"Yes." He leaned closer and closer, and reached up and touched Digby's face. Their eyes connected. He was so close. Then all at once they started making out. Thank God for Juicy Fruit! Kissing a boy was all new. First base! He only had movies and TV as his guidelines for ecstasy, and that was all purely heterosexual and totally PG. He assumed that ecstasy was a composite of busy hands, trembling body, open mouth, quivering lips, and banal dialogue.

"Kiss me Roland, you have me on fire. Yes! Yes! Kiss me!"

Roland took pity on him, and shoved a finger against Digby's lips. "Shhhh…"

At some point, the contrived moans and artifice were replaced by a raw hunger. Digby was famished and crazed, and frankly amazed to discover he was a sexual savant. First base slid effortlessly into second. He was finally good at something other than embarrassing himself and his parents, and being a fallen but still obsessed Catholic. This was his calling. He was following his bliss, which seemed to be conveniently attached to his penis. He hadn't been dead, merely dormant, a soul in sexual limbo. He'd been a hothouse flower ready to bloom, a bottle of bubbly poised to pop, a vein of gold ripe for mining, a fallow field ready to be plowed, and a pressurized gusher set to explode. He was fireworks and crashing waves. He was every cliché of sexual awakening, and then some.

Getting nasty on that sauna bench took Digby outside of himself long enough to discover and be absorbed by something greater. That moment was Heaven. It was The Rapture. It was the something more he'd been searching for all these years. Love might be forever, but this was an awfully nice quick fix. He couldn't believe that Heaven was so naughty, and so deliciously of the flesh. If this was just a trick of Satan, then kudos to him, because this slice of pearly gated paradise was very convincing. The radio station was being piped down to the lower level as well. Maybe if he wanted to get to heaven he did need to raise a little hell.

Sweat was streaming down his cheeks. He felt hot wood on his back, hot man in his hands, and an urgency hitherto unknown. Right here! Right now! This moment. This place. This me. He'd never wanted to be who or where or what he was before. Now he wouldn't be anywhere, or anyone else. After years of searching and never feeling quite right, after years of being an outsider, Digby Swank was finally home.

Tongues and hands were everywhere at once. Yes, like that. Oh, right there. Swept up in it all, he didn't recognize the opening chords of Helen Reddy's feminist anthem of strength right away, but then it hit him. He was strong. He was invincible.

He threw his head back against the hot wood in ecstasy. Sing it Helen. Sing it, you Aussie songbird. Sing it for the surging wave of emancipation rising in all person-kind. Liberation has many faces, but sometimes only one voice. Digby realized he'd been his own greatest oppressor all along. That prison was a mere memory. He'd never felt so self-assured. He wasn't pretending or second-guessing, he was doing. No one was ever going to keep him down again.

As the song climaxed, so did he, and so did Roland, and so did everything that had come before. His past didn't entirely make sense, but it didn't necessarily have to anymore. Things had changed. The need to control everything had always been so crucial to him. He'd had to know all the rules, dissect each move, analyze the playing field, and consider all the factors. It was odd to realize that he liked things a little messy, or judging from the condition of his towel, a lot messy.

When Digby discovered the freedom that came from letting go, it seemed as though every page from his past was ripped from its binder, and tossed into the air. Days, months, and years floated and fluttered about him. His pain became confetti, and his past only added to the party atmosphere. The way things had been wasn't really a part of his story anymore. It was a lousy preface, but that made the reward all the sweeter.

Repression heightened his release. When the fires of passion had found the vacuum that had been inside him, the results were explosive. His otherness and all his struggles had led to this. Was all this even possibly part of God's plan? After all, He was known to move in mysterious ways. Digby leaned back against the hot wooden wall. He now understood why people had a cigarette after sex; so they could give greater substance to their sigh of contentment.

When his breathing returned to normal Roland turned to him, "Man, that was great."

Digby giggled, "Really?"

Roland finger combed his hair, and then reached down for Digby's hand. "Yeah, really. I mean, it was only my second time, but it was way better than my first. Was that your first?"

Not wanting to appear a complete novice, despite the sexual praise, Digby shook his head. "Of course not..." He caught himself. A lie wouldn't have mattered, but the need to lie was suddenly gone. "No, you were my first."

They held hands for a few minutes until they heard someone come downstairs into the locker room area. Roland said he had to get going. His family was going out to dinner. He said they were leaving early in the morning. "So I probably won't see you again." Giving Digby a kiss, Roland rose from the bench. "You're terrific, Digby Swank," he said with a wink as he left the sauna.

Digby sat there for another ten minutes with a smile on his face. He'd never been called anything like that before.

23 - Magic Fingers

Once the glory of the encounter and heady haze of afterglow burned away, guilt tainted his sauna tryst. Digby was hardly crushed. In the Catholic Church, most pleasurable things came with a good deal of flagellation and breast beating. He was accustomed to the heaviness that arrived as the dour handmaiden of delight. Satisfaction always meant sin. But at least this sin came with a great pay off, and some personal validation. You're terrific Digby Swank! Despite his pangs of guilt, he couldn't help but think, That was so Hell-worthy.

In many ways, discovering he was actually what he thought he was surprised Digby. He was so used to not fitting in, that he somewhat expected to discover he was neither gay nor straight, but something else entirely. He worried that other gay men might see him as a freak as well. When he gave himself over to his desire, he half expected Roland to push him away. That had not been the case at all. He'd been great. Roland had said so, and he was 16 and cute, and twice as experienced. Digby smiled. He had been great, and it was effortless. Belonging was an enormous relief.

Digby actually pinched himself on the walk back to the Swank double room. Lying back on the motel bed, he figured he'd call room service in a bit. He put another quarter in the Magic Fingers slot. In seconds, he was vibrated into sleep by the rumbling that came like a purr of contentment from deep within the mattress.

Digby dreamt of a beautiful day. He was driving down a winding road beneath a canopy of trees. This was especially cool, because he didn't even have his license yet. The sun was shining through the trees overhead and directly upon Dashboard Jesus, and in that dance of light and shadow, Dashboard Jesus morphed into Dashboard Grandma Rose. Digby felt a warmth from her filling the car. She was not beige. She wore very bright colors. Having her there felt like lying on a grassy hill on a sunny spring day. It felt like perfection. Even though he had wanted to so badly, he'd never dreamt of her before.

He felt Grandma Rose smile upon him. She knew all about the events in the sauna, but it didn't matter to her. She knew, and it didn't matter. She recognized it as a part of him, and being true to that was what was important. That certainty in himself was the only faith that mattered. Belonging was really nothing more than accepting himself, and it had been an inside job all along. The moment Digby thought it, Grandma Rose raised her teacup to him, and said it was so.

Then he was no longer lying on the grass, but was back behind the wheel. He looked at the road ahead, and told her he didn't know where he was going. She laughed, and told Digby to just be himself, and he'd never lose his way. Being someone or something else causes all the problems. If you're true to yourself, you don't need the rosary for protection, or even as a weapon. She told him the important thing was to just be sure to enjoy the ride. It's over faster than you think.

In the dream, he hit a pothole and jolted awake. The Magic Fingers had stopped, but he had an enormous smile on his face. Only five minutes had passed. He wrote an abridged version of the dream on a handy Solaridome notepad, and ordered a double cheeseburger from room service. Digby remembered something that Grandma Rose had once told him. "Every dream comes from God."

It had been the best day of his life.

24 - Epilogue

The dream was all the affirmation that Digby needed for the time being. He was what he was, and that would lead him to what or who he was meant to become. No batteries were required, and no assembly was necessary. All he needed was faith in himself. The goodness would flow from there. He knew what was right. The confusion and resentment didn't arise until his voice mixed with all the others.

The crucifixion had finally been eclipsed by the resurrection. More than just a new chapter in his life had begun. This was the start of a new book in a new language—an adults only, fasten your seat belts, no holds barred, ankles behind your ears journey of self discovery. Running Falls may have been his roots, but his branches were reaching for the warmth of that sunny blue sky. He stretched his arms upward toward the white plaster ceiling.

Life usually puzzled him, but it all seemed so simple lying there. It was nothing more and nothing less than a glorious mystery unfolding. Digby sighed. He was young and freshly laid, and as such, he thought he knew it all. He'd soon discover there was much more to learn.

THE END

Trademarks Acknowledgment

The author acknowledges the trademark status and trademark owners of the following places and items mentioned in this work of fiction:

Pittman Shorthand: Sir Isaac Pitman & Sons, Limited Share Company

Woolworth: F.W. Woolworth Co.

Pabst: Pabst Brewing Company

S&H Green Stamps: Sperry and Hutchinson Company, Inc.

Zenith: Zenith Electronics, LLC

Close 'n' Play Phonograph: Hasbro, Inc.

Band-Aid: Johnson & Johnson Corp.

Old Spice: Procter & Gamble Company

Combat!: ABC Cable and International Broadcast, Inc.

Maytag: Maytag Properties, LLC

Big Chief Tablet: American Trademark Publishing

Barrel of Monkeys: Hasbro, Inc.

Buick: General Motors Corp.

K-Mart: KMart Properties/Sears Brands, LLC

Revlon: Revlon Consumer Products Corp.

Mr. Peanut: Kraft Foods Group, Inc.

Pledge Furniture Polish: S.C. Johnson & Son

Chatty Cathy: Mattel, Inc.

Zig Zag Sewing Kit: Singer Corp

Happy Family Dollhouse: Mattel, Inc.

Little Handyman Tool Kit: Small World Toys, LLC

Sears: Sears Brands, LLC

Safeway: Safeway, Inc.

Naugahyde: United States Rubber Products, Inc.

G.I. Joe: Hasbro, Inc.

Scotch Tape: 3M Company

Easy-Bake Oven: Hasbro, Inc.

Rock 'Em Sock 'Em Robots: Mattel, Inc.

Lincoln Logs: K'Nex Industries, Inc.

Plymouth: Daimler, AG

Kotex: Kimberly-Clark Corp.

Pall Mall: R.J. Reynolds Tobacco Company

Bewitched: Columbia Pictures Industries, Inc.

Kool-Aid: Kraft Foods Group Brands, LLC

The Monkees: Rhino Entertainment Company

Cray-Pas: Sakura Color Products of America

Twinkies: Hostess Brands/Apollo Global Management

NASCAR: National Association for Stock Car Auto Racing, Inc.

Piggly Wiggly: Piggly Wiggly, LLC

Frito: Frito-Lay North America, Inc.

Tiparillo: Pinkerton Tobacco Company, LP

The Dry Look: The Gillette Company

Hai Karate: Retrobrands, LLC

Chess King: Merry Go Round Enterprises

Aqua Net: Lornamead, Inc.

Pick 'N' Save: Nash Finch Company

Cub Scouts: Boy Scouts of America

Greyhound Express: National Insurance and Indemnity Corporation

Janitor in a Drum: Diversey, Inc.

Prince Edward: John Middleton Co.

Zippo: ZippMark, Inc.

Coke: The Coca-Cola Company

Orange Julius: Orange Julius of America

Sinclair: Sinclair Finance Company

Goodwill: Goodwill Industries International, Inc.

Don't Break the Ice: Hasbro, Inc.

Tip It: Mattel, Inc.

Sorry!: Hasbro, Inc.

Ants in the Pants: Hasbro, Inc.

Toss Across: Mattel, Inc.

Headache: Hasbro, Inc.

Pop-O-Matic: Hasbro, Inc.

Ouija: Hasbro, Inc.

Crock Pot: Sunbeam Products, Inc.

Impala: General Motors Corp.

Family Circle Magazine: Meredith Corp.

Texaco: Chevron Intellectual Property, Inc.

Lucite: Lucite International, Inc.

Etch A Sketch: Ohio Art Company

Ritz Crackers: Nabisco/Mondelez International

Jell-O: Kraft Food Holdings, Inc.

Quiz Bowl: Isecke, William

Ben Franklin Five and Dime: Franklin Franchising Holdings, LLC

Slinky: James Industries, Inc.

Looney Tunes: Warner Bros. Entertainment, Inc.

Elmer Fudd: Warner Bros. Entertainment, Inc.

Road Runner: Warner Bros. Entertainment, Inc.

Warner Bros.: Warner Bros. Entertainment, Inc.

Tweety: Warner Bros. Entertainment, Inc.

Wile E. Coyote: Warner Bros. Entertainment, Inc.

Sylvester: Warner Bros. Entertainment, Inc.

Daffy Duck: Warner Bros. Entertainment, Inc.

Yosemite Sam: Warner Bros. Entertainment, Inc.

Bugs Bunny: Warner Bros. Entertainment, Inc.

Volkswagen Beetle: Volkswagen Group

Stetson: John B. Stetson Company

Superglue: Chemence, Inc.

Styrofoam: Dow Chemical Company

March of Dimes: March of Dimes Birth Defects Foundation

Suzie Q's: Hostess Brands/Apollo Global Management

Rice Krispies: Kellogg North America Company

Camaro: General Motors LLC

Mystery Date: Hasbro, Inc.

Bugles: General Mills, Inc.

Tiger Beat: Laufer Media, Inc.

Sunoco: Sunmarks, LLC

Kleenex: Kimberly-Clark Worldwide, Inc.

Astroturf: Southwest Recreational Industries, Inc.

Little Orphan Annie: Tribune Media Services

Motel 6: G6 Hospitality IP, LLC

Red Roof Inn: RRI Financial, Inc.

Magic Fingers: Magic Fingers of America, Inc.

Juicy Fruit: Wm. Wrigley Jr. Company

Owen Keehnen

Writer and historian Owen Keehnen has had his fiction, essays, erotica, reviews, columns and interviews appear in dozens of magazines and anthologies worldwide. Keehnen is the author of the humorous gay novel Young Digby Swank (Wilde City Press, 2013), the gay novel The Sand Bar (Lethe Press, 2012) and the horror novel Doorway Unto Darkness (Dancing Moon Press, 2010). He also recently released the reference book The LGBT Book of Days (Wilde City Press, 2013). Along with Tracy Baim, he co-authored Leatherman: The Legend of Chuck Renslow (Prairie Avenue Productions, 2011) as well as Jim Flint: The Boy From Peoria (Prairie Avenue Productions, 2011). Over 100 of his interviews with various LGBT authors and activists from the 1990s have been collected in the book We're Here, We're Queer (Prairie Avenue Productions, 2011). He recently finished editing For My Brothers, the Mark Abramson memoir about life and love in San Francisco during the height of the AIDS epidemic. He co-edited Nothing Personal: Chronicles of Chicago's LGBTQ Community 1977–1997 (Firetrap Press, 2009), was a contributor to Gay Press, Gay Power (Prairie Avenue Publications, 2012) and wrote ten biographical essays for the coffee table history book Out and Proud in Chicago (Surrey/Agate, 2008). Keehnen was on the founding committee and executive board of The Legacy Project and is currently a contributing biographer for the LGBT history-education-arts program focused on pride, acceptance, and bringing proper recognition to the courageous lives and contributions in LGBT history. He was the author of the Starz books, a four-volume series of interviews with gay porn stars. He has had two queer monologues adapted for the stage and served as co-editor of the Windy City Times Pride Literary Supplement for several years, was a co-founder of the horror film website RacksAndRazors.com, and a featured poet in Wilde City's 2013 collection Falling Awake. He lives in Chicago with his partner, Carl, and his two ridiculously spoiled dogs, Flannery and Fitzgerald. He was inducted into the Chicago Gay and Lesbian Hall of Fame in 2012.

Also By Owen Keehnen

The LGBT Book Of Days

Gay Press, Gay Power – contributor

The Sand Bar

We're Here, We're Queer

Jim Flint: The Boy From Peoria

Leatherman: The Legend of Chuck Renslow

Doorway Unto Darkness

Nothing Personal: Chronicles of Chicago's LGBTQ
Community 1977-1997 - co-editor

Rising Starz

Ultimate Starz

Out and Proud in Chicago - contributor

More Starz

Starz

CPSIA information can be obtained at www.ICGtesting.com
Printed in the USA
BVOW02s0550251113

337222BV00001B/6/P